ACKNOWLEI

For Mo, Raven, and Caden, you three mean the world to me ... love you. And thanks, Maureen Chesser, for all of the support you've given me through this incredible journey called life. Love you. Thanks to all LE and first responders for your service. To the people in the U.K. who have been in touch, thanks for reading! Lieutenant Colonel Michael Offe, thanks for your service as well as your friendship. Larry Eckels, thank you for helping me with some of the military technical stuff in Warpath. Any missing facts or errors are solely my fault. Beta readers, you rock, and you know who you are. Thanks George Romero for introducing me to zombies. Steve H., thanks for listening. All of my friends and fellows at S@N and Monday Old St. David's, thanks as well. Lastly, thanks to Bill W. and Dr. Bob … you helped make this possible. I am going to sign up for another 24.

Special thanks to John O'Brien, Mark Tufo, Joe McKinney, and Craig DiLouie. I truly appreciate your continued friendship and always invaluable advice. Thanks to Jason Swarr and Straight 8 Custom Photography for the awesome cover. Thanks to George Stickler at Extreme Supertruck for providing the F-650 image on the cover. Beta readers ... you all rock!! Once again, extra special thanks to Monique Happy for her work editing "Warpath." Mo, as always, you came through like a champ! Working with you has been a seamless experience and nothing but a pleasure. If I have accidentally left anyone out ... I am truly sorry.

***

Edited by Monique Happy Editorial Services
http://www.indiebookauthors.com

TABLE OF CONTENTS

Chapter 1
Outbreak - Day 18
Eden Compound, Utah

Like a makeshift guillotine, the shovel's blade cut a silent flat arc through the cool morning air before burying inches deep into the rasping creature's temple. As the rotted corpse crumpled to earth, Duncan squared his shoulders, squinted against the driving rain, and poked the V-shaped cutting edge into the next rotter's sternum. Having gained a precious yard of separation from the handful of attackers, he backpedaled blindly uphill—in the direction of the white Toyota Land Cruiser which, at the moment, was keeping his two-way radio, the short barreled combat shotgun, and a half-empty bottle of Jack Daniels dry.

Hell of a lot of good they're doing ya in there, old man, he thought glumly, his equilibrium failing him. In the next instant his legs buckled, and suddenly the gloomy overcast sky was all that he saw.

"Fuck happened?" he muttered, shaking his head vigorously and spraying droplets of water in all directions. But the action had no effect on his vision, which, from the combination of alcohol, sleep deprivation, and the fine mist clinging to his aviator glasses, remained clouded and fuzzy around the edges.

Now, flat on his back, two things registered at once. To his right, wrapped in a rain-drenched sheet, was his brother Logan's corpse that he'd just tripped over. He walked his gaze along the contours of the young man's lifeless shell. Regarded the facial profile which had slackened in death, but was still unmistakably Oops—handlebar mustache and all. He noted the crimson blossoms of blood that had dried to black but had reconstituted and now ran in all directions, turning the once-white death shroud into some kind of macabre tie dye.

A half beat later he recognized that the pickle he'd gotten himself into, both figuratively and literally—the former because he'd gone ahead and left the heavy artillery in the truck, the latter because he was more than half in the bag—was about to get *exponentially* worse.

He flicked his gaze sixty yards downhill at the spot where he'd removed the triple-strand barbed wire from the fence paralleling SR-39 so that he could drive the Cruiser through. There, three disheveled first turns were heading his way, fighting against gravity, their feet slipping on the slick grass. Then his heart skipped a beat as he looked past the struggling trio and noticed another dozen flesh eaters leaving the blacktop. Slow and clumsy, they negotiated the shallow ditch and, jostling shoulder to shoulder, exploited the newly created breach.

The new arrivals to the party were deadly for sure, but it was the half dozen to his fore— spread out in a phalanx line, jaws working in eager anticipation of fresh meat—that were the clear and present danger. Knowing that he was turtled on his back with Logan and Gus lying in state nearby, one hissing monster looming over him, and another in the half-dug grave less than two feet away, sent a cold wave of dread coursing through Duncan's body.

First things first, he told himself.

Only a second and a half elapsed between him tripping over Logan's corpse and his fingers finding the knurled grip of the .45 riding high in the paddle holster on his hip. Another half-second ticked by and he had depressed the palm safety, thumbed back the hammer, and his index finger hovered near the trigger guard. By the time the weapon was clear of leather and tracking swiftly right, he had already found the trigger and drawn off a few pounds of pull, the hammer poised and ready to fall.

Flooded with adrenaline and running mainly on muscle memory, he didn't recall caressing the trigger, but the two reports crashing the still morning air confirmed it and set his ears to ringing.

The noise, like tearing paper, bounced off the Toyota's metal skin and toured the nearby trees before the shock wave rolled back over top his prostrate body. It was awakening and cathartic at once, a substance he could almost feel.

One down, too many to go.

As he watched the flesh eater he'd just blessed with a second death roll towards the Toyota, spilling brains and viscous blood from its cratered face, the female first turn he'd just poked between the breasts with the shovel point was crawling out of the freshly dug grave where it had fallen.

Over the pattering rain, the grating rasp of its clawlike hands grappling for purchase, combined with the wet rattle escaping its working maw, sent an icy jolt through his body. Shivering profusely from a combination of fear-induced adrenaline, his already lowered core temperature, and the desire for another belt of Jack Black, he dug his left boot heel in and pushed uphill. Feeling a tug slow his progress as splintered nails tore into the blue denim just below his right knee, and with a new wave of shivers wracking his body and the stink of death and decay thick in his throat, he spread his legs, a kind of half-assed mud angel, aimed between his boot tips, and pumped a round between the zombie's beady eyes.

Two down, too many to go.

He kicked free from the dead thing's grasp, rolled over onto his stomach, and clawed his way towards the SUV; his ultimate goal: getting inside and radioing for help. And then shortly thereafter, making bubbles in the whiskey.

But those things weren't happening without a fight because a pair of rotters had inexplicably looped around the passenger's side of the Toyota, flanked him, and were now doggedly lurching his way.

"Where'd y'all learn that trick?" he muttered, bracketing the one nearest him in his sights. As he drew back on the trigger, a sudden flash of reddish-orange, like a .50 caliber round fired at night, minus the sparkle and pop, entered his side vision. Momentarily convinced he was seeing ill-timed tracers—a flood of chemicals to the brain brought on by the stress of a dozen dead things wanting to eat him, or perhaps a byproduct of the Jack Daniels in his system—he held his fire, blinked his eyes, and kept them closed for half a beat. Upon reopening them the thought that he'd had too much of the latter won out because now only one rotter stood between him and the SUV.

With the throaty rasps of the dead advancing on his six, he wasted no more precious time processing what had just happened. Instead, he fixed his gaze on the flesh eater at his twelve o'clock, rose from the ground, and with the .45 extended at arm's length, took a tentative step towards the SUV.

Chapter 2
Outskirts of Mack, Colorado

Two hundred miles southeast of the Eden Compound, former-Delta operator Cade Grayson was awakened by a sustained ten-second fusillade of automatic rifle fire. Not quite fast and furious enough to be classified as a *Mad Minute*—a short but sustained volley of automatic rifle fire helpful in breaking contact during an enemy ambush—but still long enough in duration to garner his full attention.

Ears perked and listening hard, he tried to discern any out-of-place sounds he could attribute to the wire being breached. But, thankfully, he detected none of the telltale moaning of the dead or the shrill animalistic screams of the dying, and as soon as the sharp reports were swallowed by the surrounding tree-covered hillocks, the (Forward Operating Base) FOB Bastion—or "Last" as he'd heard a soldier call it—regained all of the calm of a State Park campground at first light.

While Cade pondered whether mankind had collectively produced the ammunition necessary to put down all of the walking dead, he peered into the gloom and took stock of his surroundings.

After arriving at the FOB the previous night with his family, twenty-one-year-old Wilson, his teenaged sister Sasha, and nineteen-year-old Taryn, he was immediately spirited away from the Chinook helicopter by his old friend, newly promoted to Full Bird Colonel, Greg Beeson.

Then, utilizing what little daylight that was left, he boarded a Humvee with Beeson behind the wheel and, with a heavily armored

MRAP—Mine-Resistant Ambush Protected fighting vehicle—bristling with weapons and communications gear shadowing them, received the "nickel-tour" of the base and lay of the land outside the wire.

The FOB had sprouted up on the grounds of the Mack Mesa airport, 4,500 feet above sea level and less than a mile north of Interstate 70. Equidistant to Mack to the west and Loma to the east, the base amounted to little more than a small control tower, a spartanly appointed terminal, and a handful of maintenance buildings being crowded upon by two dozen mobile homes, which, judging by the bright residential-type colors, had presumably been brought in and placed there after the outbreak. West of the living quarters was a large parking lot usually reserved for airport customers but was now being utilized as a motor pool for the U.S. Army. Running away east to west from the tower and clustered buildings was a single 2,600-foot-long airstrip, numbered 07/25. And parked next to the airstrip was a smattering of aircraft, olive drab-painted Army Black Hawks and Chinooks, and sitting static near the helos were a half-dozen colorfully painted private aircraft.

At each corner of the FOB, rising thirty feet from the desert floor, made of plywood and offering unobstructed views and uninhibited fields of fire to all points of the compass, stood four newly constructed watchtowers. Using heavy equipment liberated from an excavation company near Loma, and building from the hard lessons learned from the fall of Camp Williams in Utah, Colonel Beeson had made certain that his men supersized all of their defenses. Outside of the razor-wire-topped fencing encircling the base were trenches carved wide and deep enough into the ochre dirt to fully conceal an eighteen-wheel semi-truck. On the far side of the trench, soldiers had strung concentric rings of concertina wire complete with dangling aluminum can noisemakers—a poor man's early warning system. And when all was said and done, FOB Bastion was serving its purpose as the President's eyes-and-ears, as well as a sort of buffer between Colorado Springs, the new United States Capitol to the southeast, and the millions of dead south by west in Salt Lake City. A veritable, but very vulnerable, first line of defense responsible for interdicting and destroying anything—short of a full blown mega horde—that moved on the nearby Interstate.

Once the impromptu tour was over and they had returned to Beeson's quarters—a single-wide trailer—Cade wolfed down a quick *meal* consisting of cold MREs and warm beer and listened while his friend and mentor brought him up to speed on what to expect once outside the wire. Finally, after a couple of hours reminiscing about days gone by, and ruminating over the bleak outlook the small pockets of survivors scattered about the United States yet faced, Beeson had gone to a file cabinet and produced a pair of laminated topo-maps that detailed the countryside that lay north by west between FOB *"Last"* Bastion and the compound outside of Eden, Utah. Then, with a forlorn look, Beeson had handed the maps over and issued a stern warning that made painfully clear that, though they were friends, now that Cade was no longer wearing the uniform, under no circumstances would Beeson be able to *legally* mount a rescue should *anyone* find themselves, as the salty colonel had worded it, 'Up shit creek without a paddle.' Then the colonel had added, in black sharpie on the bottom of the map, a string of numbers followed by three capital letters: SAT. At the time Cade had smiled, knowing that it was an unspoken insurance policy and left it at that, saying nothing more. Finally sometime between 0100 and 0200, with FOB Bastion under full blackout restrictions, Beeson shuttled Cade to his temporary quarters in the Humvee, running with the lights off.

Once there, Cade had said his good byes and, resisting the urge to salute, turned on his crutches and made his way to the door.

After watching the colonel's ride crunch out a U-turn and wheel away to the west under the moon's soft glow, Cade knocked lightly on the locked door to the single-story double-wide, inside of which he guessed Brook and Raven and the others were already fast asleep. *Nothing.* Nonplussed, he conceded that a sustained and continued pounding on the door was needed before someone stirred inside. The response started as a subtle vibration on the floor that resonated all the way to the aluminum sill near his feet. Finally, footsteps, getting louder as they approached, stopped at the door and it creaked open. An unsmiling Wilson poked his head out and inexplicably let him enter without a query nor challenge to his identity.

So much for operational security, Cade had thought at the time.

But now, hours later, with the first rays of daylight probing the curtain's periphery and a considerable chill hanging in the air, he shivered under the thin sheet and looked around the cramped quarters. Noting that the accommodations were nothing more than a rectangular living room housing two rows of cots instead of the obligatory sofa and coffee table, he realized why Wilson had given him the cold shoulder when he'd come knocking. The poor kid had been trapped in the makeshift barracks for several long hours with the four females, with only Max as his wingman. Suddenly the hardened soldier felt a little sorry for leaving Wilson to fend for himself. Hell, he thought, from his experience, two against one was hard enough—to be sequestered with four of the fairer sex, in what amounted to a jail cell minus the bars, was nothing less than cruel and unusual punishment. At the very least, man-to-man, he owed Wilson an apology.

But that would have to wait. He had some shopping to do. So he hinged up and threw on a black tee shirt, laced up his remaining Danner and slipped on the walking boot, cinching the Velcro down tightly. He took a moment to look around the room and see how different it appeared now that it was awash in thin shafts of daylight. The combined living and dining room was carpeted in rust-colored shag and paneled with dark wood. In the far corner was a tiny wood stove. Through a doorway to the right was a utilitarian kitchen minus the appliances. All in all, the entire place struck him as some kind of hippie crash pad or a stop on a modern day Underground Railroad. Except for the framed photo on one wall of a girl standing in front of a man and a woman, both in their early thirties by his best estimate, there was nothing at all homey about the shack.

Adding to the *ambiance*, the group's gear and weapons were strewn everywhere. An arm's reach away, paralleling his, was a metal-framed nylon cot; the sleeping bag atop it lay open and had partially spilled off onto the floor. Next to the abandoned cot was another with two forms pressed together on its meager two-foot-wide sleeping surface. Cade recognized one of Raven's pigtails snaking from under the woven afghan blanket; at the moment it appeared she was attempting to sleep-wrestle the bedding from her mom.

A couple of yards past the ongoing struggle, near the cold stove at the rear of the room, another trio of similar-sized cots were nosed in against the wall. Judging by the red manes peeking out from under their respective blankets, Cade surmised that two of the lumps were Wilson and Sasha. And on the cot beside Wilson's, fully clothed and sleeping atop a puffy orange sleeping bag, was the raven-haired late addition tagalong to FOB Bastion named Taryn.

All present and accounted for, thought Cade. He corralled his crutches from the floor, a move that brought Max out from under Raven's empty cot. The Australian shepherd spun a half circle and leaned against Cade's good leg, then cast a backward glance full of longing at him. It was obviously a preplanned and perfectly executed move that garnered the recently adopted dog a thorough scratching behind the ears.

When he'd finished doting on Max, Cade said a few quiet words in the dog's perked ear, then shrugged on his shoulder rig and placed the compact Glock 19 in the Bianchi holster dangling under his right armpit. Next, he retrieved the full-sized Glock 17 from underneath his pillow and slipped it into the low-riding drop-leg holster, securing it within easy reach on the outside of his left thigh.

Finally, blowing a kiss towards his sleeping family and being as quiet as a man on crutches with a clunky boot on one foot could be, he rose and threaded past his sleeping wife and daughter. Stopping near the door, he fished the keys from Brook's pants pocket and couldn't help noticing the now-folded plain white envelope he'd given her the day before. Ignoring the death letter, he verified hc had the correct keys by the leather fob with the blue Ford oval. They went into his pocket, then he rooted through his ruck and retrieved a black Sharpie. He looked around for something to write on, a scrap of paper perhaps—anything but the death letter. Finding nothing he shrugged, leaned against the wall, and scrawled a message to Brook chest-high on one of the recessed vertical panels on the inside of the front door. Then, leaving Max to watchdog over them all, he slunk out into the flat light of morning.

But before he'd closed the door behind him, a second volley of rifle fire disturbed the quiet. He poked his head back inside and was relieved to find that everyone's breathing remained still and rhythmic, an indicator to how conditioned they had become to their *new normal.*

Chapter 3

The second consecutive flash of orange entered Duncan's field of vision as he was sighting on a raggedy first turn over the barrel of his .45. A microsecond later, there was an arrow buried deeply into the female rotter's eye socket, its shaft still quivering as the creature crashed to the ground, limp. Suddenly, realizing what had just taken place, Duncan smiled wide at his good fortune and said a silent prayer to Oops assuring him that they'd meet again—but apparently at a later date.

"Yo, pusbags," a voice shouted from downhill and behind the SUV. "Come and get some dark meat."

Taking a couple of long strides forward, Duncan navigated the fallen bodies and grabbed onto the rig's sloped hood for support. He looked down the length of the Land Cruiser's passenger side and was greeted by a familiar sight.

Crossbow shouldered and bouncing against his back, the lanky firefighter had swapped out for a machete and was spinning through the clutch of dead like some kind of whirling dervish trained in the martial arts. In a matter of seconds, Duncan witnessed the flashing blade relieve two of the flesh eaters of their heads, and then behind a graceful full swing saw Daymon lop off the top third of another's from the brow up.

As the severed heads bounced towards SR-39, picking up speed like a pair of hair-and-flesh-wrapped bowling balls, the third creature toppled backward, impacted the ground viciously, and entered its nearly intact brain into the downhill race.

"The cavalry is here," shouted Duncan. Aiming cross-body he dropped another pair of decaying interlopers with single point-blank headshots and added, "And it looks like he brought a knife to a gunfight." A guttural chuckle spilled from Duncan's mouth as he shook his head, another attempt at clearing the Jack-induced haze.

Out of nowhere, a jagged fork of lightning transited the pewter sky nearby. Immediately the following clap of thunder ripped the still air, reverberated off the foothills all around, and then died to nothing, leaving only the sound of raindrops pinging mightily on the Cruiser's sheet metal.

Daymon said nothing as he appeared wraithlike next to Duncan, who was now visibly wavering, about to lose his tenuous grip on the vehicle. Then, with no trouble at all, Daymon hustled the smaller man into the passenger seat, slammed the door, and backpedaled uphill and around the Cruiser's grill.

In the next instant he had the bow cocked and loaded and was tracking around to the driver's side, where, after a quick glance at the shrouded forms of Gus and Logan, let the missile fly.

The razor-sharp barbed arrow crossed space in a fraction of a second and stopped a freshly turned walker, twice-dead, in its tracks. Noticing the newly opened window of opportunity, Daymon tossed the bow to the ground and dashed for the Toyota. He hauled the door open and hastily folded his frame behind the wheel. With a pair of rotten hands reaching in, he slammed the door and locked himself inside the rig without a second to spare.

"What the hell were you thinking?" asked Daymon as he tucked his dreads behind his ears. Receiving nothing in response, he flashed an expectant sidelong glance towards Duncan and found the Vietnam-era aviator dead to the world, chin parked hard on his chest, snoring.

A flurry of white palms slapped the passenger side glass, jerking Duncan from his alcohol-induced slumber. Going wide eyed, "What the fu—" was all he could muster before the roar of the 5.7 liter engine joined the pelting drops in drowning out the rest of the expletive.

"I'm saving our butts. That's what the fuck," explained Daymon as he pinned the throttle and turned hard right, deeply cutting a clockwise pair of muddy tracks into the spongy earth.

Straightening out midway through, he pointed the center of the hood at the largest concentration of rotters, running over and pinning a number of them under the two-and-a-half-ton rig's undercarriage. Then, bouncing like a ship at sea, the luxury SUV picked up speed and careened downhill towards the zombie-choked blacktop, spitting out bits and pieces of pasty arms and legs along the way. Trying to time the power drift just right, Daymon locked eyes with the hungry throng; at the last second, he yanked the wheel hard over and with the top-heavy vehicle's pent up inertia bleeding away came a crashing of wood against metal. The vehicle shuddered from an immediate and violent halt.

Chapter 4

Walking with crutches, the half-mile trek from the double-wide to the base motor pool took Cade fifteen minutes. As he clunked along the fence line surveying the moat and the handful of Zs that had gotten trapped there overnight, a brisk crackle of rifle fire drew him off course. Ignoring the sea of vehicles dead ahead, he veered right and followed along the newly constructed and heavily fortified front gate he and Beeson had passed through the night before.

Taking into consideration the recent terrorist attacks on Schriever AFB and that he was now a civilian and dressed as such, he approached the razor-wire-topped fence with caution and a smile. Standing in the shadow of the guard tower, not ten feet from the ladder, one of the soldiers, a female nearing middle age, peeled away from her post and approached him, exhibiting the swagger he'd seen in combat veterans with multiple deployments in the sandbox under their belt. Her eyes locked on his as she challenged him in a booming voice, the business end of her M4 aimed at the ground near his feet. The action, exactly what he'd expected from Wilson the night before, actually came as a relief. Relaxing somewhat, he said, "I'm Colonel Beeson's guest. Came in from Schriever last night with my family."

Unwavering, her face a mask of seriousness, she held a hand out and said, "ID please."

Moving slowly and deliberately, keeping his hand clear of the Glock on his thigh, he retrieved the green military ID from his left hip pocket and handed it over. "I'm no longer active duty, but this is all I've got. Don't see any DMV offices opening anytime soon."

Ignoring the attempt at levity, she took the card and backed away.

Noting the separation the sergeant had created, Cade glanced over and saw the other soldiers eyeing him intently. *Good.* After the speed and manner in which Camp Williams fell to the dead, it was apparent that Beeson had articulated clearly to the soldiers under his command that complacency would not to be tolerated.

Waiting patiently, Cade removed his black ball cap and relaxed on the crutches, settling most of his weight on the rubber pads pinching his underarms. And as the sergeant scrutinized his ID, he studied her uniform. It was the newer Multicam style with multiple different earth tones intermingling over a mostly tan background. The left shoulder sleeve insignia—an olive drab star on a black shield with a full headdress-wearing Native American centered inside of the star—indicated she was Second Infantry Division. Cade guessed that she had probably been stationed at Fort Kit Carson before Z-Day and had been sent here only recently in order to help *Beeson's Boys* (Green Berets of the 19th Special Forces Group) fortify the outpost. He watched her dark eyes flick rapidly back and forth over the laminated plastic document, searching it front and back. During the process, he noticed her look up twice, presumably comparing him with the picture.

"I'll be damned," she finally said, handing the ID back, a broad smile cracking her steely veneer. "*The* Cade Grayson?"

Nodding, Cade donned his cap, snugging it low, nearly covering his eyes. Then, changing the subject, he glanced at the chevrons on her chest and addressed her by the name on the tag secured by hook-and-loop tape to her blouse top. "Can I ask you a question, First Sergeant Andreasen?"

"Fire away," she answered at once. "And you can call me Laurel." She shouldered her rifle and assumed a relaxed stance.

"What's with all of the shooting this morning?"

Her smile faded. Then she said grimly, "The Zs have been crawling out of the pits and getting to the fence. Not a lot of them ... but enough to cause me a severe case of the pucker ... if you get my drift."

He nodded but said nothing.

Andreasen went on, "Only takes one or two muzzle flashes to bring them up from the Interstate. So, if we can, we wait until first light ... put them down all at once."

"Why don't you have suppressors for your weapons?"

"A couple of SF teams headed out to recon Salt Lake a week ago and took all that we had with them. Who am I to question what the 19th does? Anyway, the colonel probably figured they needed them more than us," she explained. Then, no sooner had the words rolled off her tongue, she remembered that he was no longer a captain in the United States Army, leaned close and added quietly, "But I shouldn't have told you any of that."

"Knowing how Beeson trains his boys, they'll be back. Besides, communication's been dodgy since the Chinese satellites attacked *our* birds." The sergeant's face went slack at this bit of news. "But I shouldn't have told you that," he said with a conspiratorial wink.

A Humvee passed them by, throwing up a turbid cloud of dried grass and ochre dust.

Waving away the choking haze, Cade asked, "How are the Zs getting out?"

She adjusted her helmet. Fixed her red-rimmed hazel eyes on his and said slowly, "On the backs of the others."

"On the backs of the others?" said Cade, barely masked incredulity riding his words.

The sergeant nodded then looked towards the fence subconsciously.

"They're learning?"

She nodded again.

Holy hell, thought Cade. His gaze was drawn to the fence. He stared at it, thought for a second and finally said, "Thanks for your time, Sergeant."

"Thanks for all that you've done," she replied. "And I'm truly sorry to hear about Desantos and Gaines. They will be missed."

Cade nodded but said nothing. He cast another worried glance towards the fence and then fixed his gaze on the motor pool where he could just make out the top of the massive Ford in the distance, the sun bouncing off of its black paint.

***

Three minutes later he was zippering through the maze of static Humvees and MRAPs. He crabbed between a pair of Cougars, their slab sides painted desert tan, each towering two-and-a-half-feet over his head. After navigating by guess and happenstance he emerged from the steel canyon, pressed the unlock button on the alarm fob, and listened hard for the tone. Hearing the soft beep, he vectored towards it, hitting the button two more times before finally finding the truck without a name. Back in Portland, before the dead had come back to life, upending everything he had known as normal, Raven had taken it upon herself and named their Toyota Sequoia the *Silver Beast*; her inspiration derived from a cartoon about a girl named Maggie and her docile pet monster she called the Ferocious Beast. Seeing her smiling face in his mind's eye, he made a mental note to challenge her to coin a similarly suitable name for the Ford.

Cade popped the door, grasped the grab handle, and climbed into the seat, hauling the pair of crutches in after. He slipped the key in the ignition and the Ford fired right up, its throaty exhaust notes banging off the armored military vehicles parked on either side. *What about 'Old Faithful,'* he thought to himself. Then, a second later, the image of Jasper's truck belching steam and trying to die on the South Dakota Interstate popped into his head, instantly nixing that idea.

It took two tries, forwarding and reversing while cutting the wheel by a few degrees, before he was able to extricate the rig. Finally he goosed the throttle and with the truck belching grey exhaust sped from the parking lot. But instead of going straight, and much to the surprise of First Sergeant Andreasen and the others manning the gate, he turned left and rolled up tight to the hurricane fencing and motioned the first sergeant over.

After a quick exchange with the newest member of the Cade Grayson fan club, and a sour look from the soldier whose job it was to lower the mobile bridge system, he was outside the wire and on his way.

With the image of the bridge folding away in his rearview, Cade turned right out of FOB Bastion and drove on for a short while to the 'T' intersection he recalled from the night before where another right turn was necessary. Then, keeping a steady forty miles per hour, he maneuvered the Ford along a meandering stretch of 10 1/2 Road for almost a mile, dodging small groups of Zs and wondering the entire way, why, with so much open range, the CDOT bothered with fractions when naming their streets. As quickly as the conundrum had come to him, it diminished in importance when he came upon U-13, a north/south two-lane splitting Mack to the west and Loma to the east. He ground the Ford to a hard stop on the debris-littered blacktop just as Beeson had done the night before. He sat there for a beat staring dead ahead, past the sign reading *Loma Population 1,296*, and recalled the colonel's words. *Unlucky thirteen,* Greg had said, referring to the road by its newly earned name. Then, eyes misting over, shoulders slumped from carrying the added weight of the newly fallen, the usually unflappable Special Forces officer had added in a low and chilling tone, '*We don't go beyond thirteen ... Loma belongs to the dead.*'

Hearing those words again in his former mentor's voice, with the same inflection and cadence, stirred within Cade a healthy dose of fear which in turn produced a much needed surge of adrenaline.

Heeding the colonel's warning, Cade cranked the wheel left and proceeded down U-13, passing by wide open tracts of browned grass and tilled dirt, their neglect obviously underway well before the dead began to walk. A mile later, with the subdivision of houses he'd spotted the night before shimmering in the distance, he saw a mass of staggering Zs blocking the two-lane shoulder to shoulder. For a brief second he entertained the notion of speeding up and sending them flying like so many bowling pins, until the specter of a shattered femur or tibia puncturing one of the Ford's tires and ruining his day entered the equation. So at the last instant he braked hard and, using the truck's massive bumper like a cow-catcher, parted the rear echelon and entered their midst at a little more than walking speed. Then after enduring what seemed like a non-stop barrage of slapping palms and nails screeching against the Ford's sheet metal, he drove out the other end, tires intact but with every nerve ending in his body suddenly ablaze.

***

Less than a mile north and barely two minutes removed from the encounter with the undead herd, Cade entered the Joshua tree-lined subdivision and pulled parallel to the curb in front of a two-story Craftsman nearly identical to his childhood home back in Portland.

Nostalgia flooded his brain as he took in the sight for sore eyes. Then he shifted his attention to the late-model mid-sized SUV he'd spotted during the ride along with Beeson. It was parked on the long driveway against the left side of the house and the real reason he'd undertaken the self-centered excursion from FOB Bastion in the first place.

Disregarding the forward shambling mob in his rearview, he turned the wheel hard right and gunned the Ford over the curb. There was a harsh squelch as the knobby tires gnashed through the crushed rock parking strip and a shudder as he pulled a hard one-eighty and ground the rig to a halt atop the front yard consisting mostly of prairie grasses and ground-hugging cacti. Rattling the shifter into Park, he pulsed his window down and regarded the sight that instantly took him back to Portland. As he relived that Z-Day siege he could literally smell the stink of the dead as they surged through his front plate window and rode the splintered glass into his family room. Sitting there with the engine idling, he shuddered as Ike and Leo's screams rolled across the porch. Then he saw his neighbor Rawley taking the fight to the creatures from his front stoop. The rifle fire clear as day as it rolled across the street. There were long drawn out bursts and the dead falling and clunking down both flights of steps.

He took a deep breath of hot dry air. Feeling his heart rate ebb, he removed his hat and swiped the newly forming sweat from his brow. *For a moment there*, he thought, *the whole thing seemed so real.* Only the drapes in this Craftsman were open and he could see nothing moving in the gloom behind the still-intact double-paned windows. There were no screams or rifle fire. All in all, inside and out, the mocha-brown-and-gray-trimmed house was deathly quiet. And with no breeze to speak of, the stunted bushes bordering the side fence and mature trees opposite them were statue-still, making the whole scene—minus the putrefying monster banging around trapped inside the adjacent fenced-in yard and the approaching group of Zs still a dozen blocks distant—seem like something Norman Rockwell could have imagined.

Killing the engine, he wondered briefly if the vivid flashbacks he'd just experienced were what the doctors at Schriever had taken to calling Post-Apocalyptic Traumatic Stress Disorder. *Maybe*, he reasoned. But PATSD didn't roll off the tongue the same. So he decided to chalk it up to PTSD, call it a day, and be done with it. *Son, nobody likes a whiner*, his dad had often said.

And Dad was right. Decision made and behind him. Time to forget the past and do what he had come here for in the first place. He looked at the front door, which, like the one in Portland, was a sturdy design constructed of wide oak planks running vertically and outfitted with an antiqued brass pull and matching hinges. But sadly, destroying the illusion of home, this front door had been defaced, spray-painted dead center with a three-foot-tall white letter '*X*.' Noted in the top quadrant of the '*X*' in like color was the date the home had been searched. Cade did the math in his head and determined that nine days had passed since, presumably, anyone had entered the dwelling. Reading counterclockwise, he saw the words *2nd ID* in the left panel. *Pretty self-explanatory*. The Second Infantry Division, perhaps even the soldiers at FOB Bastion's gate, had searched the dwelling. Between the lower legs of the '*X*,' scrawled hurriedly very small, was *O-3-Zs*. He thought back to his search and rescue training from years ago. The *O* meant the Second ID had found zero survivors inside. The *3* indicated the number of cadavers they had found inside. And finally, the Z made plural told him in code that the three cadavers inside had been ambulatory. *No living, three dead, all of them Zs*. Lastly, the fourth quadrant was empty, which when he'd been trained many years ago meant that there were no dead present—or hopefully in this case—no undead present. But that was then, old training methods for sure. And this was now, when one bite spelled doom. So making no assumptions, nor taking unnecessary chances based on a bunch of spray-painted hieroglyphics, Cade decided that though time and shambling Zs waited for no one, discretion was the better part of valor. Then he heard Desantos's voice in his head: *Take it slow, Wyatt. Life is a marathon, not a sprint.*

So he did. After burning another precious minute scrutinizing the house and surrounding area, still nothing moving but the lone Z, he nudged the door open, then propped his crutches against the hinge and climbed out. Shouldering the door closed, he shifted his gaze south down U-13, quickly decided he would have five minutes or fewer inside, then armed the lock and dumped the keys into a cargo pocket.

After one last long look at the upper-story windows and a glance at the flesh eater pressing its abdomen against the pointed slats atop the neighboring fence, he nestled the crutches under his pits and clunked his way up the cement path. He carefully negotiated the half-dozen steps and stopped on the elevated front porch under an ornate oil-rubbed bronze light, the graffiti-marred front door daring him to enter.

He tested the knob and found it unlocked and figured that the soldiers of the Second ID had either A: forgotten to lock up after clearing the house; or B: the most likely scenario, had assumed that a closed door was sufficient to keep out the dead.

So he pushed the door open, stood stock still and peered into the shadow-filled foyer listening hard for any kind of movement. *Nothing.* The place seemed clear, and after an additional second's hesitation he stepped inside and back in time.

Chapter 5

Duncan came to with a crushing headache and excruciating pain stabbing his right side where the leather-wrapped armrest did the job the unused seatbelt hanging near his throbbing head had not. Stars and tracers danced before his eyes—not safety-orange arrows fired from a crossbow or .50 caliber marking rounds conjured up by his imagination—but honest-to-God, head-trauma-induced, streaks and blobs of colorful light. That his head hadn't gone through the glass as a result of Daymon's Fast and Furious-inspired sideways drift and ensuing rapid deceleration and collision with the pair of sturdy fence posts was either a testament to long-dead engineers in Japan or some kind of *miracle* he didn't deserve. *Would have better served Logan*, crossed his mind as the ethereal sky show faded and new stimuli flooded his senses.

The driving rain lessened to a sporadic patter pelting the smoked-glass moon roof as the rasps of the dead intensified. Hearing this, Duncan shook his head to blink the fog away and suddenly a blast of damp carrion-tinged air entered through the open driver's door. Looking left, he half-expected to see Daymon's body sprawled on the ground either mortally injured from the impact or being eaten by the dead.

Instead, without warning, the driver's door slammed shut with a hollow thunk and he saw Daymon crabbing sideways away from the static SUV, a two-way radio pressed to his lips, and the stubby shotgun, held one-handed, aimed head high at a crowd of advancing rotters.

Reacting to the gooseflesh-producing sound of nails rasping the window near his ear, Duncan swept his gaze right and was greeted with a multitude of snarling zombies, their teeth bared and only three millimeters of automotive glass keeping them at bay. *The Lord helps those who help themselves*, crossed his mind as he fought the numbness in his right arm and fumbled the Colt from its holster. Finally, struggling against the rig's downhill list, with his arm throbbing mightily, he wormed across the rain-slickened center console, opened the door, and slithered otter-like head first out of the vehicle. The second his chest hit the soggy ground three closely spaced gunshots set his ears to ringing. Lying in the mud, he looked left and saw that Daymon was crouched near the Toyota's rear bumper, the shotgun trained cross-hill away from the wrecked Toyota. In the next instant the shotgun belched flame and another thunderous boom pierced the air, crashing overhead. Watching the targeted rotter's head dissolve, Duncan sighted over the .45 but held fire for fear of accidentally hitting Daymon. So, after casting a quick look at the SUV, and verifying that it had indeed come to rest completely blocking the breach in the fence entirely, he moved a few feet uphill and, with his friend now out of harm's way, engaged the remaining creatures from an oblique angle.

When Duncan caressed the trigger, two things happened simultaneously. In his side vision he saw Daymon tossing the shotgun to the ground. *Empty,* he presumed. Then, almost drowned out by a deep rumble of distant thunder, a tremendous volume of gunfire sounded from below and to his right. He didn't bother looking. There was no reason. Two plus two, put together in his mind, told him that whoever Daymon had hailed a moment earlier over the Motorola had just joined the party. Then as the first bullet left the .45's muzzle, he realized that the newly turned zombie bracketed in his iron sights looked vaguely familiar. Like the Chance kid he'd killed the day before, minus the greasy blond dreadlocks and thirty or forty pounds around the middle. The pale-faced monster snarled and bared its teeth and, with its last labored step, some kind of fluid, dark and thick like molasses, pulsed from the horrific wound on the right side of its neck. Then the .45 boomed again and jerked in Duncan's fist and the top third of the Chance look-a-like's head dissolved into a viscous spray of brain and bone that mingled with the misting rain and landed with a patter, a gory strip of detritus a couple of yards long and several inches wide.

At once the gunfire below trickled off to nothing and the rain began letting up.

"Let's get the hell outta here," bellowed Duncan, turning his attention towards Daymon who was now wielding the machete and had just dropped the last standing zombie with a quick downward chop, sinking the sixteen-inch blade a fist's width into the monster's cranium. Suddenly, out of nowhere, Duncan recalled the vision he'd had of Daymon dispatching the dead on the road while he held the DHS helicopter in a hover. "Just like I remembered," he added. "Only up close and personal your handy-work is much more impressive."

"Thanks ... I think," said Daymon, slightly confused by the offhand comment.

With the surge of adrenaline ebbing quickly from his system, Duncan moved on shaky legs to the SUV and took a seat behind the wheel. From there he watched Daymon hinge at the waist to clean his blade off in the drooping grass. Then he saw more tracers as he regarded the pistol in his hand. Confused as to how it had come into his possession, he turned it over, looked at the small print stamped on the slide, and then snugged it back in its holster. Suddenly his head took a lap around his body and he saw blurred figures on the road clearing bodies away, the widening blood trails reminding him of Vietnam. Then he looked in the side mirror at where Daymon had been but he was no longer there. Seemingly, in the blink of an eye, the dreadlocked man had sheathed his machete, retrieved the crossbow from twenty feet uphill where he'd tossed it mid-fight, and then covered twice that distance towards the SUV and was standing a foot from him.

Handing Duncan the combat shotgun, Daymon noticed the look of bewilderment on the older man's ashen face. "You OK?" he asked.

Like a white light moment, Duncan had an epiphany right then and there. And as sickening as it was for him to acknowledge, considering his checkered past, he accepted as fact that he'd just lost time slipping in and out of an alcohol-induced blackout. Managing a nod he muttered, "Here we go again."

Ignoring the comment, Daymon gestured at the shrouded bodies near where the Land Cruiser's high-speed downhill journey had begun and said, barely loud enough to be heard over the falling rain, "Get the others and let's finish what you came up here to do."

Chapter 6

Cade crossed the threshold slowly as if going inside might open up old wounds. But it had no such effect. Instead he felt cheated. The entire layout was different. The mahogany stairs were not where they were *supposed* to be. The living room was misplaced as well. The house, he concluded, was a metaphor for how he was feeling just three short weeks into the life-changing event that the Omega virus had wrought on his family and the world.

When he looked in the mirror he recognized the face staring back. However, when he went introspective—like the Craftsman's flipped floor plan—everything inside him, memories, emotions, loyalties, and values, had been rearranged, changing their order of importance. So drastic the change had been that now every decision he made was predicated on a new set of rules. Guided by a constantly spinning moral compass. White lies were acceptable and had become a type of family lubricant. Real lies. Big, lifesaving lies, on occasion, had become necessary. He didn't like the direction he was headed but could do little to stop it. "You're not a Boy Scout anymore," he told himself as he elbowed the door closed and threw the lock, just in case.

He stood in the foyer and took in a deep lungful of stagnant air and instantly hit on a barely perceptible whiff of carrion emanating from somewhere inside the dwelling. *In for a penny, in for a pound* crossed his mind as he propped the crutches against the ornate bannister attached to the stairs doglegging upward to his right.

Silently, the Glock 17 cleared the drop-leg holster and then not-so-silently he hobbled towards the source of the stench, the moving parts of his plastic boot betraying his presence with every stride forward.

Along the way he saw at eye level bloody handprints, smeared and dried to black. The floors were tracked here and there with small footprints, the fluids dried glossy and flaking. After clomping across the bare hardwoods and passing under an arch dividing the living room and formal dining room, he felt the soft give of the oriental rug underfoot. He paused again to listen and was greeted with a silence with a physicality all its own. So he pushed deeper into the lower floor, the rug quieting his approach through the formal dining room as he skirted the walnut table and chairs dutifully taking up most of the space. Pausing a yard from the narrow doorway he guessed led to the kitchen, he steadied his body on a walnut built-in housing a host of very expensive-looking gold-rimmed china, looked left and saw a door with half a dozen panes of glass. Leaded and cut in diamond shapes and sandwiched between white woodwork, the entry presented a nice first impression for anyone entering from the driveway. And positioned in a breakfast nook to the right of the doorway was an informal oak picnic-style table, complete with a long bench pushed against the outside edge. Four sets of service had been laid out alongside ceramic plates featuring a desert motif of vivid reds and yellows. Three of the plates still contained half-eaten breakfast items, dried hard and shiny, no doubt a result of prolonged exposure to the sunlight filtering in from the west-facing wall of windows behind the table.

Knowing what the empty plate likely meant, Cade swept the pistol right, cautiously craned his head, and found himself peering down the length of a galley-style kitchen.

At the end were more ornate windows, sunlight beaming in. Next to the windows was an old enamel refrigerator, ivory in color, a throwback to a different era. The door leading out to the backyard opened just to the left of it. And on the floor surrounding the Art Deco-inspired item's open door was a half-moon-shaped pool of something rotten, yellowish-colored, and sprouting a thick carpet of black mold. Whatever the sludge had been, it was now assaulting his gag reflex, making his salivary glands come alive.

Trying to breathe through his mouth, he averted his eyes, steered clear of the mess and began searching for what had drawn him to the house in the first place.

Starting with the drawer farthest from the *triangle*—the recommended placement of the most important kitchen items—which in this instance consisted of the gas range on the right wall, a double-wide kitchen sink opposite it, and the putrid mess of a fridge at the tip, he began his search.

In his experience, every house had a junk drawer. And this one, which was exactly where he'd expected it to be, had a smell all its own. In addition to all of the usual stuff: small tools, old-fashioned screw-in fuses, batteries, pencils, and a myriad of other items all without a dedicated place of their own, there were a dozen patchouli-scented tea light candles mixed in. He hated the putrid earthy odor almost more than the stench of carrion. In fact, it was giving the fridge a run for its money in the offensive odor category.

After picking the candles out and tossing them into the moldy sludge, he searched the rest of the junk drawer without finding what he was looking for. So he moved on and rifled through the other drawers and again came up empty. As a last resort, he opened all of the cupboards one by one, and when he finally reached the one near the far door he found a number of eyehooks screwed into the wood, not one of them with a car key dangling from it.

"Dammit," he muttered, slamming the cupboard door. He walked back past the unfinished morning meal and scrutinized the Lincoln SUV through the side door, trying to determine if it could be hotwired. Noticing the keyless entry and guessing that the high-dollar vehicle also came standard with one of those computer-chip-embedded keys, he spit a string of epithets cursing Mister Murphy.

Crestfallen from not finding the keys to the Navigator as he had hoped, and definitely not wanting to go back to Beeson and asking for another handout, he padded through the dining room, creaked across the hardwoods, and retrieved the crutches. Before leaving the familiar-feeling house, he paused in the foyer and closed his eyes and imagined the floor plan flipped and the world righted. Thought of how nice it would be for him and Brook and Raven to be back in Portland, picking up right where they had left off. For a brief moment he experienced a respite from reality until from somewhere outside the dead and their incessant moaning had to go and ruin it.

He looked through the window inset into the door. *All clear.* So he opened the door slowly, stepped out onto the porch, and left it closed but unlocked just as he had found it.

Looking south down *Unlucky 13,* he spotted the same herd of monsters, now adjacent to the house next door, and on a collision course with the parked Ford.

With a certain urgency dictated by the events unfolding, he clunked down the stairs and through the lava rock, relying less on the crutches and placing more trust in his bad ankle. By the time he had reached the truck, the dead were stumbling over the curb, their calls becoming increasingly louder. With seconds to spare, he hit the unlock button, hauled the door open and tossed the crutches across the seat. He had just gotten inside and closed and locked his door when the Zs encircled his truck. As he sat there serenaded by the sounds of the dead worrying the truck's exterior, he closed his eyes and relived the ride along with Beeson. He retraced the route from FOB Bastion, passed by the Craftsman he was parked in front of and continued on until a four-wheel-drive shop somewhere down the road entered his mind's eye. The details were vague but the still-darkened sign shone like a Klieg light in his memory. He started the truck and powered on the navigation system, bringing up a colorful map denoting the recommended route from his present location to the GPS coordinates he'd inputted earlier. He looked at the myriad of buttons and switches and repeatedly pressed the one marked **+**. Up popped a new map, zoomed in, and not as cluttered with arterials and Interstates and side streets as the previous. He hinged forward and looked closely at an overhead view—rendered in colorful pixels—of maybe two square miles of his surroundings. Running east to west were the oddly labeled streets, all named after letters of the alphabet and each followed by the word *Road.* Some of them had fractions attached after the corresponding letter; most did not. He looked over the names in small font. To the right was an entry for the Loma post office. There was a restaurant named Lola's, presumably a greasy spoon, definitely closed for good. Then the out-of-place numbers caught his eye and he matched the rest of the text with the sign he saw in his mind. *Mesa View 4x4, here I come*, he thought as he checked the time on the Suunto. Deciding he had a couple of spare minutes to burn before Brook set the hounds after him, he selected Drive, tromped the pedal and bulled through the desperate throng, completing another one-eighty. With its off-road tires throwing rock and cactus thorns at the pursuing Zs, the Ford swallowed up the curb and Cade steered north, the two-lane leading him further away from FOB Bastion.

Chapter 7

A mile north of the Craftsman, Cade spotted the darkened signage casting its long shadow beside a rectangular steel prefab. Emblazoned in red on a yellow background were the words *Mesa View 4x4* and a phone number below. The building itself was situated smack dab in the middle of a sea of dingy gray asphalt on which a dozen spots were lined out in the same faded yellow as the sign. To Cade, the place looked like it once had belonged to one of those large nationwide outfits that used to regularly send glossy catalogs disguised as an enthusiast's magazine to his home in Portland. Far from the immaculate store represented on the catalog cover, this place had fallen into a sad state of disrepair. He reached into the center console, coming out with his Bushnell's. Placed the cups to his eyes and manipulated the center wheel, bringing the once-white building into sharp focus.

The operation looked like any other rural garage Cade had ever seen—only this one apparently specialized exclusively in off-road vehicles—which was a good thing seeing as how the two hundred miles and God knows how many Zs they were likely to encounter between FOB Bastion and the compound would chew up a normal passenger car.

Parked haphazardly on the oil-stained cement beside the garage were a half-dozen pick-ups of all different makes and models. "Gotta be keys for one of them inside," Cade muttered to himself as he swept his gaze to the glass and metal door on the far right hand corner of the building where a handwritten sign was taped to the glass. CLOSED UNTIL FURTHER NOTICE had been printed meticulously in three-inch-high block letters. He ventured to guess the person who had made the sign had taken their time in hopes that the outbreak playing out live on television that Saturday would be revealed as some kind of an Orson Wells War of the Worlds-type of prank and everything would reset to normal after the weekend. But that hadn't been the case. *Closed forever was the reality of the situation*, he thought morosely, remembering his indoctrination to the outbreak on that Saturday in July. Killing his infected neighbor Ted with an ice axe had been the most surreal experience of his life, and thankfully his survival instinct kicked in and overrode his brain as it tried to process what he was seeing at the time.

Striking the troubling thoughts from his mind, he panned left to the plate window, where, below a set of horizontal blinds, drawn half-way up and far from level, a number of sun-faded placards hawking six-inch lift kits and Warn winches and all manner of aftermarket 4x4 parts leaned out against the glass.

Left of the office window were two dirt-streaked roller doors tall and wide enough to accommodate a monster truck of Bigfoot's stature. Inset on the nearest door was a smaller two-foot square opening with a rubber flap that Cade assumed was a dog door. Stacked vertically at the top of each roller door was a pair of fairly large windows through which Cade could see a white vehicle up on the lift; the sun entering the building's skylights glinted from the curvature of its windshield.

Next, he eyed the driveway, which, unlike the rest of the operation, was a scene of order. The thirty-foot stripe of asphalt was lined with beds of recently spread mulch dotted with hardy desert flowers that lent a colorful contrast to the shop's rundown exterior.

He scrutinized the sturdy wheeled gate at the end of the drive and grimaced upon noticing the chain and padlock put there to keep people like him out. And that was good and bad, he supposed. Good if nobody had come back seeking refuge from the dead the weekend Hell decided to open up. Bad if a couple of guard dogs had been left behind to watch over the place. More so for the dog's sake than his, for with three weeks without food or water he supposed they'd be long dead anyway.

As he sat in the idle truck while watching a trio of Zs amble his way, the fact that he was going to need to ask for help (one of his least favorite things to do) in order to crack this nut became painfully obvious. On the other hand, having six people—two of them bickering siblings—and a dog crammed into the Ford would be painful in its own special way doled out like a thousand paper cuts over the course of the upcoming trip.

Weighing the pros and cons of the latter scenario in his mind, he put the truck in reverse and backed up, bouncing over the curb and flower beds in the process. Then slapping the transmission into Drive, a quick look at the Suunto told him he'd been gone too long. *Shit*, he thought, wheeling left and destroying a good portion of Mesa View 4x4's only redeeming asset, sending multicolored petals airborne as he tore off in the direction from which he'd come.

Chapter 8

Like a speakeasy patron working a bottle of bathtub gin, the hip-high mound of dark earth was greedily soaking up the rain. The first shovelful had been nothing. Number fifty was a different story altogether. Daymon's muscles burned from the exertion, therefore, number fifty-one seemed exponentially heavier and more cumbersome than the previous. But he didn't stop. In between scoops he cast a sidelong glance at Duncan who was moving a degree slower and had just cast another load of thick mud into the grave, fully concealing Logan's upturned profile. Bowing his head, Daymon followed suit, depositing number fifty-two near where he imagined Gus's feet were.

With their combined efforts, the backbreaking work filling the graves took only a fraction of the time that Duncan had spent digging them, and when they had finished, both men were muddied and tired and hungry and all alone.

***

An hour earlier, as it turned out, Lev and Chief were the ones who'd answered Daymon's mayday and rushed from the compound armed to the teeth. And after the rotters were culled, they had tossed the bodies in the ditch to be burned later.

Afterward Duncan declined their offer to help bury Logan and Gus and instead redirected their good intentions and had them go back and ready a couple of vehicles for a return trip to the quarry. *And start some coffee*, he had called out to Chief as he closed the gate to the compound feeder road behind the waiting Toyota with Lev at the wheel.

***

"Coffee sounds good right about now," Duncan said, still staring at the spot in the forest where the Toyota had entered earlier.

There was a long minute of silence during which the drizzle let up and the clouds parted to reveal a sliver of blue sky.

Daymon leaned in and said, "Don't you want to say some words first?"

Duncan removed his glasses and wiped them for the hundredth time. Pinching the bridge of his nose, he said, "God already knows my feelings for Logan ... don't see a need to tell him again."

"And Gus?"

"Didn't know Gus very well but I did think good thoughts for the both of them while I was digging."

Daymon said, "Two birds with one stone ... pretty efficient." After which he held Duncan's gaze for a second and then flicked his eyes up at the retreating clouds, trying to resist the urge to forget about the subject he wanted to broach and instead go with some bullshit comment about the weather. *Nothing doing.* This was life and death type of stuff, he reasoned. So instead of praising Mother Nature for the sunshine, he dove right in and spoke from the heart. "I'm worried about you, Old Man," he conceded. "The Duncan who I've gotten to know wouldn't have sent Lev back to the compound without restringing the barbed wire behind him. Truth be told, I'm kinda pissed that Lev didn't string it up on his own accord, but I'll cross that bridge later."

"It was a long cold night for the kid," drawled Duncan.

"No excuse for slippin' up like that."

"Hell, Daymon. His friend ... my brother ... he was murdered yesterday in cold blood. Can't blame Lev. *Besides*," added Duncan, nearly shouting, "*I* told him to git and then ran him off."

"You know ... you almost bought the farm today," Daymon said through clenched teeth. "What if you left the gate leading to the compound wide open? More lives at stake than your grizzled carcass."

Duncan remained silent, his gaze fixed on a clutch of rotters emerging from the gloom where 39 exited the forest.

"What's *your* excuse?" asked Daymon, feeling oddly like a father dressing down his kid. He glanced over at the empty Jack bottle. Said nothing more as the impulse to scream and vent his anger grew exponentially.

"I had some forgettin' to do."

"Well mission-fuckin-a-complished," said Daymon, veins bulging in his neck. "I wanted to go get us some kind of critter for dinner. Instead I'm damn near ready to host a frickin' intervention for you. What do you think of that idea? Am I out of line?"

In response, Duncan picked up the empty and tossed it into the woods out of sight. Without making eye contact, he said, "Come on. Let's hash it out over coffee." He turned and, with Daymon staring holes into his back, made his way to the crippled Land Cruiser, reached inside and came out with the half-empty bottle of Jack. Without making eye contact he unscrewed the cap and paused mid-decision, the bottle in limbo, mid-air at a forty-five-degree angle, one bend of the elbow from touching his lips. But instead of giving in to the craving for the booze and its unique ability to dull the pain brought on by the unforeseen murders and the thought of what the girls were enduring at the hands of the killers, he rotated his arm and let the amber liquid spill out onto the grass at his feet. Then, seemingly channeling the ghost of Catfish Hunter, he threw the empty overhand. It sailed at least fifty yards, a graceful arc diagonally over SR-39, bounced once or twice on the shoulder without breaking and skittered into the ditch.

Seeing this, Daymon snatched up the pair of muddy shovels, walked to the Cruiser and stowed them in the rear. Still fuming, he asked, "Who's going to cover the rest of your shift?"

"Let me see your radio."

Daymon handed it over.

Thumbing the talk button, Duncan ordered Phillip up to the road to pull a few extra hours of watch.

Cocking his head, Daymon said, "Why Phillip? I thought you had your reservations about him."

"He's capable. But if he's up here keeping watch he won't be able to tag along with us to the quarry," explained Duncan. "And that'll spare everyone's ears ... 'cause that boy can talk."

Daymon nodded, unamused, then straightened up and looked west, the low sun at his back throwing his shadow long and exaggerated. He watched the flesh eaters negotiate the slight dip in the road, and when their gaunt faces broke the crest of the rise he asked, “You have some binocs?”

“In the rig. Let me get ‘em.” Duncan ducked in and came out with a pair of oversized black Bushnell’s, unwound the strap and handed them over. Squinting into the distance he asked, “Whatcha seeing?”

Daymon said nothing at first. Then he stepped onto the SUV’s running board to gain a better viewing angle.

Watching all of this, Duncan failed to understand why the taller man was focusing on something in the shadows behind the rotters. So he asked again, “Whatcha got?”

“There’s one of those things hanging back. Where the road curves and comes out of the trees.”

“What is it doing?”

“Probably nothing,” replied Daymon. “Let’s move this thing and restring the wire.”

Grabbing a rusty strand, Duncan asked, “Are you as sick of these goddamn things as I am?”

Finished wrapping the lower run of wire around the post, Daymon unsheathed the machete, smiled mischievously and replied, “Let’s wax some rotters.”

Chapter 9
FOB Bastion

"Up and at em," bellowed Brook. In fact she was up shortly after Cade and had already dressed in a pair of weathered tan camo fatigue pants she'd dutifully tucked into her boot tops. Over her heavy black T-shirt was a thin cotton long-sleeved blouse, once white, but now a dingy tan and buttoned mid-way up. Anticipating a long day in the sun, she'd rummaged through the drawers and found a tan kerchief which was knotted loosely around her neck. A black ball cap was pulled down low, her high pony tail sticking through the hole out back. And strapped on her hip was a compact Glock similar to Cade's that had been a gift from Colonel Cornelius Shrill, her big intimidating friend back at Schriever. Unaccustomed to hearing the female master raise her voice, Max yelped and bolted from under the cot and immediately went into search mode, ears perked, teeth bared, looking for the threat.

"Everything is OK. Stand down, Max," said Brook, a half-smile curling her lip. She glanced at her watch as the liquid crystal numerals flipped from 9:10 to 9:11. "It's these other *sleepy heads* who need to fall out and fall in." Although all was said tongue-in-cheek—delivered gruffly using Cade's army-speak-infused lexicon—all humor was lost on both Taryn and Sasha as the two came up swinging, lobbing verbal barbs of their own.

"Last time I checked I wasn't enlisted," blurted Taryn, rubbing sleep from her eyes.

Sasha whined, "You're not my mom ... what time is it anyway?"

"9:12," answered Raven after checking her recently acquired Timex.

Wilson's head poked from his sleeping bag and he planted one elbow on his cot. After craning around, he fixed a no nonsense glare on his sister and said, "Time to do what the lady says ... that's what time it is."

"Looks like I've got a lieutenant doing my light work," quipped Brook. "Now someone pass the ice cubes so I can get the bed hog off my cot." The fact that there wasn't so much as an ice crystal for hundreds of miles didn't register in Raven's analytical brain. The mere mention of ice cubes used in conjunction with the words *wake* and *up,* had an instantaneous effect on the twelve-year-old, causing her to sit ramrod straight, her eyes instantly scanning the room for incoming. "Mom," she called out. "Not fair. You had me thinking Dad was up to his old tricks."

"Just making sure you *stay frosty*, sweetie."

Raven scrunched her face up. "*Not funny*," she said, flopping onto her back while pulling a big handful of blanket over her head.

Just then, sparing Brook from a full scale all-girl mutiny, the distinctive sound of their new ride reverberated outside and the Ford's shadow darkened the front of the single-story double-wide.

"Total eclipse," said Wilson. "I frickin can't believe we're going to Utah in Pug's old ride." He looked towards Sasha just as a shudder of revulsion wracked her small frame.

"Had to remind me, didn't you."

"Sorry, sis," he answered sheepishly, cheeks going crimson.

The door opened a moment later and Cade's silhouette was framed in the doorway. He said, "Gassed up and good to go." Then he looked around and saw that everyone was packed, for the most part, then went on, "Raven, will you bring me my rifle?"

"Sure Dad," she said, sliding from her bag fully dressed. "Where is it?"

"Under my cot," he said, watching his impromptu test play out.

Raven found the M4 under the cot next to hers. Pulled it out one-handed by the butt stock and then pivoted and sat on the bed with it between her knees. What she did next, while keeping the weapon's muzzle pressed against the shag carpet, made Cade very proud of her and doubly grateful for the time Brook had spent teaching her the basics.

First, Raven ejected the magazine and placed it on the floor. Then she pulled the charging handle a couple of times before leaning the rifle over to visually check that the chamber was indeed empty. Lastly, the diminutive twelve-year-old slapped the magazine home and made sure the safety was engaged before bringing it over to him, muzzle down.

"Great job, sweetie," he said. Then, already knowing the answer, he asked her, "Did Mom teach you all of that?"

Brook scooped up her pack and on the way out the door called out over her shoulder, "Damn straight I did."

M4 in hand, Cade turned on one crutch and said, "Load up. We're *oscar mike* in five."

Chapter 10

Four fucking hours, thought Elvis. *Drive all night and then spend half an hour groveling for my life trying to prove I had no intention of following through on Robert Christian's final orders. All while kissing that bastard's boots and I'm allowed only four fucking hours of sleep.* He rubbed his red-rimmed eyes and worked the controls. The blade lowered and bit into the earth. The diesel engine growled and black, dirty exhaust belched from the stack as the next phalanx of saplings and wrist-sized firs rolled under the breaking wave of rich topsoil.

In his peripheral vision he watched a pair of soldiers, clad in all black and toting like-colored carbines of some sort, pick their way to the clearing's edge. They took their time stepping over clods of dirt and uprooted ferns and halted a couple of feet from where a newly arrived zombie stood gripping the stretched wire.

"Let's see what you got," muttered Elvis who, less than a week ago, had been ripping the faces of the infected off their skulls in order to get to their salivary glands. *A means to an end*, he'd thought at the time. Anything to kill the soldiers as they cowered safe and sound inside the wire at Schriever Air Force Base.

But that one went sideways on him. He'd only managed to set off a chain reaction outbreak in the civilian quarters. To which the fucking soldiers showed up with Bradley Fighting Vehicles and Humvees and overwhelming firepower. Cowards. Just like dropping the Oakland Bay Bridge into the drink to save San Francisco. Using maximum force against their own populace in order to save their own asses—cowards one and all. And in the end his escape from Schriever undetected had been made possible because of the soldiers' unwillingness to clean up their own messes ... to do their own dirty work. Burial detail. He'd volunteered days before. *A means to an end.* Loading the infected onto Dead Sleds—massive earth moving dump trucks—and then sending them back, *ashes to ashes and dirt to dirt,* from whence they came. Nope ... nobody wanted to touch that task with a ten-foot pole. Not even the brave *warriors.* Going outside of the wire to bury the very folks he'd just infected, as much as killing his driver—the affable Private Mark Farnsworth—was also a *means to an end.* And if all went as planned, that end would be very profound and he'd finally strike a deadly blow to the heartless automatons who'd signed his family's death warrant on that Bay Bridge nearly three weeks ago.

Wishing he had an energy drink or steaming cup of black coffee, or better yet a rail of something much stronger, chemically based and white, Elvis cast a quick glance at Bishop who was watching him through a pair of binoculars from the covered wraparound porch of the giant lake house.

So, just as he had done after volunteering as a driver for the Minot mission weeks ago, he put his head down and did what he was told. *Two hours,* he guessed. Two more hours and he'd have enough of the forest pushed back and the soil packed and grated smooth that he could relax. Maybe even sleep. He smiled at the thought of putting his head down and closing his eyes. But then remembered what Bishop had said: A plat inside the security perimeter sufficient in size to accommodate a number of helicopters. The muscular former Seal had also ordered him to make it a 'flag lot,' leaving room enough for a tractor trailer to back in and still remain under cover of the trees on the 'pole part' of the clearing. But Elvis had no idea what in the hell a flag lot was, let alone the *pole* part of a fucking flag lot. Plus he'd just arrived from his cross-country drive when the orders had been issued and had been much too tired to request clarification. So he'd nodded and forced his eyes to remain open and winged it—just as he was doing now.

He raised the blade by a few degrees and set the tractor to idling. Pictured a mental image of a flag flapping in the breeze. He looked left and then right. Which corner would the pole go on? He reached into a pocket. Came out with a poker chip he'd scooped off the ground outside an Indian Casino somewhere west of the Rockies.

Left for heads, right for tails, he thought as he flipped the clay marker into the air. He caught it and slapped it on his thigh and removed his hand. *Tails.*

Right it is, he thought. *One thousand worthless dollars' worth of right.* He clanked the dozer over to the spot where the chip decided he would start the next cut. Along the way he passed by the black-clad soldiers, who abruptly stopped hacking appendages from the oblivious flesh eater and flashed smiles and bloodied blades, as if to say *Take a look at our handiwork.*

And he did, stopping the dozer broadside. He feigned a conspiratorial smile and was caught off guard by the sharp pong wafting off the corpse. Crinkling his nose, he whispered his new mantra, "Means to an end." Though he didn't want to, he found himself compelled to set eyes on the poor creature. From the neck up the thing was nearly impossible to look at. Truly a ghastly sight, minus everything fleshy: nose, ears, lips, eyelids. The zombie had been rendered aerodynamically streamlined and now resembled a demonic version of the tortured soul depicted in Edvard Munch's the Screamer. From the neck down was a different story. The sadists had hacked off the creature's forearms, leaving it looking like some kind of battlefield casualty, straining against the fence, mouth opening and closing, waving its bloody stumps at its antagonists.

Elvis threw a half-assed salute at the men, sending them back to their macabre undertaking.

Then, now knowing precisely why he was cutting the *pole* part of the flag lot into the forest, he lowered the blade and resumed razing the earth.

Watching the action through a pair of binoculars from his post near the north gate, Jimmy Foley, a newly conscripted townie, said a small prayer that whoever was driving the tractor would *accidentally* run over the pair he'd taken to calling the Brothers Grimm.

Chapter 11

A handful of things Jamie knew for certain. The first, and hardest for her to admit, was that Logan was dead. Replaying the surreal scene in her head for the hundredth time, she heard the out-of-place mechanical buzzing of the egg-shaped helicopter as it flitted left to right. The black flash of metal and glass skimmed inches above the borrowed police Tahoe. Then, like an old film, jittery and slow in motion, she saw the needle antennas quiver spasmodically from the disturbed air and the black and white SUV start rocking subtly on its springs. A microsecond later, bullets were snapping the air around her and the two men responsible for the barrage had materialized from her right side near the trio of swaybacked sheds. To her left, Logan's breath left his body, producing a drawn-out wheezy groan unlike anything she'd ever heard. Simultaneously, the fatal one-two punch registered in her side vision and she saw his black bowler hat go airborne. Instinctively her eyes tracked it as it tumbled slowly, then, a tick later, his feet followed his hat's trajectory and he was pitched onto his back, bloody red blossoms breaking out on his tan fatigue top. Then, without warning, she felt a sharp pain in her knee and was bowled over and face down on the cool concrete, wedged between Logan's inert body and Gus, who was by then flat on his back, gasping for breath, his frantic eyes seemingly begging her to run.

But she couldn't. She struggled to move but the strap on her carbine had become twisted when she fell. She remembered feeling the weight of the rifle against her back, but face down with her arms pinned fast there was no way to fight back.

Everything had happened so quickly that her mind was still collating the intense bombardment of stimuli when a dark shadow rippled over Logan's body and the light coming in through the roller doors was mostly blocked out.

The last thing she remembered before everything went black was the tempest of noise, the kerosene-tinged air and the metallic tang of Logan's warm blood as it wet her cheek and soaked into her hair.

Sometime later she regained consciousness in a helicopter with a hood reeking of blood and fear-laced sweat cinched tightly over her head, her wrists bound together so tightly that she feared a double amputation might be in her immediate future.

Next, the gravity of her situation hit her hard and fast like the bullets that had struck down the man she had grown to like and was beginning to love.

Remaining calm, she had taken immediate stock of her injuries, the worst of which had been a dull throbbing emanating from behind her left ear where she guessed the knockout blow had been delivered. From her right knee came the disconcerting sound of bone grating on bone. An injury sustained when Gus, acting heroically, had violently pushed her out of the line of fire.

Now, a sleepless night later, her brain felt like it was caroming around inside her skull and her knee was still noisy and swollen, yet remarkably could support her entire weight. Whether or not she could outrun her captors if the opportunity presented itself was a question that would have to be answered if, or when, the chance arose.

As the helicopter droned on, Jamie cocked her head towards the pilots up front and listened to their conversation, which was businesslike and spoken in a difficult-to-follow jargon. The only thing she was able to pick up on were references pertaining to their altitude and present airspeed and certain terrain features they were looking out for. Much to her chagrin, though she had hoped for some tidbit to slip, their conversation revealed nothing about where they were now, or where they were going.

After a few minutes of straight and level flight, the helicopter abruptly nosed down and banked right, dropping a big chunk of altitude in the process. Consequently the aggressive maneuver caught

Jamie unaware and, when the craft finally righted, her head moved past center and thumped against the opposite bulkhead, further aggravating the concussion and resulting in an intense wave of nausea that set her salivary glands into overdrive.

"I'm about to throw up," she croaked, her jaw beginning to lock. She tried some shallow breathing but the hot fetid air inside the hood only made matters worse. And though she could sense the man moving just inches to her right, he made no reply. So she doubled down. Made it personal by calling him by name. "Come on, *Carson.* What possible harm can I do to you? You think I'm going to open the door of a moving helicopter and run for it?" she asked, twisting her hooded head in his direction. He remained silent.

"I can't even feel my *fucking* fingers."

Still he made no reply.

She panned her head forward and called out loudly, hoping to be acknowledged by the pilots. "I need help back here. I'm going to be sick."

Nothing. Just the rotor blades beating the air overhead.

Her jaw locked open and a flurry of tremors wracked her body. Deep in her esophagus she felt the first little acidic tickle, her body forewarning her of the rising tide of bile. Then her stomach clenched tight, involuntarily doubling her over. To her right, she heard a metallic *snik* that was instantly recognizable, causing her to tense further. She imagined a gleaming eight-inch blade locking into place. Then her mind began to jump the rails, conjuring up the wolfish glare of a man whose face she hadn't yet seen. *Breathe*, she told herself. *If they wanted you dead, Jamie, they would have left your bullet-riddled body back at the quarry alongside Logan and Gus.*

Then something brushed her thigh, causing her to recoil and shrink against the helicopter's cool metal skin. She felt the hood go tight around the crown of her head. She heard the rasp of rough burlap as her head was being pulled toward the center of the chopper—towards the man she'd overheard the pilots calling Carson. Then her mind messed with her again. Tried to convince her the blade was being dragged across her neck, so real she could almost feel the flesh parting as a mortal half-moon-shaped incision was opened up under her chin. Then the blood sluicing down her chest, hot and sticky and metallic to the nose. She waited for it. Welcomed it. Instead, the hood came off with an audible pop. And as quickly as she had embraced the thought of death, the stark terror of living the rest of her life in pain while suffering through every type of degradation returned to haunt her.

The greasy sack collapsed into a pile on her lap and, for a split second before the sun behind him became too intense, she saw Carson's profile in her peripheral vision. *We're flying north*, she thought just before closing her eyes.

"You puke anywhere but in that bag and you will find yourself flying under your own power," he said, catching her wholly by surprise. His voice was gravelly and she wondered if he'd suffered some kind of injury to his vocal chords in the past. She wanted nothing more than to see her captor. To look into his eyes and gauge his resolve.

But she said nothing. Kept her lids sealed and fumbled to grasp the bag with numb hands. Then she felt Carson's hand, rough and calloused, grip both forearms. Keeping her head bowed, she opened her eyes to slits and watched as he severed the plastic tie binding her wrists with a blade all of five inches long. Black and squared off at the tip—the Tanto-style lock-blade was a far cry from the shiny twelve-inch-long butcher's model she had envisioned.

"Thank you," she croaked, feeling blood course through the ulnar and radial arteries. And as the blood continued on into the veins and microscopic capillaries in her fingers, she welcomed the sensation of tens of thousands of invisible pins and needles jabbing her there all at once. Because, she reasoned, though it was probably just a figure of speech, if she ever got her hands around Carson's neck, she hoped to feel the life slipping from him as she choked him to death.

Pushing the absurd fantasy from her thoughts, she opened her eyes incrementally and surreptitiously scanned her surroundings. At her feet on the floor of the helicopter were the black foot-locker-sized boxes she remembered seeing in the underground complex at the quarry. And also taken from the quarry compound, sitting on the fold-down seats with labels on their sides that read *Simplot Idaho Potatoes,* were a pair of sturdy cardboard boxes packed to overflowing with smaller rectangular boxes containing all different calibers of ammunition. She moved her gaze left by a degree, looked out the

Plexiglas window and saw far below the terrain which appeared almost alpine, comprised more of jagged rock and forest than the desert terrain of Utah. She saw small hillocks and lush green pine trees standing out prominently among the ground clutter.

Shifting her gaze to the right, she carefully scrutinized Carson from the chest down. His belt looked to have been a military-issue item at one time; braces ran up and over his shoulders. The whole system was supporting a series of pouches bristling with tan polymer magazines, brass glinting from the top of one of them. His pants were khaki-colored and made of thick fabric with lots of pockets, the legs of which were tucked into his boot tops and bloused smartly. His boots were lug-soled, black leather, and laced tightly. The mud caking the waffle pattern looked identical to the stuff she'd seen at the quarry, ochre red and fine like talc. And giving away which hand he favored, a holster containing some kind of desert tan semi-auto pistol with heavily knurled grips rode low on his left thigh. For half a heartbeat Jamie thought about making a play for the weapon, then remembered what he'd said to her a second ago and decided that nothing about *flying under her own power* sounded appealing. Not to mention the fact that even if she succeeded in getting the weapon from the man—which was highly doubtful considering her physical condition—she'd still have the gunmen in the helicopters keeping pace with this one to deal with.

She closed her eyes and her thoughts turned to Jordan, whom she hadn't seen since the previous day. The last thing she remembered was seeing the young woman sitting in the Tahoe, blonde hair whipping as her head followed the movements of the flitting helicopters. Lastly, before Logan and Gus were gunned down, the look of incredulity on the young woman's face morphed into one of sheer terror.

With the horrible memories of the day freshly tilled, she hinged up, opened her eyes and in a low voice asked, "Why? Why did you have to kill them?"

He said nothing.

Risking retaliation, she looked at him full on and saw a compact man crackling with nervous energy. Noticeable at once on his cheek, red and ragged near the edges, was a trio of fresh scratch marks. Then she sized him up, quickly deciding that the way he held himself—sitting ramrod straight with his feet planted on the deck a shoulder-width apart—meant he was definitely former military.

Shooting her a no-nonsense glare, he said, "Get a good look?"

She made no reply. Instead she drew the bag to her lips and faked a couple of dry heaves.

He fished a zip tie from a cargo pocket, fashioned it into a loose cuff and tossed it onto her lap. "Finish up ... then cuff yourself," he said brusquely.

She spit into the sack. Looked up and said, "You going to answer my question?"

He stared at her. Seemed to be contemplating the question. His eyes were pale blue bordering on slate gray and bored into her with a thousand-yard stare. Suddenly Jamie felt like a mouse in a room full of cats. And worst of all, she found that she couldn't break eye contact with the predator to her right. Then it struck her how Aryan his looks were—like she was in the presence of a Brown Shirt from Central Casting. High cheekbones and a squared-off jaw framed a once-aquiline nose that had obviously been broken in the past. The color of dirty straw, strands of his fine hair peeked out from under a tan ball cap sporting an embroidered caricature of a monkey brandishing a wicked-looking silenced weapon.

Suddenly she sensed his energy again. Only now it was less nervous ... more like a spring in a giant bear trap, under tremendous tension yet still keeping all of the deadly workings in place.

His eyes narrowed and he said, "I hate to be cliché but you and your friends were in the wrong place at the wrong time. Just asking for trouble leaving that Black and White in plain sight."

"They weren't my friends," she lied. "You could say it was a marriage of convenience. No way to survive out there without having any kind of numbers on your side."

"Good ... 'cause you'll make new friends where we are going. And numbers—that won't be a problem either." He shut down and turned forward. Just like she wasn't even there.

A beat later, one of the pilots called out over his shoulder, "Twenty minutes out."

Carson nodded at the pilot. Then he looked at Jamie and pointed to the cuffs.

Message received. Jamie smoothed her dark hair behind her ears, left the empty sack in her lap and worked one of the interlocked cuffs over each hand, then took the stray end of the tie between her teeth and pulled it taut.

Shaking his head disappointedly, Carson said, "Good try." He leaned over and cinched the cuffs. Then, spit and stink and all, he eased the stifling hood over her head but, showing a little bit of compassion, left it loose around her neck. The tie binding her wrists, however, was as tight as it had been before.

Cursing under her breath, Jamie sat and stewed and fantasized once again about how she'd kill him if she ever got the chance.

Chapter 12

Seven minutes after Cade pulled the Ford up in front of the double-wide, the pick-up's cab was brimming with six people, a Todd Helton Louisville Slugger, two stubby M4 rifles—one equipped with a suppressor—and Sasha's precious designer bags.

Taryn, Sasha, and Wilson were in the backseat while Brook was up front riding *shotgun*. That left Raven, who was by far the smallest of the group, stuck riding up front next to her dad who, for reasons he was keeping to himself, was hell bent on driving the first leg of the trip.

Max, though relegated to riding in the box bed, found himself a spot amongst Raven's purple-and-white mountain bike, some boxes of food and water, and the two hard-sided Pelican cases containing the additional weapons, ammunition, and gear Colonel Shrill had allowed Cade to select prior to them leaving Schriever.

Cade started the Ford and, before he'd completed the K-turn to get them headed back towards the front gate, a lively debate broke out over why the dead were walking.

"I think the Rapture backfired or something," opined Sasha with all the authority of a theology professor.

"Whoa ... hold on to that thought for a second. I need to know if I heard you right ... or if you're thinking of an old Blondie song," countered Wilson, twisting in his seat to address his sister who was occupying the center spot between him and Taryn. "So the big event ... the Rapture happens and instead of us seeing all of the clothing and personal effects of the chosen scattered all over the place, you are telling me only their souls were taken and their husks remained behind to rot and walk the earth ... and eat those that weren't called home?" He took a deep breath and waited for her response.

Meanwhile Cade bounced the truck over a curb and straightened it out and drummed his fingers on the wheel as the gate came into view.

The silence killing her, Brook twisted around and opened her mouth to speak but was beaten to the punch by the feisty teenaged redhead.

"What's your theory then, Wilson?" Sasha said in a petulant tone. "You've got an opinion on everything anyways ... and you're always telling me what to do."

Peering past Sasha, an impish grin on her face, Taryn said to Wilson, "Let's hear it, just for *shits* and *giggles*."

Looking over her left shoulder, Brook shot the tattooed young woman a look that said, *Watch your language* and then shifted her gaze to Raven, who was trying very hard not to laugh.

"All right," answered Wilson. "I bet some a-hole in a bunker somewhere let the Omega bug out."

"You mean like in the *Stand*?"

"No Sasha ... I mean like in some greedy-upper-crust-bastards who wanted all of this for themselves before the eaters and breeders sucked it all up ... purposefully released the bug on the population."

Not far from the truth, kid, thought Cade as he hung a right and brought the rig to a halt a number of feet from FOB Bastion's front gate. He killed the engine and shrugged his shoulders in response to a look delivered by one of the soldiers, who was obviously nonplussed at having to repeat the time-consuming process of extending the mobile bridge again. Then, as Sergeant Andreasen approached the truck on the driver's side, Cade opened the center console, reached in and came out with a black plastic case, about a foot in length. Once the no-nonsense soldier was at his door and looking up, he handed the case down and said, "Hopefully this will make do until Beeson's boys return from Salt Lake."

Knowing precisely what was in the box without having to open it, Sergeant Andreasen cocked her head and tried to pass it back to him. "Are you sure you won't need it?"

He put his palm up. The universal semaphore for *I'm not taking no for an answer.* "It's OK, Sergeant. I've got a couple more where that one came from. Besides," he explained, "they've got more gear than personnel at Schriever."

She nodded. "Understood. I was at Carson ..." *Bingo, thought Cade.* "... and the Zs sure did a number on us that first weekend."

"Did a number on everyone, *everywhere*, that first weekend," replied Cade. "I'll make a call to a guy I know at Schriever ... a first sergeant named Whipper. He's been pretty good about seeing to my needs lately. I'll ask him to make sure some more of those come out on the next supply bird."

"Thank you, sir ... er, um ... Cade. Colonel's already requested replacements and extra gear for us—" She paused and looked away as the hydraulic system hissed and the bridge began to fold out across the dirt chasm. Meeting his gaze, she went on, "Can't blame Colonel Beeson though ... you and I both know how slow the wheels of the Big Green Machine turn."

"Copy that," said Cade as a hollow thud diverted his attention to outside the wire just as the five ton aluminum bridge made contact with the soil, starting a dirt devil spinning. Nodding at the sergeant, he turned the key and put the transmission into gear.

"You stay frosty out there," said the sergeant over the engine noise. "Heard the 70 is thick with them due west of here. Green River's not safe either."

"Colonel Beeson briefed me," replied Cade. "But thanks. I figure we'll be doing most of our driving on the back roads." He untangled the coiled power cord and plugged one end into the sat phone and the other into the accessory outlet. Eased off the brake and, as the Ford rolled through the gate and over the fully extended bridge, he cast a quick glance towards the makeshift FOB and noted Old Glory popping in the wind over Beeson's quarters. What he failed to see, however, was the salute—totally unwarranted and against regs—given him by Staff Sergeant Andreasen as he left the relative safety of the base for the second time in less than an hour.

Inside the cab, a slightly robotic and totally unnerving female voice emanating through the Ford's over-the-top sound system said, "In two hundred feet, turn left." Then she rattled on the distance to I-70, instructing whoever was listening to take the on-ramp west.

Two hundred feet ahead Cade did not turn left. He did just the opposite. And it was an action that sparked an immediate and explosive outburst from Taryn. Gesticulating wildly with her tattooed arms, she called out from the back seat, "Where in the hell are you taking us?"

Cade looked into the rearview just as Taryn launched herself part-way over Brook's seatback and began shouting at him, "Grand Junction is this way and I do not want to go anywhere near that place ... seeing it from the safety of the helicopter was barely tolerable."

Having never heard her husband dressed down in such a manner, Brook stared wide-eyed at him, waiting for a response.

Saying nothing, Cade turned off the navigation system, a move that silenced the piped-in female voice. Half a block later, Taryn crawled back into her skin when, without warning, Cade turned north, halting further progress toward her former home.

There was a brooding silence in the cab, as if each of them, save Cade, had some kind of a preconceived notion of where this deviation was taking them but were afraid to ask.

Finally, Cade pointed to the Craftsman-style house on the northeast corner a block distant. "Anything look familiar?"

Brook walked her gaze along his outstretched arm and when she finally picked out the two-story house with the shiny SUV parked in the drive, a wide range of emotions welled up inside of her.

"Looks like our old house, Daddy," blurted Raven. "And there's one of *them* on the porch."

"Keep driving, Cade Grayson," said Brook icily.

Craning his head, Wilson added, "Looks like it's got a hold of the door knob."

After doing a quick double-take and corroborating Wilson's observation, Cade recounted out loud for everyone's benefit the behaviors he'd observed the Zs exhibit at the cemetery in South Dakota. However, he had to work extra hard to convince everyone that the Z at the crash site had in fact been stalking him. And then when he mentioned that one of the monsters had tried to open the door to Jasper's truck, he ran into a five against one roadblock with Wilson saying that it had to have been some kind of an anomaly.

"It was probably just its body coming into contact with the outside latch ... accidentally jiggling it or something," Brook reasoned.

Shaking his head and slowing the truck to a crawl, Cade answered her challenge, “No way. I’m pretty certain the door handle on that old truck was the kind that you reach under and pull up on. No way leaning on something designed like that is going to move the handle on the inside. Take a look.” He applied more brake and peered across Raven and Brook. “That’s exactly what I’m talking about.” The Z’s form now filled up the doorway and the wooden door was swinging slowly inward.

“Your point is?” said Sasha, joining the pile-on-Cade party.

“I was inside that house forty-five minutes ago.”

“And you left the door ajar ... right?” queried Brook.

“No,” he said. He thought hard for a few seconds, wondering whether he wanted to open the Pandora’s Box of worry by disclosing what he knew. Finally he decided full disclosure was what he owed everyone. He looked Brook in the eye and added, “I left it exactly how I found it. Door latched ... but unlocked.”

There were a couple of gasps from the back seat, then it went deathly quiet inside the Ford. First, Brook shot Cade a look of displeasure to which he merely shrugged. Then, she looked away and all eyes were on the zombie on the porch as it entered the house through the shadowy doorway. Finally, after Cade had seen enough, he released the brake—an action that started the familiar-looking house gliding by on the right—and everyone decided to speak at once.

Brook asked, “What does it mean?”

“Can they learn to drive?” asked Raven.

“Or shoot a gun?” added Sasha breathlessly.

“What with the tattered clothes and hanging flesh on that one ... it looked like the kind of zombie I’ve heard people calling a *first turn*,” was Wilson’s only take on the spectacle.

Cade looked over at Brook and said, “I don’t know yet.” He shifted his gaze to Raven. “Not in a million years ... especially not a stick shift.” And to Sasha, whose eyes he met in the rearview mirror, his answer, and the way he delivered it, left them all speechless. “If they learn ... or more likely remember how to operate a firearm, then all of mankind is doomed. So instead of worrying about what-ifs, let’s focus on staying alive for one more *second*. Then try stringing a few more of those precious seconds into minutes and then those minutes into hours and so on. Before we all know it the sun will be down and we'll likely be at the compound safe and sound."

"What my dad is trying to say—in way too many words—is that he wants all of us to *stay frosty*."

Smiling, Cade gave Raven a playful nudge and said to Wilson, "I think you're on to something. Maybe more of their old lives and memories creep to the surface the longer they're walking around. And if that's the case ... I hope to God it's just rudimentary low-motor-skill-type of stuff they regain."

After another long moment of palpable silence, Cade disclosed the new behaviors that Sergeant Andreasen had witnessed at the gate. Startling new revelations about the walking dead that kept them all thinking inwardly until Mesa View 4x4 and the mini-herd of zombies seemingly guarding it came into view.

Chapter 13

The turbine ratcheting up in pitch was Jamie's first clue that something was up. Then the falling sensation that came next instantly transported her back through time and she was twelve with her father at Disney's Space Mountain and being flung around like a rag doll in pitch black aboard the noisy rollercoaster—a feeling of spatial disorientation and utter helplessness that had not been surmounted until now.

And just like that she snapped back to reality and was in the helicopter—probably somewhere over Idaho—the craft in the middle of a one hundred and eighty degree turn and seemingly about to crash. She began to panic, her head spinning in the claustrophobia-inducing hood, until finally, after what felt like an eternity, the craft leveled out and she was reduced to dry heaving and begging to have the hood removed.

"Only long enough for you to empty your stomach"—Carson growled as he yanked the sack from her head, turned it over and arranged it on her lap atop her numb hands—"then it goes right back on."

Squinting against the sun, she looked down and saw rivulets of blood seeping from the deep cuts where the plastic ties bit into her wrists. Then, in order to see the full picture, she shifted sideways and *accidentally* spilled the makeshift airsickness bag on the cabin floor near her captor's feet.

"Better not puke yet," hissed Carson as he leaned over and snatched the hood from the cabin floor.

Swallowing hard, Jamie caught sight of her fingers, puffed and purple and turning black at the tips. She moaned and pitched forward and, just as Carson replaced the bag on her lap, let go with a torrent of jaundice-colored liquid the viscosity of ten-weight motor oil. She heaved and convulsed and felt the warm bile soaking through the greasy burlap and into her pants. *No time like the present*, she thought as she hinged forward and crushed the soiled burlap between her breasts and knees and flexed her arms in a calculated and covert effort at loosening the zip tie.

The crushing backhand came out of nowhere, sending her head spinning. Then, adding insult to injury, the helicopter abruptly bottomed out, and with the engine's whine diminishing, there was the hail-like noise of small debris pelting the fuselage. The rotor blades overhead slowed to a steady chop and kerosene-tinged air and dust swirled inside as the pilot in the left seat unbuckled and exited the gently shimmying aircraft.

Glancing sidelong at Carson, she realized he'd been ignoring her. He was looking out the window to his right, and beyond him, through the hazy swirls on the glass, she could see several more helicopters land and from them disembarked a half-dozen armed men. She craned her head and was able to see enough to conclude they were conducting a raid similar to the one on the quarry. A target of opportunity had presented itself, and like a raven swooping to collect a shiny bauble, the human predators were on to new prey.

There were yellow-white flashes lancing from the mercenaries' muzzles as they advanced on the log-cabin-like structure. Then a heartbeat later, Carson's men fanned out into a rough semi-circle and one of them began motioning towards the building and yelling what she guessed must be orders to surrender. And this was confirmed on the back side of that heartbeat when the front door opened and a grizzled-looking older man emerged, holding aloft some sort of long rifle, and was instantly cut in half by a hail of bullets. Jamie closed her eyes and worked on her bonds and asked, "Why?"

"Because he might have something that *we* need," replied Carson coldly, his eyes glued to the action taking place twenty yards away.

"And taking it is OK ... after all they've gone through to survive this long? You just *snuff* them out like that?"

"Dead men tell no tales. And they can't come seeking vengeance either."

"Well that's where you fucked yourself."

"How so?"

"Because the men you killed ... Logan and Gus—"

"You mean the *homo* with the bowler hat?" He paused for a second and looked out the window, focusing all of his attention on the two camo-clad men who were dragging a blonde woman along the ground.

Burning with hatred for the man next to her, Jamie said nothing. Instead she bit her lip, drawing blood, and leaned forward to get a better angle on the helicopter that looked strikingly similar to the DHS Black Hawk parked at the compound.

"That *had* to have been Logan," continued Carson. He sat back in his seat. Fixed a cold stare on Jamie. "Only a guy named Logan would feel the need to accessorize to the point of looking like one-half of Laurel and Hardy." He shook his head in disgust. "And the handlebar mustache. G-A-Y."

Ignoring the baited trap, Jamie said nothing and watched the looting taking place, grateful that the raiding party hadn't dragged out any young boys or girls.

Disappointment showing on his face, Carson continued his verbal barrage. "So, the other one was Gus, eh? Typical middle-aged former cop. Paunchy around the waist from sitting in a cruiser. Clouded in the head from toeing the line for most of his adult life. Gotta give it to him, though. He almost got a shot off. Logan on the other hand ... he wet himself."

Pursing her lips to hide the self-inflicted wound, Jamie said quietly, "Gus was ten times the man you are. And Logan ..." Her voice trailed off. She ran her tongue over her dry teeth and finished her sentence. "Logan was a gentle soul. He didn't deserve whatever you did to him."

Carson chuckled as he watched his men loading cardboard boxes into the idling helicopters.

"You're not finished with them. You know that ... don't you? His brother and best friend are hunting for you as we speak. And when they find you you're going to wish you were never even born."

"On that, my lady, you are sadly mistaken. All of your friends' corpses were cooling thirty minutes before Logan and Gus bought the farm," he said smugly. "Hell, maybe big brother gave Logan the guided tour when they were reunited ... in hell."

One of the pilots called back, "Five mikes."

Carson flashed the pilots a thumbs up. After shooting Jamie a wolfish grin, he repeated her own words. "A marriage of convenience my ass. You were an integral part of that group." He looked her over from head to toe and fished a four-by-six-inch scrap of paper from his chest pocket. It was creased and tattered around the edges and had uniformly spaced words printed in light blue on the back. He held it up, long side vertical, oriented like a portrait, then craned around and looked her full in the face. His eyes flicked back to what had to be a photo and back to her face, lingering there for a moment until the pilot called back a one-minute warning. Finally, holding the photo at arm's length, Carson made one final side-by-side comparison before putting the paper back in his pocket. Shattering the Hallmark moment, one of the pilots shouted back, "We're wheels up."

Carson nodded and looked Jamie in the eye and said, "You're right up his alley."

As the engine whine and rotor chop increased, Jamie cocked her head and asked, "Whose alley?"

"My friend's."

"Over my dead body."

"That's what the other girl said. And somehow through all of the whimpering and screaming that came afterward we got a name out of her. Said her name was Jordan." A knowing, almost conspiratorial smile creased his face. "You know, as in *Air*."

Instantly the puzzle pieces fell into place. The fresh scratches and recent comment combined with the fact that she hadn't seen Jordan since the quarry led her to the heart-wrenching conclusion that she was never going to see the impressionable young lady again. *Fucker is going to pay if he lets me near that pistol*, she thought as she watched him extract a knife and flick it open. Her hopes welled but were instantly dashed when he retrieved a new zip tie. After fashioning it into a dinner-plate-sized 'O,' he maneuvered it over her hands which by now were an angry shade of purple, and secured it somewhat loosely before slicing off the old ties. Then, with a sly grin, he mouthed, "You'll do," and pulled the soiled hood over her head.

Breathing in the acidic stench of her own bile, Jamie called out, "Do I have a choice?"

She sensed his presence first and then felt his body pressing against hers. Then he whispered through the burlap. "You have two choices. Unfortunately a quick death isn't one of them." Jamie didn't indulge him with a response. Then as the helicopter became light on its wheels and wavered subtly, Carson spoke again, his words filtering into the hood. "You can give yourself to one. Or be taken by many."

Chapter 14

"Under my seat," Cade called over his shoulder as Wilson popped open the rear passenger door. "Snip the lock and then wrap the chain around the posts once we're all inside." He dangled a zip tie out the window and added, "Secure the chain with this once we're inside."

Grunting an affirmative and none too happy to have been conscripted for the job, Wilson hit the pavement at about the same time Brook, who was armed with a short and lethal-looking carbine, emerged from around the front of the truck.

After taking the zip tie from Cade, Wilson cast a furtive glance at the Zs they'd just passed. Thinking, *Hope it holds*, he stuffed the thin plastic fastener into a pocket, rummaged under the seat and came away with the biggest pair of bolt cutters he'd ever seen. He slammed the door, then, with Brook close on his heels, looped around front and approached the wheeled gate. Once there, Brook spun on her heels and squatted next him. Wavering on her haunches, she leaned in close and said in a low voice, "Cade says there may be dogs inside ... so watch your six."

Without skipping a beat, Wilson ran the long-handled cutter's gleaming jaws back and forth over the chain-link. He locked his gaze on the distant building and when the discordant jangling finally ceased, looked back at Brook and said, "No Fido."

Focused on the approaching dead, Brook said nothing. Instead she urged Wilson to pick up the pace with a slight nudge from the collapsed butt stock of her M4.

After shooting her a sour look and again eyeing the walking corpses that were by now only a handful of yards away, Wilson went to work on the industrial strength Schlage padlock.

In the box bed, teeth bared and hackles up, Max was growling and spinning circles atop one of the Pelican containers. At the gate, attacking the lock with the bulky bolt cutters, Wilson heard the guttural growling at his back suddenly become a veritable Hounds of the Baskerville's kind of baying.

Hearing the commotion, Cade looked into the rearview and saw pale hands reaching for the snarling and snapping dog. *Not good*, he thought. In his experience there were a handful of noises the dead were especially drawn to. Mechanical sounds and gunfire and especially anything associated with fresh meat: people's voices, a baby's cries, or a dog's bark—the latter of which he decided needed to be silenced.

After threading the hefty cylindrical suppressor to the business end of his Glock, he checked for a round in the chamber and powered down his window. The stench slapped him in the face as he called out, "Max, quiet now!" Then after a quick two-count he added, "Max, down!" Then he waited, hoping two things would result from the barked orders. The first of which depended solely on whether Max had received any kind of command training from his original owners. And the second part of his plan was directly correlated to the outcome of the former. In theory, Max would cease howling and lie down out of view. Then Cade would quietly deal with the handful of dead that had been getting after the dog—which were a pittance compared to the numbers likely to be drawn if Max continued to bark.

Suddenly, as if Max knew the battle was lost, he went silent and disappeared from sight.

Then Cade's prediction came true and the dead lost all interest in the dog and filed towards Wilson and Brook, who by now had her carbine trained on them. Cade met her gaze and waved her off with a vertical finger pressed to his lips.

While all of this was unfolding, Taryn had crawled across the bench seat and sat up behind Cade just as the tops of the zombies' heads passed outside her window. "Do something," she hissed.

Cade whispered over his shoulder, "Gotta have faith ... and a *lot* more patience."

"Thanks, *Yoda*," she mumbled, casting a worried look at her man.

Cade flicked his eyes from Brook, who was now crabbing around the front of the truck, and then back to the side mirror and watched and waited as the trio of Zs tramped through the colorful flower beds. Without taking his eyes off the Zs, he gave Raven's forearm a reassuring squeeze and eased the Glock out the window. A tick later he extended his arm fully and pressed the cold steel to the first flesh eater's equally cold skin, barely an inch behind its right ear, and squeezed off a single shot.

The pistol bucked and the creature collapsed into a vertical heap, scrambled brains dribbling from the quarter-sized exit wound. The report, though not as quiet as portrayed on TV or in the movies, garnered the next Z's full attention, and before Cade could react, the monster had grabbed ahold of the suppressor and was drawing it into its open maw.

Smiling, Cade simultaneously caressed the trigger and said, "Careful what you wish for." Instantly a pink mist vented from its neck as the 9mm Parabellum caromed off jawbone and lodged somewhere in the monster's spinal column. Before the now paralyzed flesh eater hit the ground, Cade had swept the pistol to his left and double-tapped the straggler, putting one bullet into each eye socket. Lastly, he shifted in his seat, leaned out the window aiming down and delivered the coup-de-grace: a single shot to the prostrate Z's forehead.

In all, from Max's first bark to Cade's final shot, only a dozen seconds had ticked into the past. And while those twelve seconds elapsed, Wilson had cut the lock and unwrapped the length of chain.

"Let's go," Brook hissed through clenched teeth. "There's more coming." Then, leading by example, she placed the M4 at her feet, grabbed the chain-link in both hands and drew in a deep lungful of carrion-infused air.

"On three," said Wilson, grabbing some fence as well.

Eschewing the countdown, Brook bellowed, "Now!" and leaned forward, driving her feet furiously against the asphalt driveway.

Behind both of their efforts a grating sound emanated from within the channel and the wheels began to roll; finally, after what had seemed like an eternity, the entrance was clear and Cade was driving the Ford over the threshold.

Seeing the tailgate glide by, Brook grabbed her carbine and placed it on her side of the fence. Then, summoning the strength necessary from somewhere deep inside her, she grabbed hold of the fence and drove it forward until it clanged shut. She fell to the asphalt, winded and totally spent.

After looping the chain and securing it with the zip tie, Wilson called out to Brook who was now sitting Indian-style on the cracked asphalt and breathing hard. "You know that thing is supposed to be motorized."

She said nothing at first. Kept her head bowed, back arched.

Wilson didn't know if she was praying or staring at the weeds growing up through the frost-heaved cement. Finally, after a few long seconds, she said, "Just our luck," and rose shakily on rubbery legs.

Walking slowly side-by-side towards Mesa View 4x4, Wilson said matter-of-factly, "I'm afraid to find out what your husband is getting us into."

"Copy that," mumbled Brook.

Chapter 15

For the better part of an hour, as Elvis put the dozer through its paces, curling layers of topsoil away to make room for Bishop's small fleet of helicopters, the former Navy SEAL had been observing from the elevated porch behind the massive lake house. After casting cautious glances and never seeing a change in his boss's rigid stance or stoic facial expression, Elvis began to think that Bishop had somehow slipped away and left a lookalike mannequin in his stead.

Eventually Elvis put the fact that he was being watched to the back of his mind and finished clearing the main rectangle. He was dutifully plowing the splintered and broken trees to the periphery when he happened to cast an absentminded glance towards the porch and noticed that Bishop—or his doppelgänger mannequin—was no longer scrutinizing his work.

Where did you go? Elvis thought, bringing the clanking dozer to a halt. With the throbbing engine rattling his bones he took off his Husker's hat with its newly acquired band of sweat, craned his head left and, in the distance, near the north gate, spotted a pair of mercenaries hacking the arms off a newly arrived pair of walking dead, but no Bishop. He looked right and saw a flash of light off of chrome beyond the lake house. A beat later a vehicle whose profile looked vaguely familiar cut the corner, trailing a turbid cloud of dust, brown and gauze-like. Finally the boxy front end and gleaming bumper was aimed at him and he recognized the hydraulic boom protruding like a shark's fin from the bed. In the next instant he heard the engine and exhaust note and squelch of tires on gravel and it became obvious that the tow truck he'd driven non-stop from

Nebraska was now approaching fast along the lake road. Then, as if it couldn't get any stranger, the light bar flared on, strobing orange and yellow as it geared down and disappeared again behind a staggered grouping of A-frames and hewn-log structures and boat houses stretching west away from Bishop's lake house.

Because of the way the light spilling through the canopy played off the approaching vehicle's windshield, Elvis had no idea who was behind the wheel until he saw the thick neck and high brow and coal black hair of the driver, which told him unequivocally that it was none other than Bishop himself.

The tow truck crunched to a complete stop a dozen yards beyond the dozer, and the backup warning sounded even before the trailing dust cloud caught it. With a discordant beeping filling the air, the window powered down and Bishop hung his head out and expertly reversed down the thirty-foot-wide corridor Elvis had gouged out of the forest.

The annoying backup warning ceased and the emergency lights went dark. Elvis watched Bishop spill out and shoulder the door shut.

Unsure what to do, Elvis remained seated and watched Bishop walk the length of the makeshift driveway, pacing off dimensions front to back and then left to right. Apparently satisfied, Bishop flashed Elvis a thumbs up and made his way slowly towards the idling dozer, grinning.

Mired in indecision, Elvis silenced the big diesel and was preparing to dismount when he saw Bishop halt at the newly created 'T' junction, gaze west down the road and begin talking into a small radio of some sort.

Following his first impulse, Elvis walked along the tractor's muddy tread, hopped to the ground and took a few tentative steps forward, straining to hear what Bishop was saying.

But before he could get within ear shot he was met with a glare and an open palm that could only mean one thing: *Keep your distance.*

Faking an air of nonchalance, Elvis leaned against the tractor, cracked open a warm bottle of water, and fought to stay awake. Barely a minute had passed when he heard the distinct *braaap* of a big rig's compression braking coming across the narrow finger of lake from the northwest.

A short while later an eighteen-wheeler and its accompanying cacophony of engine noise and rattling couplings appeared momentarily some distance away. Trailing a tail of dust and dragging fallen pine needles along the ground in its wake, flashes of chrome and glass were evident between the houses as it traced the arc on a southeasterly heading. A minute later it passed directly in front of Elvis and there was a metallic gnashing of gears as it slowed and made the same run out to the left as the tow truck had earlier. A blast of dusty air washed over Elvis and then there was the hiss of pneumatics and the big rig lurched and shimmied to a full stop.

Then with the radio pressed to his mouth and his free hand offering additional visual cues, Bishop directed the olive-drab Kenworth into the flag cut where the driver snugged it cheek-to-jowl next to the tow truck, leaving both rear bumpers lined up perfectly.

Elvis watched on as Bishop conferred with the driver, who was wiry and compact and wore his ball cap creased and flannel shirt cut at the sleeves. In Elvis' estimation the silver-haired man was aged a hair north of fifty and was probably born in the sleeper cab of a big rig.

As the conversation ensued, Elvis regarded the two trucks of disproportionate size and functionality and racked his brain trying to figure out why Bishop had wanted them shoehorned in there in the first place. After kicking it around for a minute and coming up with no logical explanation, he leaned against the dozer's track and waited for his next task.

Elvis didn't have to wait long. He watched a wide Cheshire Cat-like grin appear on Bishop's face as he slipped the radio into a pocket and clapped the smaller man on the shoulder and sent him scurrying off across the road in the direction of a nearby garage.

After the driver was gone from sight, Elvis watched Bishop cross the road and found his gaze shifting from the man's no nonsense, hard set eyes to the semi-automatic pistol holstered low on his thigh.

Still a dozen feet separating them, Bishop called out, "You just about finished with your break?"

Swallowing hard, Elvis tried hard to think of a way for someone in his position to say no without getting himself killed. But nothing brilliant came to mind, so instead of offering potential fodder for Bishop's legendary temper, he simply nodded.

"Good," said Bishop, his disarming smile returning. "Because I'm going to need you to step it up and knock out the rest of the landing zone. Carson and the boys should be arriving within the hour." The smile faded as Bishop noticed the driver returning from the garage.

With his upper body swaying unnaturally to and fro, the graying driver walked across the road, through the golden bars of light spilling from above, in one hand a battered and dinged red toolbox, and in the other what looked like an automotive battery. And clamped under the arm lugging the battery was some kind of satchel about the size a doctor would have carried back when they still made house calls. As the driver walked the length of the cut he began to slow and favor the side with the toolbox, a clear indication that the thing held some serious hardware.

Elvis caught Bishop's eye and hitched a brow, then nodded at the man doing a Sherpa's work. A safe way to break the ice, he supposed. Not quite a prying question. And not the meek stance of silence he'd been practicing. A perfect move that left the ball in Bishop's court.

But Bishop didn't bite. Instead, he shouted, calling the driver over. Exchanged a few words with the smaller man, gripped his shoulder briefly and sent him on his way again.

What happened next made Elvis question his decision of not following his gut and fleeing to another point of the compass—*any* other point in the compass—instead of rejoining Bishop and his band of mercenaries. For when the driver turned to walk away, a boxy pistol appeared in Bishop's fist and without pause, smile widening, he fired a single shot that entered behind the man's ear and sent the hat flying one way, the body crumpling the other.

Still wearing the smile, Bishop crossed the road. Forcing a smile of his own while doing his best not to acknowledge the execution that he'd just witnessed, Elvis said, "Looks like the cut turned out OK?"

"Perfect fit," answered Bishop, holstering the pistol. "Now fire that thing up. And when you're done with the LZ," he nodded towards the house. "You see those fir rounds along the back there?"

Shifting his gaze to the breezeway between the lake house and what he guessed was a combination garage and boat house, Elvis noticed what looked like an entire forest's worth of knee-high fir rounds, each the circumference of a manhole cover. Retaining the faux grin, he nodded and asked the obvious, "What do you want me to do with them?"

More out of habit than to make a point, Bishop put a hand on his semi-automatic and said, "I'm going to need you to split those rounds down and then stack the finished product under the porch. Think you handle that?"

With the image of the driver's corpse staining the road crimson in his side vision, Elvis said nothing, accepting the job with a tilt of his head.

"Good," said Bishop. "It's going to be a cold winter up here ... you finish splitting all the rounds and then we'll sit down and have some beers. After that you can turn in. I want you well rested because I've got big plans for you tomorrow."

"I'll be ready," lied Elvis. In fact, now more than ever he wanted to bolt. He looked towards the north gate at the half-dozen guards there. Then he watched the former Navy SEAL walk the length of the semi-truck, crab between it and the tow truck and disappear from sight. Finally, shaking his head and mired in a quicksand pool of indecision, Elvis took his seat on the dozer and fired up the big diesel motor. There was a roar and thick exhaust belched toward the blue sky. He spun a one-eighty in place, dropped the dozer's blade and with the clank of treads filling the air and another few hours of backbreaking manual labor on the horizon, put his head down and started in on the final half-dozen passes.

Chapter 16

In the rearview, Cade watched Brook and Wilson close the distance to the truck. He opened the center console and retrieved a Big Box store-sized bottle of 250 milligram Ibuprofen. Defeated the child safety feature on the lid and then rattled three of the rust-colored pills into his palm. He popped them into his mouth and swallowed, then chased them down with a long pull off a bottled water. While stashing the pill bottle in the center console, he looked into the rearview, met his daughter's gaze and asked, "Were you scared back there, Raven?"

Instantly, as she was prone to do, Sasha inserted herself into the conversation. "Didn't scare *me* a bit."

Looking at her dad, Raven smiled and delivered a conspiratorial wink. "I was a little scared," she conceded.

"And that's a good thing, sweetie. A little bit of fear keeps us sharp. Too much and you're prone to freezing up." He looked over his shoulder at the slender redhead still clutching her designer bags. "Can't be too brave, Sasha. Gotta find a happy medium for yourself."

Knowing in a roundabout way that she had just been called out, Sasha made no reply.

Taryn, however, parked her elbows on the seatback and asked Cade how he kept his cool at the airport surrounded by all that death.

"Mind over matter. I put all the things I care about into a vault in my mind and heart ... seal it up and forget about them until I'm safe again. If you can't wrap your mind around that, then try envisioning the Zs in their underwear—"

"Most of them already are," quipped Raven.

Shaking her head, Taryn said, "This is not the same as getting over the fear of public speaking. Not even close. Those things wanted to eat me ... Dickless, the Subway girl Karen." She shuddered and whispered to herself, "All of them."

"Then pretend you're on the set of a George Romero movie and the dead are just extras wearing makeup."

Sasha said, "Last time I checked you couldn't shoot extras in makeup for real."

Ignoring this, Cade looked away. In the side mirror he saw Brook nearing his door, a certain swagger in her step. He glanced right and noticed Wilson in the other mirror, the Louisville Slugger held loose in one hand, sweat-stained boonie hat riding low over his eyes. He returned his gaze to Taryn and added, "Whatever works. But ultimately it's up to you to find out what that is ... or die trying."

There was a loud bang on the sheet metal and the rear passenger door hinged open. A beat later, Wilson tossed the bat in and with a subtle air of confidence said, "Gate's all locked up."

Brook stepped onto the running board on the driver's side and performed a mini pull-up in order to see in. "Get your rifle, Raven. You're coming with."

"Can I come?"

"Wouldn't expect anything else from you, Taryn," said Brook.

"Give me a second to get things sorted," Cade said quietly to Brook.

She made a face. Gave him a look he knew all too well. One that said a lot without actually saying anything.

"I want to test the ankle in my new boots."

"Better here than out there."

"I knew you'd see it my way, honey," he said with a wry smile.

She smiled. Blew him a kiss and hopped down.

"*Max. Out*," ordered Cade.

The Australian Shepherd's claws rasped against the truck's bed as he launched to the asphalt. Landing on all fours, the brindle-furred pooch performed a thorough recon of the truck's exterior, sniffing the tires and bumpers and undercarriage along the way. Stub for a tail chopping the air, he looped under the lifted vehicle one time and then returned and sat outside the driver's door and regarded Cade with a dutiful look.

"Good boy."

Max cocked his head. Shook his body expectantly.

"Sorry bud. Words will have to suffice until I can find you some treats."

Keying on the tone in Cade's voice, Max turned and trotted off towards the building where his female master and the youngsters were.

Cade reached across and grabbed the well-worn pair of size nine leather boots that one of Beeson's officers had procured for him. He loosened the laces and, as an afterthought, punched the radio on and selected the AM band and let the auto seek feature scan the spectrum.

He ripped the three hook-and-loop straps loose and removed the hard plastic boot and tossed it unceremoniously in back. As he wiggled his toes and enjoyed the cool air on his damp sock, the low hiss coming from the speakers was suddenly replaced by a human voice. He paused midway through unlacing the Danner and listened for a second. He'd heard this one before. Some Emergency Broadcast item out of D.C. Still looping, weeks old and unchanged. He guessed it was running off of solar somewhere and it would continue doing so until someone turned it off. *Doubtful.* Or, most likely, some random small part in the system failed, taking it off the air for good. Once again he hit the Seek button on the head unit, hinged over and resumed unlacing the Danner. He yanked the old boot off and slipped the new one on and laced it up. Surprisingly, it fit perfectly, like it had been custom made for him by some old world cobbler. The other boot, however, was a different story. After the first unsuccessful try, he loosened the laces entirely and forced the issue. Sweat beads breaking out on his brow and swollen ankle be damned, he jammed his foot into the new boot, forcing his toes into the cap first and then, using all of his weight, got his heel down. *Success.* The fit was beyond tight. Without the jaws-of-life or a plasma cutter he wasn't taking the thing off anytime soon. He saw plenty more Ibuprofen in his future.

As he tucked the laces inside the boot tops, the green digits on the head unit stopped scrolling and a mournful-sounding Mariachi song came through the truck's speakers. The signal was faint so Cade jacked up the volume and listened intently until the last guitar chords were strummed and the song had faded. Then, fully expecting the programming to be prerecorded and looping like the D.C. broadcast, he waited for the next south-of-the-border ditty to ramp up before yanking the keys from the ignition. Instead, taking him completely by surprise, a Caucasian-sounding male voice, deep and resonant, replaced the dead air and in an unusually cheerful manner—as if the dead weren't walking around eating people in his neck of the woods— rattled off the day, month, and year, which Cade confirmed as accurate with a quick glance at his Suunto. Inexplicably, the man continued on saying the temperature wherever he was broadcasting from was holding at eighty-nine degrees. There was a moment of dead air followed by a rustling of papers, after which the man relayed a forecast for the coming week. And judging by the ungodly high daytime temperatures coupled with the plunging nighttime lows, Cade guessed the signal was being beamed from a distant state like New Mexico, or, Arizona, or even further south than that, somewhere inside of Mexico perhaps.

The Dee Jay finished the weather report, then switched to fluent Spanish and, presumably, repeated all of the same information to his non-English speaking listeners. *Pretty optimistic*, thought Cade. Either the man spinning the records had gone crazy and was continuing his daily routine oblivious to the world outside, or some kind of sanctuary from the dead had sprouted up somewhere in the desert southwest. One safe and secure enough to embolden the Dee Jay with enough hubris to expect to outlive a week's worth of weather yet resourceful enough to keep a radio station on air in order to broadcast the fact.

After listening to the rest of the Spanish update and understanding only a few of the words, Cade assigned the station to one of the three dozen available presets and took the keys from the ignition. They went into a cargo pocket and he fished the sat phone from the bottom of the center console where it had settled. He thumbed it on and waited for it to power up. The device ran through the familiar boot-up sequence after which he checked the display, which showed that he had one new SMS text message and a single missed call with a new voice mail attached to it. He scrolled down to the call log and determined that the text message originated from the same number he'd called the day before when he had spoken with Daymon and Duncan. The missed call, however , had come from Major Freda Nash, back at Schriever, presumably. First off he read the text message and, thinking maybe Daymon was pulling his leg, smiled and said to himself, "Roger that." Next, after a moment's hesitation, he selected the voice mail, thumbed the call button and placed the phone to his ear. Through the windshield he watched Brook and Wilson conducting a preliminary recon of the building's exterior while he listened to Nash's unapologetic voice dictate a list of very explicit instructions.

Leaving the Thuraya powered on and plugged into the outlet, he tossed it in the console and out of sight. *Old habits die hard*, he thought to himself. *Who the hell is going to steal the thing out here, Grayson?*

Without answering to his inner smartass he closed the console, looked up and saw Brook staring at him, animatedly tapping her watch. Getting the hint, he pushed open the door and slipped off the seat, supporting most of his weight with a firm two-handed grip on the grab bar near his head. As he pivoted left, his gaze passed over the aluminum crutches stowed behind his seat. *Too noisy. Too encumbering. But most of all ... too easy,* the same inner voice lectured.

So he met terra firma without them. Right foot first, settling the majority of his weight on it. The moment of truth came and instead of his own voice he heard Desantos's in his head. *Suck it up,* the gravelly voice said as he let go and planted his left foot on the ground. Grimacing, he gritted his teeth as a runner of pain shot up his leg. *Bearable.* He distributed his weight evenly and, like a baby wearing that first pair of flat-soled shoes, took his own baby steps forward. *Fake it 'til you make it*, looped through his head as he walked half-speed towards Brook with a forced yet somewhat reassuring smile on his face.

Chapter 17

Duncan pulled the battered Land Cruiser up tight next to a dirt-encrusted 4Runner, also a spoil of war taken after their one-sided skirmish with the Huntsville gang.

He shut off the motor and looked to the right past Daymon. Squinting hard and craning his neck further, he said, "What do you make of that?"

"That red thing between the helicopters?"

"You call that red? Looks kind of brown to me," drawled Duncan, instantly regretting the damning admission. Then, trying to recover, added, "Someone set the thing up in the shadows. I knew it was red."

"That's not a shadow, Mister Magoo. That's Tran and he's been at it like that since I came up to the road."

After a quick mental calculation in which he was forced to perform a little long division, Duncan said, "Hell ... he's using a hand pump, not a garden hose and gravity. Even at half-speed he should have transferred all four hundred and fifty pounds of fuel into the Black Hawk half an hour ago."

"Be grateful, would you, Duncan? He's been out there cranking that thing with a couple of cracked ribs ... or bruised ... whatever. After the way you lit into him because he couldn't recall *exactly* where in Idaho Bishop was setting up shop, I'd have expected him to get out of Dodge ... or murder you in your sleep. One or the other. I'd of gone with the latter, myself."

Sounding a little like Steve Martin, stretching out his words, Duncan shook his head side-to-side and said, "Well *forgive* me ... I was *drunk*."

"Hell of an excuse," said Daymon. "I'm regretting letting you drive us here from the road."

"I ain't drunk no more," drawled Duncan, handing over the keys. "If it'll make you feel any better, you can drive us to the quarry."

"*After* I check in on Heidi."

Duncan grunted, then, favoring his lower back which was suffering greatly from digging the two graves, popped open his door and stepped gingerly onto the flattened grass. Immediately he noticed the heat from the rising sun. It had to be nearing seventy degrees and a million candle watts seemed to be focused on one area—the bald spot on the crown of his head, beneath which his brain was still throbbing from the aftereffects of his last drunk. Squinting against the sun, he looked inside the rig at Daymon, expecting another probing question, but instead saw the dreadlocked former firefighter pointing animatedly at the passenger-side door.

Ignoring the pantomimed plea for help, Duncan said, "Let's see what kind of progress Tran is making."

"A little help with the door," said Daymon, jiggling the handle. "Thing doesn't want to open."

Duncan chuckled. "You're the one who ruined it on account of your fine display of demolition derby driving."

"I saved our *asses*." There was a loud bang and then the drawn-out squeal from the pinched hinges grinding metal on metal. Rubbing his shoulder, Daymon unfolded his body from the truck, rose and stretched catlike. He snatched up his bow and machete and began walking towards the pair of helicopters where Tran was still hard at work in their shadow, his entire body hinging up and down, invested fully in spinning a pie-sized metal wheel in slow-motion revolutions.

***

Five minutes after touching bases with Tran, Duncan and Daymon were in the compound's cramped security container, drinking coffee and watching Heidi manipulate the lighted dials and knobs on the Ham radio.

"Hey hon," said Daymon to deaf ears.

Twisting in the folding chair, Heidi removed one ear pad and asked, "You get some good rest last night?"

Since he hadn't gotten good rest for weeks, he hesitated a moment to weigh the pros and cons of plopping an extra helping of worry on her plate. Then, rather reluctantly, he decided a little white lie would hurt a lot less than burdening her with the truth. Looking straight at her, he took a quick sip of his coffee and added, "Like a baby. Feels like I'm getting the old circadian rhythm back on track—"

Unwittingly saving Daymon from digging an even deeper hole for himself, Duncan interrupted. "Did you contact anyone on Logan's list?"

"I've been able to get ahold of a couple of them. I chatted with a man who is holed up with his elderly mom somewhere near Pocatello," she said. "He even mentioned seeing three or four helicopters heading west a couple of days ago."

"Pocatello," said Duncan, more statement than question. Then he looked at her over his bifocals and asked, "He say what kind of helicopters?"

"He didn't say. And I didn't think to ask. We talked very briefly, then rather abruptly he said he had to go. I'll be sure to *grill* him about it later."

"Later?"

"Yeah," answered Heidi, pinning her blonde bangs back under the headphone strap. "He promised he'd call me back sometime this afternoon."

"I bet he did," said Daymon, who was leaning against the cool metal wall, chin resting on his chest. He looked up and drained his coffee and then added, "It's amazing the effect the soothing voice of the fairer sex has on us cooped-up fellas."

Giving Daymon an affectionate pat on his thigh, Heidi held aloft a spiral-bound notebook spilling over with papers. "Then you better leave me alone, hon," she said playfully. "'Cause if we're going to find out where those creeps took the girls, I'm going to have to learn how to use this radio. And from the looks of this manual ... I've got some serious learning to do."

"One thing to be said about Oops," proffered Duncan. "He always was an anal little bastard when it came to saving paperwork and receipts and manuals. Hell, the pink slip for his first Big Wheel is probably still tucked away somewhere in here."

"Bless him," said Heidi. A pained look settled on her features as she snugged the headphones on and buried her head in the radio manual.

Taking a quick swipe at the forming tears, Duncan said to no one in particular, "I really miss the little bugger."

"We all do," Daymon replied. "Now finish your coffee, Old Man. We're going back to the quarry."

"First I need to fetch a bottle of aspirin from the storeroom."

Daymon looked to make sure Heidi couldn't hear what he was about to say. He saw her slowly moving the large dial on the radio, no doubt trying to tune in some far away frequency. Finally he said to Duncan, "There's no more of that Jack Daniels squirreled away in the storeroom, is there?"

"There is," Duncan said. "But I've done all of the forgettin' I'm going to do for now. I'll properly mourn the boy later ... maybe even pour a little out and say a few words over that pile of dirt up there."

"When is later?"

"After I put the fuckers who killed him under a pile of dirt of their own."

His face a mask of resolve, Daymon said, "Meet you topside." He kissed Heidi atop her head, gave her shoulder a soft squeeze, then ducked under the door arch and was lost in the gloom.

Duncan made no reply. Couldn't think of anything smartass to say to soften the mood. Not even one barbed quip came to him. So he took a second to study the still images from the cameras topside and then marched off in the opposite direction.

Chapter 18

Mesa View 4x4 was an easier nut to crack than Cade had presumed. Fifteen seconds using a specialized tool called a lock gun was all he needed to thwart the upper deadbolt. Less than ten additional seconds were necessary to defeat the lock on the brushed-aluminum doorknob.

After stowing the lock tool, Cade called Max over and led him to the rubber flap near the base of the first roller door.

Max entered with an eagerness that seemed to set everyone at ease—Brook especially. But a few seconds later the flap rippled and Max emerged, hair standing on end, teeth bared. He spun a couple of silent circles, then looked to Cade for new marching orders.

"Wish you could talk," said Cade. "Let us know how many are inside." *One way in.* No problem, assuming the building was a giant open-concept rectangle and not partitioned into multiple interior spaces, the latter of which Cade knew was probably the case. So he held the knob and tapped on the window. Soft at first. *Nothing.* He looked at Raven, arched a brow and shrugged his shoulders as if to say all in a day's work. And because he knew a little conditioning went a long way, he motioned her in closer.

Shaking her head and mouthing, "It's too soon," Brook stared daggers at the hobbled operator as her only daughter, her only connection to the old world, did as she was told and inched closer, a knuckle-white grip on her rifle.

Taryn whispered, "What's he doing?"

Holding his bat at port arms, Wilson looked at her and shrugged.

"Sasha ... come here," said Cade. "Let's get in touch with that healthy kind of fear."

Ashen-faced and shaking her head, Sasha shrank behind Wilson.

"Cade, no. Not now."

All eyes went to Brook.

"When, then?" he asked. "After we've fallen? I hope not because that *when* will be too late." Trying to force the issue, he decided to go the divide and conquer route. He hated to do it but knew that it was for the good of the group. So under Brook's watchful eye, he held the suppressed Glock out butt first. "Take this," he said to Wilson. "It's loaded. The safety is located on the trigger. Keep your finger out of the guard and off the trigger until you are ready to fire."

Gesturing towards the weapon, palms upturned, shoulders drawn halfway to his ears, Wilson asked, "What do you want *me* to do with it?"

"I want *you* and *Taryn* to go over to that gate we just came through ..." He pointed at the gathering dead, "... and kill every last one of those things. You have sixteen bullets. One in the pipe and fifteen in the magazine. Why don't you two make it a competition. Share the weapon and see who scores the most kills with their eight rounds."

Wilson stared, speechless. Taryn, however, stepped forward and took the weapon. Held it tentatively, like it was a baby bird and crushing it was a possibility. With the suppressor pointed groundward, she tightened her grip, turned, and walked purposefully towards the gate. Three seconds after being upstaged by a girl, Wilson's balls dropped and he trotted after.

Two birds with one stone, thought Cade. He faced Brook, winked, and said over his shoulder, "Let's go, girls." He pushed the door open and nearly tripped over Max as he bolted through the sliver of daylight. Sweeping his eyes right to left, Cade crossed the threshold into the retail area of the store, Glock 19 leading the way.

The air inside had that new car smell. Mainly tire rubber and plastics that partially masked an underlying odor of death. The causation of the latter, Cade guessed, would probably be found beyond the battered gray door which, apart from the three roller doors outside, seemed to be the only other point of entry to the garage where all of the customization took place.

But first things first, he thought. Straight ahead, illuminated fully by the eight-by-eight bar of light angling in through the skylight, was an L-shaped counter. On the glass surface were a number of telephone-book-sized catalogs, one still cracked open as if someone had just been looking up a part number. And plastering the wall behind the checkout stand were a number of glossy photos of all types of 4x4 pick-ups and SUVs—not one of them close to being as capable as the F-650 out in the parking lot. Cade retrieved his tactical flashlight from a pocket and thumbed it on. Recalling the SMS message he'd gotten from Daymon, he opened the nearest drawer and shone the harsh blue-white beam on its contents. *Nothing.* He moved on down the counter and struck out twice more, finding only pens and business cards mixed in with stacks of aftermarket wheel and off-road tire brochures. Finally, inside the third drawer, he found what he was looking for and quickly pocketed the items.

With Brook, Raven, and Sasha looking on, he closed the drawer, stepped from behind the counter, and swept the beam around the vast showroom. The windowless cinderblock walls were cream-colored and the rows of tires lining them seemed to go on forever. He peered down the right side and saw nothing lurking there. Peeked over his shoulder at Raven who was sticking to him like glue, and said, "Clear." Sensing the scrutiny, she looked up at him, caught his eye and nodded as if saying she was OK with all of this. Next, he shifted his gaze to Sasha, who was six times whiter than normal.

Head swiveling forward, Cade went into a combat crouch and listened hard, focusing all of his attention towards the back of the store. "Anyone else hear that?" he asked.

Bravely poking her head around her dad, Raven said, "Yeah ... kind of. What is it?"

Cade glanced back to verify that she was carrying her rifle safely. Satisfied with what he saw, he whispered, "Can't be sure. Sounds like something scratching to get out." For a split second he flashed back to the two-story farmhouse in Hanna. Trapped in the dark, overwhelmed by the wafting stench of the dead—and the non-stop sound of nails scratching on hundred-year-old bead board. With a frigid current tracing his spine, he met Brook's eyes and a silent message passed between them. She nodded, raised the carbine across her chest with a finger on the trigger guard, and set out for the aisle paralleling the far left wall.

Then the noise came again, but this time it echoed down the centermost aisle.

With a granite set to his jaw, Cade said, "Be ready. It's on the move and knows we are here." He swept the cone of light over stacks and rows of aftermarket wheels and tires. Illuminated a wall of shock absorbers, their garish-colored dust covers contrasting markedly against the dark brown pegboard display. Bracing the hand with the Glock over the wrist of his left hand which was holding the tactical flashlight, he shone the beam on the far aisle and crabbed to his right.

Though they could see nothing moving—not even a shadow to give the offending creature's position away— the sound, now more of a rapid clicking, grew nearer.

Behind him, Cade could hear Raven breathing hard. Then, shattering the still, Sasha started screaming. A hair-raising peal amplified by the cramped quarters and low ceiling.

Reacting instantly, Brook let her carbine fall slack on its sling, took a quick step forward and wrapped her toned arm around the hysterical teen's slender shoulders. After a brief struggle, Brook managed to clamp her hand down hard over Sasha's mouth. Shaking her head to show her displeasure, Brook met Cade's eyes and pulled Sasha's shaking frame in close and whispered next to her ear, "Pull it together or you're going to get us all killed."

Save for the stress-induced labored breathing of the group there was no more sound. Even the clicking had now ceased. *Strange*, thought Cade. There was none of the usual shuffling or moaning indicating they were sharing the 4x4 shop with one or more of the dead. And it stayed like this for a few long beats. Then the clicking started up again. Like a car's hot exhaust system cooling off. Softly at first and then louder, finally Max emerged from the catacombs, his overgrown nails raking the cement floor. Oblivious to the heightened state of tension that he had brought on the group, he sat on his haunches and regarded Cade with his dual-colored eyes.

Meeting the dog's gaze, Cade lowered his pistol and asked sarcastically, "All clear, buddy?"

Replying with a gaping yawn, Max rolled onto his side and exposed his multi-colored belly.

"False alarm," said Cade over his shoulder. "But way to go, Raven." He regarded her and then met Brook's eyes and winked. "I'm very proud of how you held it together. And Sasha ..." He removed his ball cap. Ran a hand through his lengthening hair. "We can't have that happen ever again."

Releasing her grip on Sasha who was nodding and still a little wild in the eye, Brook wiped the spittle from her hand onto her pants and said to Max, "I'm beginning to regret that I let Raven bring you home."

Knowing that nothing good would come from arguing a valid point, wisely, Raven made no reply.

"Come on girls. We've got to get this done so we can get back on the road," Cade said as he advanced past Max, ignoring him completely. Then, with the business end of the Glock following his gaze, he stepped quietly sideways, favoring his left ankle the entire way. He padded a dozen feet forward and the same distance to his right. Then, in a slow deliberate manner, he cleared each aisle, passing the flashlight's beam over the rows of vertically stocked air cleaners and oil filters and other parts needed to keep a vehicle running. After finishing his serpentine round-trip recon of the back two-thirds of the shop, he stopped front and center of the abused steel door and looked through the window into the fully illuminated garage. He walked his gaze around the gymnasium-sized structure and saw two things he'd expected to find and one that he had not. "Stay here," he said. He handed the flashlight to Raven, opened the door a crack, and slipped inside.

Chapter 19

As Taryn leveled the Glock, lining up the front and rear sights just as she'd been taught by Brook, her hand began to waver. It started as a little tremor that quickly became a full-blown twitch, causing the silencer to move in slow concentric circles as she fought its weight and her nerves to keep her aim on the zombie. And the longer she held the pistol at arm's length thinking about whom the undead elderly woman had been in life, the more pronounced her aiming problem became.

"Am I going to have to draw *first blood*?" asked Wilson, who was standing a few feet to the left and slightly behind the raven-haired nineteen-year-old.

"Do not patronize me, Wilson. I've got to get used to shooting these things sooner or later." Suddenly Taryn imagined the zombie clutching the fence in front of her minus the gaunt face and missing ear and purple-ridged bite wound to the neck. In her mind's eye she saw the woman rosy-cheeked, wispy white hair pulled back into a neat bun, and offering chocolate chip cookies to a couple of excited grandkids.

But that was not the case now. A guttural growl snapped Taryn to the present. Stalling for more time, she looked over her shoulder and asked, "Where the eff did you come up with that corny expression?"

"Some ancient movie that my mom and I watched together about five years ago. An action flick about some guy named Rambo who liked to shoot a big machine gun one-handed ..."

"A silent scream, his face all contorted in slow motion ... yeah, I remember Rambo," replied Taryn, a smile creasing her face. "Me and my father watched it one night when Mom was out late. One night of many—" Her face went slack and her grip tightened on the Glock. She was no longer clutching the baby bird gently ... she was crushing the life from it. And anticipating the report before depressing the trigger, she forgot everything Brook had passed on to her and did what most novice shooters do—she closed her eyes and jerked the trigger. The former happened so fast it had no effect on her aim. The latter, however, caused her to pull the muzzle down and to the right by a degree.

Contrary to Taryn's initial assumption, no great explosion occurred. It was more like a soft pop that dissipated even before the brass tinged against the asphalt. The devastation, however, was greater than she had anticipated—especially with this kind of close proximity. *No going back now*, she thought, opening her eyes just in time to appreciate every gory detail. There was the soft smack of the 9mm bullet striking Grandma below the left cheekbone. Then the energy from the speeding projectile whipping the undead geriatric's head left and sending a fist-sized flap of cheek and connecting tissue and muscle spinning away like a clay pigeon. But as expected, the zombie didn't fall. Instead the opposite happened. Excited by the proximity to fresh meat and the sudden silenced report, the clutch of undead behind the still-moving corpse drove it forward, pinning it against the cyclone fencing. Then the unrelenting press of the dozen-plus walking cadavers caused the unthinkable to happen: Grandma's distended belly split open like an overcooked brat, sending intestine and bile and the remnants of presumably its last victim shooting through the fence and directly at Taryn.

Backpedaling and puking a torrent of partially digested MRE pound cake, Taryn instinctively fought back by squeezing off two additional shots to no great effect. Breathing hard, she set the pistol down and dragged a forearm across her mouth. Suddenly aware of the rancid-smelling gore soiling her shirt, she tugged it away from her skin and said rapid-fire, "Fuck, fuck, fuck." Still cursing, she stripped the top off completely and threw it on the ground next to the Glock. Then, standing in the warm sun wearing only Multicam pants and a black bra, she snorted and began to laugh.

Seeing this, Wilson sat down hard on the cracked and pitted blacktop and grabbed his sides. Then, in between snorts of his own, he said, "Minus the projectile vomiting and minor striptease act, you looked a little bit like Rambo yourself."

Taryn snatched up the Glock and subconsciously adjusted her bra strap. Fixing a glare on the dead, she said, "You haven't seen the half of it." She tiptoed through the splattered guts and arrived at the fence, Glock in a firm two-handed grip, unwavering. Then, possessing a newly forged demeanor, she put one round into Grandma's head and five more into the throng of monsters grinding the pinned corpse against the fence.

Tuning out the hair-raising sounds of the remaining creatures, Taryn held the pistol out butt first. "Six ... you're at bat, Casey."

Wilson pushed off the ground and straightened up. Looking down at Taryn, he cocked his head and shot her a bewildered look.

Still holding the pistol out like an offering, she said, "The baseball universe does not revolve around your precious Mister Todd Helton."

"So who is this Casey?"

"Fictional character in a poem written by Ernest Thayer. You know, Casey at the Bat?" She let the words hang but received only a dumb stare. So she went on. "Casey is based on Mike Kelly who was the most expensive NL player of his era ... nickname was King, if I remember the story right."

The chain-link groaned under the weight of the dead.

Wilson finally took the Glock from her, pivoted to the side with the silencer aimed groundward, and ejected the magazine. He counted the remaining bullets. Saw that there were seven, plus the one in the chamber. *Eight chances to save face, Casey.* "And how much did this King guy get paid?" he asked.

"Not much," she said loudly to be heard over the hungry mob. "But like a commodity or something, they sold him to Boston."

"How much?"

"Ten thousand dollars."

Looking over his shoulder, Wilson said, "That's nothing compared to Helton's salary. How'd you learn all of this anyway?"

"If you haven't figured it out yet, Wilson." She stood on her toes and gave him a peck on the cheek. "I'm a tomboy."

"Coulda fooled me," he said with a quick downward glance at her lacy undergarment.

"Doesn't mean I can't be sexy," she said seductively.

There was an awkward silence as Wilson's jaw slowly hinged open.

After inspecting her tattooed arms for any wayward food particulates or bodily fluids, and finding nothing substantial, she met Wilson's gaze, smiled, and said, "While you finish up here ... I'm getting a shirt."

Cheeks turning every shade of red, Wilson averted his eyes. He turned on his heel and moved closer to the fence, determined to finish the job she had started.

Chapter 20

The gray steel door between the retail offerings and the garage swung open easily, but before Cade could react, hundreds—if not thousands— of small black flies enveloped his head like a funeral veil. As their burnished wings beat the air around him, the sickly sweet pong of death assaulted his nose. Glock sweeping left, he quickly pushed through the buzzing cloud and entered the sweltering garage. *Nothing to see.* So he spun a swift one-eighty to his right and spotted the dead thing just as the door settled against the rubber stop.

Curled up on the hard cement next to a pair of deep stainless steel bowls, both licked clean to a high sheen, was the decomposing remains of what Cade guessed had at one time been a seventy or eighty pound dog. And judging by the wide set eyes and pronounced snout and wiry tufts of rust-colored fur standing at attention along the jutting vertebrae, there was no doubt in his mind that he was looking at all that remained of a dead Rhodesian Ridgeback. *Great breed of dog*, he thought. In fact, he'd met a couple of them at Bagram Air Base during his first swing through Afghanistan with the 75th Ranger Regiment. Capable animals. Smart and loyal to the end. But unfortunately this one's end had not been pleasant.

Once he had taken a couple of steps into the garage and the eye-watering stench only got worse, he came to the conclusion that there was no way this weeks old maggot-infested carcass, already nearly consumed by thousands of wriggling fly larvae, could be solely responsible for the wall of stink he'd just walked into.

So, fingers spread, he raised his free hand, signaling silently to the others to stay where they were. Reaching back, he found the knob by feel and shut the door. Then, breathing through his mouth, he skirted around the front of the first bay. The lift was empty and the greasy articulated arms that would normally support a vehicle were level to the floor and splayed out over the work bay beneath them.

The next lift, however, was partially extended, its dual-chromed pistons holding a white Ford 4x4 aloft, the running boards meeting him about chest-high. And hanging off the fully extended long-travel suspension were oversized off-road tires that looked hungry for desert terrain. Off the top of his head, Cade guessed that the snazzy looking components had a foot of travel in them at least. So far, so good. The rig was the closest thing he'd seen capable of giving the F-650 a run for its money, and getting it down off the lift would be one hell of a payoff for him not having to endure two-hundred-plus miles of unchecked sibling rivalry.

Holstering the Glock, he motioned for Brook and the girls to join him. A second later he sensed a change in the air pressure and Raven and Sasha were lamenting the guard dog's demise in appropriately hushed voices. As their footsteps neared, he looped around the truck's beefy brush guard looking for some kind of a lever or switch; something obvious to throw that would release the hydraulic pressure and lower the truck to the floor. Halfway around the suspended truck, a low timbre moaning started up, setting the hair on his arms at attention and freezing him mid-stride with most of his weight supported on the sprained ankle and a sheen of sweat beading on his brow.

"Where is it?" hissed Brook, already with the M4 snugged tight against her shoulder, moving in a low crouch and checking the shadowed recesses under workbenches and behind stacked tires—any place she thought a crawler might be lurking. Finding nothing, she stood up straight and peered behind the tire mount-and-balance machine. "Nothing here," she finally called out.

"It's coming from down there," Cade stated, stabbing a finger towards the darkened pit near his feet. He thumbed on his flashlight as everyone crowded around the edge of the sunken work bay, Max included. The beam chased away the shadow revealing an overall-clad first turn, its pallid face staring up expectantly.

Still wearing blue coveralls with the name Kirk embroidered over its left breast and a patch identical to the Mesa View 4x4 sign on the opposite side, and still clutching a large socket wrench in one grease-stained fist, the male first turn looked like it had died and reanimated doing what it loved in life.

They watched in rapt silence for a few seconds as the dead thing paced fore and aft, stopping for seconds at a time either to scrutinize a hanging row of fan belts or bat at the colorful boxes of oil filters scattered on a low shelf.

"What the heck is it doing?" asked Raven, her whisper echoing in the bay.

But before Brook could formulate a vanilla answer to a sight that was freaking the shit out of her, the zombie froze mid-stride, craned its head upward and fixed its rheumy eyes on the fresh meat staring in on it. The moaning began instantly and the creature grabbed a handful of the nylon safety netting ringing the pit and looked to be figuring on a way to get at them.

"I'll do it," said Brook, bringing the M4 to her shoulder.

Shaking his head, Cade placed his hand on the carbine's picatinny rail and gently nudged it down. "No telling what kind of flammable items are down there with it. Unless someone beams him up, Kirk is going nowhere."

Raven said, "How about we lower the truck over Kirk? That way nobody will fall in and get eaten."

"I have a better idea. Raven, you and Sasha go into the showroom and find a pen and something to write on, and leave a warning on the counter for anyone else who comes poking around in here."

"I got it, Dad."

"And Sasha ... why don't you look for a set of keys with a paper tag that says Ford or Raptor on it."

Following a pace behind Raven, who was half a head shorter, Sasha nodded and flashed him a thumbs up.

Brook lowered her rifle and fought hard against the urge to follow the girls as they zippered around the far bay and disappeared into the retail area.

"They are not your own little *special operators*, Cade Grayson," she said, facing him square on. "Personally, I think you are giving our daughter *too* much rope."

"Gotta see how much she'll take and run with while we're still on the right side of the dirt."

"That's being a little grim."

"I call it being realistic. We're on our own now, Brook. Beeson can't come help us if we get into trouble. Hell, he alluded he would ... even gave me the number to his sat phone ... but I'm not holding my breath."

"What about your old team back at Schriever?"

"As far as Nash is concerned, I may as well already be dead. Even though Robert Christian is dead and buried, the nukes he stole are still unaccounted for. And right now, barring another mega horde coming out of Denver or north from Pueblo, finding them is her number one priority."

"More so than the anti-serum?" asked Brook.

"There's no denying its importance. But right now, as low as they are on personnel, Schriever is a sitting duck to whoever might want to pop off a nuke right outside their gate." He went silent for a moment, then, arching a brow, added, "And that person wouldn't even have to get within five miles to wipe the place off the face of the earth. I could see no better reason than that to get us out of there."

Brook said nothing. Because deep down she knew that if Nash called in the next second he would no doubt jump. And whether he'd ever admit it or not, getting them out of harm's way was his way of making amends for leaving them behind while he deployed on the previous three missions.

"All we have now is family," he said, jarring her train of thought.

She met his gaze. Remained silent and looked towards the open door and listened hard for any out-of-place sounds. "Just be careful with what you ask Raven to do. She's twelve ... not an eighteen-year-old Ranger candidate."

Making no reply, Cade looked down at Kirk. The monster locked eyes with him, hissed and thrust its skeletal hands through the netting, leaving traces of flesh and shiny fluids everywhere they touched.

"Done, Dad. What do you think?" Scampering over, Raven held up a yellow sheet from a legal pad. Written in big block letters, mostly colored in, was the warning: *DEAD INSIDE! ENTER AT YOUR OWN RISK!*

"Very nice, sweetie."

"What your mom said," replied Cade. "Sweet and to the point." He grabbed a roll of black electrical tape. It was thin and easy enough to tear. Handed it to Sasha. "Would you two please go and tape it to the front door."

Sasha traded Cade a set of keys for the roll of tape. "Found them under the counter. Says Raptor on the alarm thingy ... strange name for a truck."

Cocking her head as if struck with a thought, Brook walked a full circle around the white pick-up with undead Kirk watching and hissing the entire time.

Watching her, Cade shrugged and asked, "What's wrong?"

"It looks familiar ... only a different color. Still makes me think of Carl, though." She looked away and covertly swiped at the forming tears.

Cade was about to confirm what he already knew when, distracting him, a silhouette appeared in the doorway. "We're done," said Wilson and Taryn nearly in unison. "But unfortunately there are a few more coming in from the south. We should probably get," said Taryn, finishing the update for them both.

Taking charge, Cade said, "Wilson, I need you to make sure the drain plug is still on the oil pan and then lower your new ride to the floor. Be sure you steer clear of Kirk, though."

"I'll do it," said Taryn, a measure of insistence to her voice. "I know cars. Ginger here ... Mister Six Banger Lipstick Red Mustang Owner ... does not."

There was no protest from Wilson and, a couple of minutes later, after tightrope walking around the truck, Taryn confirmed that Kirk had either finished the oil change or hadn't lived long enough after being bitten to get started. After confirming that all of the appropriate drain plugs were in place, and the fluids were sufficiently topped, meaning the Raptor was good to go, Taryn found the manual hydraulic release valve which was mounted inside the pit and just out of reach of Kirk's slimy mitts. "Clear," she said, throwing the lever. There was a soft pneumatic hiss and the lift let the truck down gently.

"Thing was giving me the heebs," said Taryn as she opened the door and climbed up into the lifted 4x4.

Cade watched her but made no reply.

Raven said, "Cool. She's driving?"

"Keys please," said Taryn, her upturned palm wavering near Cade's face.

Cade shrugged, limped close and handed the keys over without giving it a second thought. "Looks like Wilson's riding shotgun," he said.

With a hangdog look on his face, Wilson edged past Cade. "Looks like I'll be getting the roller door then."

Grateful there was no pushback from Wilson, Taryn jammed the key in the ignition, more than eager to fire up the truck's power plant.

While Taryn had been inspecting the truck, Cade had sent Brook off to get some spare gas cans, extra Fix-A-Flat canisters, a few of those vanilla-scented trees he'd spotted near the register, and whatever else she deemed useful. Then, with all of the tasks delegated, he sat down next to Max and closed his eyes.

Muttering under his breath, Wilson manually disengaged the roller door's drive mechanism, hinged over and took the length of frayed nylon rope in both hands. He tensed his shoulders and was about to start the door on an upward trajectory when Brook, who had just returned with an armload of supplies, hollered an admonishment across the garage. "Wilson," she said in a matronly tone. "Lift with your knees. *Not* with your back."

Making a face, he bent his knees, kept his back vertical to the floor, and inhaled. Then under her watchful gaze, he stood up quickly as ordered and sent the metal door rattling noisily upwards in its tracks.

"Perfect," exclaimed Brook, dumping the supplies into the Raptor's box bed. "Wouldn't want to have to pull the weight of two gimps now would we, girls?" She winked at Cade but kept her face straight for Wilson's benefit.

"They do good work, eh Max?" Cade said, giving the prostrate shepherd a good scratching between his ears and earning in return a halfhearted yawn for the efforts.

Chapter 21

By the time Duncan had swapped his thoroughly muddied and drenched clothes for a set of well-worn BDUs in woodland camouflage probably issued first during Reagan's second term, the six aspirins and two bottled waters he'd downed had somewhat numbed his low-grade hangover. After cinching the trousers tight, he transferred the two-way radio, lock blade Kershaw, Zippo lighter and keys to the Land Cruiser into various cargo pockets. Deciding against the cowboy hat, he instead donned a woodland boonie that matched the surplus uniform. And lastly, after pulling on his cowboy boots, the .45 semi-auto Colt went on his hip, riding high in its paddle holster.

Comfortable in the dry uniform, Duncan entered the security container on his way topside. Sitting there on a pair of folding chairs was Heidi and Chief. She was still manning the Ham radio and he was dividing his time there between the still images on the security monitor and a thick paperback by the late Mario Puzo. Curiosity getting the better of him, Duncan stopped behind Chief and whispered, "She picking up anything?"

Shaking his head from side-to-side, Chief lowered his book and mouthed, "Nothing."

"If she raises anyone, I want you to take over. Interrogate them *real* good ... get all the info you can while you have them on the horn."

Shifting in his chair, Chief replied, "I'll glean what I can. Going back to the quarry, huh?"

"Yep," drawled Duncan. "Back to the scene of the crime. Just hope all of the supplies Logan uncovered haven't already fallen into someone else's hands."

"What if those helicopters show up again?"

"Doubt they will. All of the empty ammo boxes they left behind ... tells me they probably left with three or four hundred pounds worth. Between that and the girls, they were probably out of room. And judging from the wheel and skid marks I saw in the mud they were running pretty heavy."

Chief crossed his arms. He said, "They left some weapons behind?"

Nodding, Duncan said, "And food, clothing, Kevlar vests, bedding. There's a nice solar setup on the roof and a bunch of top-of-the-line security cameras that puts these bastardized trail cams to shame."

"We've got our work cut out for us."

"That we do, friend. That we do."

"Me and Phil will hold down the fort," said Chief. "You all hurry back now. You hear?"

Duncan squeezed the stocky Native American on the shoulder. He gently tapped Heidi's head and mouthed, "Good job," then continued on topside.

***

Shielding his eyes against the emerging sun, Duncan broke from the tree line and crossed the clearing, the damp grass wetting his boots. The newly arrived Jackson Hole Chief of Police, Charlie Jenkins, was standing alongside the dented and dinged Land Cruiser, chatting up Lev.

Calling ahead, Duncan said, "How are you this fine morning, Chief Jenkins?"

"Charlie," he answered. "My LE days are behind me."

"Respect's due to ya all the same."

"Lev and Daymon are saying you're going back up to the quarry."

Tugging the floppy brim on the boonie lower, Duncan said, "Got some unfinished business to attend to up there. I reckon one of us will be driving the black-and-white back for you."

"Suit yourself," said Charlie. "Like I said, my days of protecting and serving are over. Look where it got us all anyway."

"Jackson falling to Bishop wasn't your fault, Charlie," hollered Daymon from the opposite side of the Land Cruiser. Then the passenger door creaked, a resonant groaning of metal on metal, and the rig rocked on its springs as he claimed the passenger seat.

Charlie shook his head and, muttering something unintelligible, then leaned against the unoccupied 4Runner, hand resting on the butt of his pistol.

"Let's go," urged Daymon, his muffled voice emanating from inside the Cruiser, the door squealing as he hauled it shut.

"We can take the 4Runner, Daymon ... long as you promise not to wreck it too," said Duncan. He paused a second waiting to see if Daymon would swap rigs or fire off a surly retort and, when neither happened, turned to Lev and asked, "You coming?"

"Thought that was a given," said Lev, removing his ball cap, a yellow fabric article sporting a snake embroidered in brown with the words 'Don't Tread on Me' stitched in red directly underneath. The image had been popular on the Internet, Facebook mainly. And Duncan remembered seeing flags with the same image at gun shows in Portland before the *event* that rendered the government all but useless and the point of the message moot. "You gonna leave that *traffic cone* here? Maybe don something a little more the earthy side of the color spectrum?"

Lev said nothing. Then a beat later the yellow hat went spiraling off into the woods and the former combat veteran was ruffling his dark hair. Judging by his all-over tan and the fact he'd kept his hair closely cropped and still somewhat high and tight these last half a dozen years, a stranger would think he'd just returned from deployment in one sandbox or another. He was lean, and stood a tad over six feet in boots. He fished a pair of wraparound Gargoyles from a cargo pocket and hid his dark eyes behind the polarized lenses. "Good to go," he said. "Who's driving?"

"I got it," said Duncan. "I've seen the topography from the air. Reckon I can find that bluff from the ground. Hop in."

After placing his M4 in first, Lev took a seat behind Duncan's.

Handing his combat shotgun across to Daymon, Duncan slid behind the wheel and fired up the Land Cruiser. Then the window pulsed down and he called out to Jenkins. "We're gonna need you to protect and serve for just a couple of hours until we get back. You OK with that?"

Patting the Sig Sauer semi-automatic riding on his hip, Jenkins replied, "Don't worry ... I'll punch the clock."

***

As soon as Duncan brought the Land Cruiser to a complete stop a car length from the vegetation-covered gate separating the feeder road from State Route 39, the two-way radio in his pocket came alive and in his reedy voice, Phillip stated, "You've got visitors."

After a good deal of squirming and patting his pockets, Duncan was able to locate the device. But in the meantime, Phillip—who was a couple of dozen yards uphill hidden behind a neatly constructed blind that afforded him a commanding view of the two-lane—kept repeating over and over, "Can you hear me now?"

"Copy that," Duncan finally replied. He then added for a little comic relief, "And I heard you the eight times prior to that as well." Then he got serious and asked Phillip for a situation report before opening the gate.

"I've seen eighteen rotters since you left. Seven from down Huntsville way. All pretty fresh ... maybe a day or two dead. But get this ... all of them were kids. Three boys and four girls. I'm no expert but they all looked less then twelve. The rest were first turns ... pretty messy group. They *were* heading towards Huntsville, then suddenly about-faced and followed the kids east. My money says the kids were leftovers from the attack on Huntsville and ..."

"I get the picture, Phil."

"There's more."

"I'll bet there is," said Duncan. *There always is.* In fact after *eighteen* he'd been trying to hold it together while Daymon pretended to slash his wrists with large exaggerated horizontal cutting motions across the bulged tendons and veins there. "We've got to get going. Is the coast clear right now?"

But Phil persisted. "Wait ... you don't understand. You gotta hear this first."

With the engine idling and burning precious fuel, Duncan said rather sternly, "Sweet and to the point."

"The one that we saw earlier. Kind of frozen in place down the road."

"Yeah," said Duncan. "Is it still playing freeze tag?" He arched an eyebrow at Daymon and then craned around and asked Lev to handle the gate.

"No," said Phil after a few seconds of dead air. "You're not going to believe this."

Unable to stand another second of Phil beating around the bush, Duncan hit the talk button and said, "What in God's name is the rotter doing that is so damn special?"

"Trying to *unlock* the gate."

Used to taking most everything Phillip said with a grain of salt, Duncan said nothing at first. Then after a few seconds of silence, with everyone in the rig staring and the skeptic's voice in his head crying bullshit, he remembered that the dead had arisen and were walking the earth. Therefore, he concluded, Phillip's observation warranted further investigation.

Meanwhile, in the passenger seat, Daymon was tilting back an imaginary bottle, feigning drunkenness.

"Phil ... have you been drinking?"

After finding the one assertive bone in his body, Phillip said, "Quit busting my balls, *Duncan.* Get out of the rig and walk fifteen feet and see for your damn self what *I* am looking at. Rotter just started fiddling with it. And you went through last. Means it's got to be *locked* ... right?"

Ignoring the implied indictment, Duncan turned the volume low and slipped the radio back in his pocket and the Toyota's transmission into Park. Then he and Daymon piled out with the passenger door making that god-awful noise and joined Lev, who had a good head start and was now winding his way through steaming puddles of leftover rainwater.

Duncan was closing on Lev when Phillip's voice emanated faintly from his thigh pocket. "I think it hears you. It just stopped what it was doing ..." Then after a second's pause, the play-by-play continued, "... and now it looks like it's on to you."

Slowing his pace, Daymon looked at Duncan and mouthed, "Fucking squeaky door."

Lev, M4 at a low ready, rounded the camouflaged gate just in time to see the rotter looking around, its head on a slow swivel. He ducked back and poked his head ever so carefully around the gate and witnessed the monster take the lock and chain up with both decaying hands. And as he watched it seem to inspect each of the links individually, the thought came to him: *If I'm not imagining this we are fucked, fucked, fucked!* With the pessimistic mantra looping in his head, he wondered if maybe they should try and trap this apparent genius-level rotter. Maybe study it. Look for any weaknesses they might exploit. Then the sound of footsteps behind him, coupled with the absurdity of keeping a flesh eater in captivity, quickly brought him back to reality. That kind of shit was for the movies. And how'd that work out for them?

Having just formed up next to Lev, and carrying a heavy load of doubt towards what Phillip *believed* he saw, Duncan witnessed it with his own eyes. "Well I'll be a monkey's uncle," he exclaimed. To which the rotter stopped fondling the lock, pivoted its head slowly to the left and fixed a blank hungry stare on him. Instantly the ubiquitous dry rasping universal to the first turned reached their ears. Devouring the newly arrived meat with its soulless eyes, the seemingly semi-self-aware abomination lurched along the gate, arms held horizontal. From the west a mellow breeze kicked up, rippling the linen shirt draped on its body and delivering Duncan and Lev and Daymon each a dry-heave-inducing lungful of carrion-polluted air.

The thing had been undead for quite a while, of that Duncan was certain. Dirt was ground into the fabric of its shirt and once-plaid Bermuda shorts. Showing the miles of wear and tear from pounding asphalt during its never-ending search for prey, its feet, worn to the bone, produced a hollow clicking noise with each step. And though the rotter was on the opposite side of the fence, the fact that it was but an arm's length away and it had just been doing what could only be described as problem-solving—albeit on a primitive level—jumpstarted a tingle of dread deep in the pit of Duncan's empty stomach. Then, standing the hair on his arms at attention, the volume of its rasping increased and it hinged over the barbed wire and stalked sideways toward him, dragging its abdomen along the sharp bits of metal and leaving scraps of rancid flesh skewered on the rusty barbs.

Having just caught up with Duncan and Lev at the gate and finding himself face-to-face with the male rotter, Daymon let out a low whistle and said, "Ugly bastard, ain't he?"

"It's not the outside that's got me concerned. Something else is happening between that thing's ears. And I don't like it. Watched it messing with the lock until Old Man caught up and it heard him."

Shaking his head, dreads whipping the air, Daymon said, "Bullshit. These things are nothing but brain-dead sacks of rotting organs."

"Believe it. I saw it too," proffered Duncan. "Wasn't a figment of my imagination."

"Reminds me of that eighties movie where a bunch of Jarheads try to tame the zombie."

Lev smiled at the memory. "Bub was its name," he stated. "Prettier than this one though. Bub was more green than gray. And his neck wasn't chewed half-off, if I remember right."

"Didn't see it," said Duncan. "But I'm *dying* to know how it ended."

Excited by the sound of their voices, the nearly disemboweled rotter leaned in further, bowing the barbed wire, and took a lunging swipe at Duncan.

Daymon shouldered his shotgun and said, "Not well, I'm afraid."

"Give me that," said Duncan, pointing at Daymon's blade.

The machete changed hands and, without a word, Duncan cleaved the monster's skull nearly in two. Behind the full swing, the machete traveled clean through its crown and scrambled its brains before sticking fast against the ethmoid bone. Releasing the nylon handle which was already being ripped from his grip by the dead weight, Duncan said dryly, "Didn't want to chance ending up like the Jarheads."

Taking the embedded machete along for the ride, the rotter crashed onto the shoulder and splashed muddied water over all three men.

A tick after the walking cadaver died for the final time, the two-way radio sounded in Duncan's pocket. "Turn yours on," he said to Lev. "And tell Motor Mouth he was seeing things. No reason to alarm everyone else at the compound until we know whether this one was an anomaly or not."

"I'm from the seeing it is believing it camp, so I'm not sold. But if you aren't drunk ... and really saw what you say you did. Then I think they all deserve to be told about it," argued Daymon.

Holding up one finger, the universal signal saying he needed a moment to think, Duncan removed his aviator glasses and rubbed his temples one at a time. He replaced the bifocals and said, "Make a deal with you. If we see anything else like we just did, then I'll shout about it from the mountaintop."

After a few seconds' consideration, Daymon nodded and said, "OK."

Duncan shifted his gaze to Lev, who was holding the radio near his mouth, thumb hovering expectantly near the call button. "Lev?" To which the Iraq War veteran replied, "That's fair. The scientific method it is."

"The hell does that mean?" Daymon shot back.

"Natural science 101," said Lev. "Seek out *empirical evidence* that either proves or disproves our theory. It's all we got since Old Man here went and offed Bub."

"Eleven-Bravo my ass," said Duncan. "You were some kind of egghead scientist looking for WMDs over there, weren't you?"

"No sir," replied Lev. "I learned how to listen to my high school teachers by following Logan's lead."

Duncan made a face and said, "Lie to the man."

Lev depressed the button. Said blandly, "You were seeing things, Phil."

"You sure?" asked Phil in a skeptic's voice, much higher-pitched than normal.

Feeling a remote tinge of guilt, Lev said, "Positive, Phil. We're heading out now. Back in a couple of hours. Maximum."

"Copy that," said Phil. Then the two-way went silent and Lev said to Duncan, "That wasn't cool."

Leaving Daymon to tend the gate, Lev and Duncan walked back in silence to the waiting truck and clambered inside.

Putting the truck into Drive, Duncan glanced at Lev. "Lying to Phillip couldn't be helped. It just is what it is," he said, letting the idling power plant pull them forward. "Let's put it behind us and get a move on." Watching Daymon haul the gate open, he tromped the gas and felt the motor pulling against all that unnecessary added weight. He thought: *Leather, wood, and stainless steel. Navigation systems and Bluetooth and stereos you can hear from Mars. Who needs 'em.*

From his post on the hillside, Phil trained his binoculars on the trees to the west. *Clear.* He swept them all the way to where Route 39 crested a rise and disappeared on a downslope heading towards the quarry. Five minutes later, the rotter had been deposited in the ditch and the Land Cruiser was nosed east with the gate closed and locked up tight. Then he watched Daymon climb aboard and it pulled away. steadily picking up speed. Heard the gears cycle through as Duncan wheeled east, two wheels on either side of the dotted yellow line. Then the exhaust note dissipated as it motored down the slight grade and the burble got louder as it crawled up the other. After cresting the hill's apex the tires disappeared, then the tail lights, and finally the SUV's rear end and white roof slipped completely from view on the lee side and then silence, thick and brooding, was Phillip's only company.

Chapter 22

A throaty roar resonated inside the garage the second Taryn started the Raptor. Then a smile, the first Cade had seen in days, formed on the teenager's face as she rattled the transmission into drive. She pressed the accelerator and chirped the tires as it bumped over the splayed-out lift arms and then shot out of the garage, leaving undead Kirk bathed in the bright rectangle of sunlight shining in through the open roller door.

"Let's go. I want us all loaded up and oscar mike in five," Cade said, his words nearly drowned out by the Raptor's throbbing engine as it rolled past him. Her smile never-ending, Taryn responded with a thumb up and edged the white Raptor up close to the black F-650. *Yin and Yang*, thought Cade as the brunette hinged her door open, vaulted to the ground, and began transferring gear from the other truck. He shifted his gaze up and regarded the frayed rope dangling twenty feet overhead. Then, after deciding that closing the roller door without a very tall ladder was too much of an undertaking he instead directed Wilson to help Taryn and Sasha transfer their gear and some of the food and bottled waters into the newly liberated truck.

Noticing that Brook had already taken the initiative and was hunched over and shouldering the rolling gate open, he limped over to the F-650 and let Max into the cab. He climbed in behind the wheel, stuck the keys in the ignition, and powered the passenger window down and called Wilson over. Once the redhead was standing on the running board and peering in, Cade handed him a two-way radio and said, "Power it on and think of a number that you won't forget and set it to that channel."

There was a burst of white noise and Wilson tapped repeatedly on the rubber buttons. "OK. Now what?"

"We test them. What number did you choose?"

"Seventeen dash one."

Cade switched his radio on and cycled through the channels up from 10-1 that it had been set to and locked it in on channel 17-1. He looked up, made a face and asked, "Why seventeen?"

"Todd Helton."

"Todd who?"

"My favorite player. He plays ... played for the Colorado Rockies. I have a bat personally autographed by him." Realizing that he was obviously trying to maintain a tenuous grasp on his old life, Wilson flashed a pained smile and looked towards the gate to where Brook was waiting for him to help her. Noticing the kid's moist eyes, Cade pretended to care about the long-dead baseball player. "Helluva slugger, that Helton."

Blinking away tears, Wilson made no reply.

Changing the subject back to matters pertaining to their survival, Cade added, "Lock the channel and leave the radio on and the volume up. Make sure someone who isn't easily distracted monitors it at all times."

"I won't let Sasha near it."

"For the best," Cade agreed with a smile. "The range on these older models under perfect conditions is four or five miles—but I'd bank on no more than half of that. That being said, there should never be more than fifty yards separation between our vehicles." Then he nodded and looked past Wilson and into the Raptor's cab at Taryn, who had just finished loading her gear and had reclaimed her spot in the driver's seat. Following Cade's gaze, Wilson peered over the shorter man's shoulder.

Cade reached into the side pocket and wrapped his fingers around the knurled grip of the pistol he'd stashed there. Turning, he asked Wilson in a low voice, "Think she's ever going to give up the wheel?"

"Who knows what Taryn's going to do from one minute to the next. Hell, one second to the next for that matter," Wilson conceded.

Arching a brow, Cade shot him a look that said *Welcome to the club*. He glanced quickly at Brook and Raven and added, in a near whisper, "Better get used to it."

Nodding, Wilson said, "Thanks for the advice ... I think." Shoulders drooping, he stepped down from the running board and turned towards the Raptor.

Cade nearly let him get away but changed his mind and called him back.

"Yeah?" asked Wilson, stepping up again and poking his head into the open window.

"Take this," Cade said, passing a black nine-millimeter Beretta to the redhead. "And these." He pulled four magazines, each containing nine rounds, from the center console. He looked over at Brook, who was standing near the gate both arms up thrust at an angle—like a 'Y'—a signal he took to mean *Hurry the hell up*. Then, inexplicably, an old Village People tune began playing in his head and he wished he was back in Portland attending a Trail Blazers' game at the Rose Garden with Raven and Brook beside him and not a single dead thing in attendance. Still smiling at the absurdity of the thought, and going against his better judgment, he reached back into the console and handed Wilson a second identical Beretta. "For Taryn," he said. "Be very careful with those."

"I know. I know. Your wife's been hammering us on the rules every chance she gets."

Still smiling at the prospect of Brook following her 'Y' up with an 'M,' a 'C' and an 'A,' Cade said, "And?"

"Why are you smiling?"

Erasing the grin from his face, Cade answered, "You wouldn't believe me if I told you." Intentionally changing the subject, he went on, "Quick, tell me the fundamentals of gun safety."

"Always keep the muzzle pointed in a safe direction."

"Good ... optimally at the Zs," said Cade.

"Always keep my finger off the trigger until I'm ready to shoot."

"Good. And?"

To help with his concentration, Wilson crushed his boonie hat down tighter over his head. Screwed his face up trying to remember if Brook had covered another point. Shrugged his shoulders and said, "You tell me, Mister Delta Force."

"Former," said Cade. "Always assume the weapon is loaded and don't chamber a round until you are ready to shoot. But if she told you that ... forget the last part. We're playing by different rules now. Locked and loaded is the new gold standard. One in the pipe. Safety on ... at all times." He pointed to the ambidextrous thumb-thrown safety.

"Copy that," replied Wilson.

"Now get on over there and help my wife with the gate or she'll stare enough daggers this way to kill the both of us," said Cade. He started the engine and was struck by another thought. He reeled Wilson back to the window for the second time in as many minutes and added over the throaty roar of the engine, "You better move enough of those dead Zs to give us a clear path out of here. Last thing we need is to have a femur go through a sidewall and have to swap tires with Captain Kirk supervising."

Applying his mom's sage advice, Wilson said nothing. Instead, he nodded, jumped down from the running board, and steeled himself against the gruesome task ahead.

Chapter 23

As soon as they had crested the first ridge, the rotters Phillip had described could be seen doddering along the centerline, a small knot of pint-sized creatures in the lead with another eight or ten forming an undead Congo line a few yards behind. And in the ten-minute interim since Phillip's sit-rep, the dead had only covered a quarter mile—give-or-take.

Treating the dead like little more than an annoying swarm of gnats, an anomaly of nature that he'd only recently learned to tolerate, Duncan changed the Cruiser's forward motion by a scant few degrees and blew by them on their left, spinning a few around and sending more crashing to the asphalt, arms and legs batting the air in the process. And as the fast-moving SUV screamed past the undead kids, Daymon was the unfortunate soul who saw their ashen faces turning at once and the lifeless eyes meeting his, then the sharp crack as the passenger mirror brained one of them real good.

"One down ... seven billion to go," said Duncan grimly as he swerved back to the right and lined the center of the hood up with the oncoming yellow dashes.

Daymon couldn't resist. "Have 'em mopped up by Christmas. No problem."

Duncan looked from Daymon to Lev. "Keep your eyes peeled for the quarry sign or some kind of unmarked access road which will be shooting off to the left and climbing the bluff to the quarry."

Lev asked, "How many miles ahead do you figure that will be?"

"Not close enough for the rotters to catch up to us — if that's what you're getting at." Duncan glanced down and noted the current odometer reading, then, from memory, pulled up a mental map of the area based on what he remembered seeing from the air the day before which, considering his deteriorating mental state at the time, was very little. Because he had been so saddled with worry and guilt after allowing his little brother to go out without him, even the pertinent details of the initial search were muddled and ethereal. In fact, as soon as the first shred of discovery had been made, everything after seemed unreal, like viewed from out-of-body through a thin veil of gauze. He could see the patrol Tahoe in his mind, lonely on the gravel, its doors ajar, nobody present—living or dead.. He shook his head, trying to recall the flight from the quarry to deliver the bodies back to the compound, but that too was mostly blurred. Rage had prevailed then, and now the byproduct of that anger—the experienced bout of tunnel vision—was coming back to bite him in the ass.

A quarter mile down the road Duncan finally answered. "I'm sorry. I can't remember, Lev." He looked the question at Daymon and added, "What's your best guess?"

"I'm used to calling in airdrops from the bitch seat of a King Air."

"What does that mean?"

Pinning his dreads behind his ears, Daymon said, "That was a long-winded way of saying I was intent on being your eyes in the air yesterday. A good spotter focuses on the ground only. And that's what I was doing because I wanted to find Logan as bad as you."

Duncan remained silent—thinking hard—trying his best to pull up any small snippets from memory. All the while, off to his right, following the same twists and turns of 39 as the Cruiser, the Ogden River intermittently flashed silver through the trees. He glanced down and checked the odometer a couple more times along the way, and when three miles had spooled out behind the Toyota, thumbed his two-way and informed Phil that they were nearly out of radio range.

After Phillip's reply, Duncan pocketed the radio and scrutinized the passing landscape as the Cruiser bounced along. From light travel and the evening's rains, the desolate two-lane was left covered with damp, fragrant pine needles. It wove through forested hills, rising and falling minimally, and then shot a straight line for a couple of miles before taking on a steeper pitch where the road snaked through, what appeared to Duncan, a series of staggered V-cuts that had been dynamited into the red earth decades ago to allow the road passage.

Up on the hillsides, Duncan noticed that the patches of reddish rock where the elements had eroded the native grasses and topsoil were becoming more evident the farther they went from their valley. At last they rounded a slight bend in the road and a hundred feet ahead on the right Daymon spotted a reflective sign, the usual beehive cutout with black writing on white indicating they were still on Utah State Route 39.

Duncan slowed the SUV to walking speed.

Daymon read the first heading, "Woodruff, 11 miles."

The next line had a smaller beehive labeled *SR-16* with *Randolph, 22 miles* and an arrow indicating the town lay to the left. And below that, using the same reflective letters and numbers, the third entry read *SR-16, I-89 South, Bear River, Wyoming, 24 miles* with an arrow indicating the town was to the right at the eventual T-junction.

"Nothing about a quarry," said Lev.

Speaking in an awful faked Asian accent, Duncan replied, "Patience, grasshopper."

Two turns later those words rang prophetic when Daymon dipped his head, looking across Duncan and called out, "There. I recognize that finger of earth."

"From the ground?"

"Yep. From the ground ... it all just came rushing back to me, Lev."

Smiling for real for the first time in a long while, Duncan's eyes followed and he said, "I concur."

With his body pressed back in the seat, a result of Duncan's sudden acceleration, Daymon clicked out of his belt and racked a round into the shotgun.

"That certain?" said Lev.

"Positive," said Daymon. "Look ... right there. Looks like it's just clinging to the bluff."

There was no need for him to point out the road. For as the SUV slowed it became obvious to everyone, snaking red at about a thirty-degree angle from the State Route before the first bend, a right-hand sweeper, disappeared from sight. Another thirty feet up the bluff the road reappeared, climbing right to left, a much steeper grade that in the short run, before the next hairpin, gained a good chunk of elevation.

Lev said, "How do they get heavy mining equipment up a goat track like that?"

"No need," answered Duncan. "Cheaper to rent a heavy lift helo a couple of times than blow up the side hill in order to widen the road."

"And water?" asked Daymon as the SUV ground to a halt on the centerline.

"There's a creek behind the bluff. Heard it burbling faintly over the falling rain after I killed the helo's turbine yesterday." He stopped talking and turned left, pressing the pedal and wrestling the wheel in order to navigate the transition from pavement to the unimproved road inches thick with mud. Then, with the shiver-inducing noise of thorny branches scraping the rig's sheet metal, added, "And this is the entry."

Master of the obvious, thought Daymon as he grasped the grab handle near his head.

Duncan said, "The tire tracks I'm seeing were made by some kind of an SUV with a wide wheelbase."

"The Tahoe," Lev said. A statement, not a question.

Then Daymon made an observation, saying, "The grass in the center is crushed down. The rain alone didn't do that."

"Jenkins' cruiser sits lower than this land yacht. It's tuned for speed and handling more so than off-roading. My guess is that the grass was beaten down by the skid plates and anti-sway bars underneath the thing."

On its own accord, as if in protest at being called a land yacht, the Land Cruiser jinked left towards the road's edge and a thirty-foot drop off.

"Whoa," cried Daymon, still gripping the grab handle, his knuckles suddenly going stark white.

Narrowly averting a deadly plunge, Duncan wrestled the rig back into the established ruts and stopped dead center on the incline. Looking for a way to select a lower gear, he scanned the dash and then the center console where, next to the shifter, he spied a chromed dial labeled CRAWL. *Couldn't hurt*, he thought, rotating it to the midway point. Hearing a click, he released the brake and noticed an altogether different type of feedback through the controls. Once the SUV picked up some forward momentum there was zero slipping and sliding. And though the suspension was forgiving, and the sidewalls tall and the tire tread more suited for the city than a muddy goat track, the vehicle decried its luxury heritage and surged uphill.

"Now we're talking," said Duncan, feeling the brakes apply on their own, the ABS thwarting a fishtail on the next corner. "Technology trumping tread pattern."

Five switchbacks and ten minutes later, Duncan could sense them nearing the top. On the last turn he spotted the reservoir in Huntsville, small and distant and sparkling diamond-like. Above and to the right was the stunted hilltop peppered with a myriad of small trees clinging steadfast in defiance of gravity.

Knowing that he would soon be seeing the scene of Logan's death under a whole different set of circumstances, while hopefully maintaining a calm and collected demeanor, he went silent, steeling himself against the inevitable flood of emotions.

Chapter 24

With a pair of curious first turns shambling in from the two-lane running parallel to Mesa View 4x4's flower-lined drive, Wilson dragged the last of the rotten corpses out of the F-650's path. He stepped back and wiped the gore from his gloves on the truck with Cade inside as it passed through the gate. A moment later, the Raptor rolled onto the drive and came to a stop, leaving barely a half-foot of clearance for the roller gate to skim by its rear bumper.

It was Cade's decision to leave the 4x4 shop as near to how they'd found it as possible, and Wilson had been appointed the facilitator for this plan. So, without complaint, he grabbed a handful of chain-link, leaned in, and ran the wheeled gate closed.

Revving her engine like Danica Patrick on pole position, Taryn simultaneously eyed the approaching walkers and hollered out her window, urging Wilson to hurry up.

Panting hard from the exertion, Wilson flung the passenger door open, took a firm hold of the grab bar, and hauled himself aboard. And while they waited for the lead vehicle to start rolling, he buckled in and quickly relayed all of the pertinent information and ground rules Cade had piled on him moments before. He powered up the two-way radio, maxed the volume, and stashed it in a cubby near his elbow. He wedged one of the Berettas under his left thigh, and the other, along with two of the four magazines Cade had given him, got stashed in the glove box. Seeing this, Taryn demanded to know how he got the guns.

With a satisfied half-smile he replied, "Cade gave them to me."

"Gave *what* to you?" inquired Sasha from the rear seat.

In unison and in near perfect harmony, Taryn and Wilson replied, "Nothing, Sasha." Such words might have placated anyone under seven, but Sasha had that doubled chronologically, so predictably she pushed the issue. And, as Wilson expected, his petulant sibling wedged her upper body between the front seats and into his personal space, demanding to know what was being '*hidden*' from her.

Suddenly the F-650 blocking their exit belched grey exhaust and spun its wide tires, tilling the flower beds and finishing the destruction the undead had started. As it surged forward, knocking the two Zs off of their feet, Sasha said sarcastically, "So that must be a semi-automatic *nothing* under your leg then, huh Wilson?"

Wilson said nothing. He met Taryn's gaze and delivered the universal signal for step on it by nodding in the direction of the rapidly accelerating Ford.

Message received. Taryn pinned the pedal to the firewall, bringing four hundred of the Raptor's available five-hundred-horsepower on line. The race-tuned pick-up shimmied in place for a half second as the torque spooled up and was transferred to the rear wheels. Then two new furrows were gouged into the beds as the truck rocketed ahead, going from zero to thirty in a dozen yards.

Consequently, Sasha, victimized by both inertia and gravity, was thrown into the seatback with sufficient force to steal her wind.

"Sorry, Sash," Taryn said, a half beat before belting out a serious rebel yell.

In the passenger seat, knuckles and face turning the same ghostly white, Wilson sat speechless and dangerously close to soiling his pants.

Inside the F-650, Cade flicked his gaze to the rearview where he saw the baby Ford lurch up like a stallion and then slew sideways spitting dirt and Z body parts in its wake. Shaking his head, he whispered, "You better rein it in, Taryn."

At that same instant, great minds were running on the same track and Brook had twisted in her seat and stated the obvious: "That truck is way too much for her."

Returning his eyes to the fore, Cade arched a brow and quipped, "And how would you know ... have you been reading Road and Track magazine behind my back?" Not really expecting an answer to that, he muscled his own ride through a hard left turn that brought them back onto the tree-lined two-way heading back towards FOB Bastion.

"Because I got a few new gray hairs riding in one just like it on the way to Bragg."

A few? thought Cade. In his experience, the wild ride that surviving another twenty-four of the apocalypse had become didn't just manifest itself in the way of a few new gray hairs. In fact, nearly every person who was still living and older than thirty that he'd been around with any kind of consistency since Z-Day, himself included, had aged considerably. His normally coal-black goatee, for the first time in his life at just thirty-five years of age, was, to quote a Grateful Dead song, now showing *more* than a "*touch of grey.*" Crow's feet were now a permanent addition to his face, and when he looked in the mirror the stranger looking back possessed heavy-lidded red-rimmed eyes that gazed back with a thousand-yard-stare inherited from too many sleepless days and nights spent '*downrange*' rubbing elbows with the dead.

"I found the truck and the keys for Uncle Carl," bragged Raven, thankfully snapping Cade out of his funk. "It was the brightest shade of orange I've ever seen and parked *inside* the car place in Lumber Town. *Inside* ... pretty random, huh?"

Correcting Raven, Brook said, "Lumberton. That's where Raven saved our butts, Cade. Can't think of when I've been prouder of our Bird than that moment."

"And *that's* where Uncle Carl gave Mom the grays," added Raven, satisfied she'd picked up on the correlation.

Looking past Cade, eyes locked on the old Craftsman a block up, Brook said nothing.

Cade was doing the same. He slowed to walking speed as the duplicate of their old home crawled by. He noticed that the Z that had been loitering on the porch earlier now was nowhere to be seen. More importantly, though he didn't draw attention to it, the front door to the house was hanging open. With a palpable feeling of dread pressing him into his seat and his brain grappling with the complexities of the clear and present danger the new information represented, he pulled the rig hard to the curb and let the engine idle.

Seconds later the Ford formed up on his side, the window powered down and Wilson looked a question at Cade.

"Did you go over what I told you with Taryn?"

"Sir ... yes, sir."

With the awful memory of the IED attack that had killed Leo and Sheila instantly, and then his neighbor Rawley being gunned down as a direct result when he doubled back to help, Cade decided to let Taryn hear the grim warning from his own mouth. He rattled the shifter to Park and slid from the truck. Putting his elbows on the window channel, he made direct eye contact.

"Taryn, this is real important," he said slowly. "If we come upon any trouble, Zs or human, we keep on driving unless the road is blocked. And if that's the case ... "

Interrupting him, Taryn said rather confidently, "I stop and reverse out of the situation and then pull a bootlegger's reverse so that your monster truck doesn't get trapped. But don't worry ... I don't plan on tailgating you, so that's not likely to happen."

Stunned at the fact that she even knew the name of the maneuver he'd been taught years ago during the defensive driving section of Delta's OTC—Operators Training Course—he went silent and stared at her, trying to decide if she was parroting something she'd heard on an old Starsky and Hutch rerun or if she was actually being sincere. After a few seconds without the pendulum swinging either way towards any kind of a logical conclusion, he flat-out asked her.

"And just how many bootlegger reverses have you successfully completed in your—" He paused mid-sentence, thinking back to his youth. He remembered getting his learner's permit at sixteen and it was common knowledge that Taryn was nineteen going on twenty—so that meant she'd been driving three, maybe four years at the most. Unless she'd been brought up on a farm where special allowances are given to drive at fourteen, which Cade thought highly unlikely, because judging by the desert surrounding her hometown of Grand Junction the only thing anyone was pulling from the ground was dirt clods. After a couple of seconds, during which the two trucks engines idled and she maintained constant eye contact, he resumed his line of questioning. "So in four years behind the wheel, how much evasive driving have you actually done?"

"None," she said. "But I've raced open wheel cars on dirt tracks since I was seven and could reach the pedals."

Without wasting another word on the subject, Cade returned to the 650 and got back behind the wheel. He sat speechless for the second time since waking and, after the brief lull in both word and action, shifted into drive, and as soon as they were moving again filled a slightly amazed Brook in on the new revelation.

As the larger truck pulled away and Taryn shifted the Raptor into drive, Wilson powered up his window, looked at her with his head at an angle, and said, "Really?"

"Yeah ... *really*," she replied, her eyes glued to the road. "Every word I said was the honest to God truth."

"Shut him up real good, too," Wilson noted. "And as far as I'm concerned, my butt is glued to this seat for the rest of the trip."

"You are a badass," said Sasha from her backseat domain. "But next time ... please warn me *before* you take off like that."

Chapter 25

One heartbeat after leaving the final stretch of road with its deadly three-hundred-foot drop-off behind and entering what Duncan hoped was the final blind corner before reaching the quarry's entry, several things happened simultaneously. He nosed the Land Cruiser out of the right-hand sweeper and his attention was immediately drawn to the airspace above the quarry where a good number of raptors rode the thermals in lazy counterclockwise circles. As he straightened the steering wheel, his gaze fell next on the twelve-foot-tall concertina-topped fence looming thirty feet away. And in nearly the same instant, he saw the dozen or so rotters standing on the road between the SUV and the quarry entrance.

At first the dead remained rooted. Just staring and swaying—seemingly in some kind of state of hibernation—until the exact moment he crushed the brake pedal to the floor, bringing the nearly three-ton vehicle to a grinding halt. Then all hell broke loose. And in the microsecond between decision and action, as the dead surged forward in unison, a last furtive glance told Duncan that, prior to turning, this group had been mostly working-age folks with only a few falling outside of those demographics. That they were clothed in blue jeans and tee-shirts—sensible attire—not the kind of biker chic that the Huntsville crowd had seemed to favor, led him to believe that they had come from the east, drawn here by the recent activity.

But from experience, he knew that the lives the walking dead left behind had no bearing on their intent now. They weren't marauders from the west. Nor were they friendly survivors from points east. What they were right now was dead and hungry. Nothing more, nothing less. And he was sitting in a truck full of fresh meat only a few paces removed from them. So discarding his useless evaluation, he racked the transmission into reverse and tromped the pedal. In the next instant, as a few precious feet of separation was created, Daymon drew in a deep breath and Duncan heard Lev use God's name in vain and bitch about them nearly becoming surrounded.

Intuitively Duncan steered with one hand and craned around to look out the rear window. Then with the roar of the engine and a shrill whining from the overtaxed transmission leeching into the cabin, he ticked off two seconds in his head and again stood hard on the brakes. Lev uttered an unintelligible expletive and the distinctive click-clack of him drawing back the M4 charging handle reverberated from the back seat area. A half beat later, after the SUV had lurched to a complete stop, Duncan, with spittle flying off his lips, bellowed, "Out. Out. Out."

There was the familiar creak of metal as Daymon's door, opened followed by a soft click signaling Lev's exit. A staccato slamming of both doors came next.

Once the two had bailed out, Duncan dialed down the CRAWL feature, selected drive, and started the SUV—now three hundred and fifty pounds lighter—hurtling forward. A truck's length later he stood on the brakes and jerked the wheel hard right—an instant and aggressive move that saw the Toyota's rear end break loose. Finally, wrestling the wheel left against the slide and braking for a fourth and final time in the span of just a few seconds, Duncan let the front bumper kiss the hillside, leaving the roadway mostly blocked.

Frantically trying to create a comfortable shooting position, he clicked out of his seatbelt, clawed the .45 from its holster, and thumbed the hammer back. Motoring his window down, he was hit broadside by the wave of stench preceding the raggedy line of flesh eaters nearing the Toyota.

He braced one elbow on the window channel, had the other pressed against the steering wheel, and was drawing a bead on the nearest rotter when two things registered in his peripheral.

On his right, through the windshield's curved glass, he saw Lev's upper body—head and elbows and forearms—and then finally, completing the fluid sequence, a black carbine settled horizontally across the mud-spattered sheet metal with a dull thud, fire lancing star-like from its muzzle.

And on the left, he saw orange muzzle flashes behind a series of thundering booms that rocked the SUV, both reassuring and letting him know that Daymon had just entered the fray.

So he steadied the Colt in a two-handed grip, bracketed a middle-aged male cadaver within his sights, took a calming breath, and let loose a pair of closely spaced shots. Delivered from a dozen feet away, the perfect double-tap ruptured the thing's skull right where Duncan had been aiming, sending one half airborne behind a cascade of blood and fluid, and the other, still connected by a membrane of skin and muscle, hinging over onto its shoulder with a wet meaty slap. A microsecond later, with his spent casings still pinging off the inside of the SUV's windshield, Duncan witnessed the two-hundred pounds of dead meat collapse in place. Simultaneously, amid the cacophony of gunfire, he saw two more rotters to his immediate left receive point blank shotgun blasts, ugly face shredders creating translucent halos of airborne brain, blood and tissue.

With all of this happening around him, Duncan added three more rotters to his body count while at the same time witnessing an impressive display of shooting as Lev put down more than his fair share of walking corpses.

As the gunfire ceased and the echoes made their final rounds of the hills before dissipating into silence, Duncan stepped out onto the roadway. His gaze was drawn to the mud uphill where the twin J-shaped tire marks created by his initial evasive maneuver were filling with the blood of the twice-dead rotters. He looked high and noted the buzzards, undeterred from whatever had piqued their interest, still gliding high above the ground-hugging cordite haze. He jammed a finger knuckle-deep into one ear and wiggled, a futile effort to quell the shrill non-stop ringing the raucous gunfire had produced in his head. "Sorry about that, fellas," he said, giving his lobe a solid tug. Still talking, he repeated the procedure on the other ear. "Bastards kinda caught me flat-footed up there ... gaping at the birds and taking in the scale of the fence. And boom! They were right there in my grill ... literally."

"No worries," Lev said behind a half-grin. "Redeemed yourself with that excellent driving."

"I'll say," replied Daymon as he fished a few twelve-gauge shells from his pocket. And as he reloaded his shotgun, he nodded at Lev and asked, "Hell'd you learn how to shoot like that anyway?"

After swapping out magazines and chambering a fresh round into the M4, Lev set the safety, tossed the carbine into the backseat, and said, "Basic is where I learned how to shoot like that. The *sandbox* is where I learned how to shoot moving *people* like that. All courtesy of Uncle Sam. And when it comes to the enemy ... my philosophy is kind of like that of an alcoholic taking that first drink. You know the saying, Duncan: one is too many and a thousand is never enough."

Daymon made a face. He looked at Duncan, who wasn't biting. "That was a low blow, Lev. But these things ain't *people* and I don't see them as the enemy. They're kind of like snakes were to me when I was fighting fires, ya know ... if you gotta take off a head or two to be safe then so be it."

"Close enough comparisons. You see these ones ... how their heads popped. Brains and blood and shit spraying everywhere," countered Lev. "And they're still bleeding now. That's because these ones are fresh. Their blood hasn't congealed yet. I figure they're two days dead ... maybe three at most." He went quiet for a second. Then said, "*People*," while staring off into space.

Changing the subject, and for some reason choosing not to address Lev's jab at his booze-soaked grieving period, Duncan said, "Let's get these bodies moved off the road. This first one is real big. Lev, any help here?" He strode over to what had been by far the largest of the rotters—a morbidly obese male probably weighing upwards of three hundred pounds. How the undead Bob's Big Boy in the John Deere shirt had made it up the road, with diminished motor skills and the extra weight, was beyond comprehension. But none of that mattered now, because somehow—judging by the two dime-sized entry wounds near its hairline—the corpse was still moving even after having been struck by a pair of 5.56mm hardballs fired from Lev's carbine.

So he took a step back and gave it some room as it labored hard to roll over onto its stomach. And then it suddenly struck him as he watched it wallow, fighting against gravity, just how much the chalky white specimen with its rolls of fat leaking from under the hiked-up shirt reminded him of a beached pilot whale. Then it moaned, a bovine-like noise that stood the hair on Duncan's arms at rigid attention.

"You going to finish what you started, Lev?"

"Consider that one on me," he replied. "Pretend it's a chaser if you want."

"You got something to say to me, boy?" Duncan said to Lev. "If you do you better say it now." He thrust the Colt out at arm's length, aiming an inch behind the big flesh eater's left ear. This got Daymon's attention. He released the wrists of the corpse he'd been dragging. Left it on the shoulder, walked to the Cruiser and leaned against the rear fender.

The bucking corpse craned around and locked its jaundiced eyes on Duncan. Then it emitted a drawn-out moan that sounded suspiciously like *Noooo.*

Daymon pushed off of the Land Cruiser and racked a round into his shotgun. "No way," he said quietly.

After looking each man in the eye, one at a time, Duncan fixed his gaze back on the big rotter. "This is not the *empirical* proof you were speaking of, Lev. What we just heard was a garden-variety moan that on account of all of this flopping around came out sounding *kinda* like a word. Nothing more."

"Hope you're right."

Daymon nodded. Returned to his task of checking the bodies for identification.

Duncan's .45 boomed, shattering the still. And stilling the rotter. He holstered his Colt and said to Lev, "Lay off the booze cracks. I'm not amused."

"Copy that," replied Lev as he drew his semi-automatic. Then said nothing more and zippered his way between the fallen rotters, delivering an extra *just in case* bullet into the back of each of their heads. After the twelfth unnecessary coup de grace, he swapped mags and expended twelve more 9mm Parabellums on the unmoving bodies.

"Smartass," said Duncan as he and Daymon struggled to roll the now inert *whale* over the edge.

***

Ten minutes later and still Lev hadn't said a word. But he had helped clear the road.

"Come and check this out," called Daymon. "I thought that big one looked familiar."

Duncan looked up and said, "Whatcha got?"

"I lifted his wallet. ID says he's from Etna, Wyoming. Name *was* James Carter. I remember meeting him ... Mr. Carter, he called himself then. Before the dead started to walk he taught fifth grade at Etna Elementary."

"You went there?"

"No, Lev. We drove through there on our way down from Victor and Driggs the other day. They had us dead to rights. Fifteen guns in our faces and a school bus blocking the way ..."

Duncan was cleaning his glasses. He looked up and asked, "What happened?"

"I'm standing here, aren't I?" said Daymon. He looked up and regarded the buzzards for a second.

"And?" asked Lev, his hand making a circular reeling motion. Universal semaphore for *spit it out.*

"My good Karma kicked in ... he let us through."

"Karma my ass," said Duncan. "Look where it got him ... and Logan." Anger building, he jumped into the Toyota. "I don't need to see a death card to know that the same dirtbags who killed Oops and Gus and took the girls also sacked Etna."

"That would explain why some of the rotters had GSWs," added Lev.

"Who's getting the gate?"

"I got it, Duncan," snapped Lev. He squared up to the Toyota and looked the old aviator in the eye. "Sorry. I guess being this close to where it happened is kinda getting to me."

"Makes two of us, kid," Duncan conceded. He started the Cruiser and performed a series of short maneuvers, a combination of reversing and then pulling ahead in small increments until he had the SUV parallel with the road. Then he pulled forward a few feet and stopped next to Lev. "Apology accepted," he said.

The passenger door creaked again and Daymon sat in the passenger seat.

A minute later Lev had opened the gate which had been *locked* only cosmetically, the chain merely threaded through the fence, a piece of previously snipped padlock falsely *securing* it.

Thirty seconds later the Cruiser was through and the gate was closed and *locked* behind them.

Once Lev was back in the vehicle, Duncan urged the SUV forward and said, "Y'all ready for this?"

To which there was no reply. Only engine noise and the sound of tires splashing through puddles would accompany them to the scene of the crime.

Chapter 26

After surprising Taryn with the impromptu inquisition, and satisfied for the most part with the answers, Cade had nosed the Ford right and onto O Road, then backtracked nearly two miles west leaving the outskirts of Loma and the still-rising sun in his rearview mirror. Along the way he would occasionally speed up and brake hard, a concerted effort on his part to evaluate her reaction times. A short while later both trucks were stopped side-by-side at the intersection of Mack Road and US-6 which used to be the only thoroughfare connecting Mack with Grand Junction, Taryn's hometown, thirty miles on a diagonal east by south.

And dead ahead, finished in the late nineties and instantly making US-6 and the unincorporated community of Mack north of it obsolete, Interstate 70 ran away on a parallel tack with little more than bulletproof desert soil and tumbleweeds between them.

With a decision looming Cade, fixed his gaze on FOB Bastion off the right front fender a half a mile distant. Rising up from the desert floor, the hastily constructed front gate and makeshift guard towers all interconnected with newly strung barbed-wire looked more like some kind of World War Two internment facility meant to separate and keep safe the majority from a scant few of the population who were in fact quite harmless—not the polar opposite. He looked the length of US-6 and could see it hadn't received the same scrutiny from Beeson's boys as the other connecting roads. Like an afterthought of civilization, a number of abandoned vehicles were scattered here and there in both directions, most on the shoulder, some not. Birds fluttered around one of the nearest vehicles, squeezing their feathered forms through a partially open window to get at the sweet treats festering inside. *No go*, he thought.

So he hung a left and drove ahead a hundred yards and stopped before the westbound ramp to Interstate 70. *Three roadblocks manned by the 2nd ID and then no-man's land*, Beeson had said. *And the final one is thirty-six miles west on the I-70 and then you're on your own.* Cade looked down the four-lane which was empty and desolate, a diminishing gray scar cutting through the low scrub towards Grand Junction, over the majestic Rockies and on into Denver to the east.

He looked right and saw more of the same. Only there were no knife-edged crags magnified by the distant haze. There was mainly flat terrain. Miles and miles of desert with scattered hillocks and groves of trees lucky enough to have found a water source near which to flourish. And like the cities of Grand Junction and Denver to the east, which he couldn't see but knew were there, a number of small towns and communities dotted their route of travel, the writing on the green road sign planted in the hard soil confirming it.

Taryn maneuvered the Raptor alongside the Ford and the window pulsed down; while motioning for Cade to do the same, Wilson stuck his head out.

After Cade's window seated with a solid thunk, he stuck his head out and looked down at the redhead. "Yeah?" he said.

"We taking the Six or the Seventy?" asked Wilson. "Taryn's curious."

Cade stuck one finger in the air—the universal sign shared among his old Delta Unit for wait one minute—and then pulled his head back inside. He hinged over and pointed Brook towards the laminated maps he'd stuffed under the seat and asked her to form an opinion on which route they should take based on the map's key and the corresponding markings on I-70 and US-6 farther along to the west.

FOB Bastion

The baby-faced corporal lowered the Steiner's and called down to First Sergeant Laurel Andreasen, urging her to join him up in the guard tower.

After climbing thirteen rickety stairs that amounted to nothing fancier than one-by-fours nailed horizontally to a pair of vertical two-by-fours, she poked her head through the opening cut into the floor and accepted the corporal's outstretched hand. And once she was standing next to the southern rail on the eight-by-eight platform, she accepted the field glasses from the corporal, looped the strap over her head, and said, "Whatcha got Keefe?"

"I'm not certain," answered the corporal. He directed her to gaze down the length of his arm. "Two-thirds of a click. You see them? Two vehicles in the shadow. What do you think?"

"The nearest pick-up ... that's got to be Cade Grayson's rig. It's the right color ... plus it dwarfs the other truck. "

"What do you think about the other truck?"

"Spoils of war left by the fallen for the living to inherit. There were five other people and a dog in his truck when they left the wire. So it makes sense to me that they'd go into Fruita or Loma to liberate another vehicle."

"Which way did he say they are going?"

Wearing a mask of worry, First Sergeant Andreasen said in a low voice, "West. Towards Salt Lake."

The corporal whistled, drawn out and hollow and filled with portent. He asked, "Should I alert the pickets?"

"Good thinking," she said agreeably. Then, while the corporal consulted a laminated sheet with all of the radio frequencies on it, Andreasen put her elevated vantage spot to good use, swept the binoculars left and scanned the area around the perimeter fence. And when she reached the northeast corner where it made the first of the four sharp ninety degree bends, she witnessed a dozen or so Zs stagger lemming-like and disappear in ones and twos into the trench. Cognizant of the Zs new behaviors, and fearful of FOB Bastion being overrun like Camp Williams which had been Beeson's previous command, she looked over the rail and ordered a pair of camouflage-clad soldiers to gear up and go outside the wire and as she not so eloquently put it: *Cull the bastards before they have a chance to climb out.*

In the short time it had taken the corporal to call ahead to three different forward listening posts, and while First Sergeant Andreasen was directing the armed response to the new threat, the two trucks had started to move.

Chapter 27

"It has been decided. Interstate Seventy it is," Cade said, casting a sidelong glance at Brook. He rattled the shifter into Drive and asked over his shoulder, "Do you concur, Raven?" Waiting for her answer, he flicked his gaze to the side-view and for the first time noticed the big block letters spelling out FORD centered in the white Raptor's contrasting matte black grill. Then he stared a little too long at the reflection of the HID—High Intensity Discharge—headlights and the equally bright bumper-mounted driving lights and noted that though the sun was painting everything in a flat light, the eerie blue glow was still very intense and likely visible for miles. Blinking from the glare, he glanced up at the rearview mirror and noticed Raven, head listing a few degrees right and staring back at him like he'd been speaking to her in French or Pig Latin. The quizzical look frozen on her face, she said nothing for a long second, presumably mulling over the question, weighing its context. Finally her face lit up with recognition and she shot back, "I concur. The Interstate is wider and has a lot less stalled cars on it than the old highway."

Holding the two-way close to his mouth, Cade keyed the Talk button. "The boss ladies are telling me the Interstate is the way to go." He risked another look in the side mirror just as Taryn acknowledged with a double supernova flash of the Raptor's high beams.

Wishing he knew where he had misplaced his Oakleys, Cade placed a hand over the side mirror blocking the light hammering into the cab and said, "Before we go *anywhere,* Taryn is going to have to kill those headlights. Things are so bright everyone and their dead brother is gonna see us coming." The instant the words *dead brother* rolled off his tongue he wished he could reverse time and reword that last statement. Grimacing, he handed the radio to Brook and saw tears in her eyes. "I'm so sorry," he mouthed. "Awful choice of words. It won't happen again."

She made no reply. Took the radio and crossed her arms and turned her gaze to the scraggly roadside scrub.

A long, tense second passed in the cab before Taryn extinguished the Raptor's lights. Simultaneously, mimicking and skewering Cade's vernacular horribly, Wilson said over the two-way, "Roger, copy that ... loud and clear. The Interstate it is. We're oscar mike when you are."

Feeling like a heel after inadvertently reminding Brook of her late brother, Cade made a silent pact with himself to run anything he might say through a mental filter—*twice*—before letting a thought fly like that again. So with a heavy heart and fond memories of Carl's spirited and uplifting banter echoing in his head, Cade nosed the F-650 onto Mack Road and accelerated south. At the next intersection the two-truck convoy made the sweeping right-hand turn, blasting aside an accumulation of tumbleweeds and merging onto the westbound lanes of I-70. *Beeson's Boys did a hell of a job*, thought Cade. Both lanes for as far as he could see were clear, the inert cars and SUVs and long-haul trucks having been shoved aside onto the scrub-dotted median. While on the right shoulder the vehicles were left where they had either run out of fuel or broken down after presumably fleeing Grand Junction, Loma, or perhaps even Denver two hundred and fifty miles to the east.

The opposing lanes, however, were a different story altogether. No care had been taken to move any of the static vehicles or put down the infected still trapped inside. For all intents and purposes, that stretch of two-lane had been largely forgotten by the soldiers at FOB Bastion. *And rightfully so*, thought Cade. No reason to police more than one viable route of ingress and egress. Furthermore, putting out listening posts was another sound tactical move.

As they motored west with the AC keeping them all cool and comfortable inside the suddenly spacious cabin, Cade kept close tabs on Taryn's driving and quickly learned that she was indeed a lady of her word. Even at speeds pushing seventy, she seemed in complete control of the souped-up pick-up truck and never once did she crowd his bumper; instead, she maintained a minimum three-truck-length buffer. And apparently adhering to the adage that four eyes are better than two, she saw fit to keep the Raptor's left wheels tracking with his passenger side—a sort of vehicular right echelon stack—so that he could keep an eye on both of their sixes and she could also see the vast countryside they'd yet to cover.

Cade peered left at the Colorado River twisting and turning and glittering silver. For the first few miles west of Mack it had kept them company while the mercury continued to rise, and by the time they identified the first checkpoint shimmering wildly in the heat waves on the horizon, half an hour had passed and the outside temperature according to the F-650's onboard computer was bumping the south side of one hundred degrees.

From a hundred yards out, Cade knew that the checkpoint consisted of two opposite-facing Humvees and at least two soldiers who were dismounted and facing the same direction as their respective vehicle. One due west. One facing due east and, judging by the flare from the circular lenses, presently scrutinizing them through a substantial-sized pair of binoculars.

As the F-650 ate up another fifty yards of roadway, Cade eased off the pedal and noticed that each of the low-slung boxy vehicles had a top-mounted turret with a helmeted soldier sweltering in the sun while dutifully manning what Cade supposed was an M-240 light machine gun. And as those fifty yards were halved, the sun suddenly glared off the oddly canted ballistic-proof panes and the desert tan vehicle blocking their passage reversed onto the outer shoulder. Then, without saying a word, the dismounts stepped aside, nodded and waved both of the pick-ups through.

Barely ten seconds had elapsed and the two-way crackled to life. Cade nodded and Brook snatched it up and said, "What now?"

Wilson's voice came through the speaker. "Sasha has to pee."

Cade sighed and applied the brakes and stopped dead center in the fast lane. "Kids," he muttered. "Anyone else have to go? Raven? Max?" He felt a staccato thumping on the backside of his seat. "Max does."

"Me too," said Raven, a sheepish look on her face.

No better place than here, thought Cade. Two hundred yards removed from a half-dozen soldiers and a lethal pair of machine guns.

Doors opened and bodies jumped to the asphalt.

After averting his eyes, Cade called out, “Make it snappy.”

***

Sasha was back to the Raptor first. Then Raven sprinted across the hot pavement, scaled the F-650 and took her place in the back seat. Finally, after a long ten count, Max bolted from the brush, hackles up and growling. Crossed the two lanes in three long strides and vaulted into the open door and spun a one-eighty, teeth bared and shivering. A tick later the reason for his discontent became obvious as the upper half of a human slithered out of the shin-high scrub. It entered the fast lane five yards in front of Cade, trailing an unidentifiable softball-sized internal organ. Slowly, hand over hand, it advanced, dragging its dust- and twig-coated innards through the steaming puddles where Sasha and Raven had just finished their business.

The moment the rear door thumped shut, Cade engaged the transmission, turned a slow arcing right to avoid the crawler and then accelerated rapidly to fifty miles per hour. Taking his eyes from the road for a split second, he looked to Brook and said, “That was close.”

Remembering how Raven had nearly become Z food while peeing outside of a thoroughly looted supermarket in South Carolina weeks ago, Brook parroted something she had heard Cade and every single one of his operator buddies say at one time or another “Close only counts in hand grenades and horseshoes.”

“Copy that,” Cade said agreeably.

Chapter 28

With the first checkpoint miles behind them, and Green River nowhere on the horizon, Cade suddenly began to feel for the poor bastards somewhere up ahead baking under the hundred-degree sun. *Yep*, he thought. *Every coal mine had to have its canary*. And just like those true patriots back there, he had been on that first line of defense. His stomach clenched involuntarily and just like that he was back in Iraq. There truly was something to be said for loitering behind hastily positioned Jersey barriers at surprise checkpoints, surrounded by restless locals, most hostile, while hoping to get lucky and ensnare an unsuspecting high-value target or low-level Baath party member. *Yep*, he thought. *Being that kind of canary had its own unique pucker factor*. Because whether detonated fifty feet or fifty yards away, a SVBIED—suicide vehicle borne improvised explosive device—was usually a fatal event for anybody unlucky enough to get caught inside its blast radius. Thankfully though, the higher-ups had decided rather quickly that his unit's services were needed elsewhere and he had made it through that first deployment without getting caught on the receiving end of the enemy's most cowardly, destructive, and widely used tactic firsthand. But he had seen the aftermath of several of those suicide attacks up close and personal and right now, much to his surprise, the rapidly approaching scene looked eerily similar.

In the median, a rectangular swath of scrub brush the size of a football field had been razed by fire, and a handful of vehicles in the adjacent eastbound lanes had been reduced to nothing but soot-covered see-through metal frames resting atop pools of melted dashboard, interior panels, and tire rubber. Left of the freeway, the conflagration had spread and burned, by Cade's estimation, tens of acres of the bone-dry landscape down to the dirt. And dead ahead, several hundred feet of the once gray Interstate was blackened and had bubbled and boiled and melted in places, leaving large tracts of asphalt resembling some kind of prehistoric tar pit. He abruptly slowed the F-650 to walking speed and then stopped ten feet short of the line of demarcation where the firm roadbed ended and the soupy-looking morass began.

"Ewwww," exclaimed Raven. "Bet there are some dino bones in there." To which Brook chuckled and smiled for the first time since Cade's verbal faux pas. Then, interrupting the moment, the two-way's harsh electronic warble filled the cab. "What's up?" asked Wilson. "I thought we weren't going to stop for anything."

Thumbing the talk button, Brook said, "Pull up beside us and take it up with Cade."

"Copy that."

"Let them know that we've got company. Ten o'clock," Cade said, pointing at a tangle of scorched vehicles in the eastbound lanes.

Shifting her gaze left, Brook picked up the pair of pale figures. Watched them emerge from the wreckage and trudge across the median, kicking up dust and charred flora with each labored step. While she keyed the two-way and relayed the warning, Cade looked past her and down the embankment and regarded the hulks of a dozen cars and pick-ups that were burned and compacted nearly beyond recognition, the majority of them resting under the skeletal remains of an eighteen-wheel tandem fuel hauler—its thousands of gallons of fuel no doubt responsible for liquefying the road. And though there was no telling VW-sized crater in the road, he still marveled at how strikingly the damage resembled the work of a successful suicide bomber.

"Didn't end well for them," he said off the cuff.

"Well at least they didn't end up as one of *them*," exclaimed Raven, the resident pragmatist.

Brook shook her head ruefully and said, "I'm with Raven. I'd rather die quick in something like that ..."—she gestured towards the charred bodies and mangled metal—" ... than not *really* die ... like that." She nodded to her left at the pair of walkers.

"Let's not die at all," proffered Cade just as the Raptor pulled up smartly and stopped on a dime, leaving barely a yard between the two vehicles.

Wilson's window was already open and he was looking up and holding the Beretta at a ninety-degree angle, its muzzle almost touching the moon roof glass. Arching a brow, he nodded towards the Zs and, none too convincingly, said, "I got this."

Ratcheting the transmission into Park, Cade said, "Whoa ... slow down, Trigger."

"You sit up there and figure out how we're going to get through this sea of crap," said Wilson, gesturing with the Beretta at the ruined run of road. "And I'll get out and take care of those two pusbags."

"Not yet. There may be more where they came from. And that truck of yours ... " Cade hitched a thumb at the Raptor. "I'm not convinced it'll be able to make it across *La Brea* without getting stuck."

Taryn called out, "Let's find out. You follow those tracks and we'll follow you."

"There'll be no way for us to dig you out of this shit if you get stuck," answered Cade. *Then you'll be riding with us again*, he thought.

Hanging halfway out of the rear passenger-side window, Sasha craned her head to see over the side mirror and called out to Taryn, "What do you think it is?"

"Looks like a lake of oil to me," replied the tatted brunette as she slipped the Raptor's transmission into Park.

Once again regretting his decision to have the younger trio tag along, Cade tried his best to shut out the inane banter and followed the established set of tire tracks with his eyes. The deeply cut chevron patterns ran perpendicular from his vantage point and then straddled the breakdown lane near the center median for a couple of hundred feet before abruptly shooting off into the distance at a diagonal to the point on the shoulder directly overlooking the tangle of burnt-out vehicles.

Unable to continue following the tracks with his naked eye, he pressed the binoculars to his face and saw that the tread marks continued on straight and true, skirting the remaining stretch of melted roadway before returning to its normal muted gray which was crisscrossed by black tire marks for an additional hundred yards.

"We'll go first," said Cade. He lowered the field glasses and fixed Wilson with a no nonsense gaze. "And when we get to the other side, Taryn can follow our tracks. That way if either one of the rigs gets stuck, one of us will be on firm ground and can use their winch to pull the other out."

"Solid plan, Cade," said Wilson, tugging his boonie hat tight. "*Now* can I shoot them?"

Seeing that there were now four Zs that had made it through the maze of static metal clogging the eastbound lanes and were trudging across the dozen yards of car-choked median to their left, Cade went against his better judgment and obliged the redhead. "Got a taste of it back there and now you want more, eh?" And then laying it on thick, he added, "Go for it. Knock yourself out, *buddy*."

Hopping out as if he had something to prove, Wilson winked at Cade and walked calmly in front of the idling Raptor while holding the Beretta two-handed, its business end tracking the closest of the now rapidly approaching cadavers. He shuffled to his left and halted near the truck's driver's side front fender and set his feet a shoulder's width apart. Then, with the heat of the Raptor's engine warming his skin through his tee-shirt, he drew in a deep calming breath and caressed the trigger.

Fired at near point-blank-range, the 9mm slug covered the three feet from muzzle to impact in a microsecond and punched a dime-sized hole in the male cadaver's forehead, starting in motion a picture perfect display of Sir Isaac Newton's Law that saw the thing instantly crumple to the pavement in a vertical heap.

Meanwhile, the '*equal and opposite reaction*' component of the scientifically proven theory, visually more violent than the '*action*' component, manifested in the form of an eruption of flecked bone and congealed brain matter that fanned out and up amidst an opaque mist before finally raining back to earth in wet little clumps.

Back in the F-650, where he had a better view and feel for the unfolding action, Cade drew his Glock. He didn't bother with the suppressor, nor did he check the chamber for a round. Instead he braced the pistol against the massive side mirror, drew back a few pounds of trigger pull, and waited and watched the remaining trio of Zs.

Wilson sidestepped the first fallen corpse and backpedaled, keeping the next closest—a pre-adolescent female—a few feet in front of him and, wisely, both idling vehicles off of his left shoulder. *Good job*, thought Cade, as he tracked the delicate dance while keeping the nearest abomination bracketed in his sights.

Shuffling backward and away from the Raptor while trying to create a better angle from which to engage the Zs, Wilson's mind began playing tricks on him. Suddenly he saw not matted hair and tattered fabric and bared yellowed teeth, but a little girl in distress, all pigtails and lace and worry painting her face. His pace slowed and he shifted his gaze and fixated on the ashen withered arms peppered by horrible purple-ringed bite marks still glistening red where whole mouthfuls had been rent away. He stopped retreating and inexplicably the outthrust pistol became heavier and wavered in his hand.

Noticing the barely perceptible downward tilt to the Beretta's barrel and seeing the definite hitch in Wilson's gait was enough to set Cade's sixth sense off. Somewhere in the background—competing with the rush in his ears as adrenaline surged through his body and the scene began to slow and his vision narrowed at the edges—he heard Brook or Raven or maybe both exclaim in unison: "What is he doing?" Then he heard the unmistakable rasp of the tiny Z and, like he was watching a moment of jittery old film footage, time seemingly sped forward and the monster had covered the distance and somehow scaled Wilson's lower body. In the next instant the thing was clutching the redhead's tee-shirt with one dainty, clawlike hand, and the other had gotten ahold of the strap on the kid's ever-present boonie hat.

Head suddenly bowed under the added weight, Wilson came to, realizing that the Z had him in a two-handed embrace and its teeth were snapping dangerously close to his face. A millisecond later the reptilian area of Wilson's brain came alive and his fight or flight mode kicked in; fortunately for him, he acted on both simultaneously. Adrenaline now flooding his body, he instinctively leaned back and twisted his torso away while his gun hand traced a lazy half-arc from left to right, loosing a trio of shots rapid-fire out of the Beretta.

The first slug shattered the thing's breast bone, lifting its toes off the road. Round number two snapped its clavicle like a twig, the unleashed kinetic energy adding a reverse twist to the corpse's upward trajectory. His third unaimed shot left the gun's barrel a microsecond after the last, with his arm sweeping downward, and entered an inch lower and right of the newly shattered clavicle. The Parabellum, travelling at 1,250 feet-per-second, tore through three inches of rancid flesh and disintegrated the ball joint and bursa sac behind, and started the newly severed appendage on a flat trajectory around Wilson's back with all five fingers retaining their death grip on the cotton tee.

With all twenty years of his short-lived life flashing before his eyes and fifty pounds of snarling one-armed dead weight grating its teeth against his exposed jugular, Wilson heard a foreign sound, a kind of sonic crackle. In the same instant, coupled with the sense of falling and the blue sky tilting strangely overhead, he felt a subtle tug and then an immediate flare of white hot pain enveloped the right side of his face. Next, in his side vision, he saw the Z's temple crater inward and heard the second disruption of airspace near his face as what he would soon come to learn was the back-half of a vicious double tap.

In his side vision he saw the latter tear into the undead girl's forehead at an oblique downward angle, sending a good chunk of cranium with the rat's nest of blonde hair still attached off in one direction and what remained of the tiny infected corpse cartwheeling away in the other.

Before the noise of the first two gunshots had diminished and Wilson realized that he was still alive, another half-dozen wasp-like projectiles whistled by him and then more booming reports rolled over his head. Finally, finishing what his flight instinct had started, gravity dumped him to the ground face first. And with the trauma of the first "*operation arm removal*" fresh in his mind, he let go of his pistol, wrapped both hands around the cold arm and wailed, "Somebody get it off of me!"

With no idea the significance that the pasty arm dangling from Wilson's well-stretched out shirt represented, Cade began to laugh, and then after a few uncomfortable seconds spent watching the redhead roll around the hot asphalt with the arm flopping after, he holstered his Glock and said, "You *got that* all right, Wilson. Nicely done."

"Go to hell," Wilson shot back.

"No," Cade replied. "Those four Zs beat me to it."

"You almost killed me," Wilson said between big gulps of carrion-sullied air. He tore the shirt over his head and tossed it and the arm to the roadway.

Cade made no reply.

Wilson dragged his forearm across his cheek and it came away red with blood. Then, pasty and bare from the waist up and blushing red from the combination of the near-death experience and the embarrassment of underperforming when it mattered most, he hung his head and tramped toward the Raptor. Avoiding all eye contact, he looped around the hood and swiveled the side mirror outward on its post, dipped at the knees and inspected his neck.

In the F-650, Brook took her hands from her ears and released the breath she'd been holding for the entire duration of the dramatic melee, which had lasted a little less than ten seconds from the moment Wilson set foot on the Interstate until the Glock discharged twice and thundered and echoed about the cab around her. Pinching her nose to keep out the carrion and cordite stench, she caught Cade's eye and said, "Now *that* was close." She grabbed her first aid kit from the glove box. Zippered open the red nylon bag adorned with a white first aid cross and fished out a pair of purple surgical gloves. Snapping them over her hands, she grabbed her M4, shouldered her door open, and leaped from the cab. After giving the fallen corpses and splattered detritus a wide berth, she took up station beside Wilson, who was just beginning to show the first signs of shock. Placing a hand on his back, she asked, "Did it bite you anywhere?"

He looked away from his reflection in the mirror and set his gaze on Brook and began to shake as the spike of adrenaline ebbed. Seeing this, she gripped his shoulder with her left hand and stood on her toes. She expertly manipulated his head with her free hand, having him tilt it first left and then to the right while looking closely for any breaks in the skin. Next she called out to Sasha in the rear of the Raptor and had her pass forward another shirt for him.

"Well?" asked Wilson. "Is this the part of the show where I traipse off into the desert and put a bullet in my own head?"

"Its teeth didn't break the skin, Wilson. Looks like your show has been renewed," Brook whispered into his ear. She unwrapped a small alcohol swab and worked the towelette into the angry red fissure starting just behind his right earlobe and none too gently dragged it through to his jawline, where the projectile had mercifully parted ways with his skin before continuing on and delivering the first half of the near simultaneous double tap to the Z's head. Unaware of just how close he had come to dying—in more ways than one—he flinched and tried to pull away as Brook made a second pass to clean the edges of the puckered three-inch-long wound. Keeping a firm grip on his shoulder, she tore open a fresh swab with her teeth, spat out the foul-tasting foil packaging, and said, "You need stitches ... but I'm not comfortable doing it here."

Cade called down from the F-650. "Is the kid going to be OK?"

A big grin spread on Brook's face as she turned towards Cade and nodded slowly. "No bite," she called back. Then her smile disappeared and she added, "But one of your bullets took a chunk out of his cheek."

Making no reply, Cade poked the shifter into Drive, a move that caused the truck to rock forward on its suspension while delivering a clear signal that he was itching to get underway.

Touching the four-inch square of sterile gauze taped to his face, Wilson thanked Brook, climbed in and took his place riding shotgun next to Taryn in the Raptor.

After discarding her soiled gloves on the shoulder, Brook circled around behind the F-650 and hauled herself back into the cab. She settled into her seat, clicked her seatbelt home, and exhaled loudly. Then, as all husbands are required to do after the dreaded huff and, in this instance, mostly to avoid miles of traveling in uncomfortable silence, Cade asked, "What's the matter?"

"You shouldn't have green lit that exercise in stupidity."

"He's a grown man."

Wiping the sweat from her forehead, Brook said, "No, Cade Grayson, he is twenty. Think back to when you were twenty."

"Different set of rules ... those things were not walking around eating people back then."

"Don't you understand?" said Brook. "Proving *your* point *your* way almost got Wilson killed."

"No," Cade replied immediately. "*Wilson* almost got *Wilson* killed. *I* saved his ass from a fate worse than getting killed. And I hope the memory of this little roadside fiasco is going to keep his ego in check ... at least until we get to the compound. After that I don't give a shit how he wants to show off."

"He's looking for your approval, Cade Grayson," she said with a tilt to her head. "But you let it go too far ... and then you *shot* him."

Raven had her elbows hooked over the front seatbacks and had been following the conversation, head swinging left and right and back again like windshield wipers on high for the entire duration. But as soon as she heard her mom utter this new revelation, her brown eyes went wide and she froze, mouth agape, her gaze locked on her dad.

Ignoring the additional pair of eyes boring into his skull, Cade said, "Helluva small price to pay to learn a couple of valuable *life* lessons." He looked down into the other Ford and saw an animated and probably equally heated conversation taking place between Wilson and Taryn. And to complete the surreal near-mirror-image of his current environment, Sasha was wedged between the Raptor's front seats and striking a pose similar to Raven's.

Hunching forward, Brook shot an incredulous look his way. She waited until he took his eyes off the other truck, then asked the obvious question, "And what would those life lessons be?"

"For one, he's been shooting at those things from behind the safety of a fence for so long that he's out of touch with what it's really like out here. Hell, if we're being honest here, you all have gone and gotten a little complacent and that's got me more than a little worried."

Wanting badly to defend her own track record outside the wire, Brook decided the time and place was not in front of Raven and wisely held her tongue. Instead, she said, "And?"

"And ... we all have to be extra careful around the little Zs," said Cade, releasing the brakes. "They're a lot faster than the others. Deceptively so, as we just witnessed." He sighed, then went on, "And that's what got Mike killed. Clearly, he didn't expect a toddler to find another gear and launch on him like a meat-seeking missile. But I was there and saw it with my own eyes—" He went quiet again. Stared straight down the center of the road fixed on a point somewhere over the horizon.

"I'm sorry," mouthed Brook. "I didn't know that's how it happened."

He cupped her knee. Gave it a squeeze. "Gotta drill it into them ..." He shot a sidelong glance at Raven. Made a face at her and added, "This is for you too. Getting close to the dead out here is a whole different animal that requires a lot more concentration. 'Cause Mister Murphy *never* RSVPs his intentions."

Hearing this, and having never heard of nor met this person, Raven tore her eyes from Cade and mouthed, "Mister Murphy," at Brook while raising an eyebrow.

"I'll tell you all about *him* later, sweetie."

"RSVP?"

"Later," Brook added sternly.

Inside the Raptor, Wilson had just settled into what he thought might become his permanent station in life, forever riding shotgun with a girl at the wheel and Sasha hanging like a monkey between the front seats. He closed the door and started his window running up in its track.

Hands kneading the steering wheel, Taryn asked in a low voice, "What happened?"

"One second I was trying to move the stinking thing around so that I'd be shooting at it away from the trucks ..."

Interrupting him, Taryn said, "I saw your face go slack for a second."

"I froze up."

"Why?"

"Because I started seeing her as what she used to be ... a little girl."

"Understandable." She made a face and looked beyond Wilson at the black truck as it rolled by the passenger window. Then she fixed her gaze on him. Her face softened and a single tear tracked the contour of her cheek. "I don't want to lose you, Wilson," she said, choking on the words.

"I'm sorry," he said, reaching over to comfort her.

Trying to lighten the mood in the only way her fourteen-year-old mind worked, the queen of all ballbusters said, "Well, at least it didn't get a hold of your hair." To which Wilson whipped around and shot her a patented *Shut up or I'm gonna kill you look.*

Getting the hint, Sasha disappeared into the back and, in turn, Wilson looked ahead just as the larger truck entered the soupy stretch of I-70.

Taryn wiped away the tears and flicked her eyes to the rearview. She saw that the road was clear of vehicles but there were a couple of Zs several hundred yards back, no doubt drawn by the gunfire. Then she locked onto her own reflection and was startled by what was staring back. The combination of her red puffy eyes and the near permanent pinched and pained expression on her face made her look like someone else. More than a week in Grand Junction Regional paired with the highs and lows—mostly lows—of surviving the apocalypse had aged her prematurely. *Nineteen going on thirty*, she thought to herself.

As the F-650 in front of them wheeled around the twice-dead Zs, Wilson crossed his fingers, motored his seat forward to be closer to the AC vents, and then said a little prayer to the Gods of melted roadways.

Chapter 29

Duncan couldn't purge from his mind the idea that he was retracing Logan's last steps on Earth. And the closer he got to the rust-streaked white building where his baby brother had drawn his final breath, the angrier he became.

The facility was just as he remembered it, only coming at him from a different perspective. The water-filled quarry to his left glittered silver from the mid-morning sun hitting off the wind-buffeted ripples—a far cry from the expanse of murky blackness it presented from the air flashing underneath the DHS Black Hawk.

The black and white Tahoe was right where whoever had been driving it had parked it last, only the doors were now closed and it was surrounded by water-filled puddles. A noisy chorus announcing their arrival, gravel popped under the Toyota's tires and pinged off the undercarriage as Duncan wheeled past the Tahoe's driver's side. He looked beyond the police cruiser at the three outbuildings that yesterday, from a couple of hundred feet up, had at first seemed like kids' toys. Up close and under closer scrutiny, they exuded neglect, the wood they had been built with, gray and swaybacked, having succumbed long ago to weather and gravity. All three doors were opened up to the elements. All three locks were missing, just punched out holes where they should have been and jagged splinters where they met up with the jambs.

The oversized metal garage was quiet and dark. Before leaving with the bodies, Duncan and Daymon had snugged the roller doors shut and secured the bullet-riddled office door as best they could.

Duncan finally broke the silence. "Here we are, fellas."

Lev exhaled as they nosed in close to one of the roller doors. "This is where it all went down," he said, craning to see the building. "Where'd you find their bodies?"

"Inside," said Duncan, putting the transmission into Park and setting the brake.

Reliving the day, Duncan said, "I went in first and found them both on the concrete pad ... already bled out."

"No sign of the girls?" asked Lev.

Daymon shook his head. "Nope."

"Blood?"

Daymon answered, "Just what had pooled around Logan and Gus."

"Whoever killed them knew how to control their weapons," said Duncan. He shut off the motor. "No spray and pray happened here. They hit fast and hard, I'm guessing. Dropped the two men first with closely grouped shots. Center mass on both of them." He went quiet for a tick, then added, "That's how I would have done it."

Lev nodded in agreement. "Logan and Gus weren't wearing vests," he said, more a statement than a question.

"Nope," Duncan answered. Then, squinting against the sun or emotion or both, went on, "I told him it would be a good idea ... but he didn't listen to his big brother."

"What's good for the goose," said Daymon. "None of us are wearing vests. So who are we to be judging?"

A series of hollow thuds sounded as Lev pounded on his chest. "I am," he stated. "Been a habit that's hard to shake."

"Good habit," said Duncan, nodding.

"I plan on wearing one when we go up north," said Daymon. He clicked out of his belt and cringed as his door shrieked metal on metal when he hinged it open.

Duncan sighed and nudged his door open. "Me too," he said. "Me too." He pocketed the keys, turned back towards the others and added, "Pick one out for yourself. There's plenty of them hanging up downstairs ... and brand new BDUs and enough of those tactical elbow and knee doo-dads for all of us. Everything we need to go hunting man is in there ... except ammo. Fuckers took it all. But thanks to Oops we don't have to fret about that."

Lev smiled. "How about comms?"

Duncan slid from the SUV. Waited for Lev to do the same, then asked, "You didn't inventory that box Daymon lugged out of the Black Hawk yesterday?"

Lev closed his door quietly. Looked Duncan in the eye. Held the gaze for a second then wiped a stray tear from the corner of his eye. "Didn't hold very high of a priority with me considering all that had happened."

Fighting back his own tears, Duncan said nothing.

"Someone ... probably good ol' Logan stashed it in the back of the Tahoe," said Daymon. "Then it got overlooked by the bad guys. Or if it didn't then they had no use for some high quality communications and night vision gear."

"Sounds like something the little packrat would do," said Duncan.

Solely because he didn't want to hear the sound again, Daymon unfolded his lanky frame from the passenger seat, left the door wide open and stretched and cracked his back and neck. He looked over the SUV's hood at Duncan and said, "So what you're telling me and Lev is that when we go after Bishop and his boys we're going to look like that Delta boy, Sarge Grayson?"

"Delta," said Lev with a slight tilt to his head. "I can picture how the guy looked last time I saw him. From a distance ... he didn't really strike me as Delta."

"He's the goods," stated Daymon. "I'd tell ya some stories but then I'd have to kill you. He's *that* good."

"Lock and load," said Duncan. He slipped his .45 from its holster. Approached the office door with it held two-handed and at a low ready, hoping the situation inside remained the same as he'd left it. "Take what you want but only what you need. We don't have to hump everything back to the compound on this trip." He climbed the two stairs, hovered in front of the bullet-pocked door and rapped sharply.

Nothing.

Sensing Lev and Daymon stacked closely at his back, Duncan nudged the door open with his toe and crept into the gloom. The office seemed smaller this time around. He worked his way past pieces of inexpensive office furniture streaked with dried blood and crushed—like an ice floe of chrome and wood-grained veneer—up against the ugliest seventies-era couch he had ever set eyes on. The calendar on the wall drew his attention. However, it wasn't the mining equipment being featured in solo glamour shots that attracted it, but the month and year the calendar was open to. And save for the day the dead began to walk—that warm day in September circled on the 2001 circa calendar had changed his life forever. And in passing he felt it his duty to point it out to the others.

Daymon said, "Never going to forget that day as long as I live."

Lev nodded. Signed the cross on his chest. "It's why I joined up," he said solemnly.

"Yesterday trumped it for me," said Duncan as he rapped on the interior door. He waited a second, and when nothing went *bump* in the dark, holding his .45 near his hip, pushed through with his free hand.

Daymon asked quietly, "Whatcha got?

"Gloom and more gloom."

Daymon flipped the wall switch. "How's this?" he asked as the fluorescent tubes thirty-plus feet overhead hissed to life.

Duncan made no reply. He looked up. Regarded Edison's invention fired by what was arguably—save for gunpowder—man's greatest discovery. That it had been collected from the sun by the panels on the roof instead of taken from an overhead line made no difference. Electricity was electricity and its byproduct held his rapt attention for a second.

Lev whistled. "Solar power. We've got to unbolt however many panels are up there and take those suckers and the inverter or whatever that thing is called back to the compound."

"First things first," said Duncan. He looped around the tailgate of a gleaming white Dodge 4x4—dually and CB-equipped no less, he quickly noted—and then stood over the spot on the gray specked floor where Logan had died. Back against the roller door, he found himself staring at a dried-to-black Rorschach-like blood stain. At its widest, where Logan's upper body had lain while he bled out, the pool was oblong with thin rivulets streaming away where the cement floor had settled and folded in on itself, leaving thin capillary-like cracks that the blood had followed freely. However, at the opposite end where his feet had been, there was a dried blood trail resembling a giant brush stroke created when he and Daymon had moved the linen-shrouded bodies to the Black Hawk. He continued to fixate on the crime scene and soon felt a tickle of bile rising in his throat.

Still lost in his thoughts, Duncan flinched when Lev placed an arm around his shoulder and drew him in. "Shouldn't have happened like this," Lev said. "Fuckers had numbers, no doubt. And had no problem taking advantage of it."

Duncan said, "It was no kind of a fair fight, that's for sure. They didn't even know what hit them." He turned abruptly and padded to the southeast corner of the garage where he recalled the hidden trap door was located. He pulled the floor covering aside and flung the door open rather unceremoniously, letting it bang to the floor. "Come on ... let's get this done."

"Oh man," said Lev, crinkling his nose and rubbing his eyes. "You said you already cleared the place."

"Logan did."

"Then where's that stench coming from?"

Daymon interrupted. "There's a woman and her kids down there."

"Rotters?"

"Stationary," said Duncan. "The mom poisoned the kids. Then cut her own wrists ... fucking awful scene."

Lev replied, "Fucking awful smell." He covered his nose with his shirt. Flicked on his tactical flashlight and disappeared down the stairs, its white beam cutting back and forth, drawing and quartering the inky black. A second later, he pulled the chain to the hanging bulb below and a warm yellow light chased the shadow from the gloomy stairway.

***

Forty minutes later, with Lev and Daymon performing the manual labor while Duncan kept watch, the weapons and gear were transferred from the catacomb of Conex containers into the three vehicles they were driving back to the compound.

Remembering the old dually that he'd been forced to abandon alongside Cade's Sequoia on the road outside of Boise, Duncan said, "Dibs on the dually Dodge." Then quickly added while gesturing at the dual whip antennas, "Figure the CB in that thing might come in handy down the road."

"You're racist," countered Daymon in jest as he passed by carrying an armload of ballistic vests. "Only reason you don't like that Land Cruiser is because it's Japanese."

Duncan shot back, not so much in jest. "Blow it out your ass, Daymon. In my opinion, even after you pranged it against the fence, the thing drives like a lifted Cadillac DeVille. All pillowy and refined. Not for me, my man. Has nothing to do with slanty eyes or skin color. If Nam didn't cause me to hate 'em ... their take on what a 4x4 is ain't gonna."

"All right my Truck Trend Magazine-reading brothers. You haggle over the Dodge ... I'm taking the Silverado." Lev looked to Daymon for approval. Arched a brow in order to hasten a reply.

"Cool with me," replied Daymon. He tucked a stray dread behind his ear. "'Cause I'm easy like Monday morning. Plus, I'm used to the Tahoe. Drove it all the way here from Wyoming."

"Settled," said Duncan. "We siphon the gas and leave the worthless *DeVille* in the garage." He bowed his head and looked at the twin blood stains. Said, "But first, I'm gonna take a walk. Clear my mind and maybe go see what the buzzards are buzzin' about."

***

Duncan had been curious to see what dead thing the vultures were circling. But overpowering that was his desire to get away from the place where Logan had drawn his last breath. And as far as the buzzing part of his parting quip was concerned, he wished it had never left his lips. Because the closer he got to the patch of briars just east of the front gate where a number of colorfully hued and rust-mottled heavy earthmoving vehicles sat, the louder the buzzing in his ears became. And as he skirted the chin-high bramble patch where a couple of half-ton pickups languished, the undulating carpet of flies responsible for the incessant noise took flight suddenly, revealing to him something entirely unexpected and altogether sickening.

Chapter 30

The melted stretch of I-70 proved to be more mirage than anything else. Light playing tricks with their minds had added depth to the shiny black surface where there was none. Still, upon Cade's insistence, sticking to their plan, they transited the Interstate one at a time, slaloming between the particularly gooey areas at a snail's pace. Forty minutes later, both vehicles were sitting idle on solid roadway six hundred feet farther west on I-70, the only damage a thick coating of black tar from the wheel wells down.

"Wasn't so bad," stated Brook.

"Not a single T-Rex rose from the depths," added Cade with a wink delivered to Raven. "What's next on the map?"

Brook said, "Green River."

"Beeson said we should avoid Green River at all costs. Unfortunately we have to go over the river and skirt the city pretty close, and then just west of there we'll part ways with the Interstate."

"Then what?" asked Brook.

Cade said, "Unless conditions have degraded substantially over the last three weeks, the rural roads will be sketchy but passable."

"The flip side of that?"

"Let's not go there until we have to." Cade shifted into Drive and moved over and accelerated briskly, the yellow centerline blipping by, thin membranes of tar peeling away from the sidewalls and going airborne in lazy arcs before pattering back down.

"Should we trust the GPS navigation?"

Shaking his head, Cade said, "Not entirely. Gotta go with your common sense on the back roads ... things were known to be wrong before Z-Day."

"Then we need to stop at the first gas station or mom and pop store and try and find a local map." Brook tapped the laminated topo map provided by Beeson. "This isn't going to cut it. As it is, we'll be driving off the edge of this thing before our turnoff."

Cade picked up the two-way from the center column and pressed the talk button. "Green River will be on our right forty some odd miles ahead. Ignore it. Keep tight formation and do not stop for anything."

Wilson answered the call. "Copy that," he said.

"How are you holding up?" asked Cade.

"My first gunshot wound," replied Wilson. "I'll let you know next time we pull over."

***

Nineteen miles west of the spot they'd stopped last, Interstate 70 suddenly headed off on a northern tangent before the gray ribbon visibly doglegged off to the south. At first Cade thought the deviation was due to some kind of immovable geological feature. But after nothing became evident, he began to suspect some kind of an engineering hiccup. Perhaps the surveyor had called off sick the day the graders went through, forcing them to wing it. That is, until he saw the sign that read: Exit 187, Thompson Springs, Pop. 39. Affixed below that sign was a smaller metal rectangle, the words on it indicating that no services were available for the next twenty-five miles. *Green River*, thought Cade, as the Ford slid by the only exit from the Interstate and he saw that Thompson Springs was little more than four square blocks of clustered farm houses and fields surrounded by high desert with the Box Cliffs—a geological formation jutting hundreds of feet into the air—crushing in from behind. And as the sign had indicated, Cade saw no services near the freeway. Just flat earth and rocks and scrub. And among the clustered dwellings he saw nothing that might indicate the presence of a post office or even a telltale flagpole flying Old Glory.

All of the windows in the houses were dark, their curtains drawn. Nothing moved on the roads or the yards or in the fields. Save for the heat waves rising up from the expanse of brown desert encircling the lush green habitable area, he saw nothing moving for miles in any direction.

It didn't take more than this cursory glance to come to the conclusion that for all intents and purposes, Thompson Springs, like all of the other tiny burgs and towns that he'd had the misfortune to set eyes on during his extensive travels throughout the Western United States, was just another American ghost town.

In a blink of an eye Thompson Springs was behind them. And less than a hundred feet beyond the onramp providing all thirty-nine residents of the sprawling metropolis access to the Interstate and all points west, a second road sign rose from the scrub a dozen feet off the right-hand shoulder. Written on the bullet-riddled sign, in white reflective letters, was the same warning about the impending lack of services. Below that it read: *Green River 25 miles.* But the sign had also been defaced, and Cade had to take his foot off the gas and tap the brake and slow down a bit in order to read the second warning spray-painted in silver on the sign's bottom margin. It read: *Beware of bandits* and *River* had been sprayed over with the word *Acres.*

The sign wasn't lost on Brook. Nor was the part about bandits or the stylized skull-and-crossbones. *Green Acres, my ass*, she thought. Without a word, she retrieved her M4 from the footwell, pulled the charging handle towards her, chambering a round, and then tilted the weapon on its side and looked and made sure the safety was set. Then, with a firm set to her jaw, she looked sidelong and caught Cade's eye and nodded subtly.

Inside the Raptor, two truck-lengths behind and slightly right of the F-650, Wilson, who was growing weary of riding shotgun, also read the sign, and at once felt the first feathery tingle of fear creep into his gut.

"Did you see that?" asked Taryn, eyes never leaving the road.

"How could I miss it?" said Wilson. "Whoever wrote it used effin silver paint. Pretty eye-catching in the desert."

Sasha popped up between the seats and asked, "What did I miss?"

In unison, but not very convincingly, both Taryn and Wilson said, "Nothing."

Quarry

The sight greeting Duncan when he rounded the back side of the briar patch finished the process being near the site of Logan's murder had started. The flock of juvenile buzzards took flight first. Then the source of the buzzing, disturbed by the frantic flapping of feathered wings, took flight, changed direction and flew en masse around his head and into his open mouth.

Falling to his knees, he projectile-vomited the contents of his stomach onto the damp gravel. Yellowed bile made all the more bitter from a night of hard drinking burned as it sluiced over his teeth and shot from his nose. Thick with squirming flies that had failed to escape his mouth, the initial torrent pooled right where he had planted his hands. On all fours, back arching and falling, he emptied everything that was in his stomach—and then some. And when he was finished and had dragged his forearm across his lips, she was still there. In the same contorted pose that was instantly burned into his memory from only a split second's glance. Arms and legs twisted at unnatural angles. The sight of her, staring Little Orphan Annie-like, black jagged openings in the hollow sockets where working muscle and soft tissue used to reside, sent a chill up his spine. Her tongue was purple and flayed and rested on her chin, having no doubt been tugged from her throat by the carrion feeders.

He collapsed to his stomach and rolled over onto his back and, while watching the voracious raptors wing across the azure sky, began calling for Lev and Daymon—in a normal voice at first—then, when the shock began to dull and he'd regained a modicum of breath—at the top of his lungs.

"Get the fuck over here, now!" He crossed his arms over his eyes and added, "You're gonna need to bring some sheets!"

Chapter 31

Thirty minutes after hearing Bishop deliver his cryptic promise, Elvis had finished with bulldozing the makeshift landing spot and then jumped right into his next assigned task.

An hour and a half into his newest chore, the head-heavy splitting maul was beginning to feel like a natural extension of his body. However, swinging the eight-pound tool with the same repetitive motion to bone-jarring completion was taking its toll. Already destroyed by fifteen hours of straight driving, made worse by a measly four hours of sleep over two days, he knew from past experience—and an ever increasing flurry of twinges—that his lower back was about to go out on him.

So he thunked the axe into the manhole-sized round of wood and left it there, its yellow fiberglass handle sticking into the air. Then, looking towards the trailer Bishop had entered two hours prior, he cracked the seal on a fresh bottle of water, took a couple of long pulls, let the hot liquid reconstitute his tongue, and set it aside. With muscles aching like he'd just spent a day on a Georgia chain gang, he sat on a round, removed his Huskers ball cap and wiped the beaded sweat from his forehead. Once again he regarded the eighteen-wheeler. He drained the water and tossed the bottle on the brittle brown grass. *Means to an end*, he told himself as he worked up the courage to go and see for himself what the former Navy SEAL was up to.

After crossing the road running between the lakeside homes and the newly cleared expanse awaiting Carson's fleet of helicopters, Elvis saw Bishop leap from the back of the trailer. Mind racing to come up with one good reason—besides the truth of course—to explain why he was taking a break before he'd finished splitting the wood, Elvis stopped dead in his tracks. Pulse rising a few extra beats per minute, he watched Bishop wipe his face with the bottom of his sweat-stained wife beater then drop the tank covering his toned six-pack abs.

Busted, thought Elvis just as Bishop looked up.

"Perfect timing," called Bishop. "I was just coming to get you. I've got something that needs moving. And like the saying goes, it's more awkward than heavy."

Slowly releasing the breath he had been holding, Elvis grunted then said, "No problem." Massaging his lower back while envisioning it going out and causing him to drop whatever he had been conscripted to move onto Bishop's toes brought forth the specter of the wrath a fuckup of that magnitude would likely incur. Last thing he needed was to literally 'drop the ball' this late in the game—just about the time that he thought he had proven himself, thus avoiding a bullet to the back of the head for his past transgressions. He had failed at Schriever. That President Clay was still alive and very few soldiers had perished in the zombie outbreak he had orchestrated was common knowledge. Furthermore, he should have known, with his luck as of late, that Bishop would eventually learn of Robert Christian's order to assassinate him. Stating that he had only said yes under duress had apparently been enough to get him a shot at redemption. So here he was. Toiling away to earn the right to keep on breathing. Then, with Bishop's smile fading, Elvis heard his mother's voice in his head. *Work hard and everything else falls into place.* And then his father chimed in from the grave. *Carpe diem.*

Seize the day indeed, he thought. He nodded at Bishop and swallowed hard, trying to mask the growing pain. Then the fit and tanned stone cold killer said, "I think you're going to appreciate what I've been working on." He about-faced and retraced his steps between the two vehicles. A tick later one of the trailer's rear doors hinged all the way open, barely missing the wrecker's boom, and banged against the slab-sided trailer. "Spoils of war," bellowed Bishop, gesturing to the cargo. "Come and see."

Sparing his back from the sideways shuffle between the two trucks, Elvis took the long way around. He skirted the apparatus hanging off of the tow truck's boom and caught his first glimpse of the object of Bishop's swelling pride. Sitting there on the wood-plank floor, about chest-high to both of them, were two neat rows of footlocker-sized cases, six on the left side, and five on the right. Each box was made of some kind of brushed metal and had multiple latches on the lid. They were positioned lengthwise in the trailer and secured to the floor three feet apart at all corners with thick canvas shipping straps that Elvis guessed would be sufficient to keep a baby grand from sliding around. Box number twelve, however, was sitting horizontally near the rear edge of the trailer, its lid hinged open.

"I've got a present for you," said Bishop. He closed the lid and grabbed a handle before Elvis had gotten a good look inside. "Give me a hand. But a word of caution ... the modifications I've made require that we handle it with care." He smiled again. "That, and the fact that there's enough *boom* here to boil all of the water from the lake."

Elvis smiled as he looked into the gloom at the other eleven boxes and wondered what *twelve* boiling lakes would look like.

"OK. Lift," said Bishop.

Surprisingly the case and its contents were much heavier than Elvis had guessed. He figured his half of the box would be about fifty pounds or so. He was mistaken. The device, when combined with the weight of the lead-lined box it was nestled in, weighed closer to three hundred pounds. Elvis's back, however, seemed to think the box weighed that of a small automobile. Setting the box to the ground brought on a twinge, making the muscles rapidly contract and expand uncontrollably. A sharp stab of pain came next, shooting instantly at light speed from his lower lumbar region to his brain and nearly causing him to lose his grip.

But he clenched his teeth and sucked it up and, with Bishop manhandling most of the burden, together they wrestled the box from the trailer and placed it gently on the ground. Then, for the second time in as many minutes, Elvis released a captive breath and collapsed against the wrecker's quarter panel, his face a mask of pain.

"You going to be OK? asked Bishop.

Elvis said "Yes," but his body language conveyed the opposite. He leaned against the trailer, grimacing.

Pussy, thought Bishop as he popped open the box lid, fully exposing the hidden innards. Sitting lengthwise, held down by a pair of sturdy-looking metal bands, was a two-and-a-half-foot-long cylinder, ten inches in diameter, roughly as big around as a basketball. It was polished to a high gloss, smooth to the touch, and looked to be milled from some kind of space-age metal—probably titanium, guessed Elvis. And true to the movies, the cylinder had been labeled with the instantly recognizable trefoil symbol consisting of three magenta blades around a like-colored center radius, all overlaid atop a yellow background— an instantly recognizable visual warning pointing to its radiological nature. Coils of wires in varying colors snaked from some kind of sealed-cell battery pack to what appeared to be an Apple iPad, its display currently dark. And pointing to the work Bishop had put into prepping the thing, pieces of wire in varying lengths, some stripped of their colorful coating, most not, littered the ground around the open box.

Bishop lounged on the tow truck's bumper calmly explaining the inner workings in painstaking detail, leaving out only the *how to* part of arming the thing.

Elvis listened and nodded and felt the first tingle of adrenaline when the fact that he was being primed on the particulars of the jerry-rigged device became abundantly clear, starting him to fantasize about the havoc something like this could wreak on his enemy. Then the beginnings of a smile curled the corner of his lip, and Bishop's voice went all Charlie Brown's teacher as suddenly the possibility of righting his Schriever wrong with a much higher body count was within his grasp.

Suppressing the urge to blurt out the words, *I'll do it*, Elvis returned his attention to Bishop's technical-jargon-filled spiel.

A handful of minutes later when Bishop was finished talking about yields and overpressure and blast radius's, Elvis was invited to have a couple of beers on the porch of the big lakefront house.

With the sound of approaching helicopters reaching his ears, Elvis, praying his back would hold out a little while longer, helped Bishop lift and arrange the radiation safe box onto the tow truck using its hydraulic lift apparatus. Once it was on the deck, they secured it with the unused straps from the semi-trailer. Then, walking with a definite hitch in his step, he followed the super-fit former operator toward the house, behind which sat a quarter-cord of wood still in need of splitting.

Looking disdainfully at the dozen rounds of pine, Elvis gripped the rail firmly and scaled the stairs one cautious step at a time. Greeting him at the top stair with a sweating bottle of Corona, Bishop said, "Here. You earned it. And there's more where these came from."

As they walked the length of the rocking chair porch towards the front corner of the house, Elvis called ahead, "One will probably do. I'm not much of a drinker."

"More for me," said Bishop as he positioned a couple of wicker chairs with floral print cushions next to a weathered teak table. Chair legs scraping the pressure-treated wood, he arranged one for Elvis, and added with a nod, "You look pretty beat up. Better take a load off."

His back throbbing with pain, Elvis stayed standing for a moment.

Bishop sat down and studied the former-college football player as he tried to ease his six-foot-three-inch frame into a seated position without throwing a disc.

Seeing this, Bishop's face suddenly hardened. And like a drill instructor addressing a recruit, he growled, "For this mission to succeed tomorrow we're going to need a *youthful* Elvis to suit up and show up."

"Couple of aspirins and some shut eye and I'll be good to go by morning," replied Elvis. Then, bracing his back with one hand, the other gripped white-knuckle-tight on the low-slung chair, he lowered his butt slowly onto the cushion.

Bishop sipped his beer. Gestured with the bottle and said, "You're moving like the old jumpsuit-wearing Viva Las Vegas Elvis."

Though he wanted to explode, Elvis remained tight-lipped and ground his teeth.

After laughing at his own joke, Bishop added, "You sure we're not going to find you dead on the toilet, ass up and face down?"

"Hell, I don't think I'm ever going to get out of this chair," answered Elvis with a forced grin. "So I suppose I'll have to die out here underneath the stars."

Bishop said nothing. Wasn't his joke. He looked west across the lake where the sound of rotors thrashing the warm air carried over the still water. A beat later, moving left to right, four matte-black helicopters appeared on the horizon. Then, sun glinting from their canopies, two egg-shaped Little Bird attack helicopters, one lagging a little behind the first, left the treetops behind and descended until their skids cut the air barely a dozen feet above the lake's placid surface. And following closely—almost literally—in the smaller craft's wake, two Black Hawk transport helicopters dipped down over the trees and transited the lake, their wheels also skimming a dozen feet over the now choppy water.

Elvis covered his ears against the thunderous noise as the choppers, now just two hundred yards away, abruptly took on a nose-up attitude, slowed, and hovered in place over the lake's edge. "Thousand bucks says they're going to fit on my clearing," he said.

"I hope so," said Bishop behind a thin-lipped smile. "'Cause it's your ass if they don't." His smile faded as he regarded the impromptu airshow. Then a frown formed when he realized what a Siren's song to the walking dead the noisy helos were.

After hovering for a tick, their considerable rotor wash creating a frothy chop on the lake's surface, the noisy craft turned gracefully, gained some extra altitude and passed over the lake house before settling gently on the newly graded acreage.

"Like a glove," said Elvis smugly as the final Little Bird settled to terra firma, leaving room enough for two or three more of the smaller aircraft next to the north gate.

Collectively the whining turbine noise diminished to a throaty whoosh and the individual rotors gained definition as the rpms bled off.

When he could finally hear his own voice, Bishop began to go over the looming mission point by point. He let Elvis know that he had already entered the necessary GPS coordinates into the tow truck's navigation system and then outlined the three tasks that needed completing after reaching the target. The first of which was to lower the delicate device to the ground using the truck's boom. The second, and most important, was to enter the arming code properly. And task number three, tantamount to Elvis's survival, was to avoid contact afterward and get the hell out of Dodge. Lastly, Bishop let slip where 'Dodge' was, as well as the staggering number of casualties they could expect as a result of perfect placement of the device. When the one-sided briefing was over, Elvis was wearing a Cheshire Cat grin and the helicopters had gone quiet, their massive Nomex and fiberglass blades stilled and drooping under gravity's pull.

Bishop asked, "Any questions?"

His eyes glazing over, Elvis heard the question but said nothing. Then, still in the throes of the mental orgasm from learning that he was finally going to avenge his dead family in grand fashion, and with the beer he had just downed making everything fuzzy around the edges, the knot in his back loosened and everything went dark. He didn't see the woman emerge from the nearest Black Hawk. He also missed the hood being yanked unceremoniously from her head, allowing dark hair to spill over her shoulders. He was out cold, therefore there was no way he could know that the athletic former soldier named Carson, whom he had met weeks earlier on the Minot mission, was the person escorting the fit brunette towards the house.

Bishop, however, was clued in the moment he felt the two-way radio vibrate in his pocket.

However, the warbling that followed had a different effect on a snoring Elvis. At first he was certain he'd failed his mission. That the Guardsmen had found him out and sounded a Klaxon and were mobilizing to mount a hot pursuit. Then, as quickly as it had begun, the Klaxon died to nothing. Elvis heard the sound of boots clomping and scuffing against what he gathered were wooden stairs. They were drawing near. Slow. Deliberate. Then he heard a door suck open. And a moment later there was the distinct sound of a door slamming shut. Next, he heard more voices, strangely distant. Finally, sensing that he was about to be caught red-handed, he felt a tremor that he was certain was the device detonating. It lasted for a second or two and then the crisp images of wonton death and destruction he had wrought on his enemies took on an ethereal quality. The melting faces and contorted and crisped limbs faded away to black. The roaring tempest of radioactive winds calmed, leaving a mushroom cloud roiling up and up and casting a snaking shadow over the destroyed city. Then, out of the blue, the temblor intensified and the imagined vista from where he had witnessed the explosion began to crumble from under his feet.

Chapter 32

Elvis came to with Bishop kicking his boots, which were splayed out at an odd angle. There was also a second person shaking him from behind. In his peripheral he could see large calloused hands clamping down hard on both of his shoulders. Then he gazed up and instantly recognized the inverted face staring down at him. A cold ball formed deep in the pit of his stomach. He struggled to rise but couldn't. Then, still half asleep, he stammered groggily, "I didn't desert. Robert Christian made me ... he ordered me to leave the convoy."

Carson released his grip and walked around the chair and put his hands on his hips. Looked Elvis square in the face. "Relax, " he said. "You passed out. Started mumbling and smiling and carrying on ... in your sleep. While you were out, Bishop told me how you are going to win back our trust. Don't get me wrong, though. I'm not entirely sold that vaporizing a few thousand United States soldiers is going to wipe out your debt to me."

Shaking his head wildly, Elvis whispered, "Nothing I could do."

The veins in his neck bulging, Carson hinged at the waist and got in Elvis's face. Then, with the volume of his voice rising with each word, he said, "When I found out you had rabbited and left us a driver short with a long haul ahead ... I wanted to hunt you down and *kill* you myself."

Pulling an irate Carson away, Bishop maneuvered him towards a chair and said, "Sit. Calm down."

Carson took a minute to compose himself, then went on, "You got lucky, buddy. Robert Christian started in at once hounding Ian about the nukes. And that was just enough distraction to save your sorry ass ... from me."

Bishop put a hand up, silencing Carson. Set his gaze on Elvis and said, "When I found out about RC's idiotic play on the President—dispatching you and Pug from two different directions—I knew the house of cards in Jackson was about to fall. Then RC really started boozing it up." He shook his head. Looked at the floor and added in a low voice, "The amount of champagne and gin that he was going through tripled after the dead started walking. And the second I saw him spiraling down that rabbit hole ... blacking out and forgetting things, I made the decision. It was easy. I diverted the nukes. Had Carson truck them here. No sense letting that fool have a truckload of warheads. No use in sticking around to go down with Captain Hazelwood on that sinking ship."

Elvis was wide awake by now, but getting bored with the story. Cocking his head sideways, he asked, "Then what happened to RC?"

"Couldn't tell you. Last I knew he was holed up in his place ... *isolating*. He was *not* answering his sat phone. Then, after the bus barrier failed and the dead started pouring in—" Bishop threw a visible shudder and subconsciously his hand went to the butt of his pistol—"that was when *I* made the tactical decision to cut the drunk's umbilical cord ... so to speak. I had a duty to my men. Had to save as many of them as possible."

"Why are you telling me all of this?" asked Elvis. "And why in the hell did you wake me up? I was having the dream of a lifetime."

"Blonde or brunette?" asked Carson, flashing a sly grin.

Ignoring the quip, Bishop said, "You risked a lot in order to get here from Schriever. I have to say I'm pretty impressed. And agreeing to put your life on the line in order to take out our common enemies ... should you succeed, will be enough in my book to get you back in my good graces."

In one long pull, Elvis finished his warm beer and set the bottle aside. He made a face and belched. "I've kind of resigned myself to death one way or the other. Figured I'd either be killed by the soldiers at Schriever. Or be eaten by the dead while running from the soldiers. And to be honest with you ... the second I honked last night to get your attention ..." He went silent for a second.

Listening intently, Carson steepled his fingers.

Bishop did the same and said, "Yes. Go on."

"I thought I would be crucified before dawn. So living ... no ... that's not my motivation. And though it would be nice—neither is getting on your good side. I have three reasons of my own why I want to do this and there's no way I'm going to allow myself to fail."

"Two birds with one stone then," intoned Bishop. He looked up at Carson conspiratorially, then went on, "In one fell swoop this one blow will set things right for you, reduce my enemies to dust, and make the roads between impassable for the next ten thousand years."

Elvis paused as if in thought. He regarded the finger of lake in front of the house. It was a strange shade of aquamarine blue with cold-water eddies sullying the reflection of the surrounding landscape. Finally he turned, gingerly squaring up with Bishop and said, "When do I get my gun back?"

Bishop reclined in his chair and said, "So that you won't stray again ... you'll get it back when you leave tomorrow."

Not liking the answer, especially after being trapped in the house in Ovid with undead grandma banging around in the basement and scores of walking corpses gathered outside, Elvis shook his head and said bitterly, "That's a load of crap."

Bishop rose from his chair. Stared Elvis down and said menacingly, "It's the *only* way."

Carson also stood. Made his way to the rail and craned his head right to see how the unloading was coming along. Lined up on the ground near the smaller choppers were several neat rows of black plastic boxes brimming with thousands of rounds of the most sought-after calibers—5.56 hardball for the M4s. 9mm and .45 hollow points for the pistols, as well as a few hundred rounds of 7.62x39 mm for the smattering of AKs favored by a number of Bishop's Spartan soldiers. *Pretty good haul*, he thought to himself as he watched the two conscripts do the grunt work. In fact, they were dead men walking. Bishop had ordered them killed for riling up the walkers near the entry—but that could wait. For now, the doomed men were useful, humping the boxes into the abandoned house next door like a couple of pale overweight Sherpa.

Suddenly Carson's attention was drawn to one of the Black Hawks, where the pilot, having apparently just finished his post-flight walk around, hauled open the starboard side sliding door. There was a rasp of metal on metal and then a flurry of startled movement in the shadowy cabin. A few seconds passed, then, one at a time, the three women taken from the city near the reservoir stepped clumsily from the cabin to the ground below. Once the pilot had arranged the prisoners shoulder to shoulder, he went down the line and jerked the hoods from their heads. Instantly, eyes squeezed shut against the afternoon sun, all three fell to their knees like falling dominos.

No reason for the zip ties now, thought Carson. Though their pupils had had the time to adjust, still, all three remained hunched over, shoulders slumped, chins nearly touching their chests. Clearly all three of the twenty-something women were completely broken. Every last ounce of piss and vinegar in them gone the second he tossed the Jordan bitch, kicking and screaming, out of the helo two-hundred feet above the quarry. And to add a visual to go with the audiotrack of that bitch's last seconds on Earth, Carson had had the pilot descend while he removed the others' hoods and forced them to look at her broken form on the ground below. So that they would know, beyond a shadow of a doubt, precisely what would happen to them if they ever drew blood from him.

He traced the quartet of raised welts running from the bridge of his nose to his right ear. That he hadn't lost an eye was a miracle. In a way, giving the petite blonde flying lessons had been more satisfying than gunning down the two armed men at the quarry. Out of nowhere he felt a throbbing down below—the first stirrings of an erection.

Elvis hauled himself out of the deck chair and took up station next to Carson, eyeing the women. "Well, well. What do we have here?"

To this, Carson repeated the same three-word-quip he had used earlier. Only delivered not in a joking manner, but with all the seriousness and banality of a host at Thanksgiving offering a serving of white meat or dark. And though Elvis was dead tired, those three words, *blonde or brunette*, perked him up like a shot of epinephrine. An impish grin crossed his face. He cocked his head and said, "Both?"

Bishop caught Carson's eye and nodded subtly, like a trader on the New York Stock exchange floor giving a sell order.

Taking the cue, Carson turned and said over his shoulder, "Follow me."

Chapter 33

Interstate 70 dove south for a spell then meandered west by north, paralleling the Book Cliffs through the hardscrabble desert.

Along the way, Cade couldn't help but let his gaze wander, for short durations at a time, to the remnants of the frantic eastbound diaspora sitting inert in the opposite lanes of travel. Backed up for miles behind a horrific multi-car pileup were slab-sided SUVs, tiny foreign-made compacts, and just about everything in between. There were the obvious signs of savage zombie attacks and the bloody feeding frenzies that always followed—severed limbs, headless torsos, meat-stripped bones and remnants of shredded clothing flapping in the breeze. Doors were open with skeletal half-eaten bodies spilling out. In some of the vehicles, unfortunate attack victims who had died and then reanimated still thrashed and banged against closed doors trying to escape their metal crypts.

But this wasn't the first traffic jam of death Cade had seen, and certainly not the last. Still, he marveled at all of the crap the people had jammed inside of their vehicles prior to fleeing Salt Lake City and, presumably, points further south and west. In fact, visually, it kind of ranked up there on the absurdity scale with all of the trinkets and statues and jewelry the ancient Egyptians sent their dead into the afterworld with. Only these Americans opted to burden themselves of their own free will. A move, in Cade's opinion, that had hastened their own journey into the very same afterworld. And further making the metal column snaking east look like a modern day desert caravan, it seemed as if the occupants of every fifth vehicle had been in the process of unpacking, having piled most of their worldly belongings: suitcases, sleeping bags, tents, microwaves, televisions, and toys of every shape and size and color atop their vehicles after finding themselves trapped. *Or perhaps*, thought Cade. *Maybe the subsequent waves of survivors had come along and picked through the belongings, attempting to fortify their own provisions.*

But he'd never know and speculating just reminded him how far the human race had fallen.

Thankfully, Brook's sweet voice brought him back to the present ... the only time that really mattered now. For yesterday was gone. And he'd learned long before the apocalypse that tomorrow was never a guarantee—especially in his old line of work.

"Slow down," Brook said. "We're closing in on Green River. I think it's beyond the next rise off to the right. Hard to tell exactly relying on Miss Map here ..." She leaned forward and touched the Garmin's display. Traced the magenta line representing I-70 with her finger. "... looks like the city sits at about two o'clock. And I-70 bypasses on the left." With the visual of the map burned into her memory, she let her gaze sweep the horizon from right to left, taking in the red mesas and the smooth stripe of asphalt laid out in front of them. While not entirely evident on the pixelated screen, she recognized that the Interstate was about to enter a narrow and shallow canyon that looked to have been cut into the Cretaceous sandstone. First, she gathered, by boots and hooves and the steel-braced wheels on wagons carrying people fulfilling their Manifest Destinies. Then, more recently for certain, the natural channel had been widened by man and machine so that I-70 and the vehicles it was meant to accommodate could pass smoothly over the wave-like geological formations.

"Whatcha looking at, Mom?" Raven asked.

Brook craned around and saw that not only was Raven leaning forward on the seatback, but so was Max. He had his paws on the leather and was looking her straight in the face. She gave the dog a scratch and said, "Sit back and snug your seatbelt tight, sweetie. Mom and Dad have to talk *things* over."

Feeling the truck decelerate, while not quite understanding the reason why, was enough to convince Raven to comply without verbal protest. Pouting, she slumped into the back seat next to Max.

Powered on the iPhone she'd begged off of Taryn, jammed the buds into her ears, and let Lady Gaga take her mind off of *things.*

Cade pulled the Ford hard left to the breakdown shoulder and brought the dirty rig to a complete halt amidst a roiling cloud of dust. He chose to stop just short of the hill's apex for one reason only. To find a vantage point well back from the 'military crest' of the hill to surveil the unfolding valley without exposing a profile to anyone watching below. He had also hoped to find a stretch of asphalt relatively clear, on all sides, of the seemingly never-ending vehicular gridlock.

One out of two isn't so bad, he told himself, fixing the suppressor onto the business end of the Glock 17. "Stay here for a second," he said to Brook. He looked into the back at Raven and saw that her eyes were closed and she was attached by the ears to an electronic device that looked a lot like an iPhone. He smiled at the sight. Marveled at her resilience and her ability to relax where danger abounded. *Ignorance truly is bliss*, crossed his mind as his smile faded and he swiveled back around.

"Be careful," said Brook. She reached out and traced the curve of his cheek with the back of her hand. Her eyes left his and she looked out the rear window and spotted a handful of corpses stumbling across the median from the eastbound lanes. "How's your ankle?"

"Better."

"You sure? I can take care of the Zs while you scout ahead," she said quietly.

"I'm fine. I need to stretch it out anyway. Get the blood flowing." He gave her his patented everything's going to be OK look. The same lopsided half-grin that she'd received before every deployment overseas and more recently, whenever he went outside the wire without her. Smile fading, he gave her thigh a reassuring squeeze, popped the door and stepped gingerly onto the shoulder. *Not so bad*, he thought, settling his full weight on his left foot. Simultaneously, the Ibuprofen was lessening the pain and the swelling. *Maybe Brook's diagnosis had been wrong.* Happy to be rid of the crutches and the creaky plastic boot, he took a few tentative steps away from the truck. *So far so good.*

He looked left towards the Raptor, its engine rumbling and ticking in the hundred-degree heat. He noticed a clear liquid dripping steadily from somewhere underneath the front bumper, no doubt a byproduct of the hard-working AC unit. Unconcerned, he looked up and noticed Taryn and Wilson staring his way, looks of mild concern on their faces. Silently telling them to stay put, he held up his free hand palm out. After registering a double thumbs up from behind the grimy windshield, he took a few more steps, testing the ankle for range of motion, which he found lacking laterally. Front to back, however, was a different story, and though there was considerable pressure, all seven bones seemed to be functioning normally.

He looked at his Suunto and did the math. Twenty-eight hours until Duncan went on his own personal warpath—with or without him.

Regarding the seven flesh eaters traversing the median with only the runaway vehicle cables keeping them from crossing over, he skirted the F-650's front bumper and cut a diagonal right for them. Once he was within five feet of them he took a hard right and, with every intention of saving his ammunition for when he really needed it, followed the cable barrier keeping just outside of their reach. But as luck would have it, Mister Murphy made his presence known, and inexplicably one of the Zs found a seam between the metal stakes keeping each of the fifty-yard runs of high tensile cables taut, then the rest followed.

Hanging his head, Cade stopped in place and squared up to face the interlopers. "You are some persistent bastards," he said as the unblinking eyes devoured him. Then, fully aware of what was riding on the encounter and with his family watching from afar, he set his feet apart and leveled his Glock.

Chapter 34

Inside the Raptor, Wilson said quietly, "Thirty seconds."

Taryn tore her eyes from the scene taking place twenty yards off the Raptor's front bumper, shot a confused look at Wilson, and said, "What?"

"Duh," replied Sasha. "He's setting the over-under at thirty seconds. He's saying Cade there will take care of all of those pusbags in less than thirty seconds, and I, for one, want some of that action. Got to go with the over." She looked down for a second and pulled a wrapped stack of twenties from her handbag, and when she looked up two of the zombies had been reduced to crumpled forms with tiny dust eddies swirling around them.

Wilson chuckled. "You're on. Two down and five to go. And twenty-six *looong* seconds left for him to seal the deal. You, Sis, are hosed."

"I didn't even hear his gun go off," said Sasha, her lower lip sticking out, the first sign of the pouting session to come.

"Wait for it," said Wilson.

Shaking her head, Taryn said, "You two are sick."

Two more seconds were in the books and Cade was nearly surrounded before the black pistol bucked twice in his fist and the third Z's head dissolved into a pink mist.

"Practice what you preach, Captain America," said Wilson.

While watching Cade step over the fallen corpse and backpedal away from the rest, Taryn glanced at Wilson and asked him what he meant by the last quip.

"He dressed *me* down pretty good for letting the little one get too close to me back there. And then he lets himself get jumped like that," Wilson said. "Practice what you preach ... pretty self-explanatory."

"Duh," said Sasha. "Everyone knows the littler they are the faster they move. Brook mentioned that the other day. Weren't you listening? Or were you and Miss Tattoo too busy playing kissy face?"

"That's enough," said Wilson. He snatched the stack of crisp bills from Sasha's outstretched hand and then glanced at his watch while adding gleefully in a sing-song voice, "Three down and four to go and only *fifteen* seconds until this is *all* mine.

***

Precisely twenty-four seconds after Cade's opening salvo, the last of the unlucky seven Zs were hanging limply, tangled in the cable arrest barrier like string-snipped marionettes.

"Less than thirty seconds. Come to Papa," said Wilson as he made a show of ruffling the crisp bills. Then, to rub the win in further, he put them under his nose and inhaled deeply. "Ah ... the sweet smell of newly acquired cash money."

"Which you'll never, ever, be able to spend," Sasha shot back. "So there."

"Aren't you a little old for so-there's and I-told-you-so's, Sasha?"

Sasha made no reply. The pouting ensued.

Pressing the issue, Taryn said, "Nobody likes a sore loser."

"You don't get it, Taryn. I was put on this earth to torment Wilson," Sasha fired back. She went silent for another second and then added in a choked-up voice, "Mom told me that all the time."

Wilson had no reply for that. Instead, he focused his attention on Cade who had already moved on and was picking his way through the scrub and tumbleweeds and still staying close to the barrier.

Then the two-way radio beeped and Brook's voice came through the speaker. She told them to stay put and continue watching the Interstate behind them.

Wilson fumbled the Motorola from his pocket. "Copy that," he said. After a few seconds with no reply, he saw Brook exit the Ford and disappear from sight. Then a tick later when she reemerged she was moving at a slow trot, a pair of binoculars bouncing off her chest, M4 held closely to her body.

"What are they doing?" asked Taryn. "And why did they leave Raven all alone in the truck?"

"Safest place for her," replied Wilson. "Besides, she's not alone. Max is in there too."

Breaking her short-lived silence, Sasha said, "She's probably in there armed with a machine gun anyways."

"Jealous?" said Taryn.

"We're not a gun family. Mom said so."

Losing his cool, Wilson craned around and looked at Sasha. "Mom is dead," he shouted. "You *have* to let her go and get on with living. And while you are at it, quit being so damn bitter about anything and everything ... that's what Mom would have wanted and that's exactly what she would have said if she were sitting right here instead of me."

Momentarily stunned by the biggest display of emotion she'd ever seen Wilson display, Taryn opened her mouth to say something, anything that might diffuse the situation, but for the first time in a long time she was speechless.

Not finished making his point, Wilson pounded his fist on the dash and added in a low voice, "I'm done trying to fill in for Mom. You *will* begin to contribute and cease being a liability ... or else."

Taryn's brows raised an inch. She mouthed, "Liability." Then said, "That's harsh, Wilson."

Wilson shot Taryn a sour look, then shifted his attention to Brook who was just now catching up with Cade. He noted how she moved. How she practically oozed confidence and wished he could project just one-tenth of that. Then he turned to Sasha and said, "Next time Brook offers, you *will* let her teach you how to shoot. Because, like it or not, we have to be a *gun family* in order to survive this thing."

There was a heavy silence in the cabin as they watched Brook slow from a trot to walking speed and finally form up next to Cade, who was moving noticeably slower.

"What now?" asked Sasha.

Taryn said rather sternly, "We do as we were told. We wait and watch the road behind us."

Chapter 35

The three men sat in a semicircle, legs crossed, heads bowed. Not a word had passed between them for a long while. And truth be told, to a man, deep down, each of them hoped that the others would volunteer to untangle Jordan's corpse from the clutching thorns.

Near Duncan, separated by a couple of feet and five minutes in death, two buzzards lay dead among a bed of their own bloody feathers. Both birds were plump from feasting on the dead girl's corpse. And both birds had fallen victim to an apex predator nurturing a growing resentment and armed with a Colt M1911.

Lev looked up first. Elbows resting on his knees, his breath coming in shallow gulps, he looked at Jordan's corpse through bloodshot, teary eyes. Let his gaze linger on her face for a beat, taking in the once beautiful features now twisted into a death grimace. He focused on the red mud ground into her blond hair and wished he could find the necessary courage to take the initiative and grab one of the bed sheets and cover her. But he couldn't. Instead, he looked at Daymon, then Duncan, and asked, "What happened to her?"

"Death by rapid deceleration," answered Duncan instantly and matter-of-factly. "Once I'd finished puking I gave her body—or what's left of it anyway—a quick onceover."

"And?" asked Daymon.

Duncan made no reply. He rose, stepped around the pool of vomit and grabbed one of Jordan's dainty wrists. When he lifted the ashen arm he noticed that either the ulna or radius bone was protruding at nearly a right angle and had punctured the skin. *Greenstick fracture*, he thought. *Sure as shit caused by rapid deceleration. Hell of a way to go*. But that wasn't all that he had picked up on. He gently rolled her hand over and showed them her fingers. Even with his less-than-stellar eyesight, the blood dried there was obvious. Also, what looked like half-moons of yellowed dermis was packed tightly underneath her fingernails. And though Duncan was no CSI investigator, to him it looked like she'd put up a hell of a fight before she died.

Daymon and Lev moved close. "What is it?" asked Lev.

"Whoever grabbed her lost some skin ... at the very least. I'm sure there's some shitbag out there with a sore pair of testicles as well."

"Look where it got her," said Lev.

"From what Heidi says ..." Daymon went silent. Hung his head. *Filter, dumbass*, he thought to himself. And though he didn't want to speak of Heidi's ordeal without her permission, it was way too late to swallow his words. He looked up, cleared his dreads from his face, and regarded the water-filled quarry, focusing on the sun-splashed ripples moving east to west behind a soft breeze. After a long pause, he drew in a deep breath and went on. "Whenever Robert Christian or one of his cronies weren't having their way with her ... Bishop's boys were."

"I'm so sorry," Duncan said. "We've all got a dog in this fight. I don't care who gets to do it ... just so long as Bishop dies."

Breaking through his inhibitions, Lev said to Daymon, "She deserves to have back her dignity. Will you give me a hand?"

Daymon nodded and scooped up the sheets. Knees creaking, he rose and passed one of the stark white items to Duncan, then watched solemnly as the older man knelt next to the petite corpse and covered it from head to toe.

Together Lev and Daymon grabbed Jordan's rigor-affected arms and pressed them close to her nude body, holding them there while Duncan finished swaddling her corpse in the remaining sheets.

Standing up, Duncan drawled, "Follow me." Without a backward glance, he trudged around the thicket and set a straight course for the outbuildings.

Daymon watched Duncan walk away. Regarded the body near his feet for a second and then looked at Lev and mouthed, "What the hell."

Answering with a shrug, Lev double-timed it and fell in behind Duncan, who was obviously on some kind of a mission.

After covering the seventy-five yards of mud-puddle-pocked gravel with two curious stragglers on his heels, Duncan entered the first of the three outbuildings and ten seconds later emerged empty-handed.

With Lev and Daymon still looking on curiously, Duncan entered the middle building, was inside for a handful of seconds and came out wearing a dejected look.

"Third time's the charm," he said. He pushed the shattered door of the third outbuilding inward. This time he was inside for a couple of minutes and came out with a flat-bladed shovel in each hand. "Found them in the rafters," he said, doling out the rusty items. He disappeared inside again and returned with a pickaxe that had seen better days. The head was dulled and red with rust, its wooden handle rife with vertically running cracks. *It'll do*, he thought. Then, answering the bewildered looks directed his way, he said, "We're gonna bury her here."

Lev made a face. He said, "Why not bury her on the hill next to Logan and Gus and Sampson?"

"We will. But later," intoned Duncan. "We bury her deep enough to keep the critters away. And the same reasoning that went into that thing about the rotters learning needs to be applied here. I see no sense in letting the others know about this until we have to ... especially Heidi."

"Thanks," said Daymon. "Good call." Throwing the shovel over his shoulder, he turned and struck off for the distant briar patch.

Chapter 36

Shoulder-to-shoulder, Cade and Brook walked twenty yards beyond the parked Fords and took up a spot behind an abandoned Chevy fifteen feet short of where I-70 began the long and gradual run out into the Green River valley below.

Instinctively, Brook unlooped the Bushnell's from around her neck and handed them to Cade. Using him for support, she put a hand on his shoulder, stood on her tiptoes and pointed a few degrees right of a rising column of black smoke and said, "I saw movement." She pointed. "*There* ... to the right of the vehicles."

"What I was afraid of," said Cade. "And the reason we aren't rushing headlong down the hill ... yet." He spun around to check their six and saw the outline of Raven's head superimposed over the F-650's rear window. He shifted his gaze to the Raptor and counted three more similarly backlit silhouettes. Then pressed the binoculars to his face, adjusted the focus wheel, and scanned the retreating stripe of gray highway behind the Raptor. Nothing moved. No dead. No vehicles. Not so much as a single tumbleweed twitching in the wind. Satisfied that all was clear behind them, he turned back and squinted into the distance, trying to see anything out of the ordinary on or around the road. He searched a quick grid pattern for the glint of light off of glass that would give away a sniper's position. Then examined all of the static vehicles, giving any that weren't wearing a skirt of trapped tumbleweeds three weeks in the making a little extra scrutiny. After seeing nothing that screamed roadside bomb or even looked remotely indicative of an ambush waiting to be sprung, he shifted his gaze up and glassed the first exit servicing Green River.

There he saw a pair of SUVs of indeterminate make and model and a trio of stout-looking motorcycles parked near the shoulder. Razor wire was strung up along both sides of the off-ramp and a pile of Z corpses was stacked three deep nearby. He panned south of the Interstate where a much larger drift of death was fully engulfed, red flames licking dozens of feet into the air with fingers of oily black smoke roiling high above them.

"They've been busy," Cade said, pointing out where the median was blackened and littered with charred human remains from a point just past the onramp all the way west along I-70, downwind judging by the drifting smoke, for as far as he could see. Panning farther ahead, he noticed a few Zs meandering in from the west, but clearly evident from the size of the pyre burning, and the bodies stacked and waiting to be torched, the dead that had gathered overnight had already been culled. Same old story wherever he went. *Like moths to a flame*, as the female guard at FOB Bastion had put it.

He swung the binoculars right of the vehicles and counted five men and one woman, all sitting on colorful folding camp chairs in the shadow of a large picnic canopy erected just beyond the guardrail. And next to the guardrail was a hand-lettered sign with orders for anyone passing to stop and pay a toll before entering or continuing on. But it didn't surprise him that the Interstate was wide open. Likely the folks down there had been threatened with serious repercussions if a patrol from FOB Bastion came along and found it blocked.

Beeson had even stated the night before that due to attrition and a lack of the replacements he'd requested, he had been forced to adopt a temporary *live and let live* policy in regards to the growing sanctuary Green River had become. *The natives*, Cade had been warned, *were getting a little too big for their britches*—hence the spray-painted warning miles back.

Cade propped his elbows on the Chevy's trunk and, feeling the warmth of the hot metal through his shirt sleeves, snugged the field glasses in tight. With the magnified image blurred slightly due to the rising heat vortexes, he picked up the would-be welcoming party and scanned beyond the off-ramp. A tick later he froze and whistled softly. "It's worse than Beeson thought." He took the binoculars from his eyes and regarded Brook. "It looks like they've adopted their own brand of justice in Green River." He refocused on a flatbed truck that had been left parked haphazardly on a corner lot where both roads from the Interstate converged. *Good high visibility area*, he thought. *Maximum message delivery*. On the back of the flatbed, arranged facing the asphalt confluence, were three corpses, two male and one female. Seated on stackable lawn chairs for all to see, they had been stripped naked and posed, each sporting a different hand-lettered cardboard sign. Cade took in the macabre sight, starting with the handless male corpse on the left. The sign around his neck said: *Thief caught stealing food*. He walked his gaze over the second male corpse. Crimson red from the waist down, the man had suffered a savage V-shaped wound to the groin. The corpse's face was a mask of pain, and stuffed into the gaping mouth was a shriveled penis, the scrotum still attached. The sign clutched in the corpse's dead hands read, *Caught fucking the dead*. And the third placard nailed to the chest of a female corpse with what looked like a single rusty railroad spike read, *Adulterous murderer*.

Not wanting to describe the scene, nor thinking he could even do it *justice,* Cade passed the binoculars to Brook and let her see for herself.

A second passed and Brook let out a gasp and promptly thrust the Bushnell's back into Cade's hands. She buried her face and said, "Animals."

Cade said nothing. No way to label the folks responsible more succinctly than Brook just had. So he made three more quick sweeps of Green River, which was surrounded by what looked to be the remnants of an ancient watershed, probably last fully supportive of life when the dinosaurs roamed. The ever-present Book Cliffs rambled off into the distance north by west. Closer in, ripples of hardened sedimentary deposits lent the landscape an unforgiving lunar appearance. And in the center of it all, nestled in a twenty-square-mile gash and backstopped by red rock cliff bands upthrust on a diagonal, was a lush green diamond-shaped tract of land, treed and dotted with tired-looking businesses and nicely kept homes. Cade had received the Cliff's Notes rundown on the city from Beeson. Apparently it had once swelled to two-thousand residents in the early seventies, had enjoyed a long period of prosperity due to the mostly Air Force personnel overseeing nearby ICBM test firings, and then, with the budget cuts of the eighties, all of that had come crashing down and the city had been a veritable ghost town until the fall of Salt Lake City three weeks prior. Now bustling with refugees, the city looked busier than anything Cade had seen since leaving Portland.

A low haze hugged the hillsides, no doubt exhaust from generators he guessed had been humming along all night down there. There were a couple of vehicles moving within the city proper, trolling the side streets like predators, slowly and meticulously. Security perhaps? Dangerous for sure. Clothes drying on lines were strung between some of the houses, colorful articles brightening up the place, like lipstick on the pig of a city that was, as Beeson had put it, "A cesspool to steer clear of." And after seeing the brutality some of its inhabitants were capable of, that's exactly what Cade had in mind. But even though I-70 wasn't blocked physically, the fact that several well-armed people and a few chase vehicles were assembled near the tightest chokepoint meant it might as well have been. *This nut,* Cade thought to himself, *is going to take a little cunning and maybe some gunplay—or at least the threat of the latter before all is said and done.*

Just as they were about to wrap up the reconnaissance and return to the vehicles, Cade noticed some movement near the off-ramp. He looked through the binoculars and saw the lone woman and one of the men of the group leave the oasis of shade, head for the vehicles and climb into one of the boxy SUVs. Its headlights flared on and he watched the gray SUV—which he guessed, based on the amount of aftermarket chrome stuck on the thing, had to be a civilian Hummer—reverse down the ramp and perform a smooth J-turn and then slink away silently past the flatbed of death and into the city.

Not wanting to lose the golden opportunity of dealing with just four guards instead of the original six, Cade said, "Let's go."

Hustling back to the F-650, amid a steady stream of nods and clipped "*OKs*," Cade relayed his plan to Brook. Once they had both climbed aboard, the cab erupted in a flurry of activity as Brook keyed the two-way and filled in the others, telling them what she'd seen and what to expect. But most importantly, she made it abundantly clear to Taryn that though they might slow down, they were not stopping for *anything.*

While Brook did her part, Cade rapped the transmission into Drive and started them moving. He reached over and toggled the - key on the navigation system, zooming the map out until it presented a bigger picture that showed clearly the course Interstate 70 took past the city. After committing the particulars to memory, he toggled the system off and, with a smile, heard his father's voice in his head. Heeding that advice, he gripped the wheel two-handed—*at the proper ten-and-two position.*

In the back seat, Max, sensing something was amiss and also keying in on the scent of the recently dispatched dead clinging to his masters' clothing, emitted a guttural growl to let his concern be known.

"Max is frosty, Dad," said Raven. Then, with pigtails flopping about, she stuck her head over the seat and was hit with both barrels simultaneously when Brook and Cade barked, "Get down."

"And buckle up tight," Brook added, clicking her own seatbelt home and looping the shoulder restraint behind her head.

Glancing in his rearview just as the massive F-650 crested the hill, letting loose butterflies in everyone's stomach, Cade saw Taryn tuck the Raptor close to his ride's bumper, a racing move she'd called 'drafting' during the brief instructional conversation she'd had with Brook via the two-way a moment ago.

Speeding down the gradually sloping hill, sitting high with a good view of the surrounding countryside, Cade pictured the people under the canopy in his mind. He knew that once they heard the engine noise and looked into the sun and saw the vehicles, their minds, dulled from the monotony of watching the dead stretch of sun-baked road all morning, would burn two or three seconds processing the sight before any kind of a decision-making process would kick in. Then, depending on what kind of training, if any, they might have had in their previous lives, anywhere between three and six additional seconds would slip by. And based on his first impression of the crew down below, Cade was betting on the latter before they unfolded themselves from the low-slung camp chairs and rushed to their vehicles, of which only the Suburban concerned him.

Going by his mental stopwatch, six seconds had ticked by since they'd crested the hill. And without consulting the speedometer, his gut told him that the multi-ton truck, aided by gravity and 365-

horsepower, was picking up a great deal of speed. He looked at the speedometer and saw it creep past fifty. Closing in on sixty and figuring they'd already travelled roughly a third of a mile, and without taking his eyes from the road, he said to Brook, "I need you to glass the roadblock and give me a detailed play-by-play."

Traveling at the speed of sound—seven hundred and sixty-seven miles per hour, a mile every five seconds through the atmosphere at sea level— the engine roar ripped across the sage-covered flatland ahead of them.

Five seconds. A nice buffer, thought Cade. But since they were at altitude and the air was thinner, the dual notes reached the watchers' ears only four seconds after leaving the four-inch exhaust pipes.

Two screaming Ford power plants.

Two pickups, both technically not a color. Yin and Yang approaching, speeding up, seemingly tethered together in close formation like a couple of high-performance fighter jets.

Noticing the four heads turn in unison, on the faces expectant expressions, Brook called out, "They're onto us. A real big man is getting up. And now he's waving at us. Motioning to stop."

"No way we're stopping," said Cade. Then he smiled, knowing exactly what was going through their heads at that exact moment. First, relief in the knowledge that the trucks coming straight for them were black and white respectively, and relatively shiny versus dull desert tan and bristling with high caliber weapons. Gun trucks full of 4th Infantry Division soldiers from FOB Bastion the approaching vehicles were not. And that's why the fool was flapping his arms like a flightless bird. Cade slowed down a tiny bit. A feint. A bluff that he figured just bought them another six seconds. And shaved another tenth of a mile of closing distance.

"Now the two other men are making a break for the SUV. They both have rifles," intoned Brook. Then she added, a hint of incredulity in her delivery, "And it looks like another is going for his motorcycle."

In that instant Cade saw their actions for exactly what they were—precursors to aggression. And the only way he knew to counter aggression—the way he had been taught first in Ranger school and had honed later in the Teams—was to hit hard and fast and pull no punches. "And the fourth guy?" he asked, his decision as to their next course of action having just been decided for him.

"The big guy ... I don't see that he has a gun. And for some reason he's making a beeline on foot for the Interstate ... and just turned uphill to the west ... keeping to the right shoulder."

"Shit," barked Cade. "Keep an eye on him." He rapped the steering wheel. Checked his speed. *Seventy-five.* Twenty seconds had now elapsed and they were on the straight and level and seemingly playing catch-me-if-you-can with the heat mirage dancing in the road dead ahead.

"The two are in the SUV now. Driver's bending forward ..." She saw a puff of gray exhaust. Said, "He started the engine. But they're not moving ... just sitting there idling."

"Good," said Cade. This little tell all but confirmed his theory. He eased up on the gas, keeping the needle wavering near eighty.

The big tires thrummed against the pavement, creating a strange harmonic that sounded like an out-of-balance washing machine.

He viewed the Raptor in the side mirror. Taryn still had it nosed close in on his six.

Inside the Raptor, Sasha said, "Why is he slowing down?"

Wilson and Taryn shushed her simultaneously.

Back inside the F-650, Cade asked, "What's number four doing *now*?"

"He's still running along the shoulder, slowly," answered Brook. "He's no Jesse Owens."

Mister Murphy's taking a powder, thought Cade. Ten more seconds had elapsed and the odometer indicated the crest of the hill was, give-or-take, eight-tenths of a mile behind them. He guessed that the roadblock was two-tenths of a mile ahead and the item the man was running toward was in the general vicinity.

"The guy's got his motorcycle on the shoulder now, facing west," added Brook. "And the SUV is now rolling towards where the ramp meets the Interstate."

Cade said, "Thanks ... I can see 'em clearly now."

"Hurry up or they're going to block the road."

No way, thought Cade. *They'd have to be crazy to get in the way of all this metal screaming their way*. "Don't worry," he said. "They're going to let us drive right on by."

"Why?" asked Brook.

"Because I'm guessing they liberated some State Trooper of his or her spike strips. You're going to have to take the runner out ... before he gets to wherever he's going."

Judging by the advanced warning that the long straightaways from both east and west provided the watchers from their position, along with the ramifications of their little trap being discovered by a patrol from FOB Bastion, Cade would have bet his right arm that the fourth man still had a little ways to run to get to his no doubt cleverly hidden and instantly deployable tire-shredding roadblock.

Flashing Brook a grim smile, followed closely by a wink letting her know that he loved her, Cade coaxed some more speed from the V-10 power plant and instructed Raven to shrug off her shoulder belt and lay flat and keep her head down.

"Down, Max," added Brook. Then, in order to keep it from whipping into her face, she wrapped the M4's sling around her forearm and powered down her window.

Keeping his eye on the road, Cade asked, "You OK with this?"

Superheated desert air thundered in, creating a savage racket. "Have to be. Just keep it steady," she bellowed as she pulled her cap off and threw it to the floor. She snugged the carbine to her shoulder and flicked the selector to fire in one practiced move. Then she stuck the muzzle out first and then her head, and finally her upper body, not entirely aerodynamic, cut into the vicious slipstream.

To equalize pressure in the cab, Cade used the master controls on his armrest and lowered the driver's side rear glass, creating a sort of breezeway that helped to bring the sonic tempest down to a more tolerable gale. He saw Brook train her carbine on the cream-colored Suburban still sitting idle fifty yards off the right fender at her two o'clock. Another twenty yards ahead of the SUV and coming up rapidly, also on their right, was the black motorcycle, its rider directing a knowing look at the vehicles careening towards him.

Then the two faces in the Soccer Mom assault vehicle tracked left-to-right and Cade made brief eye contact with the driver as the F-650 blazed past the Suburban.

Seeing the man on foot begin to slow, arms flopping, head tilted back, clearly laboring for breath, Cade applied the brakes evenly and angled a few degrees to the left in order to afford Brook a better firing angle.

"I've got the runner," Brook hollered over the wind as two closely spaced shots rang out.

In clipped slow motion, Cade registered the results as he continued braking. He saw the rotund runner stop and skid, the man's back heaving, his black leather boots kicking up a cloud of ochre dust. There was a glint of metal in the man's hand and when he turned back towards the roadway and uncoiled halfway out of a sprinter's crouch, Brook's words were already trailing off and a spritz of red had blossomed on the left side of his neck where major blood delivery occurs. A millisecond later, before the man knew he had been mortally wounded by the initial 5.56mm hardball, the kill shot entered his temple left of his ear, a tumbling sixty-two grain hunk of lead that added all of its kinetic energy behind the first and sent the man sprawling onto the hot asphalt, face-down, ass up, dead as a doornail.

Instinctively Brook tracked her rifle a hundred and eighty degrees to the right and fired a four-round salvo head-high at the man on the motorcycle, causing him to dive for cover, the big Harley nearly toppling over on him.

Hot brass casings pinged around the F-650's voluminous interior. "Center mass," Cade bellowed. "No need for a head shot ... they're not Zs." From the corner of his eye, he saw the headshot corpse, and then the flare of sunlight off the spike strip which had been dragged three feet into the right lane. Instinctively he jinked the wheel hard left to avoid the vehicle-disabling device.

Back in the Raptor all hell was breaking loose. Sasha whining about speed. Wilson saying "She shot him!" over and over. Through all of this, Taryn retained her cool and also avoided the partially deployed spike strip.

Seeing Taryn match his maneuver and the Suburban nose onto the Interstate right behind her, Cade powered down his window, pulled into the right lane and slowed to fifty. Then, inexplicably, going against his earlier orders, he stuck his arm into the slipstream and waved the Raptor by.

Through the black sheet metal Cade felt the vibration of the Raptor's big engine hit his thigh as it roared past in the fast lane. He consulted his mirror and, just as the Suburban was abreast of the biker who was not injured but still righting his fallen steed, swerved left and pulled the F-650 in behind the Raptor. "Get ready," he said to Brook, watching the SUV closing fast in the passenger side-view mirror. Hands kneading her carbine, Brook nodded slowly.

When Cade figured that the Suburban had closed to within the M4's acceptable range, he shot Brook a glance and said, "In three, two, one ... "

Body coiled, face a mask of concentration, Brook snugged the carbine tight and said a silent prayer.

After abruptly slowing the F-650 to thirty miles per hour, Cade then locked up the brakes, hard, slewed the wheel right and yelled, "Light 'em up!"

Carbine leading the way, Brook leaned out the window and brought the Eotech on line as the big Ford shimmied, the smell of burnt rubber hit her nose and the world spun by her face. She kept the sight's red holographic pip centered on the approaching vehicle's windshield and caressed the trigger even as the F-650 beneath her continued shifting on axis, fully engaged in a juddering power slide. "One, two, three, four," she counted under her breath with each pull of the trigger and when she hit *five* the SUV's windshield spider-webbed and a tick later imploded behind the intense overpressure. As she watched the crumpled sheet of mostly intact safety glass lose all tensile strength and fold in on the driver and passenger, her head was jerked sideways as the truck under her came to a full and screeching halt perpendicular to the outside shoulder.

Suddenly hit with a face full of opaque glass and unable to see the road ahead, the man driving the Suburban apparently panicked and locked up his brakes.

Brook saw the blue-black smoke coming off the tires first and then noticed the ungainly SUV begin to fishtail. Then, seemingly in slow motion and suffering from an extreme amount of body roll, the SUV's rear end broke free and swerved hard to the right. Until the driver, presumably still batting the glass from his face, felt the change of inertia and overcorrected horribly by hauling the wheel in the same direction as the slide but with more vigor than necessary.

Still engaging the moving target, Brook shifted her aim right and emptied the magazine into the windshield and passenger side door. Everything around her seemed to slow to a crawl. She smelled the sharp tang of cordite. Then registered the passenger grimace and throw his hands up and then crumple over in obvious pain. She heard shell casings pinging off the door pillar to her right and felt the hot brass hitting her shoulder but didn't count how many rounds she had pumped into the out-of-control SUV, nor did she remember hearing the metallic *snik* of the bolt locking open on the empty chamber. However, the Suburban going up onto two wheels and then rolling over and over while ejecting the broken and bloody bodies of the two men amid a roiling carpet of broken glass and spilt fluids would be forever etched in her memory.

Cade looked ahead and saw the Raptor speeding off into the distance, growing smaller. *Don't stop for anything.*

He shifted his gaze right. Saw that Brook was fixated on the smoking wreckage. Her eyes were narrow slits. Her jaw was set, the muscles knotted under tanned skin. The empty M4 was still snugged tight and trained on the bullet-riddled corpses.

"Good shooting," he said. He reached over and gently helped her pull the rifle back inside the truck. Immediately she loosed her grip and her hands began trembling. "I just killed three people," she whispered.

"Their fault, not yours," said Cade, a grimace twisting his face. "And if they had anything whatsoever to do with stuffing amputated genitals into another human being's mouth—regardless of the perceived crime—they got exactly what they deserved."

"Is it over?" Raven asked meekly, still out of sight.

Exhaling hard, Cade wondered if Raven comprehended the word genitals. Then said to her over his shoulder, "Not yet. Keep down." He spun the steering wheel around to the left until it hit the stops and locked and the power steering apparatus squealed in protest. He looked past Brook and far off in the distance noticed two things. The fella with the motorcycle was struggling to get it started. Rising up off the bike's saddle, one leg extended and then coming down hard on the kickstarter. That went on for a second with no positive result. Then Cade saw the gray Hummer pull alongside the finicky Harley and pick up the rider. Knowing full well that the F-650 could easily outrun the Hummer, and confident after the recent shooting display that they could outgun the occupants if need be, he snatched up the two-way, and though it didn't need repeating, hit the talk button and told Taryn to take the next exit north and keep moving—no matter what. He released the talk button and Wilson came back with a strained sounding, "Copy that."

As Cade cast another glance at the approaching Hummer, he caught sight of Brook shakily swapping magazines. And seeing as how the last thing he wanted was for her to have to add more human bodies to her gun, he pinned the pedal to the floor, and amidst a cloud of tire smoke and with the staccato pings of rocks and pebbles peppering the undercarriage, powered the rear end around through the scrub and dirt beyond the shoulder. Once the Ford had lurched out of the abrupt ninety-degree turn and bumped back up on asphalt and was tracking west and picking up speed on the Interstate, he reached over and palmed Brook's thigh. Didn't apply any pressure. Just let it rest there, a silent sign of solidarity.

Chapter 37

There were a hundred other places on the abandoned mining site where digging a grave would have been much easier, but after taking into consideration the hell on Earth Jordan's last moments must have been, Duncan chose a spot near the edge of the quarry looking west over the valley, where the odds of a sunset gracing her grave on a daily basis was a very real possibility. "She deserves this," he stated, taking the first swing. And while he broke up the bulletproof ground with the pickaxe, Lev and Daymon shoveled away the broken-up topsoil.

Half an hour after breaking ground, they had a human-sized hole dug down to about mid-thigh on Duncan—a depth that they all agreed was roughly three feet.

Not the textbook eight-by-four-by six, thought Duncan. *But deep enough to keep the critters away.*

Lev and Daymon gently placed Jordan's body into the grave, then stood over her small shrouded form while Duncan dredged up a few words. Nothing biblical. Not because he didn't know any passages, far from it. He knew plenty of them. However, he didn't know the young lady well enough. The reason he abstained. Instead, he spoke of how nice and kind she had been during the short time he had known her. He finished with an Amen, out of habit mostly, and had shoveled half a dozen scoops of dirt before realizing that Jordan was the third person he'd interred since daybreak and suddenly felt weak in the knees.

Sensing Duncan's discomfort, and seeing him seemingly frozen, the shovel's blade hovering empty above the grave, Lev gently took the tool from his hands and helped him to the ground.

"Take a break," said Daymon. "You've done more than your share of shoveling today. Me and Lev got this."

***

Fifteen minutes later the three fully loaded trucks were parked bumper-to-bumper, five feet inside of the quarry entrance. Duncan climbed gingerly from the newly liberated Dodge and, just in case another group of semi-aware first turns had followed them up the feeder road, drew his .45 and approached the gate slowly, cutting the corner a degree at a time.

Daymon called out from the driver's seat of the patrol Tahoe. "What do you see?"

"Clear," answered Duncan, holstering his pistol. He strode to the gate. Took the piece of broken lock from the links and unwrapped the chain. Then, with Lev's help, rolled the gate two-thirds of the way open.

A minute later the three trucks were through, the Chevy bringing up the rear. This time Duncan stayed in the lead vehicle while Lev and Daymon closed the gate behind them.

Nearly two hours under the hot sun had firmed up the road. Though the ruts still grabbed their tires on the way down, threatening to send an inattentive driver into space, the going down wasn't nearly as treacherous nor slow as the trip up. Ten minutes elapsed and they were sitting at the bottom of the quarry road switching their vehicles out of four-wheel drive, grateful for the smooth asphalt of State Route 39.

Duncan fished the Motorola from a pocket and powered it on. Double-checked the channel and thumbed the call button. He said, "Left or right?"

Hearing Duncan's voice emanating from deep within a thigh pocket, Daymon lifted his butt off the seat and reached deep, grasped the radio and thumbed the button saying, "WWLD?"

"What?" answered Duncan.

From his slightly elevated spot at the rear of the column, Daymon saw Duncan crane around and imagined the deadly dose of stink eye being directed his way. Keying his radio, very slowly Daymon intoned, "What ... would ... Lev ... do?"

"He's not in the loop anymore," shot Duncan.

"Exactly. Don't you think he deserves a say in the matter?"

"Nope," said Duncan.

About to press the issue, Daymon decided to roll with it and watched the white Dodge bounce up onto the two-lane and hesitate, rocking on its springs, twin antennas moving counter to the body of the truck. Then he saw a glint off the shiny new blackwalls and his query was answered as the off-road tires cranked hard to the left.

Chapter 38

Conventional wisdom dictated that after having two vehicles fail to stop at their checkpoint and several of their own gunned down in the chase that ensued, whoever was driving the gray H2 would be calling for reinforcements before commencing further pursuit. At least that's what Cade was preparing to counter as he zippered the big Ford between half a dozen cars and trucks, all sitting firmly on shredded tires, a fate that Brook's excellent marksmanship had spared their vehicles.

After a chase lasting only a few seconds, during which the pursuers got an up close eyeful of three of their own who had been breathing just minutes prior and were now bloody corpses sprawled on the Interstate, the Hummer slowed and whipped a quick U-turn and with a puff of black exhaust sped east towards Green River.

Seeing this, Brook looked away from the side mirror, craned towards Cade and said, "What the hell?"

"Stay frosty," was his instant reply. "We're not out of the woods yet." In his mind he saw the driver and passengers, who were already jacked up on adrenaline, weighing the pros-and-cons of continuing the chase alone. A kind of hasty cost-benefit-analysis in which their lives were the cost. And presumably—the reason for their turning back—the people in the Hummer saw little benefit in tangling with the two vehicles and getting gunned down like their fellows.

Then the flip-side of the equation occurred to Cade, and he pictured the bandits not so much giving up, but making a sound tactical decision and opting to stack the deck in their favor *before* commencing any kind of a dogged pursuit. In this scenario they would slide back into town—on their mind how to add reinforcements *and* make up lost time and distance. He guessed they would discard the slow Hummer in favor of faster, more agile vehicles more suited to playing catch-up. Adding more bodies and weapons was a given. The latter most likely being of the larger caliber variety. The kind usually found abandoned at every overrun Guard checkpoint that had sprung up on the outskirts of every medium-to-large city early on in the apocalypse. And while these actions were undertaken, Cade knew that the story of the interlopers who had killed three of their own for no good reason would spread like wildfire over whatever means the denizens of Green River used to communicate.

Lastly, the top-dog, or dogs—whoever was responsible for meting out justice in Green River, perhaps the very people still with blood on their hands from hacking away genitals and cutting off hands—would whip up a frothy bloodlust among the citizenry and deputize some folks and then let loose the hounds. A modern day lynch mob, revenge their sole motivation.

Cade shifted his gaze from the retreating SUV and regarded the fast-approaching off-ramp, a fairly sharp right-hand bend that would shoot them onto US-191 North and hopefully the planned rendezvous with the kids in the Raptor. "Hang on," he said, braking and downshifting to a gear more suited to the rising road that lay beyond. He entered the right-hand sweeper with the speedo wavering near seventy and felt the first tug of g-forces at work on his body. The tires chirped, the body rolled harshly atop the raised suspension, and he felt his butt sliding on the seat.

In the back seat Raven let out a squawk typical of her namesake and then began chanting, "Oh my gosh," over and over. There was a skittering sound and a yelp as Max struggled to find purchase on the carpet.

Meanwhile, mid-way through the turn, in a cacophony of sound, empty water bottles, MRE packaging, spent brass, the laminated map, Brook's M4 and a host of other unidentified items succumbed to gravity and inertia and migrated left, the smaller items pooling against the doorframe's lower sill, the carbine coming to rest near Cade's feet.

Fresh out of the turn, the truck amazingly still upright, and with the floor flotsam and jetsam drifting slowly back to whence they'd come, Cade said cryptically, "I have an idea."

Chapter 39

Duncan smiled at Daymon's weird sense of humor. "W-W-L-D? What would Lev do, indeed." He cranked the wheel left and spun the rear tires, a juvenile move that pelted Lev's brand new Chevy with mud and rocks and ground-up scrub brush. The Dodge bumped onto the two-lane and there was a frantic beeping inside as some central-processing-unit somewhere tried to calm the crazy human's driving habits. Outside there was a staccato chirping as the rubber compound tried to grip the asphalt.

The driver's side window went down with a mechanical *whirr* and Duncan poked his head into the slipstream. The air smelled of fragrant pine with an underlying damp, mossy nose wafting up from the nearby river. He watched the road closely. Not that the appropriately named pick-up couldn't handle butting heads with a few walking corpses, but because he desperately wanted to find a few more first turns and hopefully disprove Lev's whole empirical-evidence-of-first-turns-becoming-self-aware bullshit. Not only to show them that the rotters were just automatons hungry for flesh, and what they had all witnessed at the gate to their compound had been nothing more than dumb luck and a case of wandering, pustule-ridden hands. But also to prove to himself that the rotters at the quarry gate hadn't been waiting patiently in ambush mode—a fear that had been scratching away at his gut since rounding that blind corner and coming face-to-face with them.

So he drove east along SR-39, with the river a constant companion off of his right shoulder for another couple of miles until the landscape leveled off substantially and the river and two-lane

State Route parted ways. The former jagging south by east. The latter shooting ahead straight as a plum line towards the T-junction with Utah State Route 16 near Woodruff.

Three hundred yards from the T-junction, Duncan became aware that the intersection was partially blocked by a yellow school bus that had apparently failed to negotiate the corner and now lay on its side. He looked in his rearview and tapped his brakes a couple of times to make sure he had Lev's attention and then pulled the Ram to the right. With two wheels still on the road, the other two grinding into the red-dirt shoulder, the Ram came to a complete stop two-hundred yards from the site of the single-vehicle accident.

Staring at the overturned bus, Duncan picked up movement in his side vision as the black truck driven by Lev slid in close to his door and came to an abrupt lurching halt. He also heard the electric motor go to work and saw the window glass disappear into the channel. Then there was more movement farther to the left as Daymon squeezed the Tahoe in tight beside Lev in the Chevy, then more motor noise as his passenger window motored down, creating a veritable wind tunnel through all three trucks.

Eyes still fixed ahead, Duncan said "See that?" There was movement up ahead as the group of flesh eaters, having instantly taken note of the three-truck caravan, started their slow stumbling march west—towards the mechanical noises that screamed to them the arrival of fresh meat. As they ambled down the two-lane another dozen pale forms filed in piecemeal fashion from behind the bus.

"I see rotters," replied Lev. "And lots of them." Nervously eyeing the rearview mirror, he slotted the transmission into reverse—just in case.

Ducking, Daymon looked past Lev, made eye contact with Duncan, and then called out, "You talking about what it says on the back of the bus?"

"Yep," said Duncan. He flipped up his visor. Squinted against the sun and his own compromised eyesight and read the words slowly. "Says Etna Elementary. Lincoln County, School District Number Two."

Lev said, "That's where the big boy and all his friends at the quarry gate hailed from."

Daymon added, "I remember sitting in this rig and talking to the big dude ... Mr. Carter … right in front of that very school bus. Had it parked across 89. Bunch of armed folks keeping watch. Hell, Tran nearly got us killed making sudden movements they construed as hostile."

Lev asked, "What happened?"

Daymon answered, "They looked inside the rig. Then asked Charlie a bunch of questions. Finally said *'shoo'* ... told us that they *'don't help outsiders'* and for us *'not to come back looking for food or medicine or help of any kind.'* It was kind of like that first scene from *Rambo* ... either of you two remember that movie?"

Nodding yes, Duncan said, "Remember it. I lived it for a while when I came back from Nam. Drinking and drifting. I was the original John J ... 'cept I didn't kill any sheriffs in any sleepy Pacific Northwest towns. Just ran off a lot of women folk. That's all."

"Well it was like that. Bob's Big Boy had one of his men escort us across town to a second roadblock." Out of habit born in the apocalypse, Daymon checked all three of his mirrors. *Nothing to see.* "We weren't welcome. Bottom line."

"You think they were flushed out? Had to make a run for it ... leave the safety and security of their town?"

Duncan grabbed his binoculars and glassed the bus. Then scrutinized the advancing rotters.

"Well?" asked Lev.

A gust of wind rolled in from the east, carrying with it the stomach-curdling stench of putrefying flesh. Duncan plugged his nose and said nasally, "The bus is shot up. Dollars to doughnuts says they tangled with our death-card-carrying enemies."

"What makes you so sure?" asked Daymon, trying to suppress a grin.

Still holding his nose and sounding like Fozzie Da Bear of Muppets fame, Duncan replied, "Because the bullet holes are punched through the roof of the bus. Speaks to an airborne assault."

"Helicopters," said Daymon and Lev in unison.

"X gets a square," replied Duncan to a couple of confused looks. "From an old game show ... ring a bell?"

Nothing. Lev and Daymon were speechless, shaking their heads.

Suddenly, disrupting the uncomfortable silence, another wind gust swept through, buffeting the vehicles and bringing with it a more pronounced pong as well as a chorus of disconcerting moans.

Once the wind died down, Lev said, more statement than question, "We're not going any farther ... are we."

"No need," said Duncan. "Seal up your rigs and turn on your AC. I figure we'll sit here like a trio of egghead scientists and do some observin' ... see if we can detect some more of that ... what'd Lev call it?" He cast a sidelong glance and saw Lev staring daggers at him, then, finishing his sentence, said, "... *empirical evidence.*"

Chapter 40

The narrow two-lane passing itself off as a State Route rambled on west by north. Cade looked off to the left at a wide creek bed full of dry channels twisting and turning as far as the eye could see south, presumably to where it merged with the always flowing Green River. He shifted his gaze right for a second and regarded the frost-heaved blacktop, cracked and pitted where it merged with a dirt shoulder barely wide enough to accommodate even the smallest foreign import. A couple of feet beyond the shoulder was a gently sloping dirt wall that he guessed eventually plateaued a mile east behind Green River.

A quarter-mile due north of the I-70 juncture, Cade brought the F-650 out of a right-hand turn and spotted the Raptor on the shoulder a hundred yards distant. And Taryn was hanging from the window with a black pistol in a two-handed grip, its business end pointed in his general direction. Stabbing the brakes and maneuvering left of the dotted yellow, Cade saw recognition dawn on her face and she lowered the weapon and slipped back inside the cab.

Brook said, "Where's Wilson?"

Cade pointed at the battered white guardrail a dozen yards left of the Raptor. He said, "Right there," just as Wilson emerged from the lee side of the road, shoving a pistol near the small of his back, and, with a sheepish look on his face, climbed over the barrier and onto the roadway. Approaching Cade's open window, he said, "Heard you coming ... only something didn't sound right."

"Had her in a lower gear," said Cade. He nodded at the redhead's hiding spot. "Setting up your own ambush now, eh?"

"You said not to call you on the radio unless it's an emergency."

"Good job, Wilson. Now saddle up. I don't think the folks in the Hummer are the type to be deterred so easily. We need to hustle and find a couple of stalls."

Smiling inwardly from the unexpected praise, Wilson touched his bandaged cheek and asked, "Whatcha got planned?"

"Just get in and tell Taryn to keep up."

Wilson hustled around the front of both Fords and hopped back inside the Raptor.

"What now?" asked Taryn as the passenger door thunked shut.

Wilson pointed at the F-650, already fifteen truck lengths ahead, and said, "Just follow."

***

Two miles north of the I-70 juncture they came upon a pair of cars parked indiscriminately in the right lane. There was an older model minivan, its sloped front end punched in, the chipped paint and rusted metal indicative of a previous collision. Angled at a forty-five degree angle in front of the van, and piled nearly as high with belongings, was a Ford Taurus wagon with a hideously bloated Z still trapped behind the wheel.

Head on a swivel, taking in his surroundings, Cade braked hard and stopped on the shoulder. The ridge that had been shadowing the two-lane on the right was now just undulating desert peppered with softball-sized rocks and scrub—terrain impassable by all but the heartiest off-road vehicles. The creek bed on the left had wandered away farther west a mile back; however, the rust-streaked steel guardrail remained.

"Perfect," Cade exclaimed. He waved Taryn by on the left and then made an abrupt K-turn in order to point his truck in the opposite direction. He looked Brook in the eye and pointed down the center of the hood. "Aim your rifle that way. I want you to shoot anything that moves."

Brook nodded. Then admonished Raven, who had just popped her head up, to lay flat on the seat.

Keeping the engine running but forgetting about his bad ankle Cade leaped to the hot asphalt. Wincing, he caught Wilson's eye as the Raptor ground to a halt twenty feet away. Motioning for Wilson to join him, he drew in a lungful of superheated air, clenched his jaw against the pain, and charged around front of the F-650. Taking a knee, he ripped the all-weather cover off of the winch. After twenty seconds spent learning the latching mechanism, he released the tension, grabbed a handful of cable and, ignoring the shooting pains, loped as fast as he could towards the Taurus. Wilson caught up to him and skidded to a stop as he was wrapping the cable around the wagon's left front wheel. It wasn't a AAA job but Cade figured it would do the trick.

"After I move this beast I need you to unhook the cable and secure it to the van," he told Wilson.

"Got it."

"Three things," added Cade. "Keep your ears open and eyes down the road. Watch out for the cable. If it snaps it could whip around and cut your head off. And if anyone shows up before we're done, I want you to empty your pistol into them. Remember this ... shoot the dead in the head. The living ... center mass."

"Copy that."

Shooting the redhead a funny look, Cade pushed off the car's front bumper, stood, and hustled back to the F-650. Wasting no time, he slapped the truck into Reverse and pulled the tension from the cable. Once it was laser-straight between the two vehicles and twitching slightly under the enormous strain, he goosed the throttle.

The Taurus's front end slithered right, its tires scribing the road with two identical stripes, coal-black like the light-absorbing marks beneath a wide receiver's eyes.

The Z inside moaned and pummeled the window as the Ford's tremendous low-end torque won out and the big truck angled the wagon into position fully blocking the northbound lane. Then, to release tension on the cable, Cade pulled the rig forward and waited for Wilson to do his part. He looked at his Suunto and saw that a minute thirty of the imagined lead was already spent.

Another forty-five seconds slipped away by the time Wilson was prostrate under the van's front bumper.

Hurry up, Cade thought. He then told Brook that if the imagined pursuers did show up on scene, no matter what arrived she was to take out the most distant of the vehicles. Then light up everything in-between. Nodding, but a little distant in the eyes, she wrapped the strap around her forearm and *snicked* the selector to Fire.

A minute later Wilson was scooting out of the way and flashing a thumbs up.

Cade backed the slack out of the cable and, saying, "Go to hell Mister Murphy," stood on the throttle and held the wheel tight, watching smoke emanate from the van's locked-up wheels. A tick later and the old world throwback to soccer moms and pussy-whipped dads everywhere was nosed up against the guardrail. And wedged together, the two stalls formed an imperfect inverted 'V.' A five-ton metal chevron blocking the entire road.

"We have visitors," bellowed Brook.

Hearing this, Wilson freed the cable from the van, double-timed it to the Raptor and hopped inside. He grabbed his pistol in one hand and the two-way in the other. Simultaneously powered down his window and pressed the talk button and said, "Just say the word, Cade."

"What word?" Brook answered back, the sound of a high revving engine nearly drowning out her voice.

Wilson didn't know what to say. So he said nothing.

And neither did Cade. His arms were half-raised in the universal *it should be here somewhere* posture; he was looking for a way to reel the cable in so it wouldn't get hung up under the truck when Brook said, "One step ahead of you." She reached over and flicked a rocker switch on the lower dash (right where the previous owner had decided it should be) and then there was a corresponding sound up front and the metal hook began bouncing and skittering and jangling against the roadway as the winch motor reeled it back in.

Getting Wilson's drift just as Cade initiated a high speed J-turn, Brook scooped up her carbine and powered down her window glass.

Stopping in the midst of the turn, a rising plume of blue smoke at the flat plane of the 'J,' passenger side facing south, Cade shot a quick glance over his left shoulder at the Raptor angled nose in towards the guardrail. What he saw was encouraging to say the least. Sasha was poking Raven's little Ruger 10-22 from the rear passenger window. In the driver's seat, Taryn was training her Beretta down range. And like Punxsutawney Phil searching for his shadow, Wilson was standing straight in the cab, his upper body protruding through the open moon roof. In his hand was the Beretta he'd put to great use against the monsters outside the fence at the 4x4 shop but only *so-so* against the group of Zs on the I-70 a short time ago.

Cade listened to the high-pitched exhaust notes *brapping* over the shallow ridgeline bordering the State Route south of them. The engines were being worked hard, and however many vehicles he was hearing, the carried sound said that they were drawing near. *Ninety seconds*, he thought, while hoping the bandits were farther away than the engine noise indicated.

Starting a countdown in his head, he said, "Raven, pass me the black case near your feet." In his side vision he saw Brook, M4 steadied on the oversized side-mirror. He also saw the trio in the Raptor maintaining their vigilance, their weapons trained on the blind corner five hundred yards south. A second later he had one end of the rigid case in his hands. "Thank you, Raven," he said with a forced smile. "Head down, *now*." He opened the door, lowered himself to the blacktop, rounded the front of the Ford and sat cross-legged in the dirt on the shoulder. The hood would have been optimal as a rest for the weapon but seeing as how the Ford's hood came up to his chin, the cross-legged stance he was taught in basic would have to suffice.

Seventy seconds.

Cade worked the latches and opened the lid. Inside, snugged tight in charcoal-gray foam, were six items: a black bolt-action Remington MSR (Modular Sniper Rifle) chambered for .338 Lapua, its multi-adjustable stock collapsed and folded in on the weapon. Above the compact rifle, secured in a cutout of its own, was a massive Leupold and Stevens high-powered scope. And nestled in lengthwise next to the scope was a matte-black ten-inch Titan suppressor. Lastly, below the rifle's folded bi-pod, there were three magazines riding in fitted compartments of their own, one already pre-loaded with ten rounds. A habit normally not advisable for storage, but definitely called for in times like these.

Sixty seconds.

Going through a series of regularly practiced steps—meticulous and precise like some kind of fraternal order ritual—he carefully assembled the familiar weapon that he had already used to great effect against the enemy more times than he cared to count. The stock folded into place and locked with a soft *snik*. He placed the scope atop the Picatinny rail, snugged down the quick release lever and removed the lens protectors. Grabbed one of the fully loaded ten-round magazines and carefully seated it into the magwell. Opting to forgo the suppressor, he closed the case and slid it to his left.

Forty seconds.

He calmed his breathing and rested his elbows on his knees. With the engine noise shattering the still air, he worked the recently oiled bolt open and, behind a satisfying *click,* seated the first death-dealing match-grade .338 round into the chamber.

Thirty seconds.

Five hundred yards with this weapon was almost overkill and he didn't have the time to judge windage or elevation, so he said a prayer and snugged the rifle to his shoulder.

Twenty seconds.

He placed his cheek to the weld and focused on his breathing. Started feeling himself going into the zone. And it was happening faster than he had anticipated.

Fifteen seconds.

Three vehicles materialized around the bend, ghostly shapes shimmering in a ground-hugging heat mirage. Instantly aware the road was blocked, brakes were applied.

Cade drew up a tiny bit of trigger pull and studied the vehicles as the drivers undertook frantic actions to slow and avoid a collision. As he had guessed, the pursuers had opted to go with Japanese imports. The first of which, he could see through the scope, was some kind of performance model. Out back was a squared-off whale tail. Up front, on the grill, was a constellation of stars and a slew of letters no doubt denoting a certain track pedigree. Then, ignoring everything else, Cade settled the crosshairs on the driver's head, and dropped that a couple of inches, hoping for an upper-center-mass hit. He saw the man's startled expression morph to full awareness of the predicament he had unwittingly gotten himself into. Fear crossed his face next—presumably from a sudden understanding that there was nowhere for him to maneuver to avoid the multiple weapons pointed in his general direction.

Cade caressed the trigger thirteen seconds sooner than his initial estimate. *First to the party, first to leave*, he thought morbidly as a small, finger-sized hole puckered the glass and a fraction of a second later the driver's head, collapsing inward, spouted pink mist. As Cade worked the smooth action and chambered another round, a cacophony of gunfire sounded to his right. Closer still, steady controlled pops from Brook's M4 mixed in with the sharp reports of the kids' handguns. Amidst the noise he distinguished the snappish discharge of the Ruger 10-22, telling him that at that moment Sasha's combat cherry was broken.

The four-door Japanese sedan, now sans a breathing driver, veered right and bounced and scraped through the rocks and scrub before coming to rest high-centered atop a cluster of basketball-sized rocks, its redlining engine producing a discordant oil-starved death keen.

Meanwhile, the two other fast-moving vehicles—one sporty and very similar to the first, the other a semi-lifted off-road Volvo—veered off in a 'Y,' both trying to avoid the static metal chevron.

But the evasive maneuver did the driver and passenger of the Volvo no good. They died instantly, their heads and upper torsos peppered with a hail of lead pouring from the Raptor's vicinity. Then, inexplicably, the Volvo continued on. It scraped noisily along the length of the guardrail, spewing trim and leaving a streak of forest green paint in its wake. Then, with the remains of the two in the front seats bobbing in unison, finally the out-of-control wagon plowed into the Taurus, popping its driver door and releasing the zombie inside.

Before Cade could bracket the driver of the other import in his sights, Brook had walked a half-dozen bullets along the windshield and through the open window, a number of them striking the young woman behind the wheel.

The passenger, however, in an attempt to save himself, bailed out of the little car and bounced along the shoulder, all elbows and knees and knuckles, and then somehow came up firing a pistol from within a roiling cloud of dust.

As Cade waited patiently for the dust to dissipate and leave him a clean shot, thankfully the engine of the lead vehicle blew spectacularly. He envisioned metal parts caroming around under the car's hood. Then oil fell like rain onto the desert floor.

The loud pop momentarily garnered the shooter's attention, but he continued snapping off rounds toward the F-650 until the slide on his semi-automatic locked open.

In the F-650, hearing the resonant thunks of lead piercing sheet metal, Brook threw herself across the seat. Landing flat on her back, she ejected her magazine and slammed a new one home. Still supine, she released the bolt and asked Raven if she was OK. From the back seat Raven issued a querulous and tense affirmative.

Praying her abs would hold her steady, Brook raised her upper body a few degrees into a half sit-up and then sighted over the lower sill of the passenger glass. Settling the holographic pip on the shooter, she got off two shots to no good effect just as the man swiveled around to look towards the high-centered Japanese import.

Seeing the driver of the lead car alive and sneering over the steering wheel one moment, then half of the flesh blown from his face the next brought home the enormity of the situation. Hands shaking, Sasha watched the little car veer off into the desert. Then, with a flurry of gunfire ringing out above and to the right of her, she scrunched low over the rifle like Brook had taught her. She looked down the barrel and trained it on the green car's splintering windshield and pulled the trigger. After a handful of seconds, the latter half of which she had her eyes squeezed shut, the rifle was empty and the wagon was no longer moving and had become wedged tight against the grandma car and guardrail. What, if any, effect she'd had on the outcome was lost on her. It had all happened so fast. But the front seat occupants were dead. That much was clear. Then the screaming started and as she looked on, horrified, the recently freed monster made a clumsy pirouette, staggered a couple of steps toward the smoking car, then thrust its head and entire upper body through the shattered side windows. As the wailing rose in crescendo and the rotting cadaver wormed its way into the back seat, the realization that she may have contributed directly to the deaths of the car's three occupants dawned on her, and like a hot acidic tsunami, vomit sluiced from her mouth.

Through the diminishing veil of airborne silt, Cade saw the shooter simultaneously drop the magazine from his weapon and stand and turn towards the dying car.

The former move emboldened Cade to stand as well. The latter provided a perfect silhouette for a snap shot at the shooter's center mass.

The man had turned back at about the same time Cade was getting his feet under him and, with just a hundred feet separating them, like a scene from a Spaghetti Western, they locked eyes. Cade shouldered the MSR. But the shaggy-haired shooter brought his boxy black pistol to bear a hair quicker.

Abs quivering uncontrollably, Brook cursed the first two missed shots. Then she saw the shooter's head jerk back around and in slow motion he slapped another magazine in his pistol and was tracking it towards Cade. "Make them count," she whispered, caressing the trigger three times.

With bullets crackling the air near his head, Cade saw plain as day through the scope a triangle of red welts blossom around the man's sternum. One projectile entered above his breastbone—the other two struck him near simultaneously equidistant from each other but a couple of inches lower. A millisecond after cheating death himself, Cade watched the man disappear behind the import like a trapdoor had been opened under him.

Chapter 41

Reversing the assembly process, Cade broke down his rifle, putting all of the parts in their proper places. He stowed the case in back near Raven's feet. "You need to get out for a second? Make a *real quick* pit stop?" he asked, nodding towards the roadside scrub and what little privacy the shin-high bushes might provide.

"Too late," replied Raven softly. A tick later the tears began to flow.

"It's OK honey," added Cade. "Nobody is judging you."

Max took advantage of the open door, squeezed past Raven's legs and disappeared into the desert.

There was a sucking sound as the passenger door opened and Brook clambered in. Then the door closed and she said over the idling engine, "What's going on?"

"Nothing," replied Cade as he retrieved Raven's stuff sack from behind the back seat. Meeting his daughter's gaze, he pulled her closer and gently wiped away the tears. After a semblance of a smile returned to her face, he made a show of pinching his thumb and pointer finger together and then slowly drew them across his lips, made a locking motion and pantomimed throwing away the imaginary key. "Let's go before anyone else shows up."

Brook asked, "Think they'll send more?"

"I would," replied Cade. He whistled and scanned the range beyond the road for signs of movement. A few seconds passed and then Max shot from the bushes and leaped into the open rear door, which Cade then closed with a firm push. He hustled back to the cab. Drive was engaged and he cranked the wheel hard to the right, reversed and parked alongside the Raptor so that he was looking down into the passenger side windows.

"What's up, Boss?" asked Wilson, a measure of self-assuredness now evident in his voice.

Ignoring the greeting, Cade addressed Sasha, who was looking up at him from the back seat area. "Brook's proud of how you handled yourself."

Sasha wiped her arm across her face before replying. "One of my bullets might have killed one of them," she said, brow furrowed, her voice wavering slightly.

Cade stabbed a finger at each person as he spoke. "Or one of hers or his or Brook's or mine ... doesn't matter. They made their own bed. The second they gave chase they sealed their fate. You think they came after us the second time looking for an apology?"

Sasha said nothing.

Wilson removed his boonie hat. Ran his hands through his red mane and said, "She'll be all right."

"You all carried yourselves very well from start to finish," Cade said. Then addressing Wilson, he delivered a belated apology for grazing his cheek. He finished by calling out loudly enough to be heard by Taryn over the idling motors. "You're a hell of a driver, Taryn."

The Raptor's motor *brapped* twice in recognition.

Cade imagined Taryn sitting behind the wheel, her tattooed arm in the air sending his bossy condescending ass a one-fingered salute. But the opposite was true. She was gripping the wheel with two hands, a tear running down her cheek. Not as a result of her first taste of combat but because what Cade had just uttered was what her dad said to her after every single race. *Hell of a driver.* Four words she would never hear him say in that soothing voice again. But definitely *four words* that meant a hell of a lot coming from the guy who Wilson had taken to calling Captain America.

Cade tapped a key on the sat phone and, once it flared to life, composed an SMS message and sent it to the number Beeson had written on the map. It detailed the roadblock and the antisocial nature of the people now calling Green River home. At the very least, Cade hoped the message would prevent any more attacks. But deep down he hoped Beeson's boys would roll down the 70 and deliver the top dogs there some well-deserved curb treatment.

They left the dead bandits where they had fallen, left the Subaru high-centered and still smoking, and left the high desert above Green River with the image of the lone Z, legs protruding from the import car, kicking the air rhythmically like a diver out of water as it gorged itself on the would-be bandit.

Chapter 42

More than an hour in the hot sun, burning fuel to stay cool, had only served to make Duncan feel like a fish in an aquarium. One full hour of leering faces and wanting hands pressing against the window glass. Streaks of blood and mucous and unidentifiable fluids painted every surface the dead came into contact with.

Suddenly the two-way radio sitting on the dash warbled. Daymon said, “Seen anything on your side yet?”

“Nope,” answered Duncan. He released the talk button for a second. Thought about packing it in and calling it a day when one of the creatures—a first-turn thirty-something male—began scrutinizing the passenger side door handle. Then Duncan could have sworn it jiggled.

Wanting to get back to Heidi, Daymon pressed the issue. “Can we go now, *Mister* Winters?”

“Gimme one more second ... will ya,” drawled Duncan. He released the talk button. Powered the window down a couple of inches. Looking into the rotter’s clouded-over eyes, he said, “Anybody home? Why don’t you hop in ... we’ll hit a drive through.” The creature shifted its gaze from the meat in the truck and regarded the door again. Let its eyes linger there momentarily, seemingly lost in thought. Then it looked up and its lips peeled back, revealing a cracked and chipped picket of teeth. Finally, ignoring the partially open window which Duncan had provided as a path of least resistance, the flesh eater snarled and redoubled its efforts on the door handle. Simultaneously rationalization and reason delivered a knockout punch as Duncan realized that his little experiment had just provided all of the empirical evidence they needed.

Daymon's voice again: "Well?"

Voice wavering slightly, Duncan said, "We're fucked."

"Come again."

"This thing just tried to open the passenger door ... twice."

"We telling Lev?"

Duncan said nothing. With the monster still pulling repeatedly on the outside handle, he put the Ram in Reverse and backed up rapidly, simultaneously wrenching the steering wheel left and braking, pulling a ragged looking bootlegger's reverse.

Lev looked a question at Daymon, who just shrugged and gunned the Tahoe in reverse, following Old Man's lead.

Monkey See Monkey Do was the order of the day as Lev performed a like maneuver in his purloined Chevy and took up station between the other vehicles.

With the thrumming of the off-road tires reverberating through the cab, Duncan drove on in radio silence thinking about how much—if any—of this new revelation he was obligated to divulge to the others. In no time the quarry entrance blipped by on the right. But Duncan didn't notice. All kinds of sayings were fighting for space in his head—*out of sight out of mind, what they don't know won't hurt them, ignorance is bliss*—not one of them ethical in this application.

Having finally made up his mind how best to broach the subject of the rotters' newfound tricks, another thought began needling him. And as he stopped his rig next to the gate leading to the compound, horrific thoughts of the massive damage a self-aware horde of rotters could do to the remaining pockets of mankind stirred within him an overwhelming urge to make some bubbles and do some much needed forgettin'. He turned the volume up and immediately heard Phillip's voice urging anyone listening to answer his call.

"Duncan here," he drawled. "Come on down and Lev will spell you."

"Aren't you going to put down the rotters first?"

Lost in thought while approaching the bend, Duncan hadn't even noticed the knot of fresh turns.

The radio was silent for a tick then crackled with static and Daymon said, "I'll handle them." In seconds he had parked the Tahoe between the rotters and Duncan's truck and was standing on the road, machete in hand.

The throng of monsters split in two—half veered toward the repaired fence and pressed their flesh against the barbed wire, reaching for Phillip, who was steadily walking downhill towards them. The other half, roughly seven or eight, plodded ahead on a collision course with Daymon's tempered steel blade.

Leading them east down 39, the lanky ex-fire fighter culled the shambling lot one at a time. Skull caps went spinning and bouncing across the blacktop. He decapitated the final two—a gigantic pair of undead specimens rivaling the Brothers brothers who, along with Pug, had originally abducted Heidi from the Silver Dollar Cowboy Bar back in Jackson.

He looked west down the road and saw that together, without firing a shot, Lev, Duncan and Phillip had created their own tidy pile of unmoving corpses.

He bent over and grabbed two handfuls of greasy hair. Hefting the human heads, he was struck by how much heavier they were than he had guessed. Probably a good ten pounds each. Clowning around, he pretended to tightrope walk the centerline, the still chattering heads acting as counterbalance.

A primal urge kicked in, causing Duncan to back away from the clacking teeth. Though he knew a rotter wasn't dead until its brain was destroyed, the unusual sight always gave him a scrotum-shrinking case of the heebs. "What the hell are you doing with those?"

Daymon hoisted the heads—eyes still moving in their sockets, teeth clicking an eerie cadence—over his own. He said, "Blowing off steam. Let's have some fun. I figure we'll keep them and do some experimenting."

"What are you getting at?" growled Duncan.

Quizzical looks washing over their faces, Lev and Phillip listened intently to the conversation.

One at a time, like flesh and bone bowling balls, Daymon heaved the heads down the road. Landing with solid sounding thunks, they rolled in two different directions until miraculously inertia bled off and both stopped, wobbling right-side up, the wildly different profiles positioned in a classic face-off a couple of yards apart. Shaking his head in disbelief, Daymon said sharply, "You tell 'em. Or I *will*."

"I was going to, *goddamnit*." Duncan turned a one-eighty. Faced the fresh graves up the hill and stared for a long silent minute. He turned and squared up with Lev and Phillip. Right off the bat, he apologized for contemplating keeping his findings from them. Then he described his *test* and his thoughts on the matter and their ramifications, which all together stunk on ice.

"Extinction level event ... *supersized*," exclaimed Lev. He walked away from the circle, shaking his head.

"I'll get everyone together later and tell em' exactly what I told you all," Duncan said gruffly.

After a short walk, Lev returned to the fold. He looked at Daymon first and then addressed Duncan saying, "What about what we found at the quarry?"

Duncan said, "Phillip ... earmuffs."

To which the rail-thin man cocked his head and said, "I'm not following."

Duncan jerked his chin to the side. "Please, take a walk."

Sullen. Head down. Phillip took a walk. Along the way he tried to bend it like Beckham with one of the heads but missed horribly, his boot barely grazing the ear of his intended target and setting it spinning like a top.

There was a short huddle and the trio came to a consensus. "Sorry Phillip," said Duncan. "Help us move the bodies and then we'll go inside. You'll drive the Chevy. Lev ... you get the gate. This time close it and lock it."

Lev's mouth worked silently, but he decided to let it go. *True, Duncan had been drunk at the last change*, he thought. And also true was the fact that Lev had been under the impression that the grieving man had wanted to do everything on his own. That the barbed wire wasn't secured after Duncan drove the Toyota through was a shared responsibility. So Lev vowed to himself to be more vigilant in the future. Learn from his mistakes. A few minutes later, after the twice-dead rotters were piled in the ditch with the others, Lev opened the gate and watched the three trucks disappear down the forest-lined gravel road.

He wrapped the chain, secured the padlock and arranged the foliage to fully conceal everything. Looked down the road to the west. Nothing. All clear. He looked east and saw the severed heads sitting near the shoulder, the mouths still moving nonstop. And though he couldn't see them, still, he imagined the eyes flicking left and right, following his every move. "Fuck that," he said aloud as he vaulted the barbed wire fence. "Not my job."

Chapter 43

Bishop liked to be on his feet. He was always restless as a kid. Riding his bike for hours upon hours around whatever base his father was billeted at the time had been his daily reprieve from the monotony of life as a military brat. And later on—after surviving BUDS and joining the Teams—unlike most of his contemporaries, he lived for long marches with a heavy ruck biting into his shoulders and the reassuring feel of ten pounds of lethal metal in his hands. It allowed him to think, he supposed. So when he was not out in the field and on patrol, he ran to think. Any time. Day or night. Getting his cardio going always helped him clear his mind. See things from a different perspective.

Leaving Carson and Elvis alone at the house, he jogged to the gate, where, with several of his Spartan mercenaries looking on, he took it upon himself to do the job that Carson hadn't gotten around to yet.

He called Tweedle Dee and Tweedle Dumb over and engaged them in a little small talk. Asked them if they liked the dead. If they wanted to keep one for a pet. If they liked to fuck them when nobody was looking. After all of his questions has been met with a chorus of no's and no ways and then a couple of simultaneous *hell no's*, he ordered them to go into town and clear the marina and retail area of any walking dead and then bring him back a fresh bucket of steam. The latter part of his edict was met with the usual blank stares he had been accustomed to seeing since the two showed up after having been kicked out by a group of local survivors two days prior. That they were both low-IQ dolts led to them being ostracized from the rest of Bishop's men. But every army, no matter how small it was, needed bottom feeders to burn the shit and bury the garbage—and in the case of Bishop's fifty-man army—dispose of Omega-infected corpses, a job that, to a man, nobody wanted.

Without another word, as the pair turned to go to their vehicle—to collect the bucket of steam—Bishop motioned one of his men over and relieved him of his rifle. Shouldering the black carbine, Bishop flicked the selector to burst and triggered a couple of three-round-salvos knee-high at the departing duo.

Walking left to right, the slugs chewed up Tweedle Dee's calves, pulping the muscle and severing one or both of his Achilles tendons, sending him to the dirt screaming and clutching both legs. Then, a half dozen 5.56 x 45mm hardball rounds caught Tweedle Dum a little higher, shredding both hamstrings and his right butt cheek, leaving a mass of bloodied flesh and fat and torn fabric in their wake.

Rooted in place not five feet away, Jimmy Foley's eyes went wide. And though he didn't really agree with the way the two men treated the dead, what Bishop had just done was downright evil.

With both conscripts grievously wounded and screaming and writhing on the dirt, Bishop looked directly at the balding conscript named Foley and berated everyone at the gate—including the dying duo. "I don't want another one of those dead things coming anywhere near the fence ... do you copy?" Foley nodded, as did the others. The men on the ground made no reply. Continued thrashing the dirt and bleeding out. "I want a second roadblock erected farther east. Find some heavy chain-link and string it up in the forest as well if that's what it's going to take to keep those things away from me." As the two men continued bleeding and wailing and calling out for help, Bishop spun a tight circle and looked each of the assembled men in the eye, stopping back at Foley. Then, with spittle flying from his lips, he continued, "I don't want to see another fucking walking corpse unless I decide to go outside this wire. Am I clear?"

To a man, Foley included, Bishop's fiery diatribe was met with more nods—all to the affirmative.

"Fresh magazine, please," he said to Barry, a local kid with a penchant for drinking and speeding, who promptly ripped a black polymer item from his brand new chest-rig and mutely handed it over.

Sensing what was to come, all of the men—save for Foley, who was trying to distance himself from the madness—crowded around the bigger of the two, who had gone into shock, blood pulsing from the wounds where the bullets had carved deep vertical furrows of flesh from his inner thigh. The other man, however, was far from silent. He had been reduced to a blubbering mess, all wound up into a fetal ball. And he was the one who left the world first. *Squeaky wheel gets the grease*, thought Bishop as he fired a couple of three-round-bursts into Tweedle Dee's neck and head, causing the man's body to twitch once and go limp, a dark stain marking the seat of his pants when his bowels loosened.

Handing the rifle back to its owner, Bishop bellowed, "I want them left here as a reminder to anyone who thinks it's fun to fuck with the Zs." Once again he regarded each of the men personally, then added, "Let the crows eat what they want and dispose of the bodies at change of guard."

Bishop tightened the laces on his running shoes. Motioned for the hewn timber gate to be opened and padded on down the road.

***

An hour later, give or take, Bishop was back. Pulse pounding, he stood hands on hips and breathed in through his mouth. The smell of death was heavy. Pervasive. It was one of the things he hated most about the dead. You could outrun them. As he had just proven on his jaunt outside the compound. But you couldn't elude their stench. It permeated his clothes and hair and, though it was probably just his mind fucking with him, he could almost taste it in his mouth.

Salivary glands pumping abnormally, he spat on the grass outside the gate. Still catching his breath, he looked over at the bodies of the two men he'd gunned down earlier. A murder of crows surrounded the prone forms, strutting around, their beady eyes throwing sideways looks as if aware there were more from where these two came from. One had taken station on Tweedle Dee's forehead and was laboriously working its head inside one empty eye socket. Red rivulets ran down the corpse's pallid cheek from where the raptor's claws had sunken in. It came up with a morsel, glistening wet and trailing some kind of membrane, then raised its head towards the blue sky and swallowed the treat whole and cawed mightily. Triumphantly. And though the cadavers were not yet contributing to one of the banes of Bishop's existence, in this hot sun, he knew they soon would be. "The birds have had enough," he said to the bald conscript who was opening the gate for him. Hitched a thumb over his shoulder and added for everyone present to hear, "Wait for my rotting entourage to catch up and when you're finished culling them I want those two fools buried in the same pit."

Moving the conscript aside with a sweeping motion, an oversized Spartan mercenary nodded at Bishop and stepped aside, allowing him passage.

Bishop said nothing. He used the walk to the lake house to cool down. Stopping to stretch along the way, he regarded the newly cut landing zone and the fuel-laden helicopters sitting there quiet and dark. There would be no repeat of Jackson Hole. His plan for Elvis was going to see to that. *However*, he thought. *Having the helos and pilots nearby as insurance offers me a sense of security I haven't known since before the dead began to walk.* Suddenly from the vicinity of the gate there came a fusillade of gunfire. It lasted three or four seconds and then trailed off. He went to work stretching the other leg. Working the lactic acid from his hamstring with a steady kneading, he listened to the satisfying sound of single and sporadically spaced kill shots. The hollow pops—that to him signified but a single grain of sand in the dune of dead he'd need to cull in order to be satisfied with his new sanctuary—crashed off the houses and trees across the lake and came echoing back and dissipated to nothing.

All was quiet as he mounted the stairs and entered the house through the back door. He stopped and listened hard. Nothing stirred. He walked the length of the hall past the powder room and was hit face first with a very satisfying aroma. Sage and basil and garlic instantly came to mind. Ten more paces and he was in the kitchen and saw the source. To his left, sitting atop the gas stove, was a jumbo steel stockpot and another pot a quarter its size. Steam was pouring from the large pot and he could hear the water inside roiling and making it shimmy slightly. The aroma he'd hit upon when entering the house was emanating from the other smaller pot. And sitting in a chair in the living room, that with the kitchen and dining area made up an open plan great room, was his number two, a veteran of the Iraq war who simply went by Carson. First name or last, only he and Bishop knew. And he was wearing a shit-eating grin that made the quartet of red welts marring his face fold in on themselves to resemble a vertically arranged W.

"You like?" asked Carson with a sweeping gesture.

"The view's great," he answered, looking towards the sliding glass and shimmering lake beyond.

"No ... the spread, Ian."

Looking left, Bishop noticed the wood slab dining table had been set for two. There were two napkins folded fancy. Two plates with gold trim guarded on both sides by an array of silverware, two of everything it seemed. There was even a pair of distinct glasses, one for wine, and one, presumably, for water. Peeling off his sweat-soaked tee, Bishop said, "Are you coming out of the closet on me or something? We having a date here?" He held a straight face for a second and then burst out laughing.

Failing to constrain himself, Carson also broke out in laughter, and then after a minute or so wiped a tear from his eye and said, "Get washed up. I have another surprise for you."

"I love surprises," said Bishop with a knowing look. He shifted his gaze to the lake. "Elvis?"

"Sleeping by now," replied Carson.

"Did he follow through?"

Carson smiled. "And then some. Must have found a second gear. He sent the girls out about ten minutes ago. I took them over to the boys."

Wearing a concerned look, Bishop glanced over his shoulder. "Are the girls broken?"

Carson shut down the stove. "They're a little bent. But nothing serious."

"Elvis is a go for tomorrow?"

"For sure," replied Carson. "For sure."

"Mmmm, spaghetti," said Bishop in passing. He traced his steps back. Turned a right before the back door and climbed the seventeen stairs to the second floor. He passed the first door on the right and heard Elvis snoring, deep and resonant. He got a whiff of a musky scent. A byproduct of the King's sexcapades, no doubt. *Far better than carrion*, he thought. The second bedroom was next and he noticed the door now had a padlock on the outside. A big Schlage item, the screws concealed by the hardware. Still, he imagined Carson had sunk the wood screws deep into the frame. Unless Lara Croft was behind the door, nobody was getting out of there. And since he didn't have a key, he wasn't getting in. *Dad must not want me to peek at the present before Christmas*, he mused. Pushing aside the forming mental image of the woman behind the door, he walked the length of the carpeted hall to the master bedroom and the cold shower awaiting.

Chapter 44

The overhead skylight and sliding glass door let in copious amounts of sunlight, the majority of which was reflecting off the lake and danced hypnotically, wave-like on the angular vaulted ceiling. As a direct result, the temperature in the room had risen beyond hot. Sweltering was the first word that came to Jamie's mind. Her sweat-soaked clothes clung to her body but had no kind of cooling effect. She knew she looked as bad as she felt. Passing through the back door, she had gotten a glimpse at her own reflection in the glass. Looking like a black swimmer's cap, her hair was plastered to her head and had dried that way after the hood had been removed—for good, she hoped. Put her in a flapper's dress and show her to the speakeasy and she'd blend right in, she'd thought at the time. Hell, throw in some bathtub gin as well because when she tried to swallow, her saliva was thick and viscous and a white crust had formed at the corners of her mouth. She couldn't remember ever wanting a drink of anything wet more than she lusted for one now.

In addition to the locked door leading out to the hall, there was another (also locked) leading off to the right into a Jack and Jill bathroom. This she knew because periodically she would hear the toilet water run for a few seconds and then stop, presumably a valve in the tank replacing water lost through a leaky seal somewhere. Liquid. So near yet so far. In fact it might as well have been a waterfall. And every time she heard it, her Pavlovian response was triggered, causing her to struggle against her bonds, adding new welts to the collection of old on her wrists.

The handcuffs that had replaced the zip ties were no-nonsense items. Smith and Wesson was stamped in the tempered American steel as was their place of origin—Springfield, Massachusetts.

Flat on her back with her arms cuffed high to the queen-sized headboard, she had been forced to listen to both the running water and, louder still, the grunts and groans and whimpers of a rape in progress filtering under the door from a room beyond. And sickening as the animalistic sounds and desperate female voices made her feel, they needed to be exploited. So with the noise from the ongoing attack rising to a crescendo, Jamie yanked with all of her might, trying to break a weld or compromise the curled ironwork.

Nothing.

Twenty grueling minutes passed as she fought her bonds while the assault next door continued. Finally, with the awful noises diminishing, she brought her knees to her chest, and in a last ditch effort, placed the balls of her feet against the curved horizontal top bar and extended her legs. Nothing budged except for the mattress and box springs under her. Crestfallen, she spat a few choice expletives and gave up fighting her predicament physically. Since the moment Logan and Gus had crumpled to the ground near her feet, everything seemed to be working against her.

But she was still alive.

Then her stomach growled, reminding her that she hadn't eaten anything substantial in two days. A bad thing. Weak malnourished people had no chance of escape. So she closed her eyes and, to conserve energy, focused on her breathing and visualized what she would do when the cuffs were removed. The war gaming and plotting and scheming didn't last long because five minutes into it she came to the conclusion that whatever she tried would probably do nothing more than sign her death warrant.

Two minutes after that epiphany she gave up mentally.

Sixty seconds later she was asleep and the footsteps outside the door went unnoticed.

Chapter 45

Twenty-two miles from the I-70 junction where State Route 191 passed over a tributary of the Green River, the landscape turned from dull brown to lush green and then almost instantly reverted back to the same ever-present depressing muted earth tones.

A stone's throw north of the crossing they came upon what Cade had guessed was once a bustling stop on the mostly desolate road, where, looking like nuked playground equipment, the shells of a dozen long-haul trucks sat atop acres of scorched concrete. The initial explosion, no doubt fed by the contents of huge underground tanks, had been of cataclysmic proportions. Pieces of the main building, where presumably a driver could find all manner of goods and services and other *off the books* experiences, had been blown to all points of the compass. Aluminum panels had reached the main road a hundred yards off. A carpet of glass pebbles encircling the shell of a building sparkled in the afternoon glare. After the explosion, the several-thousand-foot structure had burned to the ground completely, the only remaining distinguishable items: a pair of centrally located cube-shaped walk-in coolers. As a result of the blast, a number of the trailers had been knocked over and, along with whatever cargo they'd been hauling, had burned hot, leaving pools of molten metal, now hardened, glimmering in the sun. And to add insult to injury, like clumsy security personnel, a number of crispy Zs loitered near the sooty metal skeletons.

Clearly, the Double J truck stop had seen better days.

***

Two hours and fifty miles removed from the high desert killing fields, thankfully with all parties—especially Mom—none the wiser, Raven had recovered from her unavoidable *accident,* and was chattering on excitedly about anything and everything. After having everyone declare allegiance to their favorite pop stars—Cade's of which drew the most laughs—Raven went silent, seemingly content to just stare out the window.

Suppressing a grin, Brook looked at Cade, and said, "Michael Jackson ... *really?*" To which Raven, out of the blue and on a totally different conversational tangent said, "I think we need to name this truck." She cracked a water bottle and poured a slow steady stream onto Max's lapping tongue.

Grateful the topic had swung in a different direction, Cade humored her. "You called our Sequoia *the Big Silver Beast*, right?"

From the back seat Raven said, "Yes I did."

"How are you going to top that. *Big Black Beast* just doesn't have the same ring to it."

Brook chimed in. "*That* is not going to fly."

"How about Black Beauty?" proffered Raven.

"Taken," said Brook and Cade in unison.

"I don't care. Walt Disney is dead ... I'm using it."

Cade and Brook exchanged looks learned in the trenches called parenting and understood only by them.

"Done," conceded Cade. He looked over his shoulder and met Raven's gaze. "B.B. for short ... OK?"

Before Raven could answer, Brook blurted, "Cade, look."

Hearing this, he shifted his gaze forward and immediately saw what Brook was seeing. A little more than a mile distant, the rolling landscape started to resemble the approach to the last river crossing, the scrub sharing space with green grasses and low-growing bushes. And a few hundred yards beyond the wanna-be-oasis, he recognized sun glinting from the windows of a myriad of structures and unmoving vehicles. With the two previous firefights fresh on his mind, he eased up on the throttle and tapped the brakes, quickly halving his speed from forty miles per hour down to twenty. Keeping his eyes forward and slowing more, Cade said, "Check the navigation system."

After turning the navigation system on, Brook checked her M4 for the third time in an hour and finished her ritual by patting the extra magazines bulging her cargo pockets. Thirty seconds later, the device in the dash had shaken hands with whatever GPS satellite was providing it the info and had refreshed to show the squiggle representing S.R. 191 as well as a trio of town names stacked diagonally, ascending stair-like right to left—Wellington at the bottom, Price dead center, and then, at the top left corner of the screen, the smaller of the three, a town called Helper. All total, judging by the speed the pixelated blip representing the F-650 was moving along the State Route, Cade guessed that no more than twenty miles separated the largest concentration of lost civilization he'd seen up close in a long while.

Simultaneously, awakened from her slumber, the computerized female voice said, "*Wellington, one mile*," and on the right a sign demarking the city limits and bearing the same name with the population noted below in reflective numbers slid by.

Brook whispered, "Sixteen hundred and seventy-six souls."

"And hopefully they're all dead and have shuffled off into the sunset by now."

Grabbing the binoculars off the floor, Brook said, "Not likely. Stop here and I'll take a look."

He pulled hard to the shoulder, leaving the rig angled a few degrees left with its front tires straddling the centerline. After watching Taryn bring the Raptor to a halt a couple of truck lengths behind, Cade flicked his eyes from the rearview and asked, "What do you see?"

"Just some Zs. Nothing else."

"Nothing moving?"

"Nope. Just broken-down cars. This road runs through the middle of them all."

Cade flipped a coin in his head. Not the ideal way to make a decision considering Green River. But those folks had come from Salt Lake and Grand Junction. And it seemed to him that the ones who got out of the cities usually did so by any means necessary. Consequently, most of the survivors they'd encountered up until now came with bags packed full of bad intentions. But with Wellington, his gut was telling him something different. Using the two-way, he told Wilson that Main Street looked navigable, but the same rules that had gotten them through their previous scrapes still applied. Then he finished with a pop quiz and asked them what the most important rule of the road was.

Inside the Raptor, Sasha's mouth moved but nothing useful emerged.

Wilson looked at Taryn and shook his head. Mouthed, "We're not stupid." He keyed the radio and answered deadpan, "Don't stop for anything."

"Correct," said Cade, accelerating the Black Beauty briskly towards Wellington.

***

There was no ambush waiting for them in Wellington. Twenty blocks worth of seemingly deserted downtown were sandwiched between open fields, a smattering of quiet darkened houses, and vast tracts of land with nothing more than dirt clods and tumbleweeds to look at. They nearly doubled the posted limit blowing through every intersection—stop sign, or no—in the downtown core.

Consulting the navigation unit, Brook said, "We're in luck. We've got two choices ... stay on this and run the gauntlet through the next two towns. Or go left and take something called the Six Bypass and skirt them altogether."

"No brainer," said Cade. "Say when."

"Coming up," said Brook. "Six shoots off to the left. Looks like an overpass will take us over some train tracks—" She looked up from the GPS display and suddenly went quiet.

Muscles tensed, Cade jammed on the brakes.

The F-650's tires juddered and bounced on the blacktop momentarily and then the springs and shocks compressed under the rig's mass and a full one-thirty-second of an inch worth of rubber was laid down in the form of four smoking hundred-foot-long black streaks.

Worried that they were about to receive a vicious rear-ending, the lesser of the two evils considering that less than two hundred yards ahead, fully blocking the bypass and moving in their direction, was a full blown horde, Cade tightened his grip on the wheel and said, "Brace yourselves."

But Taryn had been alert. Looking several car lengths ahead as her father had taught her. Hands at the proper ten-and-two. Ready to heel-and-toe the pedals. And she did exactly that. However, she didn't lock them up. Instead, exhibiting an awesome display of controlled driving, she slewed her ride around the black rig even before it had ceased all forward movement. Finessing the pedals, she braked hard and hauled the wheel right, leaving four smoking black marks on the roadway before stopping broadside to the moving mass of death. Then, reacting with a sense of urgency only a phalanx of gnashing teeth and swiping nails could impart, she pinned the accelerator to the floor, held the wheel locked over and powered the Raptor's tail end around and into the front row, starting a domino-like chain reaction that sent dozens of them pin balling off of each other before succumbing to the inevitable and falling hard and vertically to the hot roadway. As the oversized bumper and boxy rear panels scythed through the second echelon of flesh eaters, the rear tires found purchase and Taryn wheeled their gore-spattered ride away from the moving wall of decaying flesh.

"That was close, Cade Grayson," said Brook, stress evident in her wavering voice.

"Hand grenades and horseshoes," he replied, tires chirping as the truck leapt backwards and, in keeping with Newton's law, their heads jerked forward. He drove fast and wobbly one-handed while looking over his shoulder and, after about twenty yards, and with the Raptor closing fast, he whipped the wheel left and hit the brakes, executing a bootlegger's reverse that Special Agent Adam Cross would have been proud of. And as the world spun a one-eighty in front of Cade's face, he saw from the corner of his eye, Taryn behind the wheel of the white truck. That it wasn't fully engulfed by the dead as he had feared brought him a palpable sense of relief. Finally feeling the inertia bleed off and the truck get light on the springs, he slammed the shifter into Drive, released the brake and sped south towards the off-ramp and a rendezvous with downtown Price, Utah.

Chapter 46

Though their small two-truck convoy had sped through the previous town unscathed, Cade attributed it to how little commerce there was in Wellington: a Gas-n-Sip, a crusty tavern with plate windows full of unlit neon, and a couple of restaurants catering to various ethnicities was about it. But Price, a college town with a population of eight thousand before Omega swept through, was a different story entirely. The going was much slower—they trudged along, barely able to make half the posted speed limit. The streets were patrolled by roving groups of flesh eaters and littered with trash and bits and pieces of putrefied corpses. Every business lining yet another street named Main had been ransacked, most of the windows reduced to razor-edged shards that littered the sidewalks.

A few blocks in, Cade was beginning to think that taking their chances with the horde might have been the more sound decision. For on two different occasions he was forced to use the F-650's angular plate bumper and tremendous amounts of horsepower and torque and fuel to bull through the clusters of abandoned vehicles clogging the main drag.

Wilson's voice came through the radio. "How much more of this?"

Brook answered back, "A few more blocks and then one more smaller town is all." She shifted her gaze right down a side street and spied a throng of Zs easily numbering over a hundred. She keyed the radio and went on, "Company on the right ... do not stop."

They slipped by the dead and a block later, near the edge of the business district, Main Street jogged diagonally north by west and became a razor-straight stretch of two-lane called Carbonville Road. After transiting eight straight miles of two-lane unimpeded by dead or static vehicles, passing by houses and fields and lastly a sprawling out-of-place country club complete with a lush green golf course and driving range, they came upon a Y-juncture in the road where Cade jammed the Ford to a stop.

A sign planted equidistant at the fork indicated that the ramp to the left merged with Utah State Route 6. Below that useful piece of information was an arrow pointing right towards the city of *Helper, population 2000.*

Cade let the truck roll forward and merged left. A tick later the voice in the box said: *Helper, one mile.*

A name that meant nothing to Cade or Brook, but nonetheless, upon hearing it pronounced in robotic syntax through the truck's speakers, the two-syllable word made Raven think of hamburger, and the two words, helper and hamburger, when combined and transposed brought to mind the talking white glove from the television commercials . Then, unable to resist the urge, she began to sing the inane jingle in a high falsetto. And as Cade negotiated the onramp and wheeled the Ford onto what he hoped would end up being a zombie-free stretch of interstate bypassing Helper, the source of his daughter's amusement, he depressed the Motorola's talk button and succeeded in infecting the heads of the kids in the Raptor with the poorly sung but commonly known ditty.

The bypass was relatively free of vehicles and walking dead and once Helper proper was behind them and the State Route had merged back onto 191, yet another country club with driving range and clubhouse all ringed by a vast empty parking lot slid by on the left. *No better time than the apocalypse to play a round*, thought Cade darkly. No groups wanting to play through. No marshals tooling the fairways looking for rules to enforce. And best of all, no one keeping count of his Mulligans. But sadly that fantasy evaporated when he noticed, with no greenskeepers to combat the desert climate, just how ratty and brown the fairways and greens of these links had become. There wasn't a single cart burdened by overstuffed bags and overweight golfers traversing the course. There were no beer girls maneuvering their carts against the grain in search of thirsty customers and the possibility of cash tips. Like the world and most of her population, this golf course was history.

Glancing in the mirror, Cade saw that Raven had her head buried in Taryn's iPhone again and was busy scrolling through the music. He looked over her head and saw the Raptor still keeping pace. Finally he let his gaze skim over the navigation system, prompting him to say to Brook, "Looks like the road splits up ahead."

She zoomed in one stop and replied, "U.S. Route Six goes off west to Salt Lake. This road we're on curls to the right past those ..."

Casting a shadow over the juncture, a coal processing plant loomed on the right. Two hundred yards beyond the towering machinery and idle conveyor belts and rust-streaked hoppers and silos was an impressive mountain of already processed coal. Seemingly sucking up every ray of sunshine, the black pyramid-shaped mound made the two trucks look like toys in comparison.

To their left was a sobering and contrasting sight that explained where the majority of Helpers' population had ended up. Stacked seven or eight deep and twenty across and stretching at least a block, the faces of dead Americans staring out of the tangle of death spoke to the harsh measures undertaken by the National Guard early on during the outbreak. The bullet-riddled bodies of infected mothers and fathers and kids and grandparents, all having been put down after the body bags had run out, had suffered greatly from scavengers and exposure to the elements.

With Raven still distracted by the device and humming away none the wiser, the F-650 and the Raptor crept by the drift of death, thumped over a set of railroad tracks and came to a complete stop, side-by-side, at yet another 'Y' in the road, where, erected in the shadow of the coal plant at the point of divergence, yet another road sign presented them with two options. After a short deliberation, eschewing the left fork that would take them straight through the heart of Salt Lake City one hundred and seven miles distant, Cade opted to suffer a few added miles and the associated time delay and backtrack slightly on US-6 and then pass through Duchesne, a town the navigation unit said was forty-six miles away north by east. After which they would stay to UT-35 and chase the GPS coordinates through a handful of small towns east of the Wasatch front to their ultimate destination a hundred and thirty-seven miles north by west near Eden, Utah. There, at the end of the proverbial rainbow, hopefully, they would find their pot of gold in the form of a fortified compound and rendezvous with Duncan and Daymon before nightfall.

Chapter 47

Duncan left his new 4x4 parked near the compound's entrance. There was a resonant thunk when he let the tailgate hinge open and fall to the stops. He scooped up an armful of the weapons they had taken from the quarry and made his way to the hidden entrance.

After delivering a series of knocks in the agreed-upon order, metal grated against metal as someone worked the inner locking mechanism. *Thing needs another shot of WD-40*, Duncan thought as the door hinged open and Heidi greeted him with a smile. Stepping up, arms outstretched, she offered to lighten his load. "I got it," he replied. "These are going into the dry storage for now." He stood in the gloom for a second and then went on, "Any luck with the ham radio?"

She shook her head. "Nothing north. I tried all of the frequencies your brother had written down. Then I freelanced a little. Talked to a guy in Nevada. Big group of survivors from Salt Lake now calling some Naval Air Base home. I guess there are a couple of hundred Marines there as well. We could use something like that near here."

Visibly bowing under the weight of the weapons, Duncan nodded and moved sideways past her and through the narrow passage. He looked over his shoulder and called, "I've got news too. We'll have to catch up as a group a little later. Thanks for lettin' me in."

"Me too," said Daymon as he stepped over the threshold, thick locks of braided hair swishing pendulum-like in front of his face. Also weighted down by an armload of long guns, he paused in front of his lady and leaned in, puckered lips parting the veil of dreads.

After pinning the unruly do behind his ears for him, she kissed him, smiled and said, "You need a hat to control that nest, my little Sherpa. Now carry on."

With Daymon hot on his heels, Duncan navigated the labyrinth and bent at the knees in front of the pantry/dry storage and placed his load on the plywood floor. Then he relieved Daymon of the half-dozen rifles he was carrying. "I'll store these," he said. "Why don't you go and get another load."

"Good call, Boss," Daymon said. "I might be a minute though. Gonna get a little more drive-by lip lock."

Duncan made no reply.

"You OK?"

Again, Duncan said nothing.

Trying to lighten the mood, Daymon said, "What was I thinking? This isn't your first rodeo. Been there, done that, right? And I do believe that you've got a Zippo older than me."

Still, Duncan remained stoic, tight-lipped, as if he were wrestling with some kind of monumental decision.

Sensing this, Daymon said, "Don't renege on your promise. Everyone needs to know what we're gonna be facing down the road."

Duncan nodded. Scooped a rifle off the floor and stepped into the darkened room. There was a flare of light as he pulled the chain dangling from the lone bulb. Squinting, he propped the rifle against a stack of five-gallon buckets. He looked at the doorway and Daymon had already gone, his footsteps faint. Receding. Then the echoes died away and Duncan found himself alone—physically and spiritually.

The voice in his head piped up a millisecond later. Deriding. Condescending. Telling him he was a failure. Telling him he'd killed Logan through negligence and dereliction of brotherly duty. He listened hard. Succumbed to the voice that seemingly had taken a contract out on his ass. The voice that wanted him dead.

It was right where he'd stowed it the day before. Insurance. His gateway to oblivion. His fingers curled around the slender familiar neck. He hefted the sack with his right and pulled the smooth vessel free with his left. Breaking the paper seal produced a brittle tearing sound, like a newly struck match igniting. *Appropriate*, he thought. *'Cause I'm about to start a fire that all the water in the quarry couldn't extinguish.*

The cap spun off smoothly. Hand shaking, he lifted the square bottle to his lips. Going down, Old No. 7 never tasted better. "To you, Oops," he said between gulps. After one last long pull of the amber liquid—during which he fulfilled his earlier promise to himself by producing a long string of roiling bubbles— he reversed the ritualistic process, spun the cap on slowly and secreted the bottle on a top shelf where it would be out of sight yet easily accessible.

Chapter 48

No matter how Jamie positioned herself on the bed or which particular wrist she chose to support her weight, she couldn't quell the dull ache deep down inside her rotator cuffs. And no matter how close she scooted to the headboard, there was no stopping the constant throbbing in her deltoids.

Entirely by design, in order to strain her muscles and stretch ligaments and hobble her, Carson had returned with two more pairs of handcuffs and had left her spread-eagled, one on each ankle secured to the footboard with lengths of nylon rope. Then he'd repositioned the handcuffs attached to her wrists higher up on the headboard, leaving her very little room for lateral movement. Finally, unable to sit on her butt and reclining flat an impossibility, she realized that the pseudo-crucified position she was being forced to endure was meant to hobble her not only physically but mentally as well. To send a message. To say: *We own you. Get used to it.* And it was working—on both accounts.

She craned her head and saw how the sunlight was now angling in off the lake from the left and illuminating the wall to her right. It told her that the sun was falling away past meridian and that west was to her left. And if everything she had been taught about the directions on the compass still held true, her feet were pointing north and the mouthwatering aroma hitting her nose was wafting under the door from the south, presumably a kitchen somewhere downstairs. And she also knew from past experience that where people cooked they also stored knives and cleavers and meat-tenderizing mallets—all high on her must-have-to-escape wish list. *Hell*, she thought. *A wine bottle would do*. Going out swinging was also high on that list. The opportunity presented to her in the helicopter had been fleeting. In hindsight she should have done it there and then. Risked everything. Gone down with the ship, so to speak.

But her mom had always said: *Good things come to those who wait.* And Mom had been right. The good thing finally did come to her—his name was Logan. And then the animal named Carson had killed him.

She drifted into a fantasy in which she was the captor and Carson the trussed captive. And she had the knife—a ten-inch single-tang item. Razor sharp. Folded metal. Tempered. She was sharpening it, the steady clatter of metal against metal comforting because she knew that to skin a man one needed a finely honed tool. The first nick drew blood. The second pass curled, scroll-like, an inches-long graft of dermis—along with it a number of veins and capillaries. Blood was spritzing on her face. Aerated droplets at first. Then a pulsing fan, hot and crimson.

But before she got to watch him die, her eyes fluttered open and she was back to being trussed and utterly helpless.

Carson hovered over her, holding a cup in one hand and in the other a half-dozen articles of ladies clothing. He said, "You were in deep REM sleep. Your eyes were going like crazy behind the lids. Creepy as hell. Had to splash you with water to wake you. Still thirsty?"

Wishing their roles really had been reversed, Jamie answered groggily, "Yes ... and I'm starving."

"Ever been to northern Africa?"

She shook her head side to side on a horizontal plane.

"You don't know starving then." Carson grinned and threw the clothing on the foot of the bed. Produced the keys to the cuffs from a pocket and started with her left foot. He paused and shot her an icy glare. He said slowly and menacingly, "You try anything and I'll strangle you to unconsciousness, then fuck you ten ways from Sunday. Then I'll throw more water on your face and wake you up and *wash, rinse and repeat* until you beg me to kill you. Then I'll oblige you. But only after you beg. *Or ...* " He let the word hang in the air.

Jamie, wide awake now, swallowed hard. She saw the boxy pistol holstered on his hip. She saw the keys pinched between his fingers.

After a long dramatic pause, Carson went on, "*Or* you can choose a nice outfit from that pile of girlie clothes there. I'll get you a washcloth so you can clean up a bit ... and then you doll yourself up a little and we'll go downstairs and you play nice and break bread with my friend. He's real nice. Tall. Dark. Some say handsome. I'm not one to judge."

She made no reply. Just stared at him trying to determine if she had enough fight in her to opt for the former. After a second spent assessing her injuries and deciding that fighting the good fight would have to wait, she nodded subtly.

"I'm no mind reader. Which will it be," he said behind a wolfish grin.

In her mind, she saw herself walking down the hall past the door to the room where something evil had happened a short while ago. Then taking the stairs down and turning a left, where her true fate would be revealed when she emerged into presumably an open living room with every available seat occupied by drooling men with bad intentions, all wearing the same disconcerting look as Carson. She threw an involuntary shudder, composed herself somewhat and lied through her teeth. "I'd love to meet him."

Chapter 49

The small group of survivors covered thirty-seven miles of State highway labeled *Indian Canyon Scenic Byway* between Helper and Duchesne in just under an hour, stopping once to top off their tanks at a quiet roadside turnout near the thirty-mile marker.

Circumventing the sage-covered natural basalt benches rising south and west of Duchesne, the State highway jogged right and the city was dead ahead. The two-truck convoy slowed, then, following the directions in their navigation units, turned right and then swung the mandated left onto Center Street North which cut the downtown core for a handful of blocks before crossing over yet another Main Street—the third so far, if Cade's memory served.

He thought about reissuing his previous warnings to the kids in the Raptor but quickly deemed it unnecessary considering what he was seeing. Duchesne City, *Gateway to the Uintah Basin* as the sign on the roadside had proclaimed, looked more post-nuclear-disaster downtown Chernobyl than a gateway to anything. A majority of the storefronts were boarded up. Some bore spray-painted apologies for closing during trying times. Most had short missives scrawled in paint warning of dead barricaded inside. Scores more were just the ventings of people pissed off at the bad cards the town had been dealt. '*Why us God?*' could be seen on more than one vertical sheet of plywood. There were also a couple of businesses papered with warnings stating: '*Looters will be shot on sight,*' which to Cade seemed highly likely considering the proliferation of firearms in most of the western states and consequently a bit odd considering all that he knew about human nature and how tight-knit most of rural America had been before the shit hit the fan.

Out of the blue, Brook said, "Kind of strange how quiet it is."

Scanning the streets and rooftops a block in advance, Cade replied, "Certainly beats the alternative." He cast his gaze down a side street and spotted a clutch of hollow-eyed first turns staggering towards him. And out of the corner of his eye he saw their prey, a scrawny feral dog, bolt whippet-like from beneath one parked car to the safety of the next. As the scene slipped from view, Cade was struck by how quickly Duchesne had become a ghost town at the hands of a little manmade virus.

After bisecting the idled city, Center Street curled left and cut a serpentine path through a greenbelt paralleling the dogwood-lined Strawberry River. The two-lane continued onward for six miles, passing by turn-of-the-century homes with rocking-chair-porches and large working fields before finally merging with Utah 35 at its easternmost terminus.

They drove on for an hour, the road numbers and distances blending together until finally forty miles north and west of Duchesne, like the fabled Bat Phone, Cade's sixth sense started ringing off the hook. Easing the Ford to the curb, he asked Brook to hand over the binoculars. With his internal voice telling him he'd been here before and his gut screaming *turn around,* he pressed the Bushnell's to his face and worked its center ring. The lush green valley spread out before him sprang into sharp focus. He started panning from right-to-left. Bordered by red earthen foothills, rectangular tracts of land in various sizes meandered diagonally for a couple of miles before the low mountains in the background closed in, creating a chokepoint in the distance where the ribbon of gray disappeared into the low forest. Cade heard the hum of tires on asphalt and then the rumble of the Raptor's engine as it sidled to a stop a foot to his left. Then the inevitable. The sound of a window whirring down followed by a, "What's up?"

Keeping his attention glued to the foreground, Cade answered, "I just wanted to look before leaping. That's all." He let the field glasses rest on their lanyard. With Brook watching him closely, he hit a couple of buttons on the navigation unit and zoomed in until nearly the same scene to the fore, only filmed by a satellite sometime in the past, was now displayed in full on the LCD screen. The lay of the land was identical. The fields were fallow, meaning that presumably the image had been captured in the fall or early winter. And the way the image was filling the screen told him nothing he didn't already know from the thirty second recon. He felt Brook's hand on his, and then sensed Raven's presence over his right shoulder. Brook manipulated the controls and the image zoomed out, showing the last city they had passed through and revealing the next one straddling the rural State Route. Then Raven, possessing arguably the best eyesight in the family, read the next town's name out loud. "Hanna," she called out. "Nice name for a town. Maybe we can stop there and stretch our legs ... let Max do his business."

Brook's head panned left ever so slowly as if she didn't want to know what kind of effect, if any, the revelation had on Cade. When her gaze finally met his, what she saw in his eyes put her at ease.

Though there was a cold ball forming in his gut, Cade remained stoic. Pushing the welling anxiety back in its box, he shrugged his shoulders nonchalantly and cast a sidelong glance at Brook. "There's no future in dwelling on the past." Then glanced over his shoulder at Raven and added, "Just because we haven't encountered many Zs since the horde near Price doesn't mean Hanna will be quiet."

"Can we stop if it is?" pressed Raven.

Massaging his temples, Cade replied, "I'll take it under advisement."

Which to Raven was Dad code for '*no,*' but stated in a manner meant to give her a little bit of hope. So she pressed harder, "Please, Dad. I think I need to go again."

"Really?" he said nonplussed. "Can't you go here?"

She said, "In the wide open, Dad? Out here in front of *everyone*?"

Then, remembering her accident near Green River, he changed his tone and added, "Only if it's safe." He looked down at Wilson in the Raptor and shrugged. Then went on and described to Wilson and Taryn as much as he could remember about the little town.

With a range of emotions stemming from what he'd gone through in the farmhouse attic with Daymon and the lawyer surging through his body, Cade rattled the shifter into Drive and set a course towards what he hoped might be a little closure.

Chapter 50

The little valley before the town of Hanna appeared to be deserted. And like in the movie *The Day the Earth Stood Still*, after the spaceship landed and the giant robot deployed, nothing down there moved for as far as Cade could see. Then suddenly a light breeze picked up and rustled what he guessed to be fields of alfalfa, creating a hypnotic waving motion that reminded him at once of the picket of aspens quaking under a fierce rotor wash, his fleeting final memory of Hanna as he escaped certain death and climbed aboard the hovering Black Hawk.

Built up alongside the State Route were hardy country homes sitting back on oversized plots of land. The yards were full of rusty farm implements and here and there they passed a hand-painted sign staked in front of a drive offering up for sale corded firewood or baled hay or freshly laid eggs by the dozen. All the kinds of things that used to be make the world go round for the folks in this neck of the woods. But unfortunately that world stopped going around when Hanna's self-sufficient economy fell to the dead weeks ago. Of this Cade was certain. He didn't need to see as proof the dead feeding on a cow carcass or the multitude of homes with darkened windows and empty clotheslines. For he had already seen dozens of the town's undead citizenry with his own eyes. Nearly half of the total population of one hundred and seventy souls had converged around that farmhouse on the hill. And in the end, after the helo had plucked him and Daymon off of the roof, Duncan claimed to have seen many more streaming in from the very road spooling out behind the Ford.

After the short climb up the far side of the valley, Cade came to find that there really was no downtown Hanna. Two and a half weeks ago he had entered from the north; at the time he had assumed the business district lay to the south. But he had been mistaken. They passed by the shotgun-style house where he'd found the Winnebago, keys and mushy brakes and all—the trio's would-be escape vehicle. A few more long country blocks down the road he saw off to the right the driveway with the aspens partially shielding the two-story farmhouse. He slowed the Ford to walking-speed and crept past the wall of trees, details of the house becoming visible by degrees. First he saw the mildew-streaked rear-end of the RV that was still wedged firmly under the left corner of the wraparound porch, the improvised escape hatch he'd fashioned with a number of rounds from his rifle still hinged up on the roof. He counted the half a dozen Z corpses decomposing on the lawn and walk where he'd felled them silently with the Gerber. Then he craned his head nearer to Brook and cast his gaze at the roof, where on the south side he recognized the flap of roofing material they were forced to saw through in order to effect their escape. A chill traced his spine and his eyes narrowed when the whole picture came together and he realized how close he had come to buying it right here.

Seeing Cade's gaze lock on the house and a second later his face harden and his brow furrow, Brook placed her palm against his cheek and asked, "You going to be OK, Cade Grayson?" And though she only knew the basics of how he got in and out of the house, upon seeing it up close she could tell that he had purposefully left a few of the major details unsaid.

"Yeah. I'm just now processing all of it for the first time. Seeing it from this perspective ... and after the fact, is a little strange. That's all." Then to change the subject, he twisted around and removed one of the buds from Raven's ear and said loudly, "You think we should stop here so Raven can pee?"

Brook winked at him. Said, "Yeah. And let Max out ... then we can all stretch a little bit too."

Back to eyeing the house, Cade said, "Done." He pulled over and stopped across the driveway. He looked past Brook and noticed a sliver of Daymon's BLM-green suburban sticking out from behind the house. In his mind he saw the special-ops motorcycle that Beeson had given him before he left Camp Williams so full of hope and fear, his only mission to find his family. It had to be back there, he told himself. Probably still propped up next to the Chevy, saddlebags full of gear, right where he had left it.

And that thought led to an idea.

Brook asked, "Who's going to clear the area?"

Cade smiled, "Great minds, honey. Great minds." He popped a handful of ibuprofen sans water and grabbed the two-way, then cracked his door. A tick later the Raptor rolled by and, with the sound of gravel crunching under its tires, parked on the shoulder just past the driveway.

Cade climbed out of Black Beauty and tested his weight on the ankle which seemed to be feeling better with each passing hour. Then he noticed the temperature had dropped at least twenty degrees. It was almost tolerable now. About eighty, he guesstimated. He hiked his sleeves up and checked the time on his Suunto. Twenty-four hours to go. *No sweat.* Before going anywhere, he scanned the State road in both directions. There was nothing to see there so he walked across the road and listened hard. Other than the soft idles of the distant engines, there was nothing to hear. None of the telltale moaning or raspy hissing to indicate the dead were on to them. Like Duchesne, Hanna looked to be a ghost town. *Hell,* he thought. *The whole world was becoming one big ghost town.*

Wilson and Taryn approached him, walking cautiously, heads on a swivel, eyeballing every blind corner. Brook had done well with the kids while he was out. He noticed that they both were carrying a bottled water and eating something from an olive drab wrapper, most likely straight out of an MRE.

With gravel squelching underneath her boots, Brook rounded the front of the Ford and greeted Wilson and his '*driver*' with a half-smile and a hug.

"Gotta rub it in, huh? I'm never going to drive that thing." Wilson looked at Taryn and gave her shoulder a playful nudge.

She smiled but made no reply.

"Someone's got to keep up the pressure." Brook's lips became a thin white line and, still reeling internally from the Green River shootout, she lowered her voice and asked, "How are you two doing after the encounter back there?"

Wilson said, "Which encounter? There were half a dozen, seemed like."

"The road above Green River."

Wilson looked away. Went silent for a moment, then said, "Like I told Sash and Tee. We did what we had to in order to survive. No telling whose bullets did them in. No sense worrying over it neither."

Eyes welling with tears, Taryn looked at Brook, then Wilson, and turned away.

Changing the subject, Brook asked, "How's the cheek?" But before Wilson could answer, the F6-50's rear door swung open and Max bounded to the pavement and charged over to Cade where he sat at his feet, stubby tail thumping furiously.

"Go ahead, boy," said Cade.

Wasting no time, Max shot off like a furry rocket in the direction of the aspens.

Seeing Raven clamber from the truck, Cade motioned her over. He slipped his backup Glock from the shoulder holster, checked the chamber, and handed it to her butt first. "It's loaded. Keep the muzzle pointed towards the ground until ... " After taking the compact pistol from him, Raven finished his sentence. "Until I'm ready to use it. Keep my finger off the trigger—which happens to be where the safety is located—until I'm ready to engage the threat."

Cade arched a brow, looked at Brook and delivered a covert wink. Shifting his gaze back to Raven, he said, "Mom sure has you dialed in. How about we go and see what Max is up to?" He bent down to Raven's height and whispered in her ear, "And while we're at it, find us a real toilet." He hauled the Glock 17 from its holster and with a quick twist attached the suppressor to its business end.

Brook grabbed his attention. She asked, "Do you have a radio?"

Cade patted a cargo pocket and said, "Roger that," then put his arm around Raven's shoulder and steered her towards the wrecked RV.

Chapter 51

Carson freed her legs first. She was certain, judging by the scratches on his face and the way he let his rough hands linger on her calves and ankles, that when the cuffs came off, deep down he wanted her to get out of line so he could follow through with his earlier threat.

His upper body hovered near as he worked the key in the cuffs. He freed her left hand first. As her hand fell limply to the bed, Jamie flicked her gaze up to the side of his neck where she could see the subtle blue line of his carotid, or jugular, she wasn't quite sure which, snaking its way vertically from collarbone to ear just underneath the skin. She parted her teeth and prayed for him to get complacent. To lean across her body in order to reach the other cuff and provide her the one opportunity she had been waiting for.

But Carson was no dummy. He finished with her left and walked around the bed and repeated the process on her right. Then, without a word, and never once taking his eyes off of her, he made her pick a dress from the pile and then ushered her towards the adjoining bathroom.

She saw him in the hall mirror, back to an interior wall, watching her undress. She peeled off her cotton fatigue pants and shrugged out of her blood-stained tee-shirt. Standing there in bra and panties, she could feel his eyes on her. Gathering up her courage, she looked at his reflection and saw that he was watching her intently. However, due to his body language and where he parked his eyes, she could tell that he wasn't doing it just for jollies. He seemed to be focusing on her hands more than anything. Making sure she didn't surreptitiously sneak a nail file, or a pair of nail clippers or anything else that she could use as a makeshift weapon. He was a professional. That much was clear. And if the man she was about to meet instilled enough fear or respect or perhaps a healthy dose of both in him to keep him on his toes, then she was pretty certain that for her to make it out of the house alive she would be needing much more than a random mani-pedi tool or sharp piece of kitchen cutlery. She sighed. Right about now her glass was half-empty, the waterline steadily receding.

Meeting his eyes in the mirror, she asked, "How does this look?"

He said nothing.

"It's kind of seventies chic, don't you think? Your friend going to like it?"

He made no reply. Arms crossed, he simply nodded towards the door.

The number she'd chosen for the big date was low cut, contained less material than a Scottish kilt, and fell across her thighs even higher. Due to the sheer nature of the fabric, something manmade, rayon or nylon she guessed, the thing threatened to reveal her feminine grooming habits with even the slightest movement.

A lifelong tomboy, jeans and tee-shirts were more in her wheelhouse than the form-fitting leggings and skorts favored by other girls. Including the one wedding she had endured as a bridesmaid, she could count on one hand the number of times she had ever donned a dress. Though she didn't let it show, up to this point in her life she had never worn an article of clothing that caused her skin to crawl more so than this throwback to the disco era.

Time to go 'all in,' she thought. Then, with Carson still watching, she reached back and unhooked her bra and shrugged it off and let it fall to the tile floor. She adjusted the top of the skanky burnt-orange dress so that a good amount of cleavage showed. Then she stepped out of her panties, kicked them away and looked in the mirror while thinking, *What's the point?* At best, the no-frills cotton articles were only going to prolong the inevitable. At worst, one of them would provide the mystery man a perfect ligature.

***

The tuxedo was on the back wall of the walk-in-closet, zippered inside a vinyl bag containing all of the necessary accoutrements: bow tie, cummerbund, dickey, and shoes. Like the jogging clothes, the formal wear was a couple sizes too small. He buttoned up the white shirt as far as possible, leaving the top two open and the seventeen-inch collar parted. From a jewelry box he took a pair of gold cufflinks and secured the starched cuffs. Then he laid down flat on the bed and zipped and buttoned the high-water slacks.

The necktie took him three tries to make presentable.

Grimacing, he squeezed the patent leather shoes on and laced them loosely.

He stepped across the master bedroom and stopped in front of the floor-to-ceiling mirror and checked his work. Service dress white uniform this was not. Judging by the recent pictures of the lake home's former owners, both well into their fifties, both packing around the extra weight accrued from half a lifetime of eating without thought of the consequences, and judging by the white ruffles and powder blue color, he guessed the era of the suit to be late seventies or early eighties. He did the math and realized that he had been a kid when the tailor made the tux for its former owner who at the time was likely in his twenties.

With a bass heavy Bee Gees track looping through his head, he adjusted the tie, turned and walked stiffly towards the door. He closed the door behind and drifted down the hall, borrowed shoes squelching against the carpet. From behind the mystery door he could hear voices. Continuing on past Elvis's room he heard a male voice filtering through the door. Then there was loud snoring followed by silence and a tick later the voice started back up. It was unintelligible but the inflection was unmistakable—urgent and demanding. Then the snoring kicked back in.

Figuring Elvis was in the throes of one hell of a nightmare, Bishop ignored the commotion and continued on downstairs. He had been there. In fact, the undead visited him every night in the form of ultra-realistic nightmares that always started with him supine and holding a pistol with no ammunition. Then like Groundhog Day, minus Sonny and Cher's opening track, the sneering faces of the dead descended on him, their cold hands clutching and tearing. Lastly, he would be out of body and watching as clawlike blood-stained hands rent steaming entrails from his abdomen. The recurring frequency and vividness of the images were taking a toll on him. Making him believe that somehow he was seeing his true fate played out every time he closed his eyes.

Born out of times of stress, he'd suffered before from similar nightmares. Only in those it hadn't been the hands of the dead literally ripping out his guts. It had been a figurative disembowelment during which his entire SEAL team was decimated by the Taliban because they had been forced to follow ridiculous rules of engagement foisted upon them by politicians who only set foot on the Godforsaken soil for a photo-op to add a sort of unearned street-cred to their own personal dossiers. But everything happened for a reason. Cause and effect. And his constant bending of those inane rules of engagement, the worst being don't shoot until you're fired upon, was seen as insubordination in some circles and eventually led to his ouster from the teams. A life event that left him rudderless and open to accepting Robert Christian's financial aid.

While the recent nightmares had yet to come true, he feared that the former had. He hadn't heard from his brothers who were still on active duty since before the outbreak. He feared that the same ROE-instituting politicians who were responsible for keeping the population in the dark and holding back the full might of the military early on in the outbreak had in effect once again tied their hands and then thrown them to the wolves. Lambs to the slaughter.

Sure, the odds against success were stacked mightily on the side of failure. Enough to make an ordinary man give up and '*ring the bell.*' But there wasn't a quitter's bone in Ian Bishop's body ... he never would have completed BUDs in Coronado a decade ago if there had been. So for now he was content to wear down the dead through attrition. Elvis's mission tomorrow would be the first blow towards ridding the United States of the only thing he feared. And if he used the rest of the devices to their full potential—placing them near the highest concentrations of the dead—the odds would begin shifting fast in his favor. He didn't care to save mankind or get back at the politicians and cry baby PC crowd who'd tried to micro manage his job over there. Nope, he just wanted to take out as many of the walking flesh bags as possible. And if he couldn't do it in his lifetime, then he wanted to make sure and leave an heir behind who could finish the job he'd started.

Leaving the seat with a view for his date, he pulled out the chair opposite and sat with his back to the lake. He poured the 1997 Silver Oak Cabernet that Carson had selected from the cellar. Noting the shiny label, he understood why his number two man had chosen it. The selection had nothing to do with vintage, or terroir or varietal. Simply put, the silver leaf embossed label screamed *pick me*. Being a beer man himself, Bishop was the farthest thing from a sommelier. He corralled the pair of crystal Boudreaux glasses Carson had also set out on the table and filled both of them to near overflowing, then carefully moved hers back to its proper place.

Satisfied with the arrangement and feeling and looking—on account of the dated attire—like a kid on a prom date, he put his hands on his lap near where he had duct taped a compact .38 caliber snub-nose pistol to the underside of the table and eyed the two rapidly cooling plates of meatless spaghetti.

Chapter 52

After checking underneath the Winnebago and finding nothing dangerous, Cade put an ear to the detritus-smeared aluminum skin just behind the driver's seat. Nothing stirring. He looked at Raven who was still holding her weapon correctly, finger braced on the trigger guard. He mouthed, "Ready?" After receiving a nod to the affirmative he made a fist and thumped on the side of the RV. Three sonorous blows. They waited a second and, upon hearing no response from within, crept past and moved along the left side of the farmhouse.

Holding his free hand up, fingers splayed, Cade met Raven's eyes and made a fist. Seeing his diminutive twelve-year-old respond instantly and freeze in place, eyes searching for the perceived threat, made Cade want to run back out front and give Brook a high-five *and* a big wet sloppy kiss. But school was still in session. He pointed to his eyes, two fingers in a 'V.' He then motioned with the same two fingers toward the far side of the inert Suburban where a pair of recent turns, low guttural moans emanating from their constantly working maws, marched in place, fighting a losing battle against a tangle of waist-high shrubs.

Raven's gaze followed her dad's gesture. She nodded subtly and remained motionless, waiting for instruction which came quickly in the form of one vertical finger pressed against his lips. She watched him creep nearer, knees bent, weapon outstretched. Her eyes went to the Zs. She saw them craning and leaning and stretching against the thick bushes, trying to see where the mechanical engine sounds were coming from. Then the dagger was in her dad's hand and he covered the final three feet at a trot.

Raven didn't look away. She forced herself to watch. Thankfully it was over swiftly and silently. Not a shot fired. Two short efficient jabs, the point of the knife piercing each creature through the eye socket, only a half second between each one's final death.

They filed by the rotten corpses, both of them hinged over the hedge as if in supplication—perhaps praying to remain dead.

A jumble of Daymon's firefighting gear was in the rear of the Suburban. On the front seat was a letter, previously folded three ways. Cade reached in the open window and snatched it by one curled-up corner. Saw that it was addressed to Heidi and, ignoring its content, promptly folded it and stuffed it into a cargo pocket for safekeeping. And hopefully future delivery.

He spun a slow one-eighty. Looked over Raven's head to check their rear.

Nothing.

He spun back around, slowly, eyes probing all points of the compass, listening hard. The truck's engines had been silenced. There were no discernable moans or rasps of the dead. No screams of the living. Nothing to hear but the aspen's soft rattle. *Things were good.*

Raven caught her dad's eye and pointed towards the desert tan dirt bike. Then a flash of recognition. The sum of two plus two fell into place and her brown eyes got wide as a knowing look fell upon her tanned face.

Cade saw that nothing was amiss. The saddle bags, though scarred from when he dropped the bike outside of Camp Williams, appeared to be sealed, protecting their contents from the elements. The bike represented one of the vague facts about his flight from Portland he'd previously disseminated to Raven. Unsubstantial, in and of itself. Nothing pointing to what went on inside the charnel house looming over them.

The bike could wait.

Raven's full bladder could not. That much had already been proven. And he had seen to it that the unfortunate result had been handled tactfully and with the utmost respect.

The back stairs led to a small porch. There was no hand rail so Cade motioned silently and had Raven wait on the first tread. Stepping only on the nail heads indicating where the under support and treads met, he scaled the seven stairs without making a sound. Bloody hand prints marred the shingles and wood casing to eye-level all around the back entry. There was more of the same and the door hung ajar and was creased vertically in the center, the victim of constant and certain pressure inflicted upon it by a couple of tons of determined dead weight.

Cade could see through the back window the damage the throng of Zs had inflicted on the kitchen table and chairs. Every piece was upended, their chromed legs bent and twisted at odd angles. More hand prints walked up and down the walls between the kitchen and long hallway leading to the destroyed front door. On the linoleum floor, two badly decomposed corpses lay among shards of broken china, their limbs intertwined, each harboring one of Daymon's arrows in an eye socket.

Repeating the dinner bell tactic he had used at the RV, Cade pounded on the windowless door. He waited and listened for a moment and heard only the sound of branches rubbing together coming through the open front door. The sound seemed to be bouncing around the expansive foyer before transiting the enclosed confines of the lengthy hall. Though the stench of decay was heavy in the house, nothing told him to turn back. His sixth sense was eerily quiet. So he brought Raven forward.

She nodded and scaled the stairs, then looked around the kitchen, mouth ajar, first taking in the destruction and then acknowledging the corpses. Finally, curiosity having gotten the better of her, she whispered, "What happened in here?"

"It's a long story," said Cade quietly. As she watched he went about the kitchen searching all of the drawers. He removed a couple of items from a far drawer and stuffed them in a pocket.

"What do you need those for?" she asked.

"For a friend," he answered. "Now follow me." He stepped over the fallen Zs, walked half a dozen feet down the hall and found a narrow door with a hole for a skeleton key. Sensitivities being a little different around the turn of the last century, residents had no problem with a toilet being so close to the kitchen. Plus, routing the plumbing with only one wall between the two was a win-win for architects and tradesmen alike.

He pushed the heavy door in with his right hand and side-stepped to his left, the hefty silencer keeping track with his gaze. "Clear," he stated. "Come on over, Bird. It's all yours."

With his back pressed to the wall across from the small first floor powder room, he peered up and marveled at the jumble of bedroom furniture and corpses clogging the stairway leading to the second floor. There were pale arms bent at strange angles reaching through the mess, some still twitching. The claw foot tub that he and the lawyer had worked so hard to uproot lay on its side where it had landed and crushed a pair of unfortunate flesh eaters.

As he waited for Raven to finish her business, the sound he had heard from the kitchen a moment prior was repeated. Only when he looked left through the empty windows framing the battered front door he saw the aspens were unmoving, their brittle leaves deathly quiet. He noticed Brook and Taryn standing near the Raptor engaged in conversation but couldn't hear a word across the distance.

A tick later the bathroom door creaked and swung inward and Raven rejoined him in the hall wearing a sour look on her face. She said, "No toilet paper," then put her hands on display and added, "Or water."

Cade said, "Sorry, sweetie. Beats squatting in the bushes or peeing yourself again." Regretting his choice of words, he passed the Glock back and with a nod towards the kitchen added, "Keep it pointed that way. I'll be right back."

With the business end of his suppressed Glock leading the way, Cade stepped over a handful of bullet-riddled corpses and then cut the corner around the baluster, keeping the front entry to his back. He swept his gaze right to the formal dining room where golden dust motes skipped between splashes of light. Speaking to the numbers of dead that had cornered them upstairs, the walnut table fit for eight had been shoved up against the far wall and around its periphery a mosaic of bloody footprints marked up every inch of a finely woven Persian rug. *It was a miracle*, he thought to himself, *that the house hadn't literally come apart at the seams.*

Then the subtle sound again. Almost like a barber running a straight razor slowly over a strap—back and forth and back and forth. Intrigued, Cade took two steps to his left, looked up, and saw a bloated gray face staring back at him from atop the mass of shattered joinery, and when eye contact was established its maw opened and once again the brittle rasp echoed about the open foyer.

He called down the hall. "Don't worry, it can't get us." Raven's reply caught him flat footed. Voice devoid of all emotion, she said, "Leave it then."

A breath caught in Cade's throat. He supposed he was expecting a little more empathy. But then again, she didn't know that the creature impaled on the picket of splintered balusters between floors used to be the man that he and Daymon had endured way too many grueling hours trapped upstairs in the hot attic with.

His name had been Hosford Preston the something or other. But Cade couldn't recall if he had actually declared a title other than attorney of law. And though Cade was no detective, how Hoss had come to be perforated diagonally through the abdomen by three wrist-thick wooden spindles was evident by the gaping hole in the ceiling directly overhead.

Stripped clean from the waist down, undead Hoss's lower body was harder to look at than his face. All that remained was a leather belt and shreds of fabric no longer resembling dress pants. There was a gaping cavity where his manhood had been, and from there on down, looking like a school of piranhas had gotten to them, all that was left of his tree-trunk-like legs was bare bone. One foot had gone missing, a rounded nub of bone and strips of opaque tendon where it used to be. Inexplicably, the other foot remained attached and still shod in a tightly laced leather wingtip.

Baffled by the fact that the lawyer's meaty head wasn't already home to a half dozen 9mm Parabellums, Cade aimed his Glock up the stairs and, before the thing could emit another hair-raising rasp, finished Daymon's job for him.

With the two spent casings still pinging across the foyer floor, he hustled down the hall, gathered Raven in one arm and ushered her from the charnel house the same way they had entered.

Now standing on the back porch, Raven screwed her face up and asked, "Who was it?"

"*Who* is not important," replied Cade. "The *it* part is what we need to remember. If me or Mom become an *it* you must not hesitate. Two to the head ... hear me? I just had to finish a job in there someone else couldn't."

"You did know *it* then."

Thinking through his answer, Cade led them down the stairs and to the motorcycle. He opened the saddle bag nearest him and looked up at Raven and said, "I knew *it* briefly." Which was as nice a way as he could think of putting it. He grabbed the single pair of goggle-like NVGs—night vision gear—and the bulging Ziploc filled with the spare batteries that went with them. He also scooped up the loose ammunition—5.56 for the Colt and 9mm for his Glock—as well as the spare magazines the armorer at Beeson's fallen command had been so kind in providing.

"If it happens," Raven said solemnly, "I think I can do it." She looked at the ground. Kicked at a pine cone, then looked him in the face. "If I *really* have to."

Handing a box of shells to her, Cade said, "I know you will." And he believed it. Had to. Because hope was all he had. All any of them really had. And the alternative—him or Brook turning and taking her with them—was unacceptable. There was no failsafe. So faith was going to have to do. He scooped up his Glock, rose from kneeling, and with one arm embracing his only child left the dirt-bike and Suburban and bad memories behind him.

Ignoring the pair of leaking corpses and following the sound of quiet conversation, they walked the drive and rejoined the others.

Chapter 53

Propping a pair of Daniel Defense M4 carbines against the door frame, Daymon said to Duncan, "That's the last of 'em."

Daymon turned to leave, then paused mid-stride and asked Duncan if he wanted to come along and hunt some game for dinner.

"I'll take a rain check," he replied. "I need some space and a little time to do some thinking ... so I can try and process all of this mess."

You mean you need to do a little more forgetting, thought Daymon darkly, as he picked up the smell of charcoal-filtered whisky coming off the older man's breath. But he didn't feel like arguing the point. There was still a lot of time before tomorrow for sobering up. And besides, what harm could he do to himself or others as long as he was only boozing it up inside the wire? So he let it go.

Duncan, hands shaking perceptibly, asked, "Anything else need to be stowed away?"

"Negative," replied Daymon. "Have you heard from the Sarge yet?"

"Haven't given it much thought," said Duncan truthfully. "He's got until tomorrow. He either shows up or he doesn't. Either way I'm going north."

"Where are you going to go?"

Duncan shrugged.

"I tried coaxing more details out of Tran this morning."

Duncan arched a brow.

Shaking his head from side-to-side, Daymon said, "No help."

"Heidi get anyone on the horn?"

Again, Daymon shook his head.

A string of expletives and another blast of alcohol-laced breath burst from Duncan's mouth. Then he reared back and put the boot to a plastic bucket filled with five gallons of rice, sending the lid and at least two gallons worth of the dietary staple airborne.

Daymon watched thousands of white grains erupt and then rain down on the plywood floor, little dainty patters filling the cramped room. Once silence had returned, he said, "Tell me how you really feel."

Cupping his face with both hands, Duncan said, "Helpless. Fucking helpless."

"Well I know one thing ... you surely are *not* gonna find your answer to that kind of problem at the bottom of a bottle."

Duncan glared at the floor. Then, without meeting Daymon's gaze, he turned away and said, "So you said earlier in not so many words. But I figure maybe this one will be the exception to the norm." He reached over his head and snatched the half-empty bottle of Jack down and quipped, "I'll let you know if I find *empirical evidence*."

"Smart ass," muttered Daymon.

Duncan spun the cap off the bottle.

"Don't forget your last promise," Daymon called over his shoulder. "'Cause Lucy ... you got some esplainin' to do to the group." Then, obviously disappointed, he shook his dreads and stalked off, leaving the hard-headed aviator to clean up his own mess.

Chapter 54

As Bishop stood still, staring out at the lake's shimmering waters, light footsteps on the stairs and then the slap of bare feet against the travertine tiles behind him signaled a start to the evening's festivities. His eyes narrowed as he imagined her brown hair flowing as she walked. He closed them and focused on the wide smile sure to spread on her face when she noticed the lengths that Carson had gone to make her feel comfortable. But since his back was to her approach and the fleeting snippets of her reflection in the sliding glass door told him little, he opted to remain still and let their introduction unfold naturally.

"You're not even going to come over and pull the chair out for me?" Jamie called ahead, a mixture of incredulity and sarcasm in her voice.

To keep her on the defensive, Bishop said nothing. Based on three things—the throw of her voice, a subtle rush of air on his right cheek, and lastly, her reflection relative to his—he put her three paces behind and a couple of degrees off his right shoulder. He also knew that Carson had a laser beam dancing between her shoulder blades and would put a .40 caliber hollow point through her the second she lunged for one of the knives in the block on the island to her left.

Used to being the pursued, not the pursuer, he remained motionless and waited.

He didn't have to wait long. As she walked by he got a whiff of musk riding her wake, then she turned and stood, back to the glass, facing him.

Anticipation rising, he walked his level gaze up her milky thighs and then to where the sheer micro-dress clung to her pubic bone and on up to her flat stomach. Trying to act the part of the gentleman, he skipped everything from there up and looked directly into her hazel eyes and was a little disappointed. He had grown fond of the girls in the sandbox. Their deep, almost impenetrable inky black eyes staring inquisitively, mysteriously, from behind a hijab. In fact, he had requested brown. And Carson had assured him that hers *were* brown. Maybe they changed with the light or her mood or the time of the month. But these were things he didn't want to immediately concern himself with. And though she wasn't anything close to being of Persian descent, his genes mixing with hers would serve to produce a capable heir. Of that he was certain.

"Aren't we going to sit?"

"Allow me." He turned and followed her to the table. Chair legs screeched on the tiles when he pulled her chair from the table. He drank in the sight from behind, taking in the nape of her neck and the small of her back and the subtle toned curve of her backside as he pushed her chair in. Then, with a discreet wave, he dismissed Carson, who was standing sentry at the end of the hall.

"Where did you get the trained monkey?" she said, gesturing towards Carson.

Full of piss and vinegar, thought Bishop. *I like her.* "I trained that monkey," he said, picking up his glass of red. "A toast. And then we eat."

Smirking, Jamie hoisted her glass to his, anticipating a cheesy one-liner or, judging by his demeanor and bearing that screamed former military, perhaps a Sun-Tzu quote. Instead, he said, "The honor is all yours."

"Whatever I want?"

He nodded.

Cocking her head, she said, "Anything?"

"Yes. Anything you want."

"To the Stockholm Syndrome, then. Cheers."

He glared.

They tapped glasses, producing a soft resonant ping.

"To Stockholm Syndrome."

She took a sip. Then, laying it on thick, said, "That's what you were hoping for ... right?"

Ignoring her question, he cut to the chase. "We're going to have to procreate if we are ever going to dig ourselves out of this hole. A dozen years from now we can begin training our kids and then take back the cities and, if we're lucky, we can reboot the United States. Minus the politicians and the Federal Reserve and all of the sheep I used to protect, of course."

He is military, she thought. *Good to know*. Then, cocking her head, she said, "So your plan is to create a utopia starting here ... wherever here is ... and make babies starting with me? Smacks of the Lebensborn program. Translated from German it means *spring of life*."

"The Aryan master race thing?" he said, shaking his head. "No. Far from it. Blonde hair and blue eyes ... not my thing."

"Well, whose thing is it then? I haven't seen my friend Jordan since Carson split us apart."

"Just like the other two who were with you, Jordan didn't make it. Carson said he was defending himself. She was more trouble than she was worth. This is a different world. I trust you understand."

Jamie took a bite of cold spaghetti. Resisted making a face as she swallowed. "OK. So if a master race isn't your ultimate plan, what is?"

Debating whether he should divulge anything else, he spun some noodles on his fork and jammed the golf-ball-sized bite into his maw. He chewed and swallowed hard and, giving in to his own hubris, said, "Starting tomorrow I am taking the fight to the enemy. We are going to use the almighty atom to disinfect every sizable city located at a crossroads in a five-hundred-mile radius from here." He saw a look of incredulity light up her face.

Jamie opened her mouth to speak but couldn't immediately form the words.

"Tell me this," he went on. "Who picked out the dress?" He shoveled more food into his mouth.

Still trying to wrap her mind around the possibility of being in the path of fallout from a nearby nuclear detonation—let alone at the epicenter of a number of them—she answered quietly, "Carson did."

Bishop took a drink of wine. He made a sour face and tossed his napkin atop his nearly empty plate. "And why no undergarments? Was that Carson's doing?"

The question struck her nearly as hard as the nugget of nuclear information. "It was my idea," she answered.

His features tightened, eyes going to slits. "What are you, some kind of *whore*?"

"No. Far from it. They are the only pair of *undergarments* I own. I figured if I was going to be raped, made sense to leave them behind."

Practical, he thought.

"Besides ... whoever this little number belonged to last wore it in the Carter administration. I doubt if there's anything but granny panties and over the shoulder boulder holders in her undies drawer now."

And funny.

She saw his face soften. *Fish on.* Then her eyes flicked to the veritable quiver of knives in the wooden block on the granite island to her left. She also noticed, next to the knives, a phone with a stubby antenna. It looked nearly identical to the ones she had seen plugged in and constantly charging in the security shed back at the compound. "What's your name?" she said confidently behind a forced smile.

"Bishop. And please, don't judge me based on first impressions. Like I said ..."

"These are different times. I get it."

He said, "Good. We're on the same page." He smiled. "To know me is to like me. Shall I call you Patty? Or do you have a real name?"

"My name is Jamie."

He admired her beauty and liked that she seemed to possess a practical nature. That she was smart was icing on the genetic cake. But what he liked most of all was her honesty. Had she given him any other name than the one the Jordan girl had screamed while plummeting to her death, he would have snatched the .38 from under the table and immediately put a third eye in the center of her forehead. "Now eat," he said. "You're going to need the energy.

Because you, my lady, are going places." He smiled. Then added a mental asterisk to his statement.

My bed, willingly.

Or up on a cross, kicking and screaming.

Chapter 55

While Cade and Raven were away, Brook and the kids' low-key conversation had somehow attracted more than a dozen dead. Returning just ahead of their arrival, father and daughter clambered aboard the F-650. A beat later the tinny calypso-like beat of palms contacting sheet metal started up. And in just a handful of seconds both trucks were surrounded and the two-way radio in Brook's hand crackled to life. "Can we go now?" asked Wilson, his voice cracking slightly.

Already one step ahead, and with the added sound of nails scrabbling and scratching the paint, Cade started Black Beauty rolling forward, its coffin-sized plate metal bumper acting like a cowcatcher and bulling a path through the entire undead delegation.

After leaving the north side of Hanna behind with more questions than answers clouding his head, Cade nosed the Ford west by north. In map view, on the navigation screen, the graphically represented road resembled a kindergartner's scribble. It bumped up and down for thirty-four miles all the way to Francis, where it intersected Utah State Route 32, which then shot straight north to Oakley where the route took a serpentine course to Peoa and finally carved a graceful arc to the left as it bypassed the Rockport Reservoir.

After the reservoir the voice in the box directed them to follow the I-80 four-lane left of a smaller reservoir until it finally merged with the run of road near Coalville that Cade had been dreading for hours. No matter how long he looked at the display—pulling it all the way out to see the big picture, or zooming it in so the unimproved forest roads and fire lanes were evident—he couldn't find a route that would let them circumvent Interstate 84.

In comparison to the desolate State Routes they'd been on most of the day, the fifteen mile stretch of I-80 was a traffic jam—albeit a passable one. Along the way, the F-650's bumper proved its weight in gold, seeing them through several Z-populated snarls without warranting a dismount or having to utilize the winch. No shots were fired and when they arrived at the cloverleaf junction with Interstate 84, Cade couldn't believe their good fortune. In sharp contrast to the eastbound lanes—where hundreds if not thousands of vehicles had been abandoned by people trying to escape the killing fields of Salt Lake City—the westbound lanes they were traveling had been cleared. In fact, it looked as if Salt Lake County DOT and the nearby ski destination of Park City had combined forces and employed their fleet of snowplows to create a viable thoroughfare. The inert vehicles they did encounter, however, were largely amassed on both shoulders, bumpers crushed in, deep V-shaped gashes creasing their sides and quarter panels.

Popping one of her ear buds out, Raven asked, "What happened here?"

Cade took his eyes from the road long enough to look the question to Brook. After a short pause, Brook said, "I've got no idea. But I'm grateful we're not going the other way." She looked at the river of dashed hopes and death flowing east. Every hundred yards or so, flashes of movement behind clouded side windows would draw her attention away from the army of Zs patrolling the warren of shiny chrome and metal.

"How much further?" asked Raven.

Cade flicked his gaze to the dash. He said, "The nav unit shows twelve miles until Morgan."

"Eyes on the road, Grayson," Brook said sharply.

Arms up in mock surrender, Cade said, "Alright Miss Bossy Pants."

Ignoring him, Brook zoomed the map out one step and said, "Exit 96 merges with Old Trapper's Loop Road north ... looks like Huntsville is eleven point six miles from the exit. And the GPS coordinates are only a few miles east of Huntsville."

"And the compound. Yeahhh," said Raven, clapping her hands and smiling wide.

Max put his paws on the back seat and peered through the windshield, apparently searching for the cause of the girl's outburst. Seeing this, Raven grabbed his ears gently and put her face near his and added, "You're going to be running wild in no time, boy."

The proximity of Raven's face and the pitch and tone of her voice proved too hard for Max to resist. He lunged up and planted a sloppy dog kiss on her face, tongue and all.

There was an immediate and opposite reaction to the show of affection as Raven simultaneously drew back and wiped her face on her tee-shirt. A tick later her face was wet, the bottled water was half empty, her head was tilted back and she was gargling away the dog spit. She pulsed the window down and spat the water into the slipstream where it was carried aloft and then deposited on the Raptor's hood and windshield.

"Close the window ... you're letting the stench in," said Cade.

"Max licked my mouth."

Swerving to miss a corpse splayed across his lane, Cade shot Brook a sly smile and said, "Wonder what Max was licking before that."

"Ewwww," cried Raven.

The smile disappearing from his face, Cade pointed to a splash of magenta bisected with a pair of parallel lines. "What's that?"

After zooming in on the item of interest, an icon representing a stylized passenger jet was evident. "Morgan County Airport," said Brook.

"How big is the city of Morgan?"

"We're about to find out."

***

Four miles from Morgan, their question was answered by a sign flashing by on their right.

"Thirty-six hundred," said Brook. "City center is off to the left. Our exit is on the right ... and so is the airport. What are you thinking?"

"Just noting it for future reference. That's all."

The number of stalls in the westbound lanes increased exponentially the closer they got to Morgan. By the time the exit north was visible, Cade was driving the Ford like a landlocked icebreaker. In the lowest gear available, he traded paint and pushed a number of vehicles aside, clearing a path for the trailing Raptor.

In the center console the radio sounded. "Are we there yet?" asked Wilson, a smart-ass tone evident in his tone.

Thumbing Talk, Brook answered back, "Soon. Less than twenty miles."

"Copy that," said Wilson. He left the channel open for a second longer and Sasha's whiny voice, tolerable only because it was in the background, transmitted over the spectrum: "We've been on the road all day."

"Less than an hour," said Brook. She looked down into a minivan full of death. The window was open and the monster in the driver's seat was reaching for the Ford's front tire as the smaller vehicle was pushed aside. Noticing the trio of car seats in the middle row, each one occupied by an undead toddler thrashing madly against the nylon straps, Brook keyed the two-way and commanded, "Do *not* look inside the van on your right."

Cade flicked his eyes to the rearview and saw the Raptor slow to a walking speed and all three heads inside turn in unison. Clearly an act of conscientious objection. Human nature was to rubberneck at an accident, so he wasn't surprised when they did. "They've got to see it all, Brook. That way when their lives or mine or yours or Raven's are on the line, they'll be less likely to freeze up. I said it once and I'll hammer it home every chance I get. A split second pause is all it took for them to get to Desantos and Hicks."

Brook said nothing.

The off-ramp was thoroughly clogged, as was the road all the way to the airport, so Cade shifted into four-wheel-drive and drove along the shoulder, churning up sod and newly planted flowers, completely and irrevocably destroying Morgan County's stab at roadside beautification.

Once they were past the backed-up airport feeder roads, the two-truck convoy bumped back onto the smooth blacktop and crossed Cottonwood Creek on a utilitarian cement bridge before the two-lane made an abrupt turn north.

As the airport slipped by on the right, Cade risked another admonition from Brook by casting furtive glances out the window past her.

She said, "You're all over the road, Cade. Pull over *or* let me drive."

And he did. After passing a single-lane road servicing the sprawling subdivision abutting the airport to the east, he brought the F-650 to a halt on the centerline between two fenced-in swaths of grassland with no walking dead in the immediate vicinity. He parked and engaged the brake and as he did so, all he could think about was how low Wilson was going to feel after seeing Brook loop around and get behind the wheel. He waited until she was out the door and onto the roadway and then, lifting his feet over the console, scooted across the seat. He glanced over his shoulder at the Raptor sliding to a stop and picked up the Motorola, keyed the talk button and said, "Mandatory driver swap."

A second or two ticked by and Taryn's voice filtered through the speaker: "My butt," she said.

The driver's door hinged open and, with an audible grunt, Brook hauled herself behind the wheel and started the process of jockeying the seat around to accommodate her small stature.

Cade dropped the radio on the seat next to him and plucked the binoculars from the passenger side footwell. He turned around and trained them on the Raptor and saw Wilson, mouth moving, arms flailing animatedly, presumably arguing for his turn at the helm. Panning right, he was amused to see a look that Brook had often given him. Arms crossed and a rock solid set to her jaw, Taryn ticked her head side-to-side, an obvious 'negative' in any language.

Hiding a smile, Cade spun around and glassed the airport, of which he could only see a thin sliver between the copse of trees at the end of the facility's single runway. The closely spaced aircraft hangars, presumably once a darker shade of robin's egg blue, were rust-streaked and weathered, their south-facing elevations inset with massive garage-style rollup doors. Sitting on strips of browned grass fronting the squat metal structures were a number of brightly colored sailplanes and parked amidst the sleek gliders was a civilian single-engine airplane, its FAA call sign, a combination of letters and numbers, emblazoned in black on its tail and wings and fuselage. And from recent experience Cade knew that where there were airplanes there were below-ground fuel storage tanks and the mobile bowsers to service the aircraft. He looked at the navigation display and made a mental note of the airport's location, then dropped the binoculars to his chest and said, "‚Home James."

Chapter 56

Twenty minutes and fourteen miles north of the Morgan Airport, Trapper's Loop Road came to a 'T' and ceased to exist. On the navigation unit, a finger's width beyond the merging yellow roads, shaped vaguely like someone's poor attempt at a snow angel, was a vast sea of blue pixels labeled Pineview Reservoir.

Thirty yards before they reached the intersection, the strange hybrid human/computer voice in the box instructed Brook to turn right. Instead, awed by the low-hanging sun shimmering silver off the vast expanse of glassy water straight ahead, she jammed to a stop on the gravel shoulder next to a road sign, one arrow pointing left towards the city of *Ogden, pop. 84,721* just fifteen miles distant, the other indicating that *Huntsville, pop. 776* was a mile to the right.

While Brook sat mesmerized by the picture postcard view, the Raptor crunched noisily to a halt on the gravel on the opposite shoulder with Taryn gesturing wildly at Cade to power his window down. A tick later, shaking her head and pointing to the sign, Taryn said, "Please tell me we're not turning left."

Cade said nothing. He pressed the binoculars to his face and gazed out the passenger window over the other Ford's hood at Huntsville, which was built up on a finger of land encroached upon on three sides by water. He adjusted the focus ring and discovered that the little burg at his two o'clock appeared no different than the smaller population centers dotting the Interstates and rural highways they'd already traveled between FOB Bastion in Mack, Colorado and nearby Morgan, Utah.

The sixty-four-thousand dollar question nagging him was what was keeping the eighty-five-thousand, presumably undead, citizens of Ogden at bay. He shifted his gaze left and studied the 'V' in the nearby Wasatch Mountain Range, where the stripe of road entered the forest and rolled up and down and beyond before finally merging with the horizon and disappearing from sight. In his head he imagined a National Guard unit, men and women, young and old, called up hastily by the President's declaration of martial law. They would no doubt be confounded at first by orders telling them to shoot the infected on sight. Fellow Americans. Perhaps even family. A feeling of helpless reluctance creeping in—or not—they were still soldiers and would have followed those orders. He let the scenario play out further in his head. He saw the squad, consisting of ten to fifteen soldiers, already dog tired from two sleepless days manning a roadblock somewhere west of Huntsville, get blindsided by word that Salt Lake—most likely their city of origin—had fallen to the dead. Then, like placing a tourniquet on a bleeding stump, the triage orders probably came down from some FEMA or Department of Homeland Security bureaucrat flitting around above it all, safe and sound in a Black Hawk. The order to procure a sizable amount of demolitions—maybe from a mining supply outfit near town or from a Guard armory—then, shaking their collective heads, the unit would dutifully follow through on additional orders telling them to bury as much of Highway 39 under as many tons of dynamited Wasatch granite as humanly possible. *At least that's exactly how I would have done it*, thought Cade. *Stopped the migrating Zs right in their rotten tracks.* But at this point it was pure conjecture on his part. For all he knew the horde of flesh eaters eighty thousand strong had already blown through the aptly named desolate cluster of structures called Huntsville—hunted it clean—and then like ants on the march, plodded on in search of the next unsuspecting town.

But speculation at this juncture—literally—was no better than throwing darts in a dark room and expecting to hit the dartboard. So he hitched a thumb to the right and said to Taryn, "Don't worry. Passing through Ogden is *not* in our plans. And it looks like this road will allow us to circumvent Huntsville as well." A look of relief supplanted the one of worry crowding her tanned features. Seeing this and concluding that Ogden and Grand Junction were roughly the same size, and that her airport ordeal was still fresh in her mind, he leaned in and read the small text at the top of the navigation screen. A beat later he poked his head back out the window, looked down and, in order to put her at ease, said, "The compound is give-or-take sixteen miles east of here. Piece of cake. We'll be there in thirty minutes ... tops." As Taryn smiled, her tatted right arm passed through the light spilling inside the Raptor's cab and went to her face and, though she was a civilian, flicked him a near-text-book salute.

And though he was no longer active duty, Cade reciprocated. As Brook moved them out, going right at the junction, Cade swiveled around and unplugged Raven from her device and relayed the same good news to her.

With a bit of fist bumping occurring in both vehicles, the two-truck convoy proceeded east, Brook driving the F-650, and the Raptor, with Wilson forever riding shotgun, bringing up the rear.

Like the blade on the Grim Reaper's scythe, the narrow two-lane dodged the city, arcing gently south before shooting laser-straight north, all the while keeping to the eastern edge of the quiet town. Soon SR-39 struck off east through the wide open rural countryside. A couple of miles outside of town, they came upon two dozen inert cars and SUVs, all pointed east, presumably fleeing the *hard place* before coming up against the *rock*. Cade brought the binoculars to bear and glassed the scene. He saw a great number of corpses still occupying the vehicles in which they had died. The lucky ones that had stayed dead appeared stiff and leathery from a combination of rigor and heat. The unlucky few that had died and reanimated inside their rides were blurry flashes of movement behind greasy cataracts obscuring the auto glass. And lastly, no doubt alerted by the sound of approaching engines, a pack of Zs suddenly showed themselves, rising up slowly one at a time, until at least ten were visible near the front of the traffic jam.

Cade settled the field glasses on the pale abominations and instantly his earlier hypothesis was blown into more pieces than he had assumed blocked the Wasatch pass to the west.

Because the *rock* that had jammed up traffic consisted of four evenly placed Jersey barriers. Ten feet from end to end, two feet wide at the base, and standing thirty-two inches tall from the ground to the narrow top where two eyehooks were embedded. Each of the four-thousand-pound poured concrete barriers could deflect a bomb blast and required a front loader for proper placement. Strangely, in addition to the wrist-sized holes punched into some of the vehicles, the nearest pair of barricades were pitted and cracked in places, almost like someone had willfully taken a jackhammer to them. Cade had seen the same type of damage up close and in person in Afghanistan. Thirty plus years of fighting one invader or another had left damn near every wall in that Middle Eastern country bullet-pocked just like the Jersey barriers blocking their advance.

Brook wheeled Black Beauty left and bumped down into the sizable ditch paralleling the two-lane. Threatening to eject the cargo from the bed, the Ford bucked and shimmied with the suspension groaning until the tires bit and clawed their way up the other side. She muscled the wheel straight and held it there, keeping the driver's side wheels on one side of the gully and the other two crunching through the gravel along the road's left shoulder. Then, with the nerve-jangling screech of rusty barbed wire raking the driver's side, and the mirrors and door handles and bumpers of the unmoving vehicles hammering against the passenger side, she tromped the pedal and made her own road.

Watching in the side mirror, Cade saw Taryn put the Raptor through the same maneuver and soon the white pick-up had closed the distance with the F-650's rear bumper.

From his elevated seat in the truck, Cade saw a number of weeks-old cadavers that the Zs had just been feeding on. And judging by the desert tan scraps of camouflage fabric and that some of the corpses still had helmets strapped to their flesh-stripped skulls, he concluded they had been National Guardsmen who had been manning the road block. Just following orders like he had done dutifully for more than a decade. *And for what?* Judging by the damage to the barriers and the sun glinting from shell casings littering the shoulder ahead, these soldiers were ambushed and murdered by their own countrymen—living, breathing wastes of skin who needed to suffer tenfold the pain they had inflicted on these patriots. Disgusted, he looked away from the dead soldiers and watched the throng of dead zippering clumsily through the traffic snarl. "Stop right here," he said sharply. "After I get out, you and Taryn are going to have to reverse out of here." Then, his voice softening, he apologized for being terse and craned around and said to Raven, "You need to be Mom's eyes and ears while I'm gone."

He drew the Glock 17 as the Ford lurched to a halt and, out of habit, ejected the magazine. *Full.* He slapped it back into the magwell and then racked the slide back a third of a pull. *One in the pipe.* Lastly, he screwed the suppressor on and nudged the door open with his good foot.

"You sure this is necessary?" asked Brook.

"Very," he replied icily. He stepped out and down and walked a few paces toward the Raptor and broke the bad news to Taryn and then motioned for Wilson to join him on the roadway.

Wilson hopped out and crushed his boonie hat down low on his head. Beretta in his right hand, he slammed the door behind him. Wasting no time, Taryn gunned the engine and sped off in reverse, spitting a hail of gravel and moist soil at their boots.

Startled by the howling exhaust note, a flock of emboldened crows took flight in an explosive flurry of black feather and attitude. Cawing and cussing, they took station overhead, cruising languid ovals as Brook, driving by feel and sound, retraced her hard-earned forward progress in reverse.

With the noise of scraping metal and breaking glass signaling the forced retreat, Cade and Wilson pushed forward on foot, approaching the dead from an oblique angle off to their right.

Leaving the thoroughly scoured carcasses to the birds, the Zs angled doggedly towards what the instincts buried deeply in the reptilian part of their atrophied brains told them was a meal of fresh meat.

Motioning for Wilson to stop, Cade said, "There was a reason the Guardsmen picked this spot to set up their roadblock. See the rocks and the steep grade on both sides of the road? Makes it pretty much impassible from this point east"—he pointed to the terrain on both sides and then to the incline beyond the Jersey barriers as he spoke—"And that means doubling back—which could take hours—and that's assuming there *is* a way around Huntsville." He paused while Wilson took it all in. "But to avoid all of that, we're going to clear a path with the winch. All of the noise is probably going to draw a lot more Zs our way. So for now, your job is to stay frosty and watch our backs." He gestured at the Zs with the silencer affixed to his Glock and stuck a vertical finger to his lips.

Wilson nodded and checked their six position. He scanned the horizon. Nothing to see. Then shifted his gaze towards the Raptor and glimpsed Taryn's form hunched over the wheel, tatted arms wrapping it in a death grip. Then the rear passenger window slid silently into the channel and Sasha poked her head out and shot him a harried look. He flashed a tentative thumbs up to her before returning his attention to the advancing cadavers.

Using the contour of the back window for support, Cade stretched his arms across the red and blue Union Jack painted atop the tiny white Mini Cooper and, feeling the heat of the sun-baked glass warming his chest and stomach through his tee-shirt, sighted down the Glock and waited. A tick later, the first of the Z procession, a shabby looking thirty-something male, squeezed its rotten torso between the closely spaced fenders of two nearby sedans.

After letting the hissing monster lead the others a dozen lurching steps into the metal and glass chute, Cade settled the Glock's tritium sights on its forehead, just below its greasy looking widow's peak, and squeezed off two quick shots. Simultaneously the silenced weapon bucked slightly in his gloved hands and the two sizzling 9mm Parabellums plowed a jagged V-shaped chasm through bone and brain. A half beat later, its bare feet left earth as the headshot body contorted into a U-shape and followed the spritz of bone and hair and gray matter airborne. With the sound of the twice dead corpse pin balling off of sheet metal, Cade shifted aim and engaged the next two behind it—a long dead female and a recently turned male teenager—with a rapid-fire pair of double-taps. The female walker received the initial 9mm round to the right temple and, as the 115-grain hunk of lead bored through bone and tumbled end-over-end, cutting a path through putrid gray matter, the second bullet entered obliquely, sending the rear half of its skull, dirty blond ponytail and all, spinning off and away like a bloody hunk of peeled orange rind. Brains dribbled from the gaping head wound as the female Z collapsed vertically to a kneeling position, wedged between the two inert vehicles, and then slowly, like a felled tree, hinged forward atop Cade's first victim.

Hands kneading the steering wheel, Brook watched the one-sided melee unfold from her high perch in the F-650. Had there been more than a dozen undead she might have climbed down and joined in. But, as always, it appeared that Cade alone had everything under control, and after the first three Zs were down and effectively blocking all passage between the two cars, he did exactly what Brook thought he might. He pushed off of the small car, and with Wilson clinging like a shadow, flanked the remaining undead. She saw him stop and square up against the line of creatures. Then, arms outstretched and sweeping left to right, he ticked degrees off an arc like a slow-moving sprinkler head, the silencer twitching once at each barely perceptible pause. The instantaneous and deadly result: a daisy chain of airborne pink mist as each of the hurtling bullets found their mark from near point-blank range.

All total, from the time Cade told Brook to stop and extricate the truck until his last shell casing had finished spinning and pinging across the pavement, a little less than two minutes had elapsed and all of the Zs were wedged chest to back, their still vertical forms leaking brackish liquids onto the blacktop. Loosening her grip on the wheel, Brook exhaled and watched Cade swap out magazines. A second later her man was stuffing the empty into a pocket and he and Wilson were on the move, crabbing past bumpers and grills, stopping now and again to look underneath the higher clearance vehicles for anything lying in wait.

The closer they got to the roadblock, the more evidence Cade was able to pick up on. Scattered everywhere were shell casings in multiple calibers. The gravel shoulder adjacent to the fallen Guardsmen had been chewed up by something. Two furrows, eighteen-inches wide and darker than the surrounding soil, had been gouged several inches deep into the sloped edge of the roadside ditch. There was also a pair of faint black smudges in the right-hand lane. They continued across the yellow centerline. To Cade, up close, they resembled interconnected chevrons—elongated horizontally. As he eyeballed the scene, he tried to picture a Humvee in his head. To gauge its wheelbase. Coming up empty, he resorted to pacing off the furrows. Then he did the same with the skid marks on the blacktop and found that, give-or-take an inch or two, both were identical.

Lastly, he paced off the width between front wheels on the nearest passenger car and discovered a two-foot deficiency on its part.

"What do you make of it?" asked Wilson, who was leaning against an old GM station wagon with a bullet-riddled cadaver slumped over the steering wheel.

"Those Guard soldiers manning this roadblock were ambushed and died right here." After a long pause, Cade pointed out the Jersey barrier closest to the right shoulder. Judging by marks scribed into the road near its base, it had been pushed back a few degrees. There were more tire marks on the shoulder, and black rubber streaks like the ones on the road marred the base of the barrier. "And whoever did this to them stole their vehicles and went east. But worst of all ... they now possess whatever heavy armament was attached to those vehicles."

"What does that mean?"

"It means that from here on out, until we get to the compound, we've got to be on high alert." Cade bent down and retrieved a massive four-inch-long brass shell casing from underneath the rust-marred front bumper of the tired-looking station wagon. It looked like it could almost double as a flower vase. He held it up in front of Wilson's face and said ominously, "Because if we run into the Ma Deuce that spit these out ... we better kiss all of our asses goodbye."

"What's a Ma Deuce?"

"A fifty-caliber heavy machine gun ... bad news to vehicles and personnel alike. It'd punch a hole clean through both of our rigs and keep going for a mile after. I figure it was probably turret-mounted on the Humvee the bandits towed from the ditch."

Toeing through a pile of smaller shell casings, Wilson asked, "How are we getting through this ... all of these cars and cement barricades?"

"Follow me. I have an idea." Favoring his left ankle, he slowly walked back and relayed to Brook what he had in mind. He disengaged the winch and, with the curved steel hook in hand, looped the 3/8-inch cable over his shoulder, leaned in and trudged forward, spooling forty feet of it out behind him. He rounded the first vehicle in the left lane and called back and had Wilson feed him an additional twenty feet.

The heavy-duty eyehooks embedded in the top of the Jersey barrier were there to make them easy for a front loader to quickly lift and position them wherever they were needed. But Cade had a different use in mind for them. He wound the cable around two of the barriers and then clicked the metal hook into the right eyehook of the barrier farthest from the Ford. Then he pulled the cable taut and let the leftover cable snake into the ditch. After having Wilson engage the winch and draw up most of the slack, Cade caught Brook's eye and pointed with two fingers in the direction of Huntsville and ducked in between the first two cars.

Message received, Brook engaged the four-wheel-drive and jammed the transmission into reverse. There was a roar as the engine's rpms rocketed upwards. Then the big Ford's rear end settled under load, the two massive tires on the passenger side found purchase on the roadway and the two opposite bit deeply into the gravel shoulder.

Simultaneously there was a resonant *twang* as the cable stretched tight, a chirping of tires trying to hold steady, and a grating of stone against stone that Cade could feel through his boot soles. A beat later, as the barriers gave in to applied horsepower and several tons of rolling 4X4, there was a sound like a bowling ball finding the gutter, only a hundred times more explosive as the barriers slapped together. Then, just as Cade had envisioned, both slab-sided hunks of white concrete did a slow motion barrel roll into the ditch.

After making a slashing motion across his throat, telling Brook to shut it down, he called Wilson forward, pointed at his bum ankle and said, "I'm afraid you get the honors. You're going to have to unwrap the cable and take it to the farthest vehicle and thread it all the way through ..."

Wilson said incredulously, "All seven of them?"

"And do it quickly." Cade pointed to a small herd of dead just topping the hill east of them.

Thankfully the barriers had landed mostly upright and it only took Wilson a few seconds to unwrap the cable and run it back. Then, on hands and knees, with Sasha who had defied orders and left the confines of the Raptor following his every move and peppering him with questions, he shuffled forward and passed the hook behind the driver's side tires of all seven vehicles.

"Better hurry," Sasha urged.

"Shhh," he hissed.

"There are more than twenty of them."

Ignoring his motor-mouthed sibling, Wilson rose from his knees and asked, "What now, Cade?"

Interrupting again, Sasha said sharply, "They're getting closer."

"I want you to wrap it around the front axle and click the hook back onto the cable. Then I need you to get inside the car and put the transmission into neutral and make sure the brake is disengaged."

Throwing his hands in the air, Wilson said, "Is that all?" He rolled onto his back and scrunched his lanky body underneath the GM wagon. Then a slew of choice cuss words later, he resurfaced with sweat dripping from his brow and blood oozing from a couple of scraped knuckles. He hinged the door open and was hit face first with a cloud of flies riding the nose-scrunching pong of weeks-old carrion. Holding his breath, he hauled the cadaver out and performed the necessary tasks inside. He shimmied off the slimy bench seat, steadied himself on the open door, and took a deep cleansing breath. Held it for a second and exhaled, saying proudly, "Done."

Seeing that the throng of Zs had closed to within a hundred yards, Cade said to Wilson, "One down, six to go." Without waiting for a negative response, Cade looked Sasha in the eye. Unsmiling, he shifted his gaze a one-eighty, let it waver on the advancing dead for a tick before completing the three-sixty and nodding the teen toward the safety of the Ford Raptor.

She put her hands on her hips. An act of defiance against the worst person du-jour on the face of the earth—the man who she perceived as trying to act like he was her dad or guardian or something.

The heat was oppressive coming from above and radiating off the blacktop underfoot. Cade was losing his patience. He stared for a tick and said forcefully, "Now!"

After spewing a flurry of excuses crammed into a few seconds with the former Delta operator's unwavering icy glare cracking her resolve, Sasha finally realized she wasn't winning this battle. Relenting, she *harrumphed* and turned and stomped back towards the second worst person du-jour on the face of the earth—the woman who she perceived as trying to replace her mother.

Six minutes later, Wilson had six of the seven vehicles ready to roll. The seventh and last in line, however, was one of those new VWs done up to look like an old VW and had a fully bloated Z occupying the driver's seat.

"Paper, rock, scissors for this one?" asked Wilson.

"I've got it," said Cade. Nearly in unison, both men gazed down the line of cars and saw that the dead were now nearly to the roadblock. Cade went on, "You can take care of them."

"I thought we needed to keep the noise down."

Cade said, "If this works, noise won't matter."

"If?"

"It will. Don't worry." He turned and put his elbow through the VW's rear quarter window. As he cleared the webbed glass with the suppressor, the monster craned around, displaying a mouth full of roiling white maggots.

Fighting a rising tide of bile, Cade swallowed back a mouthful of thick saliva and then shot the abomination between the eyes. Stomach on spin cycle, he reached inside and popped the door open. Thankfully the seatbelt hanging slack against the B-pillar spared him from having to reach across the stinking biohazard. Instead, he simply tugged on the sack of rotten meat, starting it on a three-stage slow-motion roll out the door. First the putrid cadaver folded over sideways, releasing an eruption of noxious smelling gasses from its relaxed sphincter. Second, its massive head, acting like a ship's anchor, lolled sideways, speeding up the inevitable. Lastly, a tick before the vicious face plant that would leave the thing face down on the road with a mouthful of splintered teeth and pulped fly larva, there was a faint tearing sound as the fabric and dermis and underlying flesh that had become fused to the seats peeled away cleanly.

For Cade, the unexpected sight of several pounds of marbled muscle nestled in a pillow of greasy yellowed fat quivering away on the driver's seat was the last straw. The puke came out Linda Blair-style. A thin jet of hot, bitter bile and partially digested MRE pound cake that painted the already fouled steering wheel, dash, and seat. Hands on knees, Cade emptied his stomach and then endured a few more dry heaves. Saying nothing, he wiped the spittle on his sleeve and stepped over the body. Holding his breath, he reached in and manhandled the standard shifter into neutral and disengaged the E-brake. Still holding his breath and wanting nothing more to do with the leaking corpse, he left it where it had come to rest, looped around back of the VW and stepped over the cable. He formed up next to Wilson, who wore a sour look and was digging for something in a cargo pocket.

Cade asked, "What?"

Handing over an MRE napkin, Wilson said sheepishly, "Thanks. I owe you one."

After dabbing the corners of his mouth, Cade said, "That makes nineteen or possibly twenty that you owe me ... but who's counting?" He turned and waved the napkin at Brook.

Seeing the prearranged cue, Brook released her foot from the brake and started the F-650 rolling slowly to draw up the cable's tension. When the cable snapped straight under the sum of the seven vehicles' rolling weight, she pinned the accelerator, bringing the already hard-working power plant to a howling mechanical crescendo.

Suddenly there was a rapid fire clacking as the cars merged bumper-to-bumper and then the VW's rounded rear end started rolling toward the Ford's bumper at a jogger's pace. In her side vision, Brook saw the parked Raptor slide by from right to left. She glanced over and read Taryn's lips: *Get out of the way.*

And she did. Craning over her shoulder and seeing both lanes clear, she wrenched the wheel hard right. The sharp J-turn took the Ford out of the way of the unmanned ten tons of rolling metal now tracking towards the far ditch.

Enunciating every word slowly, Raven said, "We're in trouble, aren't we, Mom?"

"The fat lady isn't singing yet," replied Brook. Thinking quickly, she shifted into Drive and matched the VW's speed for a couple of car lengths, until, like a slow motion train wreck, it went ass end into the chest-high ditch and the U-shaped slack in the cable straightened out incrementally as each car pounded into the next, their combined weight scooting the VW along the ditch while at the same time grinding it deeper into the dirt.

From forty feet away the sound of exploding Goodyears and buckling metal was loud. But from five feet away the sharp reports from Wilson's Beretta was deafening.

Cade ignored the gunfire and watched the F-650 jerk around violently. For a second he thought they would be needing a new vehicle until the cars it had been towing ground to a halt, leaving the battered Ford sitting perpendicular to the ditch.

Breathing a sigh of relief, Cade spun around and joined Wilson in engaging the dead from less than a dozen feet. Glock bucking in his fist, he suddenly heard Brook call out a warning and when he looked over she was kneeling next to the assless bloated Z, her stubby M4 belching fire.

Seconds later, after walking into the barrage of withering fire, the Zs were lying in an untidy tangle and a blue cordite haze hung heavy overhead.

Changing mags, Brook called over to Cade, "Let's get the hell out of here before more of them show up." Saying nothing, he stalked back to the truck and returned with a red gas can in hand. Still tight-lipped, he bypassed Brook and Wilson and the pile of Zs and made his way to the fallen soldiers. Once there, he stooped over each one of them and took their dog tags. He removed helmets from three of the corpses, then splashed the contents of the plastic can, five gallons of precious gasoline, liberally on the entire row.

Brook and Wilson watched Cade for a second and then headed to the F-650 to untangle the winch cable.

Head down, empty can hanging at his side, Cade passed his gaze over the dead soldiers, letting it linger momentarily on every pair of empty eye sockets. With each of their death masks ingrained into his memory, he trudged back to the Ford, tossed the helmets and empty can in the box bed, and climbed up and into the passenger seat. He clicked his belt and started to open his mouth to speak but Brook cut him off. "I know what you have to do," she said quietly. "I'll stop across from the bodies."

He nodded and stuffed the handful of jangling dog tags into a cargo pocket.

Brook waited until Wilson was back inside the Raptor before beginning the slow roll towards the roadblock.

One round from Cade's Glock was all it took to create the spark. The gas fumes ignited with a breath robbing *whoosh* and orange flames leapt up and enveloped the dead.

Feeling the heat from the impromptu funeral pyre warm on his face, Cade said a simple warrior's prayer for his brothers and sisters in arms and then powered up his window.

Sensing her man had made his peace, Brook urged the F-650 forward. They climbed the hill in silence and rolled down the other side, passing a burnt-out gas station, its yellow plastic sign the only thing left standing. And with the smoke column fading in the rearview, Brook glanced at the navigation unit and for Raven's benefit announced, "Fifteen point three miles."

Chapter 57

Daymon had the doe dead to rights. Its ears twitched as the beautiful animal tugged at the bushes bordering the game trail. *Peaceful*, thought Daymon, the sound of the nearby creek serenading him. He looked back at Chief and nodded. But when he turned around and raised the crossbow, finger tensing against the trigger, the deer went rigid, spooked by something, and then bounded away with a snort and a crashing of brush.

"Shit," muttered Daymon. He'd had enough processed food for one lifetime and could almost taste the savory sizzling venison.

Shaking his head, Chief whispered, "You win some you lose ..."

Interrupting his lament, the sound of a vehicle or possibly two on the nearby road caught them both flat-footed.

Chief's carbine was off his shoulder and in his hands in under a second. In the next breath, Daymon was fumbling for his radio but stopped abruptly and muttered an obscenity when he realized how far from the compound they were.

The State Route wound along for a dozen miles, climbing and dipping and diving while gaining no substantial elevation. Then the verdant groves of pines harboring small pockets of white aspens thickened to full-blown forest that encroached upon the road from both sides. At the fifteen-mile mark the thick canopy suddenly gave way to open sky, which by now was reflecting fiery orange from the rapidly setting sun.

The first thing that caught Cade's eye—and apparently Brook's too, as she slowed the truck immediately—was the burned-out hulk of what could only have been a Humvee, the squat blocky body and squared-out window openings the dead giveaway. Sitting on warped steel rims and listing at an unnatural angle, it looked sad and alone, discarded like a piece of trash in the roadside ditch. The smoke resulting from the conflagration had streaked the tan paint with sooty zebra-stripes. And as they rolled by the wreckage, Cade picked up on something else. There were dimpled bullet holes in the buckled side panels that spoke of an ambush involving heavy weapons and some kind of explosive device. Not the kind of chassis bending, break the vehicle's back roadside IED prevalent in the sandbox. He guessed the damage had been inflicted by something cobbled together hastily, yet deadly all the same.

Breaking the brooding silence, Brook said, "We're close ... ya think?"

Cade said nothing for a half-beat. He walked his gaze ahead, up the two-lane, over the shallow rise and then right to left along its gentle curve. Finally, he answered with confidence, "I'm dead certain that this *is* the place where Duncan and his brother tangled with the Huntsville bandits."

Brook couldn't resist. She said, "I think Duncan's and Merriam Webster's definition of the word are miles apart. Different sides of the scale. Pretty one sided *tangle* if you ask me."

"They hit first and hard. Like we did to those pukes from Green River ... they came looking for trouble and got some." Fifty feet beyond the destroyed Humvee was a burned-out SUV nosed into the ditch on the right.

Raven popped up between Brook and Cade. Her arms dangled over the seat back and her ear buds hung down in front of her. She asked breathlessly, "What happened here?"

"Stay down, sweetie," said Cade. He popped the console open and pulled out the satellite phone. Thumbed it on and resumed scanning the tree line on both sides of the road.

The two-way came to life and Wilson said, "We're not rolling into an ambush ... are we?"

Cade thumbed the talk button. He said, "Negative," and dropped the radio on his lap. He craned around, taking it all in. The whole place had the feel of some kind of hallowed ground. There was no wind rustling the boughs. The birds, for the most part, had turned in for the night, and unlike the last couple of miles where the trees crowding in on them amplified the exhaust notes, only barbed wire lined the road here and both vehicles combined to create but a whisper in comparison.

The road climbed slightly for a couple of hundred yards and when the hill's apex was within spitting distance, startling them all, the voice in the box boomed: *You have reached your destination.*

Brook pulled hard to the shoulder. She looked around and asked, "Do you see a road?"

"Negative," said Cade.

Raven added her two cents. "Why don't you honk, Mom?"

"Not a good idea," she answered.

"Where is everybody?" pressed Raven, a measure of concern evident in her voice.

"Give it a minute," said Cade. He let his eyes walk up the grass-covered hill to his left where he noticed freshly tilled soil. Then his eyes were drawn to two deep parallel tracks traversing the hill. He let his gaze linger on the crushed grass and disturbed low brush just beyond the rectangular patches of disturbed earth. "Those are graves," he added. "And just beyond them ... is where I'd place an over watch position."

Partially blocking Cade's view, the Raptor stopped abreast and the passenger window whirred down. Wilson asked, "Can we get out here and stretch?"

Brook looked the question to Cade. He nodded. Brook said, "Get out, but stay frosty."

That's my lady. Smiling, Cade returned his attention uphill. To the spot set back from the clearing. A warren of low brush and shadow. He felt a subtle tingle in his gut. Then the hairs on the back of his arms stood at attention, his sixth sense telling him that someone was indeed watching them. He tore his eyes from the hillside and regarded the sat-phone's display and saw that it had successfully shaken hands with a satellite somewhere and the signal it was receiving was strong. After cycling through the menu, he found the entry he wanted and hit the talk button. A second or two later he heard an obnoxious electronic trilling in his ear. He let it go on for a five count, then heard a tone and was forced to listen to a generic greeting delivered by an unconvincing human voice prompting him to leave a message. Instead he ended the call and met Brook's inquiring gaze.

"Nothing?"

"Nope," he admitted. "But at this point if Daymon is still alive and still has Tice's phone, he will call me back. No doubt about it." He traded the phone for the two-way. Changed the main channel from seventeen to ten. Then he set the sub channel to one. *Ten-one*, he thought. *Tried and true. The old standby.* He thumbed the talk button and said, "Anybody there?"

Nothing.

He tried again. "Old Man, are you there? It's your amigo from Portland."

A burst of static emanated from the speaker and a reedy sounding male voice replied, "Who are you?"

"Cade Grayson."

"What was Logan's nickname?" the man asked.

"Too easy," said Cade.

"*Nope.* Go fish," replied the man.

"The *question* ... was too easy," said Cade sharply. "Logan's *nickname* was Oops."

After a second or two, the man came back over the two-way. "Wait there," he said. "I'm coming on down."

Hunch confirmed. "Copy that," said Cade. He cycled the two-way back to the previous channel and told the others to expect some company. He ended the call and slipped the radio in a pocket. He snatched the Glock off the seat and checked the chamber and mag. Shielding his eyes against the setting sun, he opened the door and climbed down from the truck. He looked uphill and scanned the tree line, stopping a foot-and-a-half to the right of the spot he had pegged as the prime location to post a lookout and spotted the slender form just as it slipped from the shadows.

A minute later, the wiry man dressed in camos and wearing a tan ball cap had made his way down the hill to the fence. He passed his rifle over the fence and crawled through himself. Shouldering his rifle, he strolled to the centerline and introduced himself to Cade. After the pleasantries were out of the way, a quick question and answer session ensued and then Phillip sauntered over to the camouflaged entry.

Cade followed him all the way and then stopped in his tracks and silently chastised himself for failing to notice the wall of faked foliage overgrowing the fence for what it really was. *Clever set up*, he thought as Phillip worked the lock.

After showing Cade how to get to the gate release, Phillip swung it away quietly, faux flora and all, revealing the gravel feeder road. "It's a short drive," said Phillip. Then, inexplicably, the achingly thin man straightened up, faced Cade and delivered a pretty fair salute. "And they'll be waiting for you, sir."

Humoring the man, Cade returned the salute. "Thank you, Phillip. But the formalities and calling me sir are not necessary. In fact ... I don't recommend it."

An uneasy smile fell upon Phillip's face. Quietly he negotiated the fence and, retracing his steps, trudged up the hill and melted back into trees.

It was a tight fit but Brook succeeded in nosing the F-650 through the gate. After both trucks cleared the threshold, Cade closed the gate and, reversing the process Phillip had just shown him, latched and locked it behind them. As he hauled himself into the passenger seat, his gaze fell on the tree-lined gravel track spilling away in front of them. Then, with the memory of the cars and fencing abusing the Ford at the roadblock outside of Huntsville, he looked sidelong at her, smiled, and said tongue-in-cheek, "Go easy on the paint."

Smartass, thought Brook. Unable to think of an appropriate comeback, she ignored the good-natured quip and glanced in the rearview just as the Raptor's headlights flicked on. Eager to get to the compound and paint job be damned, she committed to the narrow one-lane feeder road and cringed as the spine tingling nails-on-chalkboard-like sounds commenced.

Inside the compound, headphones snugged on tight, Heidi, who was still scanning the spectrum for ham radio signals, failed to hear the trilling satellite phone on the shelf above. A minute later, however, the two-way radio chimed and skittered and danced all over the desktop, alerting her to Phillip's incoming call. She listened intently and, a long while later when Phillip had nothing more to add but small talk, said, "Gotta go," and ended the call.

Radio in hand, she hustled down the corridor and rousted Lev from a deep slumber. Without allowing him time to rake the sleep from his eyes, she told him about the new arrivals and how Phillip had determined they were who they said they were. Then she asked him to go up and welcome them.

Lev stretched and yawned. He ran his hands over his closely cropped hair and said sleepily, "Didn't think they were going to be here until tomorrow."

"Well ... they're here now."

"Where's Duncan?"

"I haven't seen him in hours."

Pulling on an olive-drab tee-shirt, ARMY emblazoned up front, Lev asked, "And Daymon ... where is he?"

"He and Charlie are out."

Lev asked Heidi to turn away, then he stood and pulled his pants on. "OK, I'm decent," he said. "What do you mean by *out*?"

Crossing her arms, Heidi replied, "They're hunting."

"Rotters?"

"Dinner."

Another yawn. "Oh great," said Lev. "Hope they bag something other than squirrel this time. And the others?"

"Chief and Seth are on patrol down by the Gudsons' so it's on you to greet our visitors."

Now, seemingly more awake, Lev showed a newfound sense of urgency. He slipped his boots on and without lacing them grabbed his carbine. As he scooted by her and through the entry, he called back over his shoulder, "The guy's name is Cade, right?"

"Correct," she called back. "And there are five others ... plus a dog."

"Well then I hope Daymon bags two of whatever he was gunning for," replied Lev, his voice trailing off as he wound through the interconnected containers.

There was a metallic clang in the distance and again Heidi was alone with the lone light bulb and a ham radio seemingly capable of picking up nothing but static.

Chapter 58

When Lev finally made it topside, the first thing he saw was the two trucks. One was black and giant-sized, the other white and mean-looking but smaller by comparison. They were parked side-by-side in the center of the clearing far from Duncan's helicopter and the other assorted vehicles which made up the group's rag-tag motor pool. As a precautionary measure, he chambered a round and flicked the carbine's selector from *safe* to *fire*. Putting on a smile, he approached the humongous black truck. Seeing him, the brunette woman in the driver's seat smiled back, thrust a thumb towards the box bed, and told him that her husband was already unloading.

Getting down to brass tacks. As Lev rounded the rear of the truck, the top of the bed barely level with his eyes, he nearly collided with a man wearing a black ball cap and desert tan fatigue bottoms, who was, judging by the graying goatee and sidewalls, a little older than him by maybe half a dozen years. After composing himself, Lev stuck out his hand and said, "Cade Grayson?"

Cade lowered the Pelican case from the bed to the ground, wiped his hand off on his pants, and accepted the offering. "You must be Lev," he said. "I was expecting either Duncan or Daymon."

"We were expecting *you* tomorrow. So for now you're stuck with me."

Leaning against the open tailgate, eyeing the carbine in Lev's hand, Cade asked when they were expected back.

"Duncan's sleeping and Daymon is ... speak of the devil," said Lev, nodding towards the tree line to the west. "Looks like Daymon has decided to grace us with his presence."

Turning and following Lev's line of sight, Cade picked up the lanky dreadlocked man as he emerged from the tree line. Cade waved and started across the clearing and, as the distance was halved, he recognized the man trailing Daymon from a briefing prior to the Jackson Hole mission. Only now the balding, gray-haired man wasn't wearing a badge or the blue utilities indicative of a chief of police from Jackson Hole. In fact, there was nothing Cade could see—not even a hint of swagger—that distinguished him as a lawman except maybe the semi-automatic pistol holstered on his hip.

Upon seeing Cade, Daymon picked up his pace and met the gimpy operator halfway. After handshakes and pats on the back, Cade handed over the note he'd come across in Hanna. After stuffing it in a pocket, the two shared a few words and then Daymon walked them over and introduced Charlie as the former Jackson Hole Chief of Police. "Pleasure," said Cade. He turned back to Daymon and pointed toward the far side of the clearing near where the Black Hawk sat, its massive rotor blades drooping and casting off strange kaleidoscopic shadows on the grass.

"Can I have a word with you ... in private?"

The smile left Daymon's face. He nodded and turned, following the footsteps he had just left in the grass.

"Wait up," said Cade, swallowing a couple of pills. "I'm nursing a tiny bit of a sprain."

"Tiny bit?" Brook said incredulously.

After giving Brook an aww shucks look accompanied by a shooing motion, Cade popped open the case near his feet and took out a slab of black plastic the size of a road atlas only thicker by a couple of inches. Protected all the way around by a kind of rubberized armor, it looked like a panel ripped off of a Transformer robot.

By then everyone had dismounted both trucks and was walking about and stretching. Max bolted across the clearing and promptly lifted his leg and marked the Black Hawk as his.

Lev clicked his rifle to safe and set it aside.

Shoulder-to-shoulder, Cade and Daymon walked across the clearing. Along the way, Cade brought up the fact that earlier that day he'd seen a very undead Hoss, the lawyer in the house in Hanna, and ended by saying, "I finished the job you were supposed to do." He paused for a beat to let the words sink in. Daymon opened his mouth to apologize but instead Cade raised a hand and cut him off. "Case closed. Hoss was a waste of skin. On to more important business. You kept your word in Jackson and helped me get at Robert Christian. And I in turn held up my end of the bargain and turned him over to the powers that be who honored their word, thus enabling me to get my own *pound of flesh*." He paused for another long beat.

Daymon said, "You're welcome ... I guess. Care to elaborate?"

"Negative. It's classified. However ... " He hinged open the item he'd been carrying under his arm. Powered it on and waited while the laptop screen flared a brilliant blue that contrasted sharply against dusk's failing light. "It's all right here ... on the desktop. It's labeled RCEX. Not for the faint of heart but it should bring Heidi some closure."

"This shows Robert Christian's execution?"

"All sixteen gruesome seconds of it. From drop to flop to plop. Glad I wasn't there. Heard his bowels loosened something fierce. Pretty rank-smelling."

"Can I take it?"

Cade hitched a brow. "Sure," he said. "I need it back as soon as you're finished with it." He snapped the rugged laptop closed and handed it over.

"Thanks again," said Daymon, a troubled look settling on his features. "About Hoss—"

Cade said nothing. Locked eyes with Daymon and shook his head slowly side to side.

Tucking a stray dread behind his ear, Daymon said, "Daylight's fading fast. Let's get you unloaded and we'll fire up some canned chili and vegetables."

Cade's stomach growled at the mere thought of eating anything other than MREs or Schriever mess hall chow, which was barely a notch above a TV dinner in his opinion.

With twilight falling quickly and everyone helping, the trucks got unloaded and the gear stacked outside the compound entrance.

Chapter 59

Stubby carbine in hand, Brook entered the compound a step behind Raven. After pausing a tick to let their eyes adjust, they caught up with Charlie who had paused in the communications room in order to introduce them to Heidi.

Heidi, who had seemed to find purpose in monitoring the radios, seemed truly delighted to meet them. "Want to see our eyes and ears to the outside?"

"Sure," Brook lied. In reality she just wanted to find a dark place and lie down and close her eyes and quiet the little voice that kept reminding her that she had killed three people a handful of hours ago.

The introduction to the ham radio and Motorola two-way radios was far from necessary. Focusing on an urn of coffee whose aroma had been calling to her since she stepped foot into the room, Brook heard maybe one word in three. Even Raven seemed to tire quickly of the narrative; however, Brook's interest was soon piqued when she learned the group would soon be returning to a nearby quarry in order to relieve it of its solar panels and high-tech closed-circuit camera system.

When Heidi had finished, she led them from the communications room to the container the Grayson family would be calling home. The low-ceilinged affair happened to be in the farthest corner, near the rear of the compound, diagonal from where the kids would be staying.

Heidi opened the door for Brook and said, "The guy who was staying here took his ball and his family and went home."

Brook set her canvas duffel on one of the low-slung bunks. Somewhat confused, she looked a question at the blonde.

"Oh. Sorry," proffered Heidi. "He was a bit of a pacifist. Didn't like Duncan's proactive approach to handling our problems around here. And the fact that Duncan used the heavy artillery against the Huntsville thugs was too much for him to handle... so the day before yesterday he loaded his family into his airplane and flew the coop."

"Where to?"

"Anywhere but here were his exact words."

"What did Duncan do?"

Heidi paused. Unsure if the lady could handle what she was about to divulge. But hell, the dead were walking the earth topside. If this gun-toting super-fit thirty-something couldn't handle the truth then what good was she?

Based on second-hand knowledge, Heidi described the ambush in a Michael Mann fashion. Leaving nothing out, first she exaggerated the propane tanks exploding and catching the vehicle on fire. Her graphic description of Chance's head and helmet bouncing down the road and spinning away in two separate pieces, even in Raven's presence, was hardly tempered. Then, to wrap it up, she mentioned the fifty-caliber decapitation job Duncan had wrought on the driver of the Toyota. And when she'd finished telling the tale, she removed her hat, looked up to the ceiling, and waved a little elbow-wrist waggle to an imaginary airplane and said, "Good effin riddance Bob ... and thanks for the empty bunks."

Then Brook disarmed Heidi with a smile of her own and, as if she had read the blonde's mind, finished her thought off with words strikingly similar to the prejudicial thinking her host had engaged in first. "Besides, if they can't pull their weight then what good are they?"

Throwing a shiver, Heidi changed the subject and said, "God willing we'll be cooking some fresh meat over the fire later tonight. Hope to see you there."

Salivating at the prospect of flame-broiled *anything* and barely able to contain her enthusiasm, Brook looked at Raven, smiled, and said, "Yes you most certainly will."

***

After helping Wilson, Sasha, and Taryn get squared away in their new digs at the end of the wing just left of the front entry, Cade retraced his steps, stopping briefly at the comms container to get directions to Duncan's quarters. As he listened to Heidi, two things of almost equal importance leapt out at him. One, a thin black satellite phone resting on a shelf just below his eye level. And two, a coffee machine warming a half-full urn of inky black goodness, its pleasant earthy smell filling the room and taking him back to Portland, before all of this mess started. He thanked Heidi, but before carrying on he addressed both of his observations in order of importance. "That phone, he said. "Is it Daymon's?"

Heidi nodded.

"Heard any incoming calls recently?"

She shook her head side-to-side. "Nope."

He took it off the shelf and fiddled with it for a second and then replaced it. "Thing's no good with the ringer cycled to mute. There's a missed call ..." He saw her face go pale, then added, "Don't worry, it was me and it'll remain our little secret."

"Thanks," she said with a wan smile. "I've been trying to get ahold of some ham radio users Logan had been in contact with before word of the black helicopters started filtering in." The color returning to her cheeks, she went on, "Logan left a whole page full of notes ... all pertaining to different frequencies ... or handles. Whatever they're called."

"Call signs," said Cade. "Any luck?"

"Nope."

"Keep trying," he said. Then he touched upon the second item of importance. He asked, "Can I relieve you of two cups of your wonderful-smelling coffee?"

Without a word she smiled, poured two mugs to the rim and passed them over. Then she placed the headphones over her ears and sat back down, safe and secure, free from all physical contact with the outside world.

Chapter 60

Cade followed the map in his mind and arrived outside a closed door mere moments after talking to Heidi. He stood there, a mug in each hand, steam wafting to his nose, barely able to constrain his impulse to drink both on the spot. Instead, he tested the door with his toe. Balanced precariously on one foot, looking like one of the Flying Wallendas—only grounded and with scalding coffee sluicing over his knuckles—he managed to get the door moving without crying out in pain. He stepped over the threshold and crept into the gloom. Inside, the air was still and smelled strongly of whiskey and flatulence. Ragged snoring was coming from a darkened corner.

Cade took three steps into the room and felt the soft tickle of something dragging across his face. Unable to see a place to set the mugs, he tilted his head sideways and a few passes later, looking no doubt uncoordinated like a kid bobbing for apples, was rewarded for his efforts by finally seizing the dangling length of errant string between his teeth. He backed up until the string went taut and there was a click and the single bulb flared to life.

The retinas, he was reminded, like everything else, were also affected by Newton's law. Their sudden contraction and the pain to the optic nerve made him squint, which in turn caused an involuntary flinch that started a new mini-torrent of pain-inducing caffeinated liquid sheeting across his exposed skin.

Once again stifling a yelp, he set both mugs on a nearby footlocker and cast his gaze over the sorry sight. Still wearing his aviator's glasses, fully clothed in some foreign army's surplus uniform, and still clutching a near empty bottle of some kind of booze, Duncan Winters snored away, presumably stone-cold drunk.

After unsuccessfully trying to wrestle the bottle from Duncan's firm grip, Cade resorted to a bit of dirty pool. He grabbed one of the mugs and, practicing guerilla warfare of the highest order, placed it next to the older man's head, making sure the wispy tendrils curled over his cheek so he would have no choice but to inhale the heady aroma.

Three slow steady breaths later, Duncan smiled yet his eyes stayed closed. Then, a tick after Cade removed the mug, Duncan's eyes opened briefly and, retreating from the sixty-watt glare, closed back to two thin slits. There was a long moment of silence and Duncan said, "You, Captain Cade Grayson, are in violation of Army regulation six-seventy-dash-one. Your sideburns must not be below the lowest ear hole." He cackled and looked longingly at the bottle.

"You're drunk," said Cade. "And I'm no longer taking orders. I've gone civilian."

"And hippie," stated Duncan.

"Far from it," Cade shot back. He changed the subject and addressed the reason he was here. "Are you going to be good to go tomorrow?"

"Is a frog's ass watertight?"

Cade laughed at that and offered the cup of joe.

After swinging his legs over the edge of the bed, Duncan waited for a couple of beats for his brain to stop bouncing around in his cranium, then worked at sitting upright. He accepted the mug and took a long pull.

Having been around a few folks battling the bottle, Cade had a feeling he knew what to expect next. And he was right.

The bottle that Duncan had so firmly clutched during sleep seemed to have a stronger appeal upon waking. With no apparent remorse, he added the remainder, two fingers' worth of the amber liquid, into his coffee. He stared hard at the floor, as if he were making a decision right then and there. He cupped the mug. Considered chucking it at the steel wall. But he wasn't ready yet. He hoisted the concoction, looked at the metal ceiling and said, "To Logan."

Cade grimaced. He knew from those intervention TV shows that threats and coercion would get him nowhere. The decision was Duncan's, and Duncan's alone to make. So he hung his head and looked on with disappointment as his friend took a serious breath and a greedy gulp of the Jack Daniels-laced coffee. He waited until Duncan drained his cup. It didn't take long. Then Cade acquiesced, hoisted his coffee and said, "To Logan."

Duncan placed the mug next to the empty bottle, hoisted an imaginary drink and said, "Indeed. To Oops."

Finished with the coffee and craving more, Cade looked at the Vietnam-era aviator squarely and said, "None of us are going anywhere and nobody's going to pay for what happened if you're not sober enough to fly by tomorrow. Forty-eight hours ... that was our deal. Remember?"

"What day is it?"

"The day you got sober ... and stayed sober."

Shaking his head, Duncan said, "I'm a grown man. I can handle my own affairs."

"You need to come to a decision." Cade let the words hang for a minute then went on. "If your mind is not made up by twenty-three-hundred-hours I am going to load my gear into my pick-up and take whoever wants to go and leave without you." He didn't wait for a line of bullshit. Or another excuse. He had a job to do and he was determined to see it through to the end, whether he got there by plane, train, or automobile. Without another word, he bowed out of Duncan's quarters, closed the door softly behind him, and headed for the Grayson family's new billet.

Chapter 61

Grateful his twelve-hour *sentence* was over, Jimmy Foley parked his Jeep in the driveway. Though he was technically still *'inside the wire'* as he'd heard the mercenaries say, he stayed in the rig until he was confident there were no zombies lurking nearby.

Satisfied he was alone, he hopped out and climbed the creaky steps to the back door. Beginning his newly adopted ritual, he paused outside and listened hard. *Nothing*. He slipped his key in the deadbolt, unlocked the door and went inside. Once inside with the door locked behind, out came the .40 caliber Springfield XD.

From being sealed up all day, the still air inside the two-story A-frame-style guest house was hot and made breathing a chore. Pistol leading the way, Foley transited the hall and stopped at the door to the stairway leading down to the single-car garage, mudroom, and half-bath on the lower level. Finding it locked, he padded back the way he'd come, boots tapping a quiet cadence on the tiles underfoot. Cutting the corner, he made his way down the hallway that shot straight off the back entry, passed the empty powder room on his left along the way before emerging into the front half of the open-floor-plan home. To his immediate left was an open kitchen sporting a large quartz island with a trio of bar stools pushed against it. Ignoring the thought of rewarding himself with a warm beer for enduring another day conscripted to Bishop's group, he skirted the dining room table and threaded between the sofa and coffee table to the front of the home. Concluding his ritual, he inspected the sliding glass door set below the massive wall of windows that afforded a fair amount of lake view between the waterfront homes across the way.

Still locked. And he found the makeshift security bar (a wooden dowel he doubted a shambler could thwart) still in the channel where he had placed it earlier. Leaving the door secured, he used a long pole specially designed for the job and opened all of the upper windows, letting the evening breeze in. He put the pole aside, turned and looked up towards the loft where the master bedroom lorded over the living room. Nothing seemed amiss. *Times like these, one can't be too careful.*

Something about returning to an empty house when there were dead things walking the world unnerved the hell out of him. And that was why he was allowed to pick any home on the peninsula. And that was also why he eschewed the larger, more opulent homes across the gravel lane in favor of this one. *The fewer rooms to clear before turning in*, he reasoned, *the better.*

The stairs to the loft were massive oak slabs perched centrally on a thick steel beam. A triangular-shaped door below hid a wall of electronics—his favorite part of the new digs. He thought about watching *Heat* again, but decided against firing up the generator and instead opted for a good night's sleep so he would be sharp for some patrol Carson was sending him out on. Probably another full day as *initial entry* while the Spartan guys placed bets on whether or not he'd get bitten, or the daily over under on how many walking dead would scramble from the door as he stepped aside. It wasn't fun work, but it beat the alternative. Plus, if there ever was a way of escaping this fate that had befallen him, getting past the gate was the first hurdle. And doing so unscathed alongside a dozen heavily armed men carrying a set of legitimate orders might be the only way. *Marathon, not a sprint*, he reminded himself. He'd either get bitten and then eat a bullet. Or he'd catch the Spartan boys slipping and steal away into the forest.

With feet sore and heavy from an entire day of standing, sunup to dusk at the east gate, he climbed the stairs and sat on the bed and kicked off his boots. His belt and pistol, still in its holster, went on the nightstand. He fell heavily into the bed fully clothed and, just before nodding off, remembered to say a prayer for his wife and kid, both early victims of the Omega virus.

Chapter 62

The clearing was alive with activity. Raven was zipping back and forth along the makeshift packed-earth airstrip, the tactical flashlight Cade had zip-tied to the handlebars casting a blue-white cone of spastically juddering light dozens of feet in front her. Slaloming through the grass, instincts suddenly alive, Max would spring from out of the darkness, enter the light spill and nip at the mountain bike's front tire just as the diminutive twelve-year-old initiated a wide looping turn.

Just inside the tree line near the compound's entrance, Daymon stirred a big pot of chili-con-carne, all the while wishing it was instead a haunch of venison roasting slowly on a spit.

As usual, the *security trio*—the moniker Logan had bestowed upon Lev, Chief, and Jenkins—were sitting on camp chairs around the fire, talking about their next mission to the quarry and how best to remove the solar panels off of the high roof without damaging them.

Near the entrance, Cade was getting his kit in order. "Hand me the night vision goggles and the spare batteries, please," he said to Brook.

Glancing away from Raven, who up until then had garnered her undivided attention, Brook rummaged around in the Pelican case and handed the items over. "Are you going to take my advice and slow down after this one?"

"That's my plan," said Cade. "Once the threat is gone."

"How long do you foresee yourself being out there?"

"One day."

"Why the comms and NVGs if you're only gone one day?"

"OK. Twenty-four hours. Give or take." He placed the goggles he'd retrieved from his bike in Hanna into the box next to the two pairs Colonel Cornelius Shrill had given him prior to leaving Schriever. Alongside the goggles he put an extra box of ammunition for the Modular Sniper Rifle which would also be accompanying him for this mission.

"How's the ankle?"

"I'll live," he replied.

"I hope so," Brook said. "For Raven's sake." She rose and without another word stalked off towards the fire.

Cade watched her go. Then he shifted his gaze and regarded Raven for a second. Burned her smiling face into his memory for later retrieval.

Daymon sauntered over and placed the armored laptop inside the open Pelican container.

Cade stopped what he was doing, arched a brow, and looked a question at the taller man.

"She's still processing it. And you were right ... it was a messy affair. I could almost smell the puddle of shit through the display."

"I'm sorry."

"Don't be. She needed to see it." He tucked an errant dread behind his ear. His face suddenly softened as he added, "*I* needed to see it."

There was an uneasy silence between the two men.

"Ten minutes," said Daymon as a smile cracked his face. "This ain't no mess hall. So bring a plate and a spoon."

Simultaneously Cade nodded and realized his salivary glands were going crazy. The smell of smoke and the sound and aroma of the pot of chili bubbling twenty feet away was distracting him from the task at hand.

As he removed a tangle of communications gear from the box, there was a mellifluous rustling in the darkness next to him. Instinctively his hand went to his Glock and suddenly a wiry Asian man whom he hadn't yet met invaded his personal space and hammered down onto his haunches, butt an inch from the ground—a cultural thing, Cade guessed. The man stared for a second. Liquid black eyes studying and gauging. Assessing threat perhaps.

Cade's headlamp illuminated the man's face from the nose up. Slightly misshapen, his upper cranium looking like a ball peen hammer had been applied to it in random places. And from the long horizontal gash between brow and hairline, foul-smelling yellowed puss oozed between the puckered skin. Cade finally broke down and introduced himself.

After a quiet few seconds the man said, "I'm Tran."

"Good to meet you," said Cade. "You worked for Robert Christian, right?"

Tran nodded.

"He was a piece of work, wasn't he?"

"*Was?*" whispered Tran through swollen lips.

Shaking his head, Cade said, "*Was*." He opened the laptop and, while it powered on, transferred a few smaller items from the big box into the one that would be going with him in either the truck or the helo—the answer to which would be evident shortly. He glanced at his watch: 2145 and still no Duncan.

Tran crowded closer as the screen flashed blue and the Schriever logo and desktop icons appeared.

Cade opened the file labeled: RCEX. There was a whirring sound as the hard drive went to work. After a moment a box with an opaque *Play* button hovering over a blurred image filled the entire screen. Placing the pointer over the arrow, Cade clicked the button and turned away, leaving Tran to watch the execution alone.

As Cade arranged the remaining items in the box, he heard the charges being read aloud to Robert Christian. Then the pleading he remembered followed by a loud *thunk* and silence. A second later the clip was replaying and Tran was watching as tears streamed down his face.

After clicking the case containing his gear shut, Cade heard the *thunk* again, then Tran asked, "Bishop?"

Meeting the smaller man's gaze, Cade shook his head and said, "Not yet."

Tran's face tightened. His eyes looked up and away. He appeared to be trying to draw something from his memory.

"Do you know where Bishop is?"

Tran shook his head. He said, "Gee six."

Cade thought for a half second and said, "Gee six ... you mean Gulf Stream Six?"

Tran nodded and smiled, showing off a mouthful of broken teeth.

"What happened to you?"

Tran said, "Bishop's men beat me."

Cade made no reply but seethed inwardly.

"Time to eat," called Daymon.

Tran rose and wandered off towards the wildly dancing firelight.

Cade saw Brook herding Raven over and made a mental note to ask Brook to see to Tran's wounds. Then from behind he heard the steel door hinge open, followed at once by Sasha chattering excitedly about something. His eyes followed as the girl and the new lovers, Taryn and Wilson, walked by, barely acknowledging him. He pressed the light button on his Suunto and checked the time in its soft blue glow: 2210. There was another rustling from behind and a hand gripped his shoulder. A voice from the dark, low and with a southern drawl said, "I owe you one, Grayson."

Cade said, "You owe yourself. I had nothing to do with it."

Hands on hips, Duncan said nothing. He swiveled his head towards the fire.

Seeing the fire reflected off Duncan's glasses and reading the body language as belonging to someone not entirely defeated, Cade said, "We better get it before it's gone."

Nodding, Duncan left Cade alone with his gear and walked off towards the gathering crowd.

Cade watched him go and pulled out his satellite phone. After powering it on and acquiring a signal, he scrolled through the menus and selected a preset. He tapped out an SMS message and hit send. Leaving the phone powered up, he locked the keys and stuffed it back into his pocket. Stomach growling like a cornered wolverine, he rejoined the small band of survivors to enjoy his first good meal in a long while.

Chapter 63

After many hours of conversation—most of it forced—Bishop led Jamie back to her room. With the soft steady hum of the generator serenading them, there was a moment outside of the door when she could tell by his body language that he wanted to lean in and kiss her. She sensed him exuding a certain nervousness totally out of character for someone who had survived SEAL training and several deployments in the recent wars. *Hell*, she thought. *Someone who survived the Omega outbreak and rose to lead his own group of mercenaries should be fearful of no man—or woman.* But now that she knew he was one of those naturally awkward ones, she decided to use it to her advantage. String him along to a certain degree. She said, "I think it's working."

He said nothing. But his head cocked a little, showing a measure of intrigue.

"The Stockholm thing. I'll never forgive Carson for what he did. But you ... like my mom always said ... life gives you a bowl of lemons, you make lemonade." Guts churning, full of disgust at what she was about to initiate, she stood on her tiptoes and kissed him on the cheek. In the process, the shred of fabric passing itself off as a dress rode up to the small of her back, leaving bare everything below. She figured him falling for her advance was perhaps a 50/50 proposition. And if he did, she put the odds of him grabbing her and dragging her into the room caveman-style at probably 80/20 for.

The former happened at once as his inhibition crumbled. His hand went to her bare backside. Her stomach clenched and adrenaline flowed freely in her body. She saw lust in his eyes, indicating the latter was dangerously close to happening. Until she had a split-second epiphany. She gently pushed his hand away and said the four words that in her experience had the power of kryptonite to even the horniest of men. "I'm on my period."

There was a moment's hesitation on his part. She could almost hear the gears turning in his head. However, the lust leaving his eyes was impossible to miss. His smile turned to a grimace. *Throw him a bone,* she thought to herself. "It's at the end, though."

Still he made no reply. He seemed to be wavering on some kind of decision she knew would end badly for her so she pushed all of her chips in and said, "I haven't been fucked since the world went to shit." Which was the truth and it appeared that he bought it. "So what's one more day? You reserve the table and pick out the wine, and when we retire tomorrow night it will be together in the same bed. Deal?"

More hesitation on his part. The same amount of words—none. His eyes were boring into hers. Finally he said, "Deal." He opened the door and made a grand sweeping gesture indicating she should enter.

Rubbing the welts on her wrists, Jamie asked, "Are you going to handcuff me?"

Outside there was a long burst of gunfire. It resonated for a moment, the echo amplified by the proximity to water. Then a tick after it dissipated a wicked grin appeared on Bishop's face. He said, "We'll save that for tomorrow. Consider tonight a test of your loyalty."

Definitely one of the tactics employed by the Symbionese Liberation Army who had held the newspaper magnate's daughter hostage. They gave her some rope but not enough to hang herself. Let the sense of inclusion, over time, help win her over. Breaking Jamie's train of thought, Bishop's grin disappeared. He promised, "If you so much as crack this door I'll let the boys have you. And when they're done ... if you survive ... I'll have them feed you to the dead."

Somehow remaining stoic despite the visual his threat conjured in her mind, she mouthed, "Thank you," flicked on the light and backed into her room.

After the door closed, Bishop remained there for a moment, listening, half-expecting to hear the slider hauled open followed by hasty footsteps across the porch roof. In fact, deep down he welcomed it. Welcomed the chase that would ensue. After all, like she'd said, *'What is one day?'* And that's all it would take for him to find her and take what he coveted anyway. But, slightly disappointed, he heard nothing. Not a peep.

Before retiring to his room, he padded to the door by the stairs and heard the loud rumble of Elvis's snores. Then he went downstairs and retrieved the pistol from under the table. He stuck it in his waistband near the small of his back and blew out the candles, leaving only the faint glow of the moon off the lake's surface to guide him. He negotiated the furniture carefully, their placement still foreign to him. Scaled the stairs and paused in front of Jamie's room. *Nothing.* Not even a choked sob or the sound of crying reached his ears. Not that he really expected it. She was proving to be a worthy opponent—and after he had finally broken her completely—she'd be a worthy mother to his children as well.

He made his way to the master bedroom and, once the door was closed behind him, called Carson on the two-way to let him know that the usual test was a go. It was a kind of controlled experiment that up until now had ended badly for every single one of the women he had deemed worthy to bear him children.

The .38 caliber revolver, now relieved of its bullets, he left in plain view on the nightstand closest the door. His semi-automatic Sig Sauer went under the pillow that was to be Jamie's if she lived to see the day.

Content in the knowledge that the next day was going to be glorious—in more ways than one—he put his head on his pillow, closed his eyes, and let sleep take him.

***

Ten minutes after the shock of being left to her own recognizance without any form of restraint had worn off, and a full twenty since being let into her room, Jamie decided the second shoe wouldn't be dropping tonight. So, willing herself to breathe normally, she leaned over and put her ear to the door. She heard nothing in the hall. The Jack and Jill, however, was a different story. The snoring coming from the room beyond was the loudest she'd ever heard.

She searched the room and discovered that her clothes and boots were gone. The closet was full of bedding and curtains and crafting supplies. There was nothing useful under the bed—unless dust bunnies counted as a deadly weapon. The lamp was a flimsy item branded as Scandinavian but made in China. *Useless.*

Fuck it, she thought. She padded to the door and tried the knob. It moved freely. She pulled the door slowly toward her, exposing the hall in small slices. Expecting to find herself staring down the barrel of a gun, she poked her head out and looked first left and then right. Seeing nothing there, she tiptoed down the hall and took the stairs down at a glacial pace, one at a time, pausing for half a minute on each tread to listen hard.

At the bottom she saw a blue rectangular spill of moonlight on the floor by the back door. She paused there, bathed in its glow, gazing into the inky black outdoors.

"Do it," said Carson softly. He turned Ozzy down and shifted in the Escalade's supple leather seat. "Please do it. You want to run. And I want to catch you in the act." *The act*, he thought with a sly grin, *would be a messy affair*. He would have nothing less.

Her hand touched the cool brushed nickel knob. The generator throbbed outside. Then there was a long burst of automatic rifle fire. It died off quickly but, as she stood frozen in front of the door peering out the glass, sporadic single shots continued for a full minute after the initial volley.

Seeing the dark-haired beauty's resolve crumbling before his eyes, Carson chanted, "Fuck. Fuck. Fuck." He pounded the steering wheel softly and, along with the distant gunfire, felt the throbbing erection tenting his pants slowly subside.

Standing at the door, knob turned halfway to freedom, another of her mom's sayings popped into her head. *Slow and steady wins the race.* And slow and steady would let her live to see another sunrise. And tomorrow or the next or the day after that, she'd find a vulnerability that would allow her to extract her revenge.

Reluctantly, she let the knob snap from her grip. Then she pushed away the earlier thought of getting a knife from the wood block—he would notice it missing anyway—and about-faced and crept back up the stairs to her room.

Without her arms and legs cuffed to the bedposts, sleep came easy and instantaneously.

Ozzy was back on the stereo and riding the Crazy Train. In Carson's mind, he still saw the woman's silhouette in the window. Then she cast a surreptitious glance about. And with her dress riding up around her waist, she was through the door and taking the stairs two at a time. He was on her heels in a half-beat. Shouting for her to stop. Yet she ran blindly into the woods.

His hand worked furiously at his crotch, trying to awaken his flaccid member. To facilitate the lost blood flow's return. He imagined he caught hold of her toned, tan arm and was dragging her to the ground, the dress now over her head.

Another ragged burst of fire shattered his concentration and ruined the moment. His radio came to life and a voice said calmly: *The Zeds that squirted around the gate have been contained. Mopping up.*

"Copy that," replied Carson. Nonplussed and unsated, he put his junk away and zippered his pants. Cracked an energy drink and fixed his gaze on the empty window, hoping she had only decided to give it some time and make her run for it at zero-dark-thirty. The witching hour when studies showed most people let their guard down.

He drained the last of the Red Bull and tossed the can unceremoniously onto the floor. He traced the welts on his cheek and thought to himself, *Bring it on, bitch.*

Chapter 64

Lying on the bunk, face-to-face with her mom, Raven asked in a sleepy voice, "When is Dad leaving?"

Brook's eyes snapped open but the view didn't change. Though an impossibility, the space inside the Conex seemed darker than the insides of her eyelids. After realizing there would be no adjustment to the gloom nor eye contact to affirm and back up her words, she gave up trying to locate Raven's features in the dark and said, "Just know that he will be back."

"Why is he going?"

"Because some bad men hurt his friend's brother and some other people who used to live here."

"And why does that make it so Daddy *has* to go?"

Brook wanted to say: Because the motherfuckers killed people for the guy President Clay just had hanged. The same man who was indirectly responsible for setting back the production of antiserum weeks or months, and perhaps extinguished that glimmer of hope forever. Instead she said half-truthfully, "Because those men also had something to do with your Uncle Carl's death."

Raven yawned, then said, "But I thought Uncle Carl died in a fire."

Time for the whole truth and nothing but. "He was murdered first."

There was a silence heavier than the oppressive shroud of darkness.

Forgetting where she'd put her headlamp, and feeling an overwhelming need to look her daughter in the eye and tell her everything was going to be OK, Brook searched the bunk for it with one hand. Finding nothing atop the cool sheets, she batted the air near her head and felt the rubberized backing and then walked her hand up the elastic band and extricated it from the spring she'd hung it from.

"I'm about to switch the headlamp on ... shield your eyes."

There was no answer. She put her arm protectively across Raven's sleeping form and, still wearing the headlamp, drifted off to sleep herself.

***

"Are you sure she's asleep?"

Wilson said, "Positive." He shrugged off his shorts and marveled at the softness of Taryn's cool skin against his. "Want some covers?'

Nodding in the dark, she pulled on a corner, accidentally exposing his backside. "As long as we're quiet," he said, letting his hands wander. "There's no way she'll know. It's too dark in here."

Their legs and arms intertwined, Wilson ran his hands over Taryn's tatted bicep, feeling the raised scar tissue and imagining in his mind's eye the permanently etched skulls and dragons residing there.

Stifling a giggle, Taryn lost herself exploring his mouth with her tongue and for a moment she forgot about everything. The walking dead were of no relevance. The cold pit she'd been carrying in her gut since escaping the airport disappeared. For a few minutes everything was all right in the world.

An arm's length away, everything was not all right. Every time Sasha nodded off she was awakened by a man's face splitting in half under a barrage of bullets. Not a direct representation of the first and hopefully last human she would be forced to kill, but damn close. And this she knew because a millisecond after she'd pulled the trigger the first time her eyes clamped shut on their own accord. But before they did, however, she'd seen the face of one of the occupants in the second car implode and break in two. And this, she supposed, was where her subconscious had picked up the horrific image it had seen fit to cut and paste, seemingly at will, onto the insides of her eyelids.

Now though, mercifully, she guessed, every time her lids fluttered the metronomic metallic squeak from a loose bolt in the other bunk bed dispelled the encroaching visions. So she lay staring in the dark and listening to the subtle rasp of fabric against skin and trying to decide which was worse. Succumbing to sleep and enduring the visions of mayhem. Or fighting it tooth and nail to stay awake and having to endure the sounds of lovemaking that only served to further remind her how alone she really was.

Chapter 65
Outbreak - Day 19

As dawn broke and the horizon turned from a dark blue to purple and the sliver of rising sun spilled golden light across the clearing, Cade was surprised to find Duncan already up and giving the Black Hawk her pre-flight inspection. He called out from a dozen yards away, "She gonna fly?

Looking up from his task, Duncan adjusted his glasses and waited for Cade to cover the distance between them, then replied, "Oh she'll fly alright ... question is how far." Cade cracked the seal on a bottled water, took a long pull and tipped the mouth toward Duncan. Declining the offering, Duncan went on, "What's with the all-black getup? Is this some kind of mission impossible which requires you to look like a modern day ninja?"

"All my other gear is olive or desert. Not going to fly where I think we'll be going."

Interest piqued, Duncan stopped what he was doing. He looked up and in a serious tone said, "Sounds like you've got a handle on where this Bishop prick is."

"I got a pretty good lead from Tran last night." He paused a beat. Removed a small plastic bottle from his cargo pants. He looked up, arched a brow and said, "If I heard him correctly. And that's a big if—"

Duncan said, "Yeah, that boy was pretty busted up and I guess damn near death when Daymon and his crew found him."

Working the child safety cap on the ibuprofen bottle, Cade went on, "Tran said ... well, it was more like a mumble ... but what I took away was that Bishop escaped Jackson Hole aboard Robert Christian's G6." He swallowed a handful of pills, grimaced, then took a long pull off his water.

"G6? As in Gulf Stream G650 which is one of those sixty million dollar Learjet-looking planes the CEOs and one-percenters like Donald Trump used to tool around in?"

"And *billionaires* like Christian. Affirmative."

"And how are you going to find this G6?"

"Are there any aeronautical maps aboard this bird?"

Duncan shook his head. "Nope. I left Schriever with GPS coordinates and the DHS manual covering the UH-60 platform. That's it."

"Logan stockpiled everything else ... did he have any detailed maps?"

Hearing Logan referred to in the past tense brought on a wave of sadness. "Negative," drawled Duncan. "There's only a couple of maps of Utah and Wyoming. One of 'em has a sliver of Southern Idaho on back."

"No help there," replied Cade. "You're going to need to find fuel for this bird, correct?"

Nodding, Duncan said, "I was planning on hitting the Air National Guard base in Boise. There's gotta be underground tanks there."

Seeing the devastation, a whole city aflame in his mind's eye, Cade said, "Boise burned pretty bad, remember?"

Duncan shivered visibly. "Don't remind me. We barely escaped that one with our hides intact."

Cade unwrapped a breakfast bar and took a bite. Said with a mouthful, "Wasn't the first time and surely it won't be the last."

"Shhh. You'll piss off Mister Murphy."

"Murphy blew his wad in South Dakota," said Cade. "More shit went wrong there than I care to remember." He finished the bar.

"You're alive. How'd you manage that?"

Cade opened the port door and adjusted the seat forward a bit. "You got four or five hours?"

"Save it for later ... around the campfire."

After tossing his pack in the back with the rest of his kit, Cade said, "I have an idea."

"Here we go again," said Duncan. "Do tell."

Cade described the Montgomery County airstrip he'd passed the day before, including the fact that he'd spied a pair of fuel bowsers parked near the hangars. "Figure one of those ought to have some JP in it. At the very least we'll be able to obtain an aeronautical chart from the airport or scavenge one from one of the airplanes there. Use that to find an airstrip capable of handling that Gulfstream. Can't be more than three or four of 'em in Idaho, anyway."

Duncan clucked his tongue. "Good idea. Heading back to Boise held very little appeal for this good ol' boy."

"Reminds me," said Cade. "I brought you a present, Old Man." He hustled to the F-650, opened the driver's door and leaned inside. Coming back, he handed Duncan a small paper sack, a clatter sounding as something inside it shifted.

After testing the bag's weight, Duncan reached in and said, "Hell is this?"

"Something you couldn't have benefitted from last night ... since you were wearing a thick pair of beer goggles."

"Glasses?" said Duncan, holding up a half-dozen pairs in different styles and materials and no doubt thicknesses.

"Sneaky Daymon sent a text message to my sat phone. Mentioned you're way past due for a new pair."

"Yeah, but where'd you get them?"

"A lost and found here. A junk drawer there. That old house you rescued me and Daymon from ..."

"Yeah ..."

"Two pairs in the kitchen drawer there."

"Well let's see. Pardon the pun, of course." He removed his Aviators and tried on pair after pair, saying, "nope, nope, nope," after each one that did nothing to fix his near sightedness. Then, getting towards the end of the lot, he tried on a pair with large oval rims and the necessary horizontal line demarking the long distance half of the prescription from the up close viewing part of the lens. He tried them on and fixed his gaze on the vehicles thirty yards distant and then focused farther yet at the very end of the airstrip two football field lengths away. *Wow,* he thought. Then he peered down at the grass near his feet and could make out the individual blades. *Holy hell.* "These are going to work just fine. How do I look?"

Suppressing a smile, Cade heard the song *Rocket Man* cue up and begin playing in his head. "Great," he lied.

Concealed behind the foliage-covered blind, the door to the compound opened with a resonant grating noise of metal on metal. Soon, Daymon, Lev, and Seth, all three dressed in surplus woodland camouflage BDUs circa the late eighties and carrying backpacks and various weapons, emerged from the gloom. Once they'd crossed the dew-laden grass and stood under the Black Hawk's drooping blades, Seth, whose normal job watching the radios and trail cameras had been recently taken over by Heidi, wished the group good fortune and continued on his way towards the motor pool.

Duncan snugged his flight helmet on, adjusted his new glasses, and directed a question at Lev. "Is Seth relieving Chief at the road?"

At first sight of Duncan's new look, Lev's eyes bugged. Holding back laughter he said, "Yep," then bit his lip, nearly drawing blood.

Testing out his new pair of eyes, Duncan gave the three-man team a visual inspection. "Looks like we got ourselves a ninja and a couple of Cold War-era troops here. Y'all said your goodbyes to your ladies?" He fixed his magnified bloodshot eyes on Cade, who remained stoic and said nothing. Duncan looked at Daymon, who merely nodded an affirmative. "Well shit. Let's kick the tires and light the fire then." *If I can remember the proper procedure.*

Lev took a seat on the starboard side near a window, donned a flight helmet, and strapped himself in. Peering sidelong across the cabin, he watched Daymon climb aboard and slide the door closed. He cracked a smile as the dreadlocked man battled to tuck his hair into the helmet, finally succeeding just as the turbines overhead coughed to life. After flashing Daymon a thumbs up, Lev closed his eyes and said a quick prayer, asking, in a general way, for his God to see to it that good prevailed over evil.

From the port-side front seat, Cade watched the kids file into the clearing with Raven and Brook bringing up the rear. He caught Raven's eye, smiled broadly, and flashed her a thumbs up. He blew a kiss in Brook's direction and then strapped his helmet on and drew down the smoked visor to hide the welling tears. Then he started the process of shoving all of the things he held dear—anything and everything that might cause a lapse of judgment or a moment's hesitation—deep into an imaginary vault in the deep recesses of his mind. The dial spun in his mind's eye and the tumblers clicked and everything and everyone was on hold for the duration of the mission—or so he hoped.

As the RPMs spooled up and the blades overhead became a seemingly solid moving disc, Duncan craned around and said, "Mike check?" To which he received a chorus of 'Copy's' and three thumbs up. Satisfied, he pulled pitch and the Black Hawk juddered slightly and left the earth amidst a rising cacophony of sound and the pungent smell of kerosene-tinged exhaust.

Then, inadvertently blasting the nine upturned faces with rotor wash, Duncan dipped the helo's nose and began a gradual left-hand turn across the clearing, gaining elevation while positioning the rising morning sun at his six.

Speaking into his boom mike, Cade said, "Before heading to the airport will you please take us west?"

"To Huntsville?"

"No, beyond. I want to see what the Ogden Canyon pass looks like from up here."

Duncan said, "I've only been as far west as the National Guard roadblock this side of Huntsville. Any guess how much farther the pass is?"

"According to a sign I saw near the reservoir, Ogden is fifteen miles west of Huntsville. I figure the pass is somewhere in between."

Lev entered the conversation. He asked, "What's at the pass?"

Cade answered, "I'm not certain. But whatever it is, it's holding eighty thousand of Ogden's finest at bay."

Duncan said, "Three mikes and you'll have eyes on the pass," then, with gloved hands finessing the stick, he finished the turn, straightened the Black Hawk out and resumed level flight, following the two-lane until it disappeared into the verdant forest below. The DHS bird thundered west, and near the burned-out gas station he'd seen earlier, Cade picked up a group of Zs at least thirty strong lurching eastbound. A tick later, the Black Hawk overflew the gawking creatures and then the roadblock and the ditch filled with listing vehicles slid by on their left. Pressing his helmet to the glass, Cade regarded the tangle of charred corpses lining the south side of the raised roadbed and said a second prayer in as many days for the men and women who'd died in service of their country.

***

Less than a minute after overflying Huntsville and the glassy waters of the Prineville reservoir, a natural slot appeared in the mountains where from more than a mile out Cade could see movement on a large scale. "Put us in a hover," he said sharply.

Duncan said, "Roger that," and nosed the Black Hawk up and quickly dropped some altitude before holding a semi-steady hover. "I'm going bring the FLIR (Forward Looking Infrared) camera on line. You've got a hat switch on the stick to move the pod."

"Copy that," replied Cade. He grasped the stick and found the switch with his thumb. A half-beat later the center display facing him lit up, showing a full color view of the canyon ahead. He gently thumbed the hat switch until the slot was centered perfectly on the monitor. To the right of the road rose a steep, nearly vertical cliff face, scrub and gnarled trees clinging to it tenaciously. Opposite the face, beyond the guardrail, the canyon dropped off sharply an indeterminate number of feet. And entirely blocking the dull gray four-lane in between the two was a wall of rust-colored shipping containers. Four abreast, three deep, and stacked two high in an inverted 'V,' the twenty-four steel Conex containers created a formidable-looking barrier, its point facing a jostling logjam of death that looked to be at least a thousand strong. *Not enough to move the barrier*, Cade thought to himself. *But still something worth keeping a close tab on.*

Duncan whistled slowly; a mournful sound befitting the sight. He said, "Zoom in on the outside guardrail."

Cade panned the FLIR pod left and zoomed in on an eight-inch gap between the scraped and dinged white metal rail and the vertically ribbed wall of the nearest container. One thing that stood out to him instantly, because of the sun glinting from them, was the carpet of spent brass covering the road several feet in every direction on the near side of the barrier.

In the span of less than a minute, they witnessed a Z being pushed through the gap under force from behind. It fell hard to the road face first and then clumsily picked itself up and marched east, joining the ragged line of creatures preceding it. Consequently, as a result of the sudden forward surge, a half dozen Zs went over the guardrail, cartwheeling into space.

Giving voice to Cade's thoughts, Duncan said, "I figure those Huntsville bandits had to come out here pretty regular to keep their numbers down. And these things have been accumulating since Bishop and his boys dealt those death cards here the other day."

Lev entered the conversation, "What do you figure, a couple hundred new ones show up every day?"

"At least," replied Cade. "Good for us more spill over than squirt through."

"Just a matter of time before enough of them show up and that gap starts getting wider," added Duncan. "Someone should have dynamited the hell outta that wall and sealed it off for good."

Great minds, thought Cade. Then he said, "Everyone seen enough?"

Duncan switched off the FLIR feed and nudged the stick. As the helo took a sharp left turn and started to descend, he said, "Next stop Morgan County Airport."

Chapter 66

Nearly thirteen hours of uninterrupted sleep had left Elvis with a banging headache; a sort of hangover minus the reward of a wild night of partying.

He dressed quickly, pulling on a pair of Levis and then a red Huskers tee-shirt he'd found hanging in a destroyed truck stop south of the Nebraska state line. Laced up his boots and donned his lucky Huskers ball cap.

Feeling naked without the .45 pressing the small of his back, he took the stairs down two at a time, walked through the house and joined Bishop outside on the deck overlooking the cobalt blue lake.

"Take a seat," said Bishop, his voice devoid of the menacing tone from the night before.

Feeling the rising sun warming his chin and cheeks, Elvis pulled a chair out and took a load off. There was a pot of coffee and a couple of mugs as well as a six-pack of canned energy drinks, dew rolling off their aluminum skin. In the center of the table was a platter containing some kind of sausages, a rasher of bacon, and a fluffy mound of scrambled eggs. "May I?" asked Elvis, reaching for an energy drink.

Bishop smiled, obviously pleased with himself for procuring such a meal. "Help yourself. Mi casa su casa," he said. "And thanks to our neighbors to the east, the eggs are always fresh."

Elvis took a Red Bull and filled a plate. He held aloft a stiff strip of well-marbled bacon, examining it front and back.

"No cook bacon," admitted Bishop. "Who knew it would take a zombie apocalypse for me to stoop so low."

Elvis chuckled.

"Did you enjoy the girls?"

"I was so tired I had to make them do all of the work." Then, changing the subject. "When am I leaving?"

Bishop flicked his wrist. The key fob arced from his hand, hit the table, bounced once and then skittered under the lip of Elvis's plate. "After you've had your fill, you're free to go. The tank is full and the spare cans are strapped down in back. Gives you about fifty gallons total ... more than enough to get there and back. There's a couple of MREs and some waters up front and you'll find your pistol and two spare mags in the glove box. And to make it easy on you, the coordinates are already programmed into the Tom Tom. Get within one mile of your final destination and lay up somewhere safe until just after sunset ... twenty-one-hundred hours ... or nine o'clock, and then proceed the rest of the way. I want you to activate the device at nine-eleven sharp."

Cocking his head with a harried look on his face, Elvis asked, "Won't they see me coming ... be using some kind of night vision goggles or overhead drones or something?"

Bishop shook his head. "Negative. You won't see their base because it'll be blacked out. Besides, the coordinates I inputted are BVR of the base."

"What's a BVR?"

"It means beyond visual range. So unless you do something stupid and honk the horn or trigger the light bar or set off fireworks, you can go in all the way and deposit the device and arm it without anyone seeing or hearing you."

"Why nine-eleven?"

"Easy enough to remember, don't you think?"

Nodding, Elvis said, "What if I come up against a patrol?"

"They lock the base down at dusk. No one goes in or out." Bishop smiled. "So no patrols."

"No patrols." Elvis was the one smiling now. Thinking about the damage he was going to inflict, he asked, "What's the code to arm the device?"

"One, two, three, four. Also easy enough to remember. Input that and you'll have one hour to get twenty miles away."

Grinning ear to ear, Elvis stood up, extended his hand and said, "Thanks for believing in me, sir."

"No. Thank you, Elvis," said Bishop. He rose and shook Elvis's hand. "We're stretched pretty thin here. Carson and the guys have their hands full with the dead and locals alike. What you are doing for me will be remembered and rewarded ... handsomely."

Chapter 67

Bishop was a man of his word, that was for sure. Elvis found the fuel needle pegged at full. The .45 and the spare mags for it were right where they were supposed to be. Resting demurely in the passenger side footwell was an AK-47 with a folding wire stock and two full thirty-round magazines for it. *Bonus. Apparently*, Elvis thought, *I'm back in Bishop's good graces and thusly there will be no bullet to the brain to account for my past transgressions.* And when all was said and done, the only thing more staggering than the body count will be the amount of tail he was going to get upon returning.

Wearing a big *I belong here grin* and without being given so much as a second look, Elvis pulled up to the southwest gate and put the transmission into Park. *I really am one of them now*, he thought, as Carson smiled big and approached his side of the truck.

Inside the lake house

For the first time in nearly three weeks, Jamie awoke to something other than the dark insides of a dirty sack or the pitch-black interior-of-a-casket kind of darkness she'd gotten used to at the subterranean compound. Now, after being dragged from her sleep by the throaty exhaust of a diesel engine working laboriously somewhere outside, she found herself squinting against the onslaught of early morning sun spilling in from the skylight above.

The split second of feel good was instantly supplanted by a wet blanket of dread as she realized what was most likely in store for her at the day's end.

Southwest Gate

Unable to sleep soundly the night before, Foley was now paying dearly. He felt his lids getting heavy and then, as was par for the course whenever he was saddled with the mind-numbing task of manning the gate, his mind began to wander. Suddenly he was on a beach somewhere tropical, his family by his side, a cold beverage in hand and white sand underfoot. And best of all, for the time being, the walking dead were out of sight and mind and he wasn't beholden to a bunch of *Lord of the Flies*-type thugs—grown men who operated as if everything was for their taking and every survivor their subject. Suddenly the crunch of tires on gravel tore him from the blissful moment and a full-sized American-made tow-truck sat idling on his side of the gate.

He straightened up and waited for the inevitable order to open the gate, but oddly enough none came. A tick later, a shiny Escalade pulled in behind the tow-truck and Carson (who was rarely seen around this gate) stepped out and hustled forward. Stopping at the driver's door, he shot the driver a forced smile, then, further confusing Foley, the two shook hands and shared a quiet conversation.

Watching the glad handing with mounting disgust, Foley sized up the new guy in the blood-red Cornhusker hat and wondered to himself what kind of pillaging mission he was being sent out on. Most likely batteries and ammunition, which, next to cigarettes, were the new gold these days. But the more he thought about it the more unlikely that seemed. The vehicle was all wrong. No bed or crew cab to stow the loot. And then he got a glimpse of the sturdy looking trunk on the back of the truck. Instantly he recognized the radiological symbol affixed to it and felt a cold tingle charge up his spine.

Then the order he'd been expecting was delivered. "Foley," bellowed one of the Spartan mercenaries who was known to be excessively cruel to the McCall conscripts. "Open the gate."

Seething inwardly, Foley checked for dead and, seeing none, nearby, pulled the three pins and laced his fingers through the blood-and-detritus-streaked chicken wire. Putting his back into the effort, he dipped his shoulder and kicked imaginary postholes into the gravel roadbed as he drove the steel and wood barrier outward. Slightly short of breath, and dreading the forthcoming order to close the gate, he watched the wrecker cross the threshold, turn left and speed away, its heavy-duty radials thrumming against the pavement.

Leaving the enclosed perimeter behind and not knowing where in the hell he was going, Elvis resorted to following the directions doled out by the sultry female voice. After passing through the deathly quiet resort town of McCall, where the only things moving were a roving pack of flesh eaters, he saw in the distance a gauze-like haze hovering over the road. As he got closer to the edge of town it became evident that the blight on the sky was an enormous flock of ravens, crows, starlings, and many other carrion-feeding birds he couldn't name. And traveling another quarter of a mile Elvis saw what was drawing them. Nailed to crosses made from railroad ties and stuck upright into the hard soil, a trio of naked men had been left to die a painfully slow death. Already gone to the birds were their eyes and ears and lips. The cavities once containing soft organs vital to sustaining life had been mined of everything save scraps of sinew and glistening ribs and knobby vertebra. As he passed by the warnings to anyone contemplating crossing Ian Bishop, he found it impossible to tear his eyes from what could have easily been his fate if Carson had had his way.

***

Twelve miles and fifteen minutes later, with the visual of the eviscerated examples still a strong imprint on his mind, the small town of New Meadow rose from the heat shimmer. Thankfully a few hundred yards shy of the city, the voice of the Tom Tom had him go right off of Idaho State Highway 55 and merge onto State Route 95, a north/south four-lane that a large orange road sign warned was currently under construction.

And it had been. But was no longer. For the first three miles, in addition to a steady stream of southbound zombies, he passed various colorful pieces of idled heavy equipment. There were diggers, graders, dump trucks, and a roller with a shiny steel drum big enough to flatten a herd of walking dead and keep on rolling. The fantastic visual supplanted that of the crucified and brought a rare smile to his face.

Chapter 68

Refueling at Morgan County Airport was a far cry from what Cade and his team had experienced more than a week ago at Grand Junction Regional. For one thing, a fuel-laden jetliner hadn't landed short and plowed through the perimeter fence trailing flames and strewing luggage and body parts the length of the runway.

Here, two hundred twenty air miles removed from the killing field that was GJR, the total opposite was true. The fencing around the single-strip facility was intact, and whoever left last had taken care to lock all points of entry behind them. The asphalt runway and helicopter pads southwest of it were clear of obstructions.

Duncan brought the Black Hawk in slow and low just over a copse of forty-foot-tall trees west of the airport, and put it down softly thirty feet north of a pair of painted-on circles meant specifically for the airport's rotor-wing aircraft. After the engines spooled down and the rotor noise subsided markedly, Cade hashed out a game plan and assigned Daymon and Lev each a task to perform.

Cade gave the perimeter fencing a quick once-over with the Bushnell's. Nearby, just south of the landing pad, a small number of Zs were clutching the fence and looking in. A few hundred yards behind them, on the airport feeder road, at least two dozen more flesh eaters slowly ambled closer, no doubt drawn in from the highway by the helicopter's noisy entrance. All total, Cade counted more than thirty and deduced with a cursory glance that the hurricane fencing would most likely hold them at bay for the time being. Which was a good thing because he had no desire to experience another hot refuel like the one at Grand Junction. Then, with one eye on the dead and the avoidable death of his former teammate Maddox fresh on his mind, he stepped from the helicopter and instinctively ducked his head as he loped under the blurred rotors towards the nearby fuel bowser.

He drew his Glock on the move and, once he'd covered the distance, stretched to full extension and banged the butt of the polymer pistol high up on the fuel tank's smooth skin. At the curved apex, near the top fill line, the sound rang hollow. However, halfway down, just above his eye level, the raps from his gun returned music to his ears in the form of a bass heavy report indicating there was still plenty of fuel inside.

He flashed a thumbs up towards the Black Hawk and, as planned, Lev leaped out and sprinted across the tarmac. Together they ran the hose to the chopper and Cade plugged the nozzle into the port which contained a mechanism that automatically opened the valve and started the flammable fuel flowing into the tanks, a risky proposition under normal conditions made more so with the howling turbines and a quartet of blades cutting the air overhead.

While the transfer was taking place, Cade cast his gaze beyond the rubber-streaked runway to the pair of single-engine Cessna airplanes, the nearest of which bounced up and down slightly on its tricycle-style landing gear. A minute later the plane stopped moving and Daymon stepped from the door, wearing a wide grin and clutching a thick stack of what to Cade looked like the kind of folded maps you'd find for sale at any corner gas station.

Three minutes later the DHS bird's tanks were full, and with Lev's help Cade ran the hose back to the bowser.

Back inside the chopper, Cade shrugged his harness on and plugged his helmet into the comms jack. He craned over his shoulder and confirmed Lev and Daymon were aboard and buckled in, then flashed Duncan a thumbs up. Instantly the turbines spooled up and whined noisily and the fuel-laden bird's wheels parted with the tarmac and it rose steadily skyward, nose already spinning northward.

Cade said, "How many charts did you find?"

Thumbing through them, Daymon replied, "Four."

"Nicely done, gentlemen," said Duncan as he leveled out the lumbering bird and kicked the turbines up a degree. With the ground and distant trees whipping steadily by, he looked over at Cade. "Where to, Boss?"

"Boise," answered Cade. "Closest possible strip I know of that'll handle a G650." Then, addressing Daymon over the comms, he said, "I need you to go through the charts and find all of the airports in Idaho. Start at Boise and work north."

"Done," replied Daymon as he clumsily unfolded the first map that was supposed to contain detailed information about every airstrip in the state, from the small public affairs like Morgan County all the way up to facilities like Boise with multiple runways capable of handling even large commercial jetliners.

Shrugging, Duncan said, "The man spoke. Boise it is."

Chapter 69

The knife-edged ridges of the taller peaks to the west reflected the rising sun as Elvis left the small towns of Pollock, Riggins, and Lucile in his rearview. Then, with the Salmon River and the low mountains scribbling along off his left shoulder, he chose a desolate zombie-free strip of 95 on which to pull over and piss.

***

Thirty-three miles north up 95 and forty-five minutes after leaving the puddle of steaming urine on the centerline, the voice in the box instructed him to deviate from the highway and turn left onto the Johnston Road Cutoff in order to, he presumed, bypass the nearby city of Grangeville showing just to the east on the Tom Tom's display.

Taking the nav unit's advice, Elvis left 95 behind and motored due north with huge fenced-in tracts of freshly tilled flatland scrolling by on each side. He'd only made it three-fourths of a mile down the straightaway when he came upon a dozen vehicles blocking the road. And behind the vehicular wall were twice as many walking corpses, a good number of them pressing against the far fence line.

What to do, thought Elvis. He stopped the tow truck and looked the scene over for a good ten minutes. There was not one kernel of broken safety glass on his side of the block. He didn't see so much as a smudge of rubber on the roadway to indicate that any of the associated vehicles had committed to any kind of hard braking prior to coming to rest in such a haphazard fashion. And as far as he could tell, the same could be said for the other side of the snarl. Suddenly he concluded that these vehicles had been placed here in order to force someone, such as himself, into taking the path of least resistance. To make turning around and going through Grangeville—where certainly something more dangerous than twenty-some-odd rotting pusbags—look like the lesser of two evils.

So he figured he had two options, and no matter which he ultimately chose he would need to be facing south in order to execute it. So he K-turned and parked facing south and sat in the cab with the window half-open and Jerry Garcia serenading him through the speakers. He pulled his hat down against the sun spilling in the window and balanced out the pros and cons in his head, unaware that his music had gotten the creatures agitated to the point where, clamoring for fresh meat, they crushed into one another in such a manner that two of them—a grade-school-aged male and a petite African American female—were inadvertently boosted up and over the trunk of an inert Chevy. Both monsters spilled to the road face first, arms and legs askew, and then somehow managed to get their sickly looking limbs to cooperate and dragged themselves to their feet. Mouths working and eyes locked on the fresh meat, they advanced on the truck from the driver's side.

As the band harmonized about a long strange trip and Elvis's thoughts drifted to a warm tropical beach, something cold brushed his Adams apple, causing him to start. In the next instant his hat slid from his head and seemed to levitate its way out the window.

It only took a millisecond longer for him to regain his composure and lean away from the window without losing a good chunk of flesh in the process. "Think you caught me sleeping, did you? Well I wasn't, you motherfuckers," he bellowed. "I was just resting my eyes."

As he fumbled to get ahold of the .45, which lay on the seat next to him, the undead duo hissed and reached into the window, their hands leaving greasy slug tracks on everything they touched.

Enraged, Elvis screamed, "You're gonna pay for that, bitches." He jacked a round into the chamber and poked the muzzle through the open window. Instantly, the female grabbed ahold of both the gun and his hand and drew them towards its gaping maw. "It's all yours." His lips curled up and he pushed hard, wedging three inches of the barrel in deep and pulled the trigger—twice. Small bits of vertebrae and flesh and blood sprayed in a flat arc from the side of its neck as the thing crashed to the asphalt in a vertical heap, paralyzed from the neck down, spinal cord completely shredded.

He put the smoking .45 on the dash and reached one hand out the window and palmed the kid zombie on the forehead, a move he'd used effectively on his kid sister many times when they were growing up. Then with his free hand he extracted his boot knife and thumbed it open. Finally, with the little monster flailing and snapping away, behind a brutal thrust, Elvis buried the four-inch blade into little Johnny's eye socket.

Pissed off at himself for letting the abominations catch him sleeping, he donned his Husker cap, kicked open the door, and stepped over the bodies, taking care to stay well clear of the female's still-clicking teeth.

Seeing its eyes tracking him, he clucked his tongue and knelt down on a bloodless patch of highway and in a sing-song voice said, "Look what we went and got ourselves into." Two quick thrusts of the blade into one of the roving eyes followed up by a thorough twist of the wrist scrambled its brains and stopped the incessant clicking.

Feeling nothing for who they might have been or who they loved nor who loved them, Elvis cleaned the blood and brains off on the kid's Minecraft tee-shirt and clipped it back onto his belt. *What a sorry sight*, he thought. *Gives new meaning to misspent youth.*

Standing there on the lonely stretch of road with the noon sun beating down and the murmurings of the nearby dead competing with the idling engine, he came to a decision.

He leaned in and turned the volume to 8, which was more than loud enough to start the creatures slam-dancing into each other again. He stalked around to the passenger side and retrieved the AK-47 from the floor and racked a round into the chamber.

Bracing a thigh on the Chevy's rear quarter-panel, Elvis opened fire point-blank on the moaning crowd. With the spent brass collecting around his boots and the front row of zombies falling fast, the second echelon unwittingly took advantage of the situation by crawling over the backs of the fallen. Listening to the awful sound of flesh and bone hitting pavement, Elvis back-pedaled several feet to a new position against the fence to his left and watched the zombies spilling over the Chevy's smooth trunk. After collecting himself, he resumed firing until the magazine was empty, then switched to the .45 and finished off the remaining few with single bullets to the brain.

As the sound of the gunshots dissipated, Elvis made his way back to the truck and, using the lift apparatus, lowered the device to the road.

After an hour spent hooking and unhooking cars and trucks, he'd created a passage north. Ten minutes after that he had the device secured to the tow truck and was accelerating away from the roadblock with the lyrics sung by the Grateful Dead taking him back to early days of the outbreak. *What a long strange trip*, indeed.

Chapter 70

From the Morgan airport the Black Hawk hammered a straight line north through the morning sky, overflying Huntsville, where Cade noticed a few more Zs patrolling the streets than there had been earlier. He cast his gaze left at the Pineview reservoir which, contrary to the sad state of the sacked town below, glistened silver and calm, a sharp contrast to the black smudge on the horizon a number of miles to the northwest.

Seeing the haze in the distance, Duncan deviated a few degrees right and a minute later Eden was slipping by off the starboard side. Down below in an isolated sub-division abutting low hills on the town's west side, a raging fire jumped from house to house, the trees, lawns and surrounding scrub tinder-dry from a long hot summer providing the perfect catalyst.

By Cade's estimation, already twenty or thirty structures were involved and there appeared to be no end in sight. He asked the resident firefighter, "Think Eden will be gone when we come back this way?"

Looking up from the map spread across his lap, Daymon said, "Who's gonna stop it? I just hope it doesn't jump into the *Cache*. If it does, the compound could be at risk."

"What do you think the odds are of that?"

"Pretty low," said Daymon. "I've explored the canyon south and west of the compound pretty extensively. There's a creek flows through and the woods down there aren't dry like all of those dead lawns back there."

After toying for a moment with the thought of calling the compound and putting them on alert, Cade finally decided not to because of the undue stress it would create.

***

The Black Hawk cruised along in radio silence for a good twenty minutes before Cade finally broke it. "Daymon ... any luck with the airports?" he asked.

"This is some small-assed print," he said, flattening out a crease. "Plus everything is vibrating. I'm doing my best."

Cade replied, "Keep looking. We've got time."

Below them an unidentified road snaked south to north, interconnecting a number of smaller cities that Cade guessed were bedroom communities to the rapidly approaching sprawl. He looked at Duncan and asked, "What city is that."

"Logan," said Daymon over the comms. "Couldn't miss that one on the map."

Inwardly Cade cringed, and out of respect said nothing.

Seemingly unaffected, Duncan drawled, "City of about fifty thousand. And no, my bro wasn't conceived there nor does the city have anything to do with his name."

The flood gates opened, Lev piped up, "Refresh my memory, Duncan. Why did your dad name him Logan?"

"After some stupid Sci-fi drivel about a bunch of folks who have gem stones in their palms."

Looking up from the map, Daymon asked, "Surgically attached ... or are they just holding them?"

"I've no idea," conceded Duncan. "But what I do know ... if the palm gem goes black on ya then it's Reaper time."

Cade said, "Now that Daymon went and opened Pandora's Box, I've got to know, Duncan. Is this trip about revenge, or justice?"

Duncan remained quiet and dipped the helicopter towards the ground and turned a few degrees left. Then he regarded Cade and said, "Great big helpings of both."

Sun flared off of Cade's visor as he nodded in agreement.

"Holy shit," exclaimed Lev. "Port side ten o'clock."

"There has to be at least fifty thousand of them," said Cade. "Haven't seen numbers like that since Castle Rock."

Daymon chuckled then said, "Which I bet is still glowing."

Craning his head groundward, Cade began to feel a sense of vertigo course through his body. With the memory of the recent crash still at the forefront of his mind, he cinched his safety harness tight. *Lot of good that did Tice*, he thought, seeing the Spook's crumpled body in his mind. Grimacing, he fished the sat phone from his pocket. It was still turned on and a tap on the number pad lit up the display. "Bingo," he said. "Forget Boise. Inputting coordinates." He leaned forward and tapped a long string of numbers into the flight computer. "Way point is set." He cycled through the basic functions and shook his head. "But the maps for Idaho, Washington, and Oregon aren't in here. I'm only seeing software updates that cover Nevada, Colorado, California, and New Mexico."

"Roger that," said Duncan. "I'll fly by compass while you find it on the map. Hell, before computers and GPS, all we *had* was laminated squares of plastic." After gently carving an arc in the airspace over infested downtown Logan, Duncan pointed the helo's nose northwest and kept the altitude a steady eight-hundred feet.

"How do we know where we're going then?" said Daymon.

Cade passed the phone back and said, "You tell me."

A couple of minutes spent poring over the maps and Daymon came back on the comms and said, "These GPS coordinates are for the McCall Airport in Idaho. Looks to be two-fifty or three hundred miles northwest of us. But Cade"—Daymon handed the phone forward—"Tell me what this second message is all about."

Rather cryptically, Cade replied, "'Stand by, detailed images to follow.' Speaks for itself ... don't you think?"

Already thinking two steps ahead, Lev took his eyes off the horde below and leaned back, knowing that his skills would be coming in handy, sooner, rather than later.

Chapter 71

They'd been airborne in the DHS Black Hawk for close to two hours and were now following a diagonal flight path northwest towards the new GPS coordinates that Cade had inputted over the outskirts of Logan, Utah.

Millions of acres of Cache National Forest were behind them. They'd overflown dozens of small cities, all seemingly inhabited by nothing but walking dead. Then in the blink of an eye the scenery went from inhabited land crisscrossed by stripes of empty highway interconnecting farms and small communities to a vast volcanic plain spreading to the horizon.

Breaking over the comms, Lev said, "Craters of the Moon. Me and Oops camped there once."

Cade replied, "Looks like the 'Stan to me ... minus the folks wanting to blow us outta the sky and cut our heads off."

Lev said, "You had to go there, didn't you?"

"I never left there."

Duncan added, "I haven't had those kind of nightmares for quite a while. However, some of the sights and smells lately have taken me back to the Nam with my eyes wide open. And I can't decide which one is worse —"

Lev said, "I have 'em ... but thank God they slip away the second I wake up."

"Lucky you," said Duncan.

For a long minute nobody spoke as the Black Hawk engaged in a futile race with its own shadow. The black shape would morph, stretching and shrinking, an illusion created by the rifts and cracks in the ancient volcanic flows below.

After a short while, Daymon said, "I'm no expert. But that sure looks like the moon down there."

Cade opened his mouth to reply but was silenced as the helo encountered a thermal and bucked like a bronco for a split second. Cinching his harness tighter, he felt a slight vibration against his thigh. At first he attributed it to the natural flight characteristics of a craft boldly defying physics. Helicopters were no stranger to shaking and groaning as they fought gravity and their natural inclination to drop from the sky. So Cade had learned long ago not to pay heed to all of the different sensations—such as the jostling created by the pocket of rising air—and instead take the cues pertaining to the Black Hawk's airworthiness only from the pilots. But after experiencing the same sensation in the same place for the second time in as many minutes, he realized it for what it was. He extracted the sat-phone and saw on the screen that he'd missed two calls and there were two corresponding unread messages. He thumbed the four-digit code, unlocking the Thuraya.

With Duncan casting quick glances his way and the unforgiving landscape below slowly giving way to sage and grass, Cade read the two SMS messages. The first was several paragraphs—almost a book by modern texting standards—and greatly buoyed his hopes of them finding the needle in a haystack as vast as the state scrolling by under the helo. The second, much shorter correspondence, caused a pit in his stomach the likes of which he hadn't experienced for quite some time.

Duncan cast a sidelong glance and asked, "Everything OK?"

Cade replied, "For now. Find a place to land and take us down."

Duncan said incredulously, "Here?"

"Here and now."

Daymon asked, "What's up?"

Cade said nothing as Duncan slowed the craft and the ground steadily rose up to meet them.

Cade unbuckled and, with the sagebrush whipping madly in the cyclonic rotor wash, he opened his door and leaped from the bird the second its tires hit Terra Firma.

The side door slid open before Cade's hand hit the handle. Then Lev appeared, the smaller Pelican case in hand. Cade received it without a word and loped south thirty yards. He set the box on the volcanic soil and turned a quick three-sixty. Nothing to see but sagebrush and grass and tan rock for miles around the emergency LZ. Farther off to the northwest, the Sawtooth Mountains rose up, their eastern-facing flanks and sharks-teeth-like crags catching the full force of the afternoon sun.

Consulting the compass feature on the Suunto, Cade found due south and scribed a line in the earth with his toe. He heard the whine of the turbines drop a few octaves to a low howl and then detected footsteps and Lev was at his side with a second, medium-sized Pelican hard case in hand.

In seconds they had both boxes open and, working silently, had extracted the larger pieces from their eggshell foam interiors. Working as a team, Lev assembled the desert tan-colored dish and positioned it facing the azimuth etched in the soil while Cade cracked open the armored Panasonic laptop and plugged it into a port on one side of the dish.

Powering on the computer, Cade said, "Thanks. You reading my mind?"

"Recognized the boxes. That's all," Lev said. "I went on a couple of joint ops with an SF team during my second deployment."

Cade nodded. Then the computer got his undivided attention. He tapped on the keys and waited. Then a few more keystrokes and a topographical map dominated the screen.

"We could use a printer," said Lev.

Tapping his flight helmet, Cade said, "This is my printer." Using the arrow keys, he scrolled the image up and down then panned it left and right. Lastly, he zoomed way in and sat in front of the static image, letting it burn into his memory. Eighteen minutes from setup to tear down and everything was stowed and everyone was aboard the Black Hawk. A minute later amidst a storm of sand and bouncing tumbleweeds, they were airborne and Cade was fielding the questions, reluctantly.

Chapter 72

The house Elvis settled on was five miles southeast of the final destination. Wary of being trapped again, he made certain there were no walking dead in the vicinity before turning off the highway and barreling up the paved drive.

Like the house in Ovid, this two-story clapboard affair was set back on a hillock with commanding views of the highway. The house was surrounded by a sturdy looking post and beam fence, while the drive leading toward the garage was bordered by both a chain-link fence and the dense strip of hedge that, over time, had completely engulfed it.

He parked the truck and killed the engine and, though the music coming from the speakers was barely above a whisper, turned off the stereo as well. Sitting in silence with the field glasses trained on the highway below, he witnessed hundreds of dead stagger by over the span of just forty-five minutes, the vast majority of them heading in the direction from which he'd just come.

Finally satisfied that he hadn't been made by the dead, he grabbed his pistol and quietly exited the truck. He tucked the .45 in his waistband and scaled the wooden fence. The walk to the house was brick, the mortar between tinted green with a thin veneer of moss. There was a rise of six stairs leading to the back door. Gun drawn, Elvis took them two at a time and peered in the window. Nothing to see but a barren back room, one wall of shelving holding rows of glass jars containing home canned fruits and vegetables. The other, a hook full of coats and assorted brooms and mops and the like. The kitchen beyond seemed unused. There was nothing in the sink that he could see and the counters were devoid of small appliances. After rapping on the glass quietly, nothing dead arrived so he tried the knob. *Locked.*

Instead of breaking the glass, he jumped to the browned lawn and curled around front. After scaling the same number of steps, he stood in front of a wooden door sporting a posted notice of foreclosure. *Someone didn't pay their note*, thought Elvis. He noticed its posting date was two weeks before the outbreak. Bad for the previous occupants. But good for him. He ripped the notice in two and broke into the house.

For a foreclosure, someone sure left a ton of shit behind.

But that was a good thing. He liberated a chair from the kitchen. With its chromed legs and a red vinyl seat brittle with age and showing more fault lines than California, it was plain to see why it had been left behind. The same could be said for the few pieces of furniture in the living room. There was a side table and coffee table—both far from Amish quality. A lamp with a pea-green tasseled shade. Definitely not a keeper.

He dragged the chair across the scarred wood floor. Spun it around and planted it in front of the grand west-facing picture window. Cracked seatback pressing against his chest, Elvis propped his chin on steepled fingers and watched the dead march south.

Chapter 73

For a long while they continued on, the Black Hawk keeping roughly the same heading. The new GPS numbers, Cade said, were going to leave them south and east of the McCall airport where they would need to find a place to safely secrete the helo for future use.

The miles ticked off quickly and the closer they got to their final destination the lower Duncan seemed to fly. The drop in altitude was gradual, but if another fifty miles were added to the trip the big UH-60 would eventually plow into the earth.

Cade looked to his right and said, "Hey Dunc, how are you liking your new glasses?"

Keeping his gaze locked dead ahead, Duncan replied, "The VA hospital couldn't have nailed the prescription any better. Guess I owe you a big thanks."

"Or a sloppy kiss," said Daymon.

A broad smile formed under Cade's smoked visor. "Wasn't my idea," he conceded. "Yesterday I received a message from Daymon saying Mister Magoo needed new glasses and that I was supposed to pillage a LensCrafters."

Daymon chuckled. "I just said to bring glasses. And Sarge here came through with flying colors ... orange and yellow with streaks of red."

"I'd wear a pair of Groucho Marx shades if they helped me see up close like these ones do."

Laughing, Lev said, "With the big plastic nose and bushy black 'stache and brows?"

"Affirmative," Duncan shot back.

Lev said, "Logan would have gotten a kick out of that."

"And Jamie and Jordan and Gus. Hell, if we find Jamie alive ..."

Setting his jaw, Cade said, "We will."

Duncan made no reply. Jordan's death grimace had just flashed in front of his eyes. He saw her wildly contorted form, bird-ravaged and tangled in the briars. Consumed with rage, he suddenly found forming a coherent thought let alone some kind of positive affirmation way too much work.

Save for the thumping blades and hardworking twin turbines, the cabin remained deathly quiet as Duncan threaded the bird through the jagged Sawtooth mountains.

***

Duncan covered the final twenty miles to the end waypoint with an impressive bit of near NAP-of-the-earth flying. And considering that Cade had informed him earlier of the presence of two AH-64 Apache attack helicopters parked on the tarmac at the nearby McCall airport, who could blame him.

In fact, Cade was rather pleased that from his perspective in the left-hand seat it appeared that Duncan was flying well within the *edge of the envelope*, not beyond.

Seeing the lake dead ahead reflecting the afternoon sun, Cade said, "At least Tran got the lake part of this right."

"That's not saying much," said Duncan. "Even a broken clock is right twice a day."

"That's not fair," said Daymon. "If it wasn't for him fingering the getaway plane I'd still be wrestling with the charts and we'd all be crisscrossing the state with our dicks in our hands."

Cade nodded. *The dreadlocked man has a point.*

"Five minutes," said Duncan.

Cade flashed an open hand at the passengers. Universal semaphore reiterating what the pilot had just said verbally. Then added, "Lock and load."

Lev said, "You can take the man out of Delta ... "

The other men, Cade included, finished the thought by saying in unison: "*But you can't take Delta out of the man.*"

Cade used the duration of the flight pondering the mental image he'd spent five uninterrupted minutes memorizing. In his mind he saw Payette Lake, an inverted 'V,' the west half larger by half than the east. The three-mile-long forested peninsula splitting the lake stretched south to north. At its south end, from shore to shore, the finger of land which was mostly all State Park was a little over a mile wide. Three miles north of that it gradually tapered off, leaving a narrow passage between the two halves of the lake at the point of the inverted 'V.' He recalled the arrows and notations overlaying the precisely rendered imagery, presumably put there by the wizard of Schriever's 50th Space Wing herself. On the southeast side of the peninsula were a dozen very large lake-front homes, each with their own wooden dock and narrow stretch of beach. And directly across the lake from the homes bordering the State Park were three dozen west-facing houses, all with big lots and beaches and docks offering the same instant lake access.

But the biggest tell of all had been the four black helicopters sitting atop a rectangular landing pad gouged out of the forest northeast of and equidistant to the west-facing homes.

Yes, he concluded. *Nash came through once again.* And now it was his turn to put the intel to use. So, as he'd done hundreds of times in the past, he drew up the battle plans in his head, ad-libbing for the time being the bits and pieces of the puzzle she hadn't been able to provide. *Time to practice patience*, he thought. Because very soon, if Mister Murphy behaved, they'd be close enough to have eyes on their target.

Duncan flared the Black Hawk a split second before the flight computer chimed letting him know he had arrived on target. Hovering seventy-five feet above what appeared to be a thirty-six-hole golf course with the nearly dead closely cut fairway grass rustling in the down blast, he asked, "You sure this is it?"

Cade pointed to his ten o'clock and said, "Affirmative. Put her down there on the green."

As the helicopter side-slipped over the fairway, Daymon elbowed Lev in the ribs and said, "You bring your sticks?"

Lev said nothing for a half-beat as he stared out the window at the browned grass and stark-white sand traps gliding by below. Then he shifted his gaze to Daymon and then the crossbow before patting his own carbine. He smiled and said, "You use your stick and I'll use mine."

"I meant your golf clubs. Some people call them *sticks*," Daymon explained.

Lev made no reply as the Black Hawk began its descent.

With the gently undulating green rushing up, Duncan began his countdown. "Five, four, three, two, one. We are wheels down." And as soon as the helicopter settled on its suspension and the turbine noise dissipated and the rotor slowed markedly, he looked to Cade and asked, "Shut her down?"

"Affirmative," said Cade. "Lev, you and Daymon unload your gear first. I'll pull security while you three cover the bird." He drew his Glock and twisted the suppressor onto the threaded barrel. "From here on out we have to be as quiet as possible."

"Copy that," replied Lev, passing a Kevlar helmet over to Daymon.

Nodding his affirmative, Daymon tore off his flight helmet and shook out his dreads. Tucking them behind his ears, he scrunched the Kevlar helmet on and muttered, "These things have got to go."

Hearing this, Duncan halted his shutdown procedures and looked over his shoulder and said, "You better not. Haven't you heard? The hair makes the man." Then, after delivering one of his trademark cackles, he removed his own helmet to reveal a wispy tangle of sweaty graying hair.

Sliding open the door, crossbow in hand, Daymon answered back, "I see your point. Nice glasses by the way."

***

Five minutes later they'd concealed the helicopter with the swath of tan camouflage netting.

Now wearing his tactical helmet with a pair of NVGs affixed and flipped up out of the way, Cade knelt on the edge of the green, head and eyes moving constantly. On his back was his desert tan pack with the MSR sniper rifle folded down and secured on the outside by a couple of bungees. In his MOLLE gear, six spare magazines rode diagonally on his chest in easy-to-reach pockets. And in his gloved hands was his trusty M4, a stubby tan camouflage suppressor secured to its business end.

After setting all four of their comms headsets to the same frequency, Cade passed them out along with the other two pair of

NVGs—Duncan going without the latter. "These are voice activated," Cade said, tapping the mike. "Just talk softly and everyone will hear you."

Slipping the headset on, Duncan said, "Keep the chatter down, though. I'm still nursing a headache."

His voice containing a measure of *I told you so,* Daymon said, "You mean still nursing a hangover."

Duncan made no reply. He snatched up his shotgun and walked away.

Lev said to Cade, "Want me to grab the Panasonic?"

"Negative," Cade replied. "With that bulky dish it's too much to carry. Besides ... odds of an updated map coming in this late in the game are slim to none." Tapping his helmet he went on, "It's all up here anyway."

Duncan said, "Better hope your '*up here*' doesn't take a bullet."

Cade said, "OK Duncan. Grab only the laptop. Hump it along if that'll make you feel any better."

Waving one hand in a shooing motion, Duncan said, "Forget about it."

"I'll grab it," said Lev. He hustled back to the chopper and was back in a matter of seconds, stuffing the rugged Panasonic into his ruck.

Daymon looked to Cade and asked, "Wheels?"

Shaking his head, Cade replied, "Five miles on foot. And no complaining ... I'm three days removed from one hell of a sprained ankle." He regarded the map in his head and then the sun over his left shoulder and struck out to the northeast.

They walked as if on patrol. Cade on point with Duncan and Daymon in the middle, and Lev bringing up the rear and tasked with watching their six.

They were barely two fairways removed from the landing zone when the first wave of Zs found them.

Vectoring in from the north and east, the pallid corpses trickled from the trees in small groups at first and then in seconds their numbers increased exponentially; dozens of lurching Zs were spread out across the fairway, a moaning, moving wall of decaying flesh completely hampering any chance of forward progress.

So with the odds of backtracking and outrunning these kinds of numbers dwindling, Cade made a hard and fast decision. He chose their present location—one particularly wide spot in the dog-leg right—for them to make their stand.

He dropped his pack on the dying grass and went to a knee. He passed the suppressed Glock to Lev, then waved Daymon and his crossbow to the left where the creatures were fewer and farther between. Then, feeling a trickle of sweat tracing his spine, he snugged the M4 to his shoulder and settled the Eotech's holographic pip on the closest Z. As he clicked the selector to fire, there was a flash of movement in his side vision and a quick glance over told him Lev and Daymon were in position.

Together, Lev, Daymon, and Cade formed a rough semi-circle with Duncan in the center, rear-facing, his combat shotgun to be used only as a last resort.

Opening fire first, Cade engaged the Zs taking up space in an imaginary slice of the green directly in front of him. His first suppressed volley sent a half-dozen shamblers to a second death. Brass tumbled lazy arcs through the sky as he emptied the thirty-round magazine in a matter of seconds.

At the apex of their position, the proverbial *tip of the spear*, Lev wisely held his fire, opting to wait until the monsters were within effective range of the Glock—which for him, a fan of the long rifle—was going to be much too close for comfort.

Meanwhile Daymon was firing and notching fresh arrows as fast as possible. But these weren't bear and he found that the trifecta combination of their sheer numbers, inconsistent and hard-to-predict actions, and stilted movement made targeting their brains a little difficult. Shooting a little under fifty percent, he poured through a dozen arrows in just a couple of minutes without making much of a difference on his side. Five rotters down and out of arrows, he cursed at the creatures and fell back.

Just as Cade cast a glance over his left shoulder, the fight on that flank devolved to hand-to-hand combat. He saw Daymon drop the bow and backpedal to tighten up his side of the arc. In the next instant the dreadlocked man brought his neon-handled machete into the fight. Then, kicking and slashing, Cade witnessed him kill another half-dozen abominations. In fact it seemed as if Daymon was going to be fine until one creature grabbed ahold of a strand of his dreads and he was toppled off balance.

Hearing Daymon cuss into the comms and then call for help in the next breath, Lev took his eyes off of his sector and rushed over.

Seeing this, Cade dropped an empty magazine and slammed a fresh one home. With the rising carrion stench assaulting his nose, he snapped the bolt forward and resumed firing, fully content to let Lev help where he could. And as he double-tapped another three Zs, sending a trio of frothy pink halos airborne, he heard three distinct closely spaced booms directly behind him. *Duncan.* Forcing himself to concentrate on the task before him, he put down another three Zs, shifted left a few degrees and engaged the ones Lev had been forced to abandon.

With a berm of death building in front of the tiny force, and a haze of cordite wallowing in the still air, Cade turned to help the others and was surprised to see an equally large drift of ashen-faced corpses with Lev in the middle swapping out magazines.

"So much for quiet," said Daymon as he rushed forward to harvest his arrows.

Cade said, "Cut the small talk. "We have to move out, *now.*"

Loading fresh shells into his shotgun, Duncan quipped, "You change your mind about the *wheels* yet?"

Saying nothing, Cade engaged the flip-up 3x magnifier, leveled his carbine, and glassed beyond a burbling water feature a fairway over and spotted another wave of Zs staggering from the nearby gated neighborhood. Letting his rifle hang from its single-point sling, he accepted the Glock from Lev. Then, rethinking the driving thing, he stepped around the pile of leaking corpses and led them due east towards the clubhouse—a massive stone and wood structure that looked as if it had been plucked off the slopes of the Swiss Alps and dropped right here smack dab in the middle of Nowhere, Idaho.

Chapter 74

For three hours, wondering where in the hell they were coming from, Elvis watched the steady procession of dead trudging south towards McCall. *Surely*, he thought, *the two cities to the west, Lewiston and Clarkston, with a combined population of thirty-one thousand couldn't possibly be the only source.* Then he remembered that the Tri-Cities were just over the Idaho border in eastern Washington. And though it had been a number of years since he'd been there, if his memory served correctly, before the Omega outbreak those cities combined were home to two or three hundred thousand people. Which went a long way towards explaining what he was seeing now.

But still a couple of other things nagged at him. One, the base, purported to be nearby, should be attracting the dead like moths to a flame. And two, though he wasn't complaining—because one man, a pistol, and an AK-47 were no match against a squad of soldiers—where in the hell were the patrols? He hadn't seen so much as a single Humvee or helicopter all day. Hell, this close to a base of any size there should have been some kind of activity. A mission or two outside the wire to forage for supplies or sweep for survivors. He half-expected to see columns of black smoke presumably caused by some lowly private setting fire to fifty-five-gallon drums containing diesel-soaked human excrement. Or maybe the rising exhaust from tractors working hard to dig enough holes in the ground to bury the infected. Even the fools at Schriever were running similar operations during every second of available daylight.

Then he had a fleeting thought. Maybe he'd followed the directions wrong. Given what little he knew of the technology involved, it still seemed next to impossible to him that a satellite overhead beaming directions straight into the navigation box would have led him off course.

So he got up for a second and meandered to the tiny bathroom and dropped a load. "Fuck," he bellowed. "No ass wipes." *Look before you leap, genius.* He punched a hole in the lathe and plaster wall and then finished the necessary task with his left hand. Considering that he'd been rooting around elbows deep inside infected cadavers just a few days ago, being soiled with a little of his own shit was no big thing.

Walking a little funny, he went back to the window and retook his perch. He glanced at his watch and smiled wide and then resumed his lonely vigil with a giddy anticipation welling within him.

Chapter 75

With the moans of the pursuing dead rising in the background, the four-man team scaled the steps in single file. In wispy flowing font, the word *Whitetail* was etched in the glass atop the massive oak double doors, and when Cade reached out to grab the wrought iron pull the opposing door swung slowly inward. In disbelief, Cade stepped back and leveled his Glock at the figure responsible.

Empirical evidence, thought Daymon as he halted on the second step and gaped at the sad sight staggering from the gloom.

Still recoiling from the sudden start, Cade first noticed the unmistakable smell of bourbon and then took note of the pair of hands reaching out for him. They were large and calloused, probably scarred from a lifetime of manual labor. Then, shaking mightily, they beckoned him inside with a sweeping motion.

Still in sort of a daze and with blood trickling into his eyes as a result of the near scalping, Daymon drew back a few pounds of trigger pull and sidestepped Cade to get a better angle. Suddenly Cade blurted out, "Hold fire."

Your lucky day, dude, thought Daymon, lowering the bow.

One at a time, a little jumpy and still full of adrenaline from the recent brush with death, the makeshift team followed the obviously inebriated man. Once over the threshold and acting purely on survival instinct, Lev and Daymon pushed past him and rushed into the circular foyer. Lev called out "Clear!" and then the two fanned out, poking their heads into each individual room and making sure they were indeed alone.

Meanwhile Duncan closed the front doors, reached into a nearby display and grabbed a handful of graphite shafted clubs—five-hundred-dollar drivers with ridiculously large heads. Feeling something heavy impact the door, he quickly slipped a number of clubs through the interior door pulls, his way of augmenting the single deadbolt.

In seconds, Lev and Daymon had returned from their cursory recon and had taken station next to Duncan, who was listening with amusement as presumably the last remaining denizen of Whitetail Country Club offered them all a warm yet rather incoherent welcome.

Lev handed the Glock back to Cade, who was listening and trying to mine pertinent details from the man's rambling narrative.

Accepting the Glock, Cade swapped magazines and checked the chamber. Loaded. After looking around the entry, Cade locked eyes with the blabbering fella and asked him his name.

"Walter," replied the man, casting his gaze through a grand arched doorway towards the deeply polished mahogany bar beyond. "I used to keep the greens. Now I *own* the joint."

Cade looked the drunk in the eyes and said slowly, "Pleased to meet you, Walter. Lovely joint you have here." Then he asked the next question even more slowly, but with an added measure of authority. "Do you have keys to *any* of the cars in the lot?"

The man processed the question for a long while, during which Cade could almost hear the gears working inside his booze-soaked gray matter. Finally, while heavily slurring his words, the man said, "Hell no. I'm not giving up my car keys. I've only had one or two tonight, officer."

Taking a different tack, Daymon crowded in, bloody face and all, and said in as nice a tone as he could muster, "I need to get to the hospital. Will you drive me?"

Something clicked and the man staggered across the foyer and into the bar area. In a few moments, with a jangling noise preceding him, he returned and shook the keys at eye level and said, "Let's go."

While he was gone, the entry doors had started to tremor slightly. Then the golf clubs shoring them up began to rattle, the vibrating alloy heads producing a tinny resonance.

After snatching the keys from the man's grasp, Cade rifled through them and found what looked like an ignition key. Only it was a basic black, probably a backup cut by Ace Hardware and not behind the dealer's counter. Therefore there was no proprietary logo stamped there. So Cade asked the man what kind of car he drove.

Thinking hard, the man looked at the rafters and ran his hands through oily slicked-back hair. A tick later there was a flash of recognition in his eyes and, still slurring his words, he replied, "Yes. It's parked around back."

No help, thought Cade. He said, "You stay in here. We'll come back later and shoot the shit. Maybe even tip back a nightcap with you."

His face lighting up behind already reddened cheeks, the man said, "Perfect. I'll be waiting with shots lined up." Then he looked Daymon in the face, swiped a finger through a rivulet of blood there and said, "You better go to a hospital. I can drive you."

At once four resounding *No's* echoed through the overhead beams.

Keys in one hand, Glock in the other, Cade hurried through the foyer and threaded his way between the white linen-shrouded tables of what had once been a four- or five-star restaurant. With the others close behind, he negotiated the kitchen, passed through a narrow dish room clad all in stainless steel, and then found the back door which he guessed led to a receiving area where there just might be a vehicle waiting.

And there was. A quick peek through the peephole showed the distorted image of a boxy SUV-looking thing. So they moved what seemed like a hundred pounds of boxed russet potatoes blocking the door and tugged it inward.

Glock leading the way, Cade stepped out first. He looked left then right and called out, "Clear." As the others filed out behind him, he lowered his body from the loading dock to the grease-stained parking pad and made his way to the vehicle.

Stumbling over one of the Simplot boxes, Duncan made his way through the door and onto the loading dock. Daymon emerged next and when he saw the vehicle he threw his arms up in disgust and said, "Pontiac Aztek. You have got to be shitting me."

After instructing Walter to shore the door with the boxes of potatoes, Lev threw the lock and closed it behind them. He passed by Daymon and said, "Wheels are wheels."

There was no alarm fob so Cade tested the key in the rear hatch first. *Success.* He placed his ruck inside and circled around, opening the other doors along the way. Completing the circuit, he placed his M4 in the footwell, Glock on the dash, and slipped behind the wheel. In no time the others had stowed their gear and the hatch was shut and Cade had coaxed life out of the engine. A beat later he found Reverse with the shifter and was backing rapidly out of the confined space.

After pulling a quick J-turn, as a courtesy to Walter, Cade wheeled the man's ride around front, passed underneath the covered valet area and brought the Aztek to a halt. He rolled down his window and whistled and cat-called to the gathered dead pressing on the double doors. After acquiring their undivided attention, he proceeded east with the needle barely registering a numerical speed on the gauge.

With the Pontiac's back end just out of their reach and the radials clicking a slow steady cadence against the pavers, all two dozen staggering messes gave slow speed pursuit.

Chapter 76

Contrary to Daymon's opinion, Cade found the Aztek, although a hell of an eyesore, to be a fairly capable ride. With four adults and all their gear and guns it was cramped inside for sure. And come to think of it, kind of squeaky and rattily. But capable nonetheless.

After goading the undead into the unwinnable goose chase and keeping them enticed until the clubhouse was out of sight (and hopefully out of mind), Cade sped up and drove east through the parking lot and past a dozen luxury sedans.

At the entrance, he turned right and jinked the ride around a pair of doddering first turns and continued east, still negotiating the golf course roads for a spell, then passed by an algae-choked water feature, its aerial display fountain no longer in business. Finally they came to a stop sign at a 'T' with one of McCall's four-lane arterials. There, Cade consulted his mental map while watching a trio of dead wade after the geese floating in the dormant water feature. Finally after a long pause, during which the Aztek's engine purred quietly, he hung a left, once again sending them on a winding northeasterly tangent on Boyostun Drive through a verdant canyon of pines blocking their view of the lake to the right.

After five minutes on Boyostun, Daymon broke the silence and called out from the back seat, "Why are you keeping us in the dark, Boss?"

Cade said, "I'm just trying to maintain focus. That's all."

Stopping short of delivering an elbow, Duncan turned towards Daymon and said, "Let the man work, would ya? He saved our collective asses back there on the links."

Recalling how Duncan had sprung into action, saving his ass with three perfectly placed shotgun blasts—all without hurting an additional hair on his head—Daymon decided to practice what Heidi liked to preach and quit sweating the small stuff. "My bad," he said.

With the Panasonic on his lap and hinged open on his lap, Lev zoomed the satellite image in a couple of stops. After tilting the screen to get a better viewing angle, he read one of the notations on the overlay and said, "We're looking for Sylvan Beach. It'll be on the right ... a couple of miles ahead."

Dabbing his head wound with a swatch torn from his tee-shirt, Daymon instantly forgot his previous pledge to self and asked Lev, "What's at Sylvan Beach?"

"I'm not in Cade's head ... but from what I see here I'm guessing that's where we're going to cross the lake."

Cade nodded, then gazed right and noticed shadows darken the lake's surface as the sun slipped behind the peaks to the west.

Daymon said, "We'll be sitting ducks crossing before dark."

"It'll be OK. Besides ... they won't be expecting callers," drawled Duncan. He looked at the driver. "Right, Delta?"

Keeping his eyes on the road, Cade said, "Affirmative." Then suddenly a little worry slipped through his self-imposed mental barrier. His thoughts raced. In them Brook was mourning him. Then, as if in a time machine, the vision fast forwarded and Raven was grown and seemingly surviving the apocalypse on her own. Snapping him back to present, Lev said, "Sylvan Beach ... next right."

Seeing that their encounters with the walking dead had fallen off substantially the farther north they travelled, Cade decided to ditch the Aztec here, a quarter mile short, in order to assure a stealthy approach. "Lock and load," he said. He pulled into the nearest side road where a hundred yards east the massive rear facade of a two-story house blocked most of the lake view.

Once again they donned helmets and packs and inspected their weapons. Once again Cade handed Lev the suppressed Glock and then unslung his suppressed M4. Staying inside the tree line, they cut through a handful of yards and were at the Sylvan Beach parking lot in a little under ten minutes.

Stopping at the south end of the parking lot, Cade knelt down next to an overflowing garbage can, wrestled the Bushnell's from his pack, and surveyed the scene. To his left, beyond a picket of broadleaf trees, he saw a couple of red clay tennis courts. Dead ahead there was a public use restroom built of cinderblocks and painted a bland shade of yellow. Arranged outwards from the structure, like the spokes of a wheel, were a contingent of hunter-green picnic tables. To the right of the bathrooms, stretching nearly to the lake's edge, was a very large swimming pool surrounded by a built-up wooden deck, its still waters slightly murky with algae. And beyond the pool, across a couple of hundred yards of open water, was the tip of the heavily wooded peninsula he'd so far seen only in the overhead image.

Glassing the gently curved stretch of beach ahead, Cade spotted the two things that had piqued his interest in the satellite image. Stretching a dozen yards out over the water and built up on telephone pole pilings was a stark-white dock. Tied up and bobbing on the water on its lee side was some kind of low-to-the-water two-man power boat, a giant chrome-plated engine sitting out back. Closer in still, upside down on the sand, were a dozen wooden rowboats identical in style and size, but varying vastly in color. Cade guessed they were most likely rented out to the throngs of tourists either by the day or smaller increments thereof.

Thinking back to the '90's John Candy comedy *The Great Outdoors*, Daymon so wanted to quote a line from the movie and start chanting '*kick ass drag-boat*' over and over. But seeing as how that might give them away to the dead, he kept it to himself.

Seeing Cade lower the field glasses, Lev said, "What next?"

"We cover each other and cross in the boats. The State Park over there"—he pointed to the overgrown finger of land on the other side of the narrow channel—"as best as I can tell from the imagery, *that* is the western boundary of Bishop's territory. And on the opposite side are some houses and across the lake from them is where he is holed up. We'll pick a house adjacent and start observing."

"And?" asked Daymon.

Though there was more he could add, Cade simply said, "And we move on them when the opportunity presents itself."

Shaking his head, Daymon put his bow aside and sat on the curb. He removed his helmet and discarded the bloody knot of fabric he'd stuffed inside. He tore another piece from his shirt and applied pressure to his wound.

After checking his Suunto, Cade said, "We're oscar mike in five."

Duncan cracked a water and sated his thirst in one long, drawn-out gulp, all sixteen ounces, followed by a stifled belch.

Conversing quietly amongst themselves, Cade and Lev agreed to split up. He would cover Lev and Duncan who would be crossing first in one boat. Once on the other side, Lev and Duncan would extend the same courtesy and provide security until they were all four on the peninsula.

"Looks good on paper," conceded Cade.

"Remember ... Mister Murphy's got scissors," quipped Lev.

Shaking his head at the prospect of crossing open water in daylight, Daymon positioned the makeshift bandage and cinched his helmet down as best he could.

Five minutes later, two boats, one pink and the other black, bobbed in the water next to the dock.

"Age before beauty," said Lev.

Saying nothing, Duncan steadied himself by bracing the pair of oars across the boat's gunwales. Then, after pushing them off, Lev hopped in and sat down quickly on the center thwart and rowed as fast as he could.

Cade glassed the far shore, looking for movement or a glint of light off of glass. Seeing nothing, he lowered the binoculars and prepared to board what he'd secretly dubbed, on account of its pink splendor, the Good Ship Lollipop.

After navigating the still narrows, the two men clambered ashore and Lev gave the signal.

Already in the boat and with the oars chocked in the oarlocks when Cade jumped in, Daymon started rowing immediately. Taking fast and deep cuts in the water while Cade trained his M4 on the receding shoreline, Daymon put them on the white sandy shore of the peninsula in half the time it had taken Lev.

After taking care to stow the boats in some low bushes a dozen yards from shore, the ragtag team melted into the trees.

Chapter 77

With Cade walking point and practicing proper noise discipline, the trek from the landing site to the State Park entrance burned an additional sixty minutes of daylight.

Raising a clenched fist, the age-old silent signal meaning *stop at once*, Cade halted and went to a knee beside the trunk of an old gnarled pine. He craned his head over his shoulder, made eye contact with the spread-out line, and whispered into the comms, "Vehicle approaching."

Lev turned to their rear and took a knee, keeping the Glock trained down the trail.

Duncan and Daymon both went to ground two yards behind Cade. The former crouching next to a hearty pine and the latter on his butt, cross-legged, with his crossbow parting a low-to-the-ground clump of ferns, its deadly end aimed at the nearby strip of asphalt.

In the few seconds it took the team to react to the engine noise it ceased getting louder and a couple of beats later, died off altogether.

Surrounded by deepening shadows under the double canopy, they remained frozen in place for what to Duncan, who was itching to make someone pay for Logan's death, seemed an eternity. He looked at his watch and saw the minutes slowly crawl by. A full thirty minutes passed before he saw movement ahead, but shortly into the thirty-minute wait the cravings had begun. First just a thought. Then something washed over him and he wanted nothing more than to open up a bottle of Jack Daniels and forget.

After staying still and silent and hearing nothing more for a full thirty minutes, Cade rose from the needle-strewn floor. He motioned silently for the others to follow and padded forward on the same course paralleling the single-lane road from several feet inside the tree line.

Three hundred yards south, Cade repeated the same routine. But this time, after taking a knee, he looked and listened for just a couple of minutes and then called Lev up front.

From a dozen feet away Daymon watched as the two former soldiers conversed. They must have turned off their comms because their mouths were moving but he wasn't hearing the words. However, he followed Cade's arm movements and tried to read his lips, picking up on only a smattering of words—among them, *house* and *go* stood out prominently. Before they had finished their exclusive tête-à-tête, Daymon saw their only two suppressed weapons once again change hands.

As Lev crept past Duncan and Daymon, suppressed M4 in hand, he whispered, "Cade's going forward to recon some houses up ahead. He asked me to tell you two to '*stay frosty*.'"

Watching Cade pulling items from his ruck, presumably in preparation for his impromptu foray, Daymon muttered, "Never heard that one before."

Leaving his pack behind, Cade stuffed a flashlight and a half dozen zip ties into a cargo pocket and crept towards the road, being careful to maintain a low profile along the way.

He stopped and looked, first left and then right. Nothing to see here but shafts of ambient light dappling the road with an eerie pattern resembling clawlike hands ready to trip him up.

He padded south to a darker stretch of roadway with a good deal of cover on the opposite side and sprinted across in a combat crouch, Glock leading the way.

A couple of hundred yards east he could see a trio of houses separated by great expanses of lawn and beautiful landscaping and surrounded by wooden picket fencing. Beyond the houses he could see the lake and small structures he guessed to be boat houses. Docks with personal watercraft tied to them reached dozens of feet into the lake.

A trio of garages nearly the size of his home back in Portland sat sentinel nearer the road, one belonging to each lakefront mansion.

Cade padded across a carpet of fallen needles, ducked through a grouping of tired-looking rhododendron bushes and found himself standing in front of the guest house of the middle mansion. Built in an A-frame style with the double-car garage below and what looked to be guest quarters above, the structure was much bigger than he'd originally thought.

Sitting in front of the right-side garage door, parked on the cement pad, its hood still warm to the touch, was a boxy SUV, the tags on the back proclaiming it to be a Jeep Commander. *New to me*, thought Cade. The only rig he deemed appropriate to associate the venerable Jeep name with usually had a soft top, a roll bar, and a vertical grill between closely spaced headlights.

Nonetheless, the *Commander* would do.

Stopping at the bottom of a flight of stairs angling up to the right of the structure, he listened hard but heard nothing. So he scaled the steps, heel and toeing it to the top, silent as a ghost.

Chapter 78
McCall, Idaho
Forty minutes prior

Another monotonous day in the books, thought Foley as he nosed into the driveway, disappointed. There had been no mission with Carson and his men. Therefore he had experienced none of the excitement and adrenaline rushes that came along with going house-to-house and clearing out the dead. No, this day had been more of the same: too many grueling hours standing under the hot sun interspersed with mad minutes of gunfire and then the inevitable back-breaking work of digging graves to bury the infected in.

He climbed the stairs, hopefully for the last time. Then he initiated his ritual, also hopefully for the last time. The house was quiet. The door was still locked. He turned the key in the lock and upon entering the A-frame was hit square in the face with a blast of carrion-free super-heated air. Thankfully everything was as he had left it. The downstairs and sliding doors remained locked and the loft above was unoccupied.

He looked at the massive television with attached Blu-Ray player and the shelves crammed full of movies and thought to himself, *fuck Heat.* There was still more than enough of it trapped inside the house. Besides, there were other more important things on his agenda tonight and priming and starting a generator was not one of them.

Instead he pulled two warm bottles of Bud from a twelve-pack on the island. Cracked one open, waited for the pungent nose to waft away, and drank half of it in one long pull. After a long, drawn-out belch that echoed around the room, he downed the rest—frothy backwash and all—then promptly unlaced his boots and left them on the floor beside the island.

With a newfound pep in his step and the beginnings of a slight buzz hitting him, he took the slick wooden stairs two at a time.

After spending a minute upstairs, Jimmy returned to the kitchen carrying a black backpack stuffed full of all his worldly belongings: a handful of pictures of his wife and daughter, extra ammunition for the pistol, two changes of clothes, and a high powered headlamp that had already come in handy for searching the deep dark recesses of unfamiliar abandoned homes where things reeking of death hungrily laid in wait.

He was leaving on foot, that much he'd already decided. So he opened some bottled waters and filled his hydration pack. Then he broke down a couple of MREs and placed the individual items in the pack's side pockets. Lastly, he took his XD from its holster, removed the mag, and cleared the chamber. He stripped the pistol into four separate pieces and cleaned each one. When he was finished, he reassembled the parts, inserted the magazine, and placed the handgun on the island.

He opened another beer and set the alarm on his wristwatch for 3 a.m. *Full dark*. The time of night when alertness wanes and nearly every sentry starts to bemoan his loss of sleep and pray for dawn to arrive. And also a perfect time, Foley had decided, for him to make a run for it.

Two beers later he snatched up his pistol and scaled the stairs. In less than a minute, the waning daylight gleaming faintly through the adjacent bank of windows, he was sound asleep.

***

Foley's eyes snapped open. In his nightmare, his daughter, Samantha, had been chasing him again. It was always a slow motion, almost comical, pursuit through his old home. Around the island first, her hands outstretched and reaching. And then he fell. The visions were always the same and played out exactly as they did in real life weeks ago. Only this time he didn't shoot her dead. In the dream he tripped on something and she was atop him. Clawing and scratching until her bent fingers got tangled in his short beard. He decided in his subconscious state this time to let her live. And it was his undoing. Sam pulled closer, teeth clicking. Then, though he hadn't gone to get his gun from the safe yet, for some reason he could smell gunpowder. And in the twisted reality of his dream that was now bordering on nightmare, the stench was inexplicably on her breath. So he gave up. Accepted his fate, willing to join his family at last. But once again the same subconscious that had been terrifying him nightly since he'd pulled the trigger in real life wouldn't let him die in the ethereal one.

Coming to, he focused his sleepy eyes on the silver-dollar-sized oval trained on him and came to the frightening realization that it was real. And then it became evident the cordite stench clinging to the matte black cylinder was also real, not Sam's breath nor a part of his nightmare. The slightly wavering oval was made of metal, quiet and deadly and of this world. As was the man in black brandishing the pistol it was affixed to. A tick after waking, Foley heard, "Planning on leaving soon?" He nodded, then moved his head an inch left. Looked the length of the barrel and admitted, "Yeah ... but it looks like I should have left earlier."

Cocking his head, Cade said, "Let's hear it." He put the lock gun that he'd used to gain the quiet entry back in his pocket and came out with a pair of cuffs modeled from zip ties. Lastly, he set the cuffs on the man's chest and ordered him to put them on.

Reluctantly, Foley acquiesced. He clenched the rigid plastic tip of the first tie in his mouth and pulled it tight. After doing the same with the other, he looked up at his captor and arched a brow as if asking silently, *Now what?*

Cade checked the man's work, then added a couple more clicks for good measure. Satisfied, he took the man's pistol from the small of his back where he'd temporarily stowed it. Removed the magazine and checked the pipe. *Clear.*

Cade replaced the weapon in his belt and took a seat on a chair kitty-corner from the cuffed man. "Let's start with your name."

After meeting Jimmy Foley, former IT professional and outdoor enthusiast formally, Cade had him detail Bishop's operation, beginning with which house across the lake was his and how many others were present and where they stayed. Cade committed these details to memory, then rifled through Foley's wallet. He looked at the Idaho license and asked, "Why this place? Looks like you used to stay in southwest McCall."

Foley shook his sunburned bald head. A tear showed at the corner of his eye. "Couldn't go back there ... after—"

"Something bad happened there?"

Foley nodded. He was sitting up on the bed now, fully clothed in camo shorts and a thin cotton shirt of the same pattern favored by hunters, his chest rising and falling, obviously fighting to keep the awful memories of that day from tearing him apart.

"Something bad happened everywhere," said Cade. "But I'm going to need your help here."

Foley straightened up, nodding.

Already having cross-checked the many details divulged by Foley and deciding the man was who he said he was, Cade asked the most important question.

Once again Foley nodded. "Yesterday," he said. Cade nodded to that and said, "Thank you. Now I'm sorry I have to do this but unfortunately I have no choice."

Foley closed his eyes and turned away, waiting for the darkness.

Chapter 79

Being down four capable people at the compound, Chief made the executive decision and nixed the campfire the younger folks, Raven especially, were clamoring for.

So Brook used the time between dinner and lights out to go over the basics of field stripping her stubby Colt carbine. With Raven and Sasha sitting cross-legged at the ground near her feet, and the two love birds Taryn and Wilson dang near spooning each other a few feet removed, she held the rifle up for all to see and popped out the takedown pin. "Do not drop ..." The old saying *do as I say, not as I do*, entered her mind the moment the little black pin squirted from her grip and was lost from sight in the matted-down patch of grass.

"I got it, Mom," said Raven as she went to all fours and started combing the ground where she thought she saw it fall.

Soon all five of them were searching for the piece with the beams from a pair of headlamps added to the mix to augment the day's failing light.

Five heads nearly touching and as many pairs of hands feeling around, Brook thought the odds of finding the crucial component seemed a sure bet.

But that wasn't the case. It seemed as if Mister Murphy was in attendance tonight. *Better he's mucking things up here than somewhere else*, she conceded to herself. Then she tried to imagine what her man was doing at this very moment and came up blank. She removed her hat and plopped it on the ground to mark the spot and said, "Everybody inside. We're done here for the night." Leaving the search for the pin for the morning, she policed up the parts of her rifle and rose. Taking

Raven's hand, she called for Max and began the lonely walk back to the compound entrance.

Chapter 80

Lev heard Cade's voice in his earpiece: *Bring my kit and meet me halfway.* So he picked up the pack and carbine and set out towards the row of bushes Cade had entered a few minutes prior.

Before leaving the guest house, Cade extracted his sat-phone and typed out a quick text message. Stowing the sleek device in a cargo pocket, he peered through the back glass. *Clear.* With his ankle starting to throb again, he took the steps at a leisurely pace, crossed the lawn, and met up with Lev near the fragrant rhododendrons. He shrugged on his ruck and clicked his M4 to the center-point sling, then held a quick huddle with the others after which he traded the suppressed Glock to Lev for the laptop and accepted the blood-soaked helmet from Daymon for safekeeping. With a fist bump and a few words of encouragement, he sent Lev and Daymon off on a separate mission of their own.

Once the pair were out of earshot, Duncan asked, "You sure that's going to work?"

"It's got to," answered Cade.

"I figure we're outgunned ten-to-one. No way to win a shootout against those kind of numbers."

"Try fifteen-to-one," proffered Cade.

"With no air or arty to call in ... just starting out we'll be fighting an uphill battle."

To which Cade replied, "Have faith in me, friend."

"You have an ace?"

Remaining stoic, Cade said, "Desantos always practiced what he preached. And he liked to say: 'Keep your cards close to your vest and a derringer up your sleeve.'"

Duncan said ruefully, "It's a shame I didn't have a chance to get to know that fella."

Talking as he walked back towards the guest house, Cade agreed, "He's missed. That's for sure. But we've got to go on if we're going to somehow reverse this extinction-level event we've found ourselves in." He started up the stairs, carbine banging his thigh, and gripping the rail white-knuckle-tight, letting his upper body strength counter the extra stress on the ankle. Grimacing, he craned over his shoulder and went on, "Cowboy had a favorite MacArthur quote ... want to hear it?"

Pausing on a stair, Duncan said, "I'm all ears."

"Usually after beating some young swinging dick in a shooting competition or out on the O-course (obstacle course), Cowboy would say: 'Age wrinkles the body; quitting wrinkles the soul.'"

"So true," said Duncan. He followed Cade through the door and once inside marveled at the triangle of custom glass opening out onto the elevated deck. Tugging on his collar, he said, "If we're staying here until full dark then we really ought to open some of those windows."

"That's my plan," Cade said behind a grin. "Go on upstairs and check out the arrangement."

Duncan said, "I've had it with stairs."

Chuckling, Cade said, "Quitting wrinkles the soul."

Shaking his head, Duncan said, "Fuck off." Then relented and began to climb the oak stairs, muttering the entire way.

Cade put his carbine aside and placed his backup compact Glock 19 at arm's reach on the island before him. He was in the midst of assembling the MSR when Duncan called down to him from above asking, "What's this hot mess up here?"

"Jimmy Foley. Says so on his Idaho driver's license."

"What'd he do?"

"Ask him."

Looking at the sweating mess with equal measures of empathy and anger, Duncan removed the washcloth from the man's mouth. Bald head beaded with sweat, arms and legs zip-tied at four points, Foley's chest heaved as he drew in an unimpeded breath of fresh air.

Duncan interrogated Foley in much the same way as Cade had. Finally, after all of his questions had been answered, he went silent and hung his head.

Foley stammered, "Don't kill me. I can help you. Anything that I can do ... I will."

"Have you killed a man?"

Eyes bugged and locked with Duncan's, Foley shook his head wildly side-to-side.

Duncan called down to Cade. "I think he's being truthful."

In the process of hauling his gear up the stairs, Cade replied, "That's what my gut was telling me."

"Cut him loose?"

Having just cleared the final step, Cade dumped his gear on the bed and opened the laptop, placing it on a side table. He cocked his head and looked at Duncan. "Ya think?"

Gradually Foley was coming to the realization that he might live to see another day. His head, ever so slowly, began bobbing up and down, his chin hitting his chest with force.

Duncan pulled a lock-blade knife from a cargo pocket and sliced through Foley's bonds, feet first. While removing the flex cuffs on his wrists, Duncan leaned close and whispered, "Don't make me have to kill you. Because I will."

Rubbing his wrists and sensing he was ahead of the game, and not wanting to foul it up, Foley simply nodded and watched the man in black move about the room.

While Duncan was looking at the satellite image on the open laptop, Cade was pulling the drawers from a shaker-style dresser. All six ended up in the far corner, their contents, once nicely folded clothes and bedding, spilling out on the floor.

Looking at Foley, Cade said, "Give me a hand with this."

Without a second's hesitation, with Duncan watching him like a hawk, Foley rose from the plush chair and grabbed the dresser's end nearest him.

Cade said, "We're going to place it perpendicular to the ... " then suddenly stopped speaking. He placed his end down and pressed one hand over his earpiece. He nodded, obviously listening to someone, somewhere. This went on for a moment before he responded, "It's your call. Kill or capture."

Still holding up his end of the dresser while looking quizzically at the man calling himself Cade, Foley tried to figure out what these two men, who appeared miles apart in training and composure, were really up to. He had already come to the conclusion, due to the nature of the earlier questioning, that Bishop and his men were the hunted.

But given the disparity in numbers, he was beginning to question his earlier assumption that had him living to see another day.

Picking up his end of the rather sturdy dresser, Cade resumed where he'd left off. "As I was saying, I want to place this perpendicular to the railing here." They dragged it across the room and positioned it slightly angled to the right. "Do you know how to open those windows?"

Foley nodded. He said, "You want all of them open?"

"Negative," said Cade. "Only the long one in the center."

Foley shuffled across the room and went down the stairs, then retrieved the pole from where he'd left it the day before. The system was simple but required time and patience. He slipped the curved end of the ten-foot pole into the eye hook affixed to the box just below the rectangular window that housed a screw-drive mechanism. One end of the pole had an egg-beater-style hand crank of the sort found on old-fashioned hand-powered drills. He started in conservatively. Then found a rhythm and cranked the window fully open. Instantly a cooling breeze rolled in over their heads, hit the back wall and supplanted the hotter air, chasing it down and out of its realm.

Cade said, "Perfect." He flipped down both stubby legs of the bipod and placed the Modular Sniper Rifle atop the dresser, its lengthy suppressor pointing in the general direction of the center house five-hundred yards distant.

Duncan said, "You sure you don't want to move closer? Set up in one of the other houses?"

"No need," replied Cade, "The angle and range from here is optimal. Now all I need is a target." He pulled the floral chair to the end of the dresser, piled some of the spilled bedding on top of the seat cushion, and took a load off.

After acquiring the target house he tweaked the optic, drawing the slightly shimmering image into sharp focus. Through the clear glass railing surrounding the covered porch he saw a table and chairs. With no reason to their placement, a dozen beer bottles sat atop the table. To the right, dominating most of the front level, were sliding doors, all glass, designed to open wide, presumably to let nature in. He pressed his cheek to the rest and leaned in and trained the optics on the bank of upstairs windows where he saw some movement. After a few seconds of watching a dark-haired woman moving about the room, Cade was convinced the woman he was looking at was Jamie. "Duncan," he called out. "I think I see our girl."

Chapter 81

There was a loud knock at the door. Nothing cheery about it. All business. Reluctantly Jamie put down her book and padded across the room. "Who is it?" she asked.

"Ian," came the muffled reply. "Won't you join me downstairs?"

"Give me a minute." Suddenly Jamie's fight or flight instincts revved up. She took a couple of calming breaths, slipped out of the shorts and dressed in the jeans that had been provided her earlier in the day. She pulled her hair into a high ponytail and looked at herself in the mirror. "That'll do."

There was a trio of knocks at the door, closely spaced. Urgent. With a little edginess to his voice, Bishop said, "Everything OK?"

Jamie swallowed hard and opened the door. What she did next was planned. She wanted to deliver a knee to his groin but was presently unsure of herself. Bottom line, her level of desperation hadn't risen there yet. So instead, sticking to her original plan—to further the idea, in dribs and drabs, to her tall, dark, and handsome suitor that capture-bonding was indeed taking place—she stood on her tiptoes, gripped his bicep, and delivered a peck to his cheek. *Hell,* she thought. *If female spies can use their feminine guiles to get what they want, so too can I.* And right now what she wanted more than anything was to carve the fucker into little tiny pieces. She'd killed to protect herself on two separate occasions already since the world went to shit, and this one, if she got the chance, was going to be very different from the others. It was going to be very gratifying.

Smiling, Bishop said, "Cheeses and crackers and a surprise after sunset. Does that sound good to you?"

Mind racing, Jamie held her composure and said, "I love surprises. I think I can get used to this treatment." Then, thinking she'd laid it on too thick, she felt a cold pit forming in her stomach.

Bullshit, thought Bishop. His smile turning wolfish, he said, "Let's get some fresh air." Stepping aside he swept his arm in a kind of grand gesture and ushered her ahead and followed her down the hall.

Chapter 82

Cade moved aside so that Duncan could get his eyes on the target house. The suppressor on the end of the MSR tracked left to right in tiny increments as the old aviator glassed the house. "I can't see a thing," he finally said.

"Because of your vision ... or there's nobody *to* see?"

"The latter. I wasn't blowing smoke when I told you these glasses were doing the trick."

Interrupting, Foley said, "Just yesterday Carson and his crew brought three women back from their foraging trip."

Suddenly wishing he hadn't played his cards so close to his vest, Cade asked, "Why didn't you divulge that earlier?"

"You didn't ask."

Cade straightened up and ran a hand through his dark hair. After a beat he said, "Enlighten me."

Foley repeated what he'd overheard the other guards say about the women, leaving out the vulgar descriptions of certain parts of the women's female anatomy.

Across the lake

Once downstairs, Bishop followed Jamie through the kitchen and living room, then through the slider. That she'd eyed the block of kitchen knives along the way wasn't lost on him. At the rail he sidled up behind her and whispered, "Have you ever seen a sunset so grand?"

Playing along—for now—Jamie answered, "Why no. No, I haven't."

He pressed closer, grinding against her now.

Though the temperature had dropped a few degrees in just a handful of minutes, the shiver Jamie threw was one of revulsion. Then his cheek brushed hers and he pointed over her left shoulder north by west and said cryptically, "In a short while you and I are going to be blessed by a sky show few humans live to tell about."

Reacting to the absence of direct sunlight, multitudes of insects seemed to come on the scene at once, buzzing the two of them.

Pushing back against Bishop's advance, Jamie said, "The bugs are killing me. Can we go inside?" There was no word of warning. Not so much as a grunt, but suddenly she found herself freed from his weight and following him back inside, her hand in his.

Foley's place

As the sun sank from sight somewhere far away in the west, the windows across the lake broadcast the event, reflecting the oranges and reds of the fiery evening sky. Meanwhile, inside the A-frame guest house overlooking Mother Nature's stunning sky show, Duncan said, "The way you described the brunette ... athletic, medium height ... gotta be Jamie." No sooner did the young woman's name roll off his tongue than he was staring her in the face. And that face, amazingly, was unmarred. There were no obvious signs of abuse, only a pinched smile and a hard set jaw—subtle tells of the stress she was no doubt under. *Nothing like Jordan though*, he thought. The image of her death mask he'd no doubt carry with him for a long time. "I have eyes on Jamie. And I think I've made the Bishop fella too."

"Carson?" asked Cade.

"Nope. Just the two. They just stepped onto the porch. And oh how I wish I could kill the bastard right now." Then, recognizing the fact that he was observing them with Cade's scoped rifle, he rose and backed away from the dresser. "Shoot the fucker. Please take the shot," he pleaded with Cade.

Taking position behind the rifle, Cade switched frequencies on his comms. He clicked the send button twice and, after less than a second, was relayed instructions from somewhere on high. Responding with a quick, "Copy that," he switched back to the frequency shared by his small team, clicked the send button twice, and then answered Duncan. "Timing's got to be just right if you want Jamie to come home with us alive."

"Cade ... you've gotta make sure she's not harmed," said Duncan. "You know Logan was smitten with that girl."

Foley blurted, "Can I go with you ... wherever *home* is? I've got nothing here."

"Stay in line and out of the way and I'll consider it," answered Cade. A half-beat later, in his earpiece, he heard a pair of soft clicks. He answered with a pair of clicks of his own and snugged the rifle in and put his face to the scope. *Too late.* He watched helplessly as Jamie, following closely behind Bishop, disappeared back into the house. A few seconds later he saw a flare of light inside. Brilliant at first, then the single flickering flame became two and the original died out.

He saw Jamie sit down, her face a golden mask of beauty illuminated by the flickering candlelight. Then Bishop pulled out a chair and sat down, his head and upper body eclipsing her entirely.

Chapter 83

Hearing the two clicks he'd been anticipating, Lev clicked back twice and when his response was answered in like fashion, he flashed Daymon a thumbs up. They'd agreed ahead of time that Daymon would start the ball rolling and Lev would join the party only if necessary.

Twenty feet away, concealed in some low brush, his woodland BDUs and rangy mop of dark hair effectively breaking up any kind of outline the faint light of dusk might illuminate, Daymon received the signal. *Just a bear*, he told himself. In fact, if the man at the gate had to be compared to any animal—a bear would be the logical choice. Easily over six feet tall and weighing in well north of two hundred pounds, the bearded man had already displayed a nasty streak in the way he'd been toying with the arriving dead. Instead of sticking a dagger in their brains like the other, much smaller, guard had been wont to do, Big Beard was fond of carving pieces off of them first. *Not a way to treat your former fellow Americans.* And though the man appeared to be an asshole of the highest order, no matter how hard Daymon tried to dehumanize the man in his mind, the thought, however doubtful, that the sadist might still have kids or a wife somewhere gave the former BLM firefighter reason to pause.

Sighting through the bow's optics, Daymon could sense Lev's eyes on him, beaming the chanted words, *do it, do it,* straight into his brain. Then he remembered that these men may have been the ones who'd kidnapped Heidi. Who'd held her against her will and defiled her after Robert Christian had his way and cast her out like yesterday's trash. At the very least they were guilty by association.

Something shifted in him. The last modicum of empathy melted like an ice cube on the surface of the sun. Suddenly he was full-of-rage Daymon. The very same guy who had sacrificed the fat lawyer to the dead in Hanna. *Bye bye Ursa*, he thought, drawing up a few pounds of trigger pull. Then, with the crosshairs centered over the bearded man's throat—targeting the soft, fleshy indentation right below where the whiskers stopped growing—he sealed the deal.

Silent, save for a barely perceptible twang which was followed by a slightly louder crack, like a twig giving underfoot, the arrested tension was released and the barbed arrow shot from the carbon fiber bow, covered the short distance in the blink of an eye, and found its mark dead on.

Buried to the feathers, blood pulsing in sheets around the fiberglass shaft, the arrow quivered for a second until Big Beard's hands instinctively came up and grabbed ahold.

Whether due to the commotion or the coppery smell of blood, or both, the dead on the other side of the gate reacted instantly. Their moans intensified and they thrust their stick-thin arms between the horizontal slats.

Busy notching another arrow, Daymon hadn't been witness to the actions of the dead or the bearded man's eyes rolling back into his skull. Nor did he see the man's mouth working frantically to draw a breath against the torrent of his own frothy blood that was effectively drowning him.

Daymon finished reloading and snugged the crossbow to his shoulder and targeted the smaller man, who by now had turned a one-eighty and was watching the life drain from his companion's eyes.

As the realization that he had crossed over and was now a killer of men settled heavily on Daymon's shoulders, he hovered the crosshairs on the little guy's ribcage, right side, below the arm and above the hip. Just a grouping of muscles and a few slats of horizontal bone protecting a whole mess of important organs. Seemingly unfazed and presuming he was out of the line of fire, the second guard raised a radio to his lips. *Too late and wrong assumption*, thought a changed Daymon. *I'm behind you, fucker.*

From a spot of concealment thirty feet from the gate and with his finger tensed on the Glock's trigger, Lev watched as

Daymon channeled his inner Grim Reaper and put an arrow into the second guard's right side. The reaction was instantaneous as the guard dropped his weapon and another item he'd just pulled from inside his fleece vest and then fell over onto his left and curled up into a fetal ball.

Instantly Daymon popped up and sprinted towards the gate.

Lev covered Daymon's approach and once he'd taken a knee beside the second guard, broke from cover and hustled over there as well.

Having already disarmed the guard, Daymon held up the silent two-way radio and said, "I don't think he got the call off."

"Let's find out," said Lev darkly. Over the moans of the agitated Zs and the guard's whispered pleas for help, he grabbed the arrow shaft, gave it a tug, and hissed, "How many more men are inside the perimeter?"

The man's glassy eyes suddenly gained some cognition. Mouth moving, the man shot a hate-filled sidelong glance at Daymon but said nothing substantive, just pained grunts and groans escaping his mouth.

Twisting the shaft, Lev hissed, "*How many?*"

Looking around, worried reinforcements were soon to emerge from the lengthening shadows, Daymon said, "Cade wants us to get these guys out of sight and then get right back."

Hoping to get some extra intel, Lev ignored Daymon and jiggled the arrow, an action that was met by a shriek and then a beat later a muffled, "Thirty or forty," left the man's mouth between gasps.

Addressing Daymon, Lev said, "You can look away if you want." He unsheathed his matte black blade and without pause drew it across the doomed man's throat, pressing hard enough to produce the sound of honed steel dragging against bone. Blood sprayed everywhere, hot and sticky. After a handful of seconds the man went limp and the bleeding let up, signifying the end of his life.

The stench of the dead when combined with the stink of loosened bowels and the metallic tang of the freshly spilt blood was enough to make Daymon's stomach clench. Wondering to himself if the acts he'd just committed, or the byproduct of those acts, was the responsible culprit, he swallowed against a throat full of rising bile.

"You going to be OK?" asked Lev as he wiped away the blood and sheathed his blade.

Nodding, Daymon grabbed the smaller guard's arms and draped the limp dead weight over his neck in a fireman's carry. Then he rose slowly, straightened his arms and heaved the warm corpse over the gate where it was received with open arms and gnashing teeth.

It took a combined effort to drag the bear-sized guard into the underbrush, and when they were finished both men were fighting for breath.

Without a word, Lev tossed the smaller guard's weapon into the mass of feeding dead. On the run back to the guest house the radio went into his cargo pocket. Then, broadcasting the mission's success, he clicked the transmit switch on his headset twice.

Chapter 84

Finger tensed on the trigger, Cade felt the faintest of stirrings in his chest, a sensation like no other, certainly one he'd never forget. The first time he had experienced the unique harmonic overpressure, which was the way his mind interpreted it, Mike Desantos had been on this side of the dirt. The last time he'd had the pleasure was at the NBL in Canada, when, exhausted and nearly overrun by the dead, the glorious sound like no other signaled his Delta team's imminent rescue.

He breathed in deeply, filling his chest with warm, still air. Held it in check for a tick then exhaled, a whisper of breath escaping slow and steady. Between heartbeats, he drew off the remaining trigger pull, saw the barrel jump and felt the considerable recoil pummel his shoulder and send gooseflesh rippling down his ribcage. Upstairs in the loft, the suppressed report sounded like a single hand clap, sharp and attention-getting and, before it had made the rounds and finished echoing off the slanted ceiling, Cade saw the grievous damage inflicted by the .338 Lapua round. First to take the brunt was the sliding glass door as the bullet riding the air at a supersonic pace punched through both sandwiched panes, causing the entire 4X7 sheet to web first then splinter and fall inward, leaving him an unobstructed view of what came next.

When the bullet struck Bishop, his right arm was raised to shoulder level; whether he'd been talking with his hands, about to strike Jamie, or shoveling food into his mouth, Cade wasn't certain.

In the time it took Cade to draw in his next breath, three things were going on inside the target house. First he saw Bishop's upraised arm jerk violently forward towards Jamie as his entire bulk, reacting to the kinetic energy behind the sudden mule kick, followed suit, hinging forward over the table, scattering china and service as the dark wood slab reared up on one end and he disappeared from view, pulling everything down atop himself. Next, in slow motion, Bishop's form was replaced by a spreading pink cloud of mist and Cade saw, clear as day through the powerful optics, Jamie's expression go from one of taciturn acceptance, to surprise, to sudden revulsion as the expanding cloud of flesh and blood pelted her from the neck up.

As Cade worked the MSR's bolt back, simultaneously sending the spent piece of smoking brass on a tumbling journey to the floor and the next match-grade shell smoothly into the breach, he witnessed two things. First Jamie disappeared from view, her slight form slipping behind the teetering table. In the next instant, a black angular shape, the source of the harmonic disturbance, crossed the night sky smooth and dangerous, its near silent rotor wash rattling the open windows and frothing the lake's placid surface.

A half-beat later all hell broke loose northeast of the lake as well as in Cade's ear bud when unexpectedly, over his team's shared channel, he heard, "Good shooting, Wyatt. Target is down." Then the voice he recognized as belonging to Ari said, "In five, four, three, two ... " At *'one'* Cade saw the black shape flare and level out over the target house and instantly there were a pair of fast ropes uncoiling snake-like from the aircraft's open doors. He blinked and two forms, all in black, weapons strapped across their chests, rode the ropes to the ground below. Then, a second after the first pair appeared, another two ninjas exited the hovering Ghost Hawk and rode the ropes to earth.

For a second the radio was silent in Cade's ear. Then a voice he recognized rattled off a couple of orders and the comms went suddenly quiet—for a second.

"What was that all about?" asked Daymon over the comms.

Finally seeing the black shape for what it really was, the lone remaining Ghost Hawk, Duncan whistled low and slow and stated, mostly for Daymon's benefit, "Cade's been holding out on us. That there is the cavalry and I'd give my left nut to sit in the pilot's seat of one of those birds."

Still cuffed at the wrists, Foley crabbed past the furniture and had just taken up station, nose to the sliding glass, when an explosion, lighting his face up red, rocked the house immediately left of the target house. Then there was a continuous laser-straight red and orange stream of fire lancing groundward from the orbiting Ghost Hawk and the house on the right side of the target suddenly caught fire.

After the fast-moving shock wave rippled the water and rattled the east-facing windows, a muffled *'Whoomph'* rolled over the guesthouse. Cade heard the loud thumping of what could only be a Chinook and then it came into view far left of the lakefront homes. And as licks of small arms fire lanced up towards the lumbering chopper, in his ear bud, he heard whom he guessed was Ari's co-pilot speaking in clipped syntax, directing the action on the ground.

Then there were more explosions to the north and more chatter and then again he heard Lopez's unmistakable tone and delivery followed by, "Copy that," which, deep and sonorous, could only belong to the surfer-boy-looking Special Agent Adam Cross. All of a sudden Cade imagined an old Thin Lizzy song befitting the battlefield reunion taking place, then he heard the unmistakable thundering cadence of a new pair of Chinook helicopters entering the airspace over the lake. *The boys are back in town*, *indeed*, thought Cade as the all too familiar combat tingle returned. Juices flowing, he shrugged on his ruck, snatched up the MSR and Lev's M4 and said, "Let's move." The newly flowing adrenaline countering any latent ankle pain, he hustled downstairs following Foley's shiny bouncing dome. At the bottom of the stairs, the man of the house turned a one-eighty, held his hands in the air, and shot Cade a *what about me* look.

In answer to that, Cade cocked his head and stared into the older man's eyes. Seeing no signs of deception or malice in them, he pulled his Gerber and sliced through the man's cuffs.

"Two coming in," announced Lev over the comms.

"Copy that," replied Cade as a soft knock echoed in the hall. As a precaution, he watched Foley rub his wrists as Duncan disappeared down the hall to get the door. Then there was a sharp snick of a lock being thrown and a subtle creak and the noise of clomping boots and labored breathing invaded the guesthouse.

Stopping and turning where the hall spilled into the great room, Duncan furrowed his brow and asked, "Done?"

Face white, like he'd seen a ghost, Daymon held his blood-stained hands up, palms forward, and whispered, "Done."

From across the lake came the steady popping of small arms as a firefight raged between troops on the ground and the occupants of the house flanking Bishop's. Tongues of orange leapt from windows on the second story. In the next second, silencing the opposition, red tracers, seemingly connected like links in a chain, poured from the sky somewhere above and behind the house full of holdouts.

"They're not going quietly, are they?" observed Cade.

Shooting a rueful look Cade's way, Duncan asked, "Your boys are really taking it to them. When do *we* get some?"

After switching frequencies and holding a separate private conversation with someone over the comms, Cade looked at the men assembled around him, met each expectant stare and said, "Police up your gear and lock and load ... we're *oscar mike* in *five*."

Chapter 85

The second Bishop stood and reached across the table for her, Jamie knew her worst fears were coming true. She'd seen it in his eyes. The sparkle of hope that had lit up the room the night before and had been there to a certain extent when he'd met her at the door upstairs was gone. A look of menace crossed his face as he said: *I've survived dozens of encounters with liars better than you. I've been taught how to win hearts and minds and it's become evident with you I'll do neither.* And when he looked down the hall over her right shoulder, she instantly knew why he had sent Carson upstairs. And that there were a pair of handcuffs in her immediate future followed shortly by a lifetime's worth of agony and degradation and torture, both physical and mental.

Several things happened at once. Her epiphany, given away by the look on her face, was followed by a devious grin spreading on Bishop's shadowed features. Then she instinctively pushed away from the table and tried to stand. But by the time those impulses crossed synapses on their way to make it so, she was wearing most of the former Navy SEAL's right shoulder and clavicle in the form of blood and flesh and flecked bone.

Blinking against the onslaught, she cried out as tiny razorblade-sharp bone splinters bombarded her face and eyes. Then simultaneously two things happened. Stifling her scream, a sizeable hunk of shredded pectoral muscle, firm and warm, entered her mouth and lodged in her windpipe. And the cause of all the damage crackled the air by her ear and impacted the heavy-gauge stainless skin of the Wolf refrigerator with a solid sounding slap.

As she instinctively gagged and spit the plug of flesh from her mouth, she noticed the glass spilling like a wave from the destroyed slider. Then, like a slow-motion scene from a Matrix flick, food and china and silverware bunched together at the low end and crashed to the floor as the table, looking like a sinking ship, reared up and followed her captor over backwards, a look of utter surprise painting his face.

Fight or flight. The question didn't register in her brain as an audible cue. Nor did she realize she had made a decision until a second after the endorphins flooded her brain and she acted.

Hearing Carson cursing upstairs and then his footsteps pounding out a hollow cadence above and behind her, she shifted her gaze left to the block of knives on the island. Midway through the sweep, her eyes had fallen on something interesting on the underside of the upended table. Her subconscious mind instantly knew what it was, but not until she stared at the black lump for a second did she realize her incredibly good fortune.

Elvis

Waiting for a break in the river of dead, Elvis sat in the truck, thinking. After a couple of minutes wrestling with more questions than he had answers for, his patience wore thin and he started the big engine. Lights off, he nosed the rig down the drive and turned right at the 'T,' charging hard against the trudging tide of decaying flesh. The effect his presence had on the creatures was comical as he zippered through the flow of flesh eaters, causing a bullwhip-like chain reaction when they clumsily about-faced and gave chase, all shoulders and elbows and hips battling for a clear lane on the blacktop.

The reversal of flow intensified and as he sped away, in his rearview, Elvis saw what looked like an undead orgy taking place in the center of the road.

After driving two straight miles nudging dead from the tow truck's path with the bumper guard most of the way, he came to another 'T' and the sultry voice in the box told him he had arrived at his final destination.

"What the fuck," he said aloud, banging the wheel while the dead slapped the flanks of the truck. Panic welling within him, he wildly scanned the horizon while weighing his options. Blackout restrictions or no, he figured he would see at least the silhouette of a military base, however distant. A guard tower maybe, standing out boxy against the blue-black night sky. A fence with coils of concertina perched strategically atop. But he saw nothing. No base. No soldiers in the distance having a smoke. No vehicles in the foreground where he assumed a base would be. And worst of all, starting the slow creep of chill into his stomach, he saw nothing to indicate there had been, save for the traipsing dead, any activity whatsoever near here for quite some time.

For just a tick he entertained flashing his headlights as he had upon arriving at the lake two nights prior. But knowing he wasn't a tactician, nor would it serve him to pretend he was, he quickly discarded the foolish notion.

Instead he turned right and drove madly for a quarter-mile until he came upon a county road blocked by a swinging gate intended to keep out vehicles, mainly. The gate had a sign bolted to it warning that trespassers would be prosecuted to the full extent of the law. *Throw the book at me*, thought Elvis with a morbid grin.

Beyond the gate was a winding gravel road that meandered up to a squat, earth-tone-painted cinderblock building he guessed was home to water pumps or controls of some sort. And best of all, the windowless structure was on a slight rise and surrounded by a cyclone fence, which in his opinion presented him the perfect location to arm and abandon the device.

He shifted into low gear and used the truck's bumper and a ton of torque to breach the gate. It popped noisily and rocketed inward as Elvis sped through. He followed the gravel road to the building and stopped short of the entry. After a quick K-turn he nudged the gate open with the wrecker's rear bumper.

Leaving the engine running and the front end blocking the newly forced opening, Elvis leaped out, stuffed the .45 in his belt, and went to work.

Jamie

The second that she knew what she was looking at, fight won out over flight and she ripped the stubby looking gun, tape and all, from the table's exposed underside. Without giving thought as to why it was there in the first place, she thumbed the hammer back and aimed the revolver at the air above the table's edge where she suspected Bishop would eventually surface. In the interim, she reached her left hand out and snatched up a medium-sized knife from the block. *Not too big to swipe with*, she reasoned. And long enough to hit a vital organ. It would do the trick, she decided.

The air in the great room had taken on the all-too-familiar smell of spilt blood. Breathing through her nose, Jamie listened hard and detected movement on the stairs. She knelt down, the island pressing her back and Bishop struggling to pull himself up with his one good arm to her fore.

Outside there was a loud explosion. Very near, she surmised. Then, coinciding with a few long, drawn-out chainsaw-like sounds, the horizontally mounted windows on each side of the house lit up red and orange like eyes on a Jack-o'-Lantern.

Carson's voice: "*Bishop?*"

With one elbow hooked over the table edge, Bishop's head slowly broke the plane. Instantly the image reminded Jamie of the old Navy recruitment commercial in which a team of SEALs emerge from black waters, deadly and wraith-like. This was nothing of the sort. Bishop looked pathetic. His face was drained of color and his mouth moved fish-like, fighting to draw a breath.

In her side-vision Jamie saw the toe of a tan boot followed by a shin and knee and finally a man's thigh, all muscled and flexing under the desert tan camouflage fabric.

"Bishop?" said the owner of the leg, only this time with an, *Oh fuck what happened to you* kind of delivery. Not agitated sounding, but drawn out and filled with compassion.

Knee, thigh, or head?

Jamie chose thigh but her aim was off. Instinctively she crunched her eyes shut as the report, sandwiched between the table and island, roared back and forth, seemingly using her ear canal as a pass through.

Semi-deafened, Jamie squeezed the trigger two more times as Carson fell sideways. The first shot she would find out momentarily passed through his scrotum mid-stride. The second she witnessed (between blinks) punch through the soft meat of his hamstring, instantly turning the pants leg crimson and bringing forth a shrill, gut-wrenching scream.

Both hands allocated to holding together his nutsack, Carson let his semi-automatic fall to the floor where he joined it a beat later with a third catastrophic bullet wound to the left hip.

Willing herself to move, Jamie scooted along the blood-slickened floor and snatched away the boxy pistol. She rose on shaky legs and crabbed around both men, tiptoeing through splintered china and around the upended table.

Standing hands on hips with shouts and gunfire rising to a crescendo outside, she smiled big at the fallen men. For an instant she contemplated crowing about how *Karma's a bitch* or spouting something witty like *you reap what you sow.* But she didn't. Trembling with rage and aware of how Bishop, on orders from Robert Christian, had left Heidi for dead in Jackson Hole, she went to work with the knife.

"This is too good for you, Bishop."

"You don't have the balls to kill a man," he managed to say through a mouthful of crimson froth.

Even over the ringing in her ears, Jamie heard the backdoor come off its hinges. Undeterred, she hissed, "I just grew some, asshole." Fighting off the dying man's one good arm, starting with Logan and finishing with Jordan, she drew the keen-edged kitchen knife from one ear to the other, slowly whispering the names of the three who had fallen beside her at the quarry.

"Drop it," called a stocky Hispanic man clad head to toe in camouflage and Velcro and body armor. He trained a stubby machine gun on her and repeated the order, louder and more forcefully. Then, still glaring at her, he talked to someone out of sight over his high tech communications gear.

After seeing the American flag on the man's uniform, Jamie dropped the knife and inched away from Bishop's pale corpse. Immediately a second man dressed all in black with a weapon to match helped her to her feet. He turned her head and checked her for injuries. A second later he nodded to the Hispanic soldier and whispered near her ear, "You're going to be OK."

Shaking slightly, Jamie shot a long nod at Carson and asked the soldier in black matter-of-factly, “Is he going to die?”

Having just zip-tied the blonde mercenary’s hands behind his back, the Hispanic soldier rolled him over. He stuck a gloved finger into the hole in the crotch of Carson’s blood-soaked pants. Grimacing, he examined the other more visible gunshot wounds and finally said, “He’s got a few minutes. Ten max.”

Chapter 86

Across the lake, Cade took two strips of what looked like reflective tape from his pack. He peeled the backing to expose the adhesive and stuck one strip to Foley's chest over his heart and then another on his back. Lev and Duncan said nothing. Both peeled the backing and stuck a strip to their BDUs over their hearts.

Daymon snugged on his helmet and shot Cade a quizzical look.

Flipping his NVG's over his eyes, Cade answered, "Infrared reflective GloTape. It's already on our helmets ... the rest is for good measure. We wouldn't want our friend Foley to be mistaken for a bad guy and take a bullet and buy the farm before we get a chance to interrogate him."

Foley felt his stomach flop as he was herded out of the house with the sharp barrel of a gun against his spine.

Between the recent sunset and the moon's inevitable rise, without any ambient light from street lights of nearby McCall, the night sky had gone inky black. Listening to the distant sounds of battle—and kind of disappointed he was missing out—Cade flipped down his late-gen night vision goggles and descended the stairs as quickly as his ankle would allow. Once at the bottom and standing on the cement parking pad, he pulled two identical items from a pocket. About the size and weight of a double pack of Wrigley's chewing gum, the devices, made from high impact plastic, had a flat bottom and an elongated clear plastic dome on top.

After flicking a switch and peeling a strip of backing paper from each one, Cade stretched tall and placed one atop the Jeep, centered on the roof sheet metal just aft of the windshield. As he placed the second device on the roof near the rear hatch, Duncan hopped in the passenger seat and Lev and Daymon bookended Foley in the backseat.

As expected, rendered in bright yellowish-green as seen through Cade's goggles, there was a flare of stark-white light from the overhead dome when the doors hinged open. Working quickly to extinguish the light, Cade got behind the wheel and used his Gerber to pry the plastic lens away and then dug out the tiny bulb with its sharp point.

Reacting instantly, the goggles adjusted and the brilliant corona subsided; he could see the dash and controls presented in a dozen varying shades of green. *So far so good.* In his ear bud he could hear brief snippets of conversation, the practiced commands and calls of a well-honed team presumably clearing one of the houses across the lake.

He started the truck up and asked Foley: "*Is anyone we encounter going to recognize this rig?*" A nod from the bald man registered in the rearview as Cade J-turned out of the driveway and shifted into Drive. In less than a minute, driving south, lights out, they were approaching the T-junction. Sweeping his gaze right, Cade noticed the gate some distance away. He also saw the logjam of death pressing up against it. Bright eyes in hollowed sockets, all the more evil-looking through the NVG's optics, swept left in unison as the monsters detected the exhaust note of the approaching vehicle.

"That's some Boris Karloff shit right there," stated Daymon. "All green and glassy-eyed."

Without prompting, Foley proffered, "Turn left here."

"Think the gate's going to hold?" asked Duncan as Cade took the left at speed.

Foley said, "Not for long. We have standing orders from Bishop to cull them on sight."

"Not everyone follows orders," muttered Daymon.

Remembering the vision of the two men Bishop had gunned down earlier and hearing their cries in his head as they died, Foley said, "Anyone caught not following orders were made examples of ... either crucified or shot on sight by Bishop or Carson."

"Carson?" asked Cade.

"He likes to say he's into *'procurement'* ... supplies and women. Especially women."

"I hope your D-boys roll him up," said Duncan.

"Me too," Cade agreed, meeting the older man's gaze.

The Jeep cut through the darkness under a thick canopy of trees. On their left vacant houses flashed by, the lake beyond appearing as green slivers of light between them.

They encountered no resistance travelling the curving arc of road between the roadblock near the peninsula and the first few houses making up the lake front compound where fires were raging and a mopping-up operation was underway.

Then a hundred yards from the action and two houses removed from the target house they encountered the security perimeter, where a trio of Army Rangers wielding M-203 grenade-launcher-equipped automatic weapons lit them up with what seemed like a million candlepower light.

Shielding his eyes in front of the goggles with one hand and holding the wheel tight with the other, Cade braked hard, bringing the Jeep to a crunching halt a dozen feet short of colliding with both bullets and vehicles.

"Hands out where we can see them," shouted one of the soldiers whom Cade could not see.

Cade flipped up the goggles and then with both gloved hands poking into the night air and a light like a locomotive's blinding him, suddenly sensed a presence on his left. Then he heard: "*Name?*"

"Cade Grayson ... United States Army, Retired."

"Wyatt?"

"Affirmative."

The soldier pressed, "Ground call sign?"

"Anvil."

Though Cade couldn't see it, the Ranger nodded. Then he said, "And the civilians?"

"They're capable."

The Ranger said nothing to that. A few seconds passed as he walked around the vehicle. Finishing the lap, he returned to the window, the light flicked off and he said, "IR beacons ... nice touch, Grayson."

Cade said, “Didn’t want the SOAR boys in the Chinooks to open us up like a tin can.”

The Ranger, a first sergeant whose name tape said *Fleishman*, turned and over his shoulder said, “Follow me in.”

Cade followed behind the sergeant at a walking pace, then wheeled the Jeep up to the rear of the target house where he was met by a face he knew very well. “Lopez! How’s it hanging, amigo?”

“Longer than yours, Wyatt.”

The two men embraced. Cade noted the captain’s tabs on the smaller operator’s collar. “Captain Lopez. Has a nice ring to it. Congrats,” he said, nodding.

Wearing a wide smile, Lopez crossed himself and pointed skyward.

In full understanding, Cade gestured towards the lake house and asked, “Cross inside?”

Still beaming, Lopez tilted his helmeted head in the same direction. “He’s in there ... prepping Bishop for his body bag.”

Cade’s brows crowded together. “Prepping? I thought I only winged him.”

“You’ll see. First I want to fill you in on the broken arrows. Man, Wyatt ... you were right. Where the G6 goes so goes Spartan. Funny thing is they thought they’d concealed the truck. But you and I both know there’s no hiding from a KH-12 and the keen eye of one of Nash’s determined imagery techs.”

With the distant flames casting flickering shadows at their boots, both men said in unison, “Or Nash.”

Smiling and shaking his head, Cade shifted his gaze to the olive-drab tractor-trailer. He let his eyes wander over the dozens of corpses, Spartan mercenaries who had fought hard but had ultimately paid the price for their betrayal. After the long pause, he said, “Bishop should have known he couldn’t hide that truck for long. Wonder why he even tried.”

Lopez shrugged. “Hubris? That’s my best guess.” Then the smile returned. “You shoulda seen Nash, though. She was giddy as hell that you came through ... said she held *you* to your word.”

Ignoring that, Cade asked, “Are the nukes inside?”

Shaking his head side-to-side, Lopez conceded, “I don’t know. The Geiger counter thinks so. But we’ll have eyes on the inside in a couple of mikes." He went on and was in the middle of bringing Cade up to speed on a couple of previous missions and the status of the Fuentes antiserum when a Chinook, drowning out their conversation, flew low and slow, passing directly overhead.

Chapter 87

From his seat in the thundering Spec-Ops-configured MH-47 Chinook being piloted by a highly skilled SOAR aviator, combat engineer and explosive ordnance expert Army First Lieutenant Larry Eckels peered out the port-side window as the lake below, black as polished obsidian, passed by slowly against the Chinook's counterclockwise orbit. Through his NVGs he saw flames from the helicopters and wheeled vehicles burning near the north gate, casting ghostly clawlike shadows across the newly graded tract of land. And beyond the gate, no doubt drawn by the firefights and explosions and glowing an eerie green in his goggles was a spectral army of the dead, swaying back and forth as they marched nearer.

Having had his fill of the destruction brought on by Delta's lightning-fast sneak attack he shifted his gaze right as the pilot maneuvered on approach and instantly recognized the squat tractor still hitched to the squared-off trailer parked amongst the tall pines, its metal skin showing up a slightly lighter shade of green and contrasting against the darker forested backdrop.

Near Eckels' feet, Hudson, his German Shepherd trained in explosives detection, yawned and looked up expectantly.

"Soon, boy," said the recently promoted lieutenant as the MH-47 banked sharply and bisected the lake west to east on approach. Then over the comms he reminded the chalk of Army Rangers under his command of the sensitive nature of the cargo inside the trailer.

The dual-rotor bird slowed and Eckels's stomach visited his throat as the pilot flared and said, "Target is at our two-o'clock. Wheels down in five, four, three, two ..."

At *'one'* there was a soft hiss aft as the flight engineer actuated the hydraulics and started the rear ramp on its downward journey. A curl of wood smoke infiltrated the cabin first thing. "Go, go, go," shouted a Ranger sergeant as the thirteen eager soldiers from the 75th Ranger Regiment poured forth, and like spokes on a wagon wheel each claimed his position, carbines locked and loaded—to a man fully ready to meet any resistance with the force necessary.

With the sonic shriek of the twin turbines diminishing and fresh from turning the Pueblo horde away from Schriever, Eckels ducked his head and hustled down the ramp, Hudson at his heel.

Instantly a barrage of different odors assaulted Eckels's nose: jet exhaust, cordite, burning flesh, and the ever-present underlying stench of death—a harsh reminder of the new world in which he was living.

After witnessing the twin-rotor behemoth glide in and settle neatly, Cade beckoned the four other men from the Jeep and over the diminishing turbine whine introduced them to Lopez one at a time. When he was finished, he turned and they all followed the stocky Delta captain into what he'd already described as a '*charnel house*.'

Which it was, Cade quickly found after nearly slipping and falling in the Lake Erie-sized pool of blood painting the dining room floor. Lying prostrate in the coppery smelling fluid, his face already gone slack, was Ian Bishop, whose presence was infinitely smaller in death. Cade knelt and rolled the corpse to the left to inspect his handiwork. The entry wound between Bishop's right bicep and scapula was torn open completely, a mess of jagged bone and cartilage. Up front, left of his sternum from Cade's perspective, the exit wound sprouted a crimson and white bouquet of shredded flesh and feathery lung tissue. Strangely, Bishop's left shirt sleeve had been cut off cleanly, revealing a fresh bloodless crater where a cantaloupe-sized oval of flesh had been excised from the shoulder. Finally, craning over, Cade rotated the corpse's head and saw the ultimate cause of death—a second mouth smiling out at him, severed muscle and sinew and yellowed trachea glistening under the artificial light cast by Adam Cross's head lamp.

"Whatcha got there?" Cade said, trying to find a face behind the glare.

Unfolding the blood-soaked length of camouflage fabric, Cross revealed his prize—or rather—Bishop's posthumous punishment. There, cradled in his palms atop the blood-soaked fabric, was the missing plug of flesh, stark white, and tattooed on it permanently in black ink, a Budweiser—the SEAL symbol consisting of an eagle clutching in its claws a U.S. Navy-style anchor, trident, and flintlock pistol. "He never deserved it," said the former Navy SEAL. "In my opinion he was never one of my brothers."

Cade asked, "What'd he do? Before all of this ... of course."

"He stopped being a team player a long time ago." Cross paused and folded the fabric over. "He was doing shady stuff over there trying to establish contacts for after service. Stepped on a lot of toes."

With the others now standing in a loose semi-circle and listening in, Cade asked, "And?"

"Another member of his team took a couple in the back in the kill house during training. Came out later it just happened to be the junior shooter who dimed on him."

Shaking his head, Cade stepped over the body and approached Carson, who was unconscious and pretty pale. "And this one? I recognize him from Nash's briefing."

Jamie stood up from where she'd been crouched in the corner and said, "He killed Logan. And the fucker admitted he made Jordan jump to her death from a hovering helicopter."

Cade made his way over to Jamie and whispered something while pointing over at Foley. She shook her head and continued talking rapidly and gesturing towards the fallen man.

Lopez had opened his mouth to speak but then stopped abruptly and held up a finger and walked off, apparently talking with someone over his comms. Then he turned, his face slack and devoid of color as he called across the room to Cade. "That was First Lieutenant Eckels," he said in a low voice. "Says we've got an empty quiver."

Cade crunched across the field of broken glass and kneeled over Carson. Thinking, he regarded the man for a moment and then looked up at Lopez and asked, "How many?"

"Looks like only one."

Game changer, thought Cade. And though he didn't let it show, his mood went south in a millisecond.

Getting the drift of the ABC conversation, Daymon saw himself into it and blurted out, "Only one. I broke *only* one bone ... that's an *only* situation. I *only* have one girlfriend ... that's an *only* situation. But one missing nuclear bomb doesn't fall under the *only* category. Where in the *hell* is it?"

Trying to shush Daymon earned Duncan an angry glare.

Foley stepped forward and described to Lopez and Cade what he saw earlier at the southwest gate. He included the tow truck in detail, including the driver and the cargo.

Foley's description of the man, compounded by the fact he had dark hair and wore a red Cornhusker hat caused Cade to say to no one in particular, "Elvis."

Daymon frowned, then said with a certain amount of reverence, "What's the *King* have to do with this?"

"Smelling salt ... now," Cade said to the medic, who was attempting to keep Carson from dying on him. "And I need you to shoot him up with epinephrine and stand back."

Nodding and disregarding the fact that Cade carried no rank, the medic got into his bag and administered the shot as if following a superior's orders.

Carson stirred almost immediately.

Sticking his entire hand into the gaping hole in Carson's crotch, Cade grabbed ahold of something down there and hissed, "Where is the missing nuke?"

After a second, Carson's eyes fluttered open. But he said nothing.

Crunching the smelling salts between the two fingers of his free hand, Cade waited a second for it to activate and then in one quick motion jammed it deeply into Carson's left nostril.

Still looking on from her spot in the corner near the shattered window, Jamie thought, *that's for Gus.*

Carson's mouth moved, then quietly he asked, "What time is it?"

Cade removed his helmet. Put it aside and then stuck a finger into the bullet wound in Carson's hip. He rooted around while Carson squirmed until he found a nerve that caused the mercenary to pound the ground with a fist and eventually shit himself. "Time for you to tell me where the nuke is ... *now!*"

"What time is it?" repeated Carson, the stench of his own excrement wafting up from the spreading puddle of watery brown fluid.

Lopez said, "Nine o'clock sharp."

With an icy hand twisting his guts, Cade confirmed this on his Suunto. "Why?" he hissed, probing the finger deeper, feeling bone grating against bone through his tactical glove.

Eyelids fluttering, Carson said, "You'll see."

Cade cracked a second capsule. Rolled it in his fingers and balanced out Carson's nose by inserting it into the unobstructed nostril.

Wincing from the ammonia sting, Carson said, "Nine-eleven ... you'll see."

Chapter 88

The low timbre thrum of the idling engine combined with the hydraulic whine of the tow apparatus as he lowered the device to the dirt was a siren song for the passing dead. As he worked, the steady crunch of feet on gravel drifted up from the winding road below.

He popped open the case and hinged the lid over. There, its metallic skin throwing the light of the low moon, was the mother of all pay back. Whether he could see them or not, he had to believe they were down there. And they were all going to get a very rude awakening.

When he powered on the tablet, its soft glow illuminated his face. He swiped the icon just as Bishop had demonstrated, bringing up a benign-looking rectangle of numbers that hinted to none of the destructive power that would be unleashed in just sixty short minutes. Couldn't there have been flames represented there? Like the ones oft painted on a custom hot rod. Or some wicked looking barbed wire? *Anything*, he thought to himself, *to make inputting the moronic four-digit code seem more ominous.*

He looked around for a subtle tell that he'd been made by some night-vision-wielding soldier. *Nothing.*

Finger hovering over the ten-digit keypad, a sudden tinge of doubt fluttered like a single minuscule butterfly in his stomach. Was his sixth sense telling him something? The desire to get even with the sleeping assholes whose presence he could almost feel overpowered the obvious until all four digits were inputted and a graphic reading *Armed* flashed up at him from inside the box.

Elvis, you stupid fucker, he thought. "Noooo!" he screamed.

The dead, having just arrived, fanned out and took station, eyeing him greedily, their bony fingers kneading the chain-link fence, making it rattle.

That he'd been duped hit him like a sucker punch. And that there were tens of thousands ... maybe even ten times that number of walking dead converging on the 'T' from places distant dawned on him. He laughed because he had become the world's most lethal suicide bomber—and there was nothing he could do about it.

Stupid fucker. He had been conned. Every word of Bishop's and Carson's good-cop bad-cop routine on the porch over beers rushed back at him. Bishop, momentarily playing the bad cop, had chastised his condition after no sleep and a day's worth of work and said: *For this mission to succeed tomorrow, we're going to need a youthful Elvis to suit up and show up.* Then Carson had piped up: *Blonde or brunette?* and he was hooked.

"Shit! There are no fucking soldiers," he bellowed, further exciting the dead. *And that,* he thought, *explained the ridiculously easy approach.* He was for all intents and purposes now an accidental martyr in Bishop's personal jihad against the dead, and there would be no squeaking out of this fix. Nope, all of the Kamikaze pilots and the disaffected with a grudge and a package truck full of TNT combined couldn't hold a candle to the damage this device was going to do—on the already dead. He spat on the ground and cursed the dead as the fencing quaked and quivered under their pressing weight.

Bemoaning the fact that he could have detonated the device outside of McCall and taken Bishop and at least three or four dozen former military pricks with him, he turned his thoughts to his family and how they had died. Cold and alone in the waters of San Francisco Bay. Adjusting his Huskers ball cap as a tear streamed down his cheek, he glanced down at the quickly scrolling numbers on the timer. His watch indicated it was four minutes past nine o'clock. Sensing his life slipping through his fingers and disgusted at himself for not following through, he drew his pistol. It was loaded, that much he knew for sure.

The muzzle was bitter in his mouth from the mixture of oil and burnt gun powder. Twisting his wrist slightly, he bit down on the muzzle and said sorry to his kin for the last time. The hammer, on line with his right ear, made a mechanical click as it dropped, causing him to twitch ever so slightly. The resulting detonation punched an opening the size of a softball in his skull, taking his left eye and ear and everything connecting the two sensory apparatus with it. Dermis and flesh and muscle splashed over the device and, now deafened, he fell in a vertical heap, legs and arms kicking and pawing at the dirt—autonomous functions created by the massive brain trauma.

But he wasn't dead when the fence failed and the moaning flesh eaters dug in with their cold probing digits. In seconds, his entrails were spread out on the ground around him, one big sloppy dirty mess. His legs and arms continued to twitch as he lived in intense silent agony with the timer counting down to zero, with all of the bad deeds, of which there were many, flashing before his remaining eye. He felt his body go cold at the three-minute mark. With two minutes to go until detonation, he saw stars flitting behind his lids as his mortal self passed and the Omega virus began working to bring him back. His body convulsed, mostly from the meat being rent from his bones, as the prions wormed their way to his brain. Luckily—or unluckily, depending upon how you looked at it—Elvis turned quickly and would get to attend his second death. Shrugging off his feeding brethren undead, newly turned Elvis rose on unsteady feet. Then a single drop of crimson blood oozed from his shattered orbital bone, traced the ridge of his powder-burned nose, and freefell to the device, inexplicably splattering on the glass tablet where the timer now read 00:01:33—a full fifty-eight some odd minutes shy of those Bishop had promised.

Chapter 89

Cade's Suunto read 21:09. *If the bomb is nearby*, he thought sadly, *then I have two minutes to live and will never again hold Raven and Brook. Or maybe*, he reasoned, *Elvis somehow transported it to Schriever and in less than two minutes hundreds of good people will die a horrible death.* Either way, sad as both scenarios would be, Carson was going with him. Another pound of flesh excised from the Earth. *Or*, he thought grimly. *Two minutes go by and nothing happens and the real interrogation begins.* No matter what, Carson would never see another sunrise.

A minute passed and nothing.

Though a cooling breeze flowed in off the lake, the air inside still stank of fear-laced sweat and shit and drying blood.

Fifty more seconds became history and the room had grown so quiet a pin hitting the floor could have as well been a cymbal crash.

Counting down the last ten seconds in his head, Cade instinctively shifted his gaze from the lake's rippling black waters to the nearly identical-appearing blood-slickened floor tiles behind him.

Out of the blue, though the possibility of surviving a danger close nuclear detonation with only flash blindness was remote, Lieutenant Eckels—who had up until then remained on the sidelines—called out, "Avert your eyes, *now!*"

After hitting one and ticking off a few more seconds to the negative, Cade exhaled and opened his eyes. A half beat later, before craning around, a flicker of light shone off the glassy crimson pool at his feet. And amazingly, for a split second it seemed bright as the Ranger's hand-held spotlight had been as it refracted away and lit up the stainless steel appliances. And like the nuclear detonation forty miles north of Schriever, there was no initial sound. No explosive concussion. No muffled *Whoomph. Nothing.*

Just a continuing flicker of white and orange over the horizon north by west.

The entire episode from flicker to realization took three seconds. After those three seconds, the room erupted in an explosion of movement and excited chatter.

"Where was the detonation?" Lopez demanded.

"Wait one," answered Lieutenant Eckels. Then, shaking his head, he added. "Comms are all messed up."

Lopez asked. "How long will they be down?"

"Minutes. Maybe an hour or more depending on the atmospheric bounce," answered the lieutenant. "We'll be OK here ... *for now.* The remaining devices are being loaded onto the Chinooks. The women who were found in the rape house have agreed to come along to Schriever in the third helo."

"And us?" Cade asked, looking at Lopez.

"You'll be getting a ride to wherever you want with us on Jedi One-One."

"And Carson?"

"I'd call General Nash and clear it with her ... but the comms are *down.*" He winked and made air quotes when he said '*down.*' "At any rate, after hearing what your friend Jamie had to say about Bishop's operation, I wish we could bring that pendejo back from hell so you can send them both back as bunk buddies."

Smiling morbidly at the thought, Cade offered his hand and said, "Thank you, Captain Lopez. I owe you one." Instantly regretting saying that one three-letter word, *owe*, that was such an indicator of character if followed through on—and had gotten him into so much trouble with Brook in the past—he lowered his hand and returned Lowrider's sharp salute.

"You can take the man outta Delta—" said Lopez.

"—but you can't take Delta out of the man," finished Cade.

Seeing this, Cross called out across the room to the third member of the Delta team, a fully bearded operator the size of a small mountain. "Lasagna," he said. "Help me get this sack of shit to our ride." Then, grabbing a handful of Carson's torn pants, he winked at Cade and said in a near perfect Schwarzenegger, "You'll be back."

Knowing full well the call of duty would once again whisper his name while simultaneously wishing for it never to happen again—for both Raven's and Brook's sake—Cade clapped Lev on the shoulder and, still favoring his ankle, put an arm around Daymon and together the three of them followed Duncan and Jamie to the waiting Ghost Hawk.

Chapter 90

As they walked towards the matte-black chopper with its lazily spinning rotor cutting the air, Duncan commented about how quiet it was. "I felt that black demon in my gut but had no idea what it was until it was too late."

"That's the point," said Lopez behind a wry smile. "Wyatt could tell you some stories about our Jedi Ride."

Duncan said, "I bet. But then he'd have to kill me, right?"

Lopez smiled and went about his business, readying the flight.

After watching an ecstatic Foley accept a hand up into the chopper, Duncan let Jamie take a seat ahead of him, then chose an open spot on the floor next to Carson's prostrate form.

The bird was pretty crowded by the time the big bearded operator everyone called Lasagna boarded and shut the door behind him. *Strange*, thought Cade as he swapped out helmets and plugged the comms wire into a jack near his head. The operator across from him didn't have Italian features, nor, judging by his muscular physique and slim waist, did Cade think the nickname derived from a penchant for that type of cuisine. So craning over covertly, he read the name on the man's Multicam blouse: *Lasseigne*. He nodded and smiled while tightening his harness.

"Strap in and hang on," warned Ari over the shipboard comms. Then he leaned back and repeated the ominous-sounding orders for the benefit of those not wearing a flight helmet. Finally he looked at Cade and added, "We've got us a celebrity flying Night Stalker Airways. Everyone give Wyatt a round of applause and please

... save your autograph requests until after we arrive back at Schriever."

"So I'm being shanghaied," said Cade playfully as he pressed a boot into Carson's ribs, producing a long, drawn-out moan. *Still alive ... good.*

"Just yanking your chain," replied Ari. "Where to?"

"Golf course. Northwest of the lake," Cade said. He hinged at the waist and looked out the port side as the helo lifted smoothly from the makeshift landing zone. He saw the Chinooks already nosing off to the east, their insect-like silhouettes framed against the rising moon. Then the northeast gate drifted by and he noticed in the light of the still-burning fires the unchecked dead seemingly forming a step up with their bodies and the others behind them spilling over the gate.

As the burning structures and black glassy lake spun from Daymon's view, they were replaced outside of the window by a gathering of dead, and he witnessed the same behavior Cade had just been privy to. He grabbed Lev's attention and stabbed a finger groundward and mouthed, "Empirical evidence."

Flying at an extremely low altitude, Ari buzzed the dormant water feature. Below, illuminated ghostly white by the rising moon, the Zs were still wading the waters, giving slow chase to the handful of geese unwilling to give up their habitat. Shimmering swirls marred the surface as predator and prey maintained the ongoing dance.

Ari broke in over the comms and said, "Next stop the eleventh hole. A difficult dog-leg right with ball-hungry traps on the left and flesh-hungry hazards surrounding the green."

"Can you take us over the clubhouse first?" Cade said into the comms.

Ari said, "Roger that," and the helo banked right and seconds later was orbiting a hundred feet above the grand building.

"Keep going," said Cade sadly upon seeing the staggering mess below. Dressed in the same coveralls and sturdy work boots, but minus the golf hat and any semblance of life, the Z that had been Walter looked up lazily and opened its mouth, no doubt moaning at the mechanical thing flitting overhead.

After saying a prayer for the man who had offered them sanctuary and in a roundabout way the use of his vehicle, Cade pushed it from his mind and looked for the Black Hawk.

Still covered in netting, their ride was right where Duncan had parked it. Cade also confirmed visually the presence of a dozen Zs in the vicinity. He took the opportunity afforded by their altitude to scan several fairways surrounding their chopper and saw that they were also overrun by rotten shamblers. *Going to have to work fast*, he thought, quickly swapping helmets.

Announcing their imminent touchdown, the whine and thunk of the landing gear deploying sounded through the cabin. Then Ari began his countdown, all business.

On *'one,'* clutching his M4 close, Cade thumped Lasagna on the chest and mouthed, "Thank you." As the bird settled softly adjacent to the DHS Black Hawk, Cade stepped onto the brittle grass, went to a knee and flipped the NVGs over his eyes. Hearing the others running across the grass at his six, he shouldered his carbine and began picking off glowing green forms at distance.

With help from Lopez and his Delta team, in no time they had the netting rolled up and Carson was transferred, trussed and blindfolded, into the Black Hawk.

After the transfer and once Duncan had gotten the Black Hawk's rotors spinning, Ari launched and orbited the area, Jedi One-One's port-side minigun throwing a barrage of hot lead into the approaching Zs.

Five minutes after the transfer, Duncan had the DHS Black Hawk airborne and was holding a hover over the eleventh hole green with only the rising moon lighting the ground below.

Communications having just come back on line, Ari's voice sounded over the comms. "Cade ... you owe me a detail for this bird. My customers say your man bled all over back there."

"Copy that," said Cade. "I'll throw in the cash for the undercoating spray and a vanilla-scented tree for your mirror." He looked right and saw a smile spread on Duncan's green-tinged face.

After a long bout of laughter, Ari replied, "See you soon, Wyatt." The comms went silent, and after spotting Ari give the Jedi Ride a little intentional waggle on axis, Cade watched the Ghost

Hawk, shimmering a bright green in his goggles, turn hard south and climb away rapidly.

"Where to?" asked Duncan. "Knowing you, I think you've got something special planned for this Carson fella."

Regarding Jamie through robotic-looking eyes, Cade said, "Think he needs a bath?"

Nodding and looking down at the golf course below, Jamie said, "Yeah. But go lower. I don't want him to die from the impact like Jordan did."

"Copy that," said Duncan. "Get that lady some night vision goggles so she can enjoy the show."

***

Duncan held the Black Hawk in a ragged hover thirty feet over the algae-filled water. The down blast from the rotors frothed the surface and did what the dead had been unable to: sent the geese away with a chorus of angry honking and a flurry of beating white feathers.

The kerosene-scented exhaust entered the cabin when Cade hauled open the door. He nodded at Jamie while Lev scooted the prostrate captive to the curled metal lip. Not realizing the significance of his words in golf parlance, Cade said, "You've got honors," then shifted his gaze to the tiny mushroom-shaped cloud far, far away in the distance.

After yanking the scrap of saliva-soaked fabric and enduring a stream of whispered epithets from Carson's maw, Jamie regarded his green-tinted features and said, "For Logan." There was no hesitating. She rolled him off into space behind a firm nudge from her boot.

His scream pierced the night air for a two-count, then went silent.

After seeing the dead pile on and the whitecaps below turn a lighter shade of green from the warm blood, Jamie backed from the precipice and sat down hard, tears welling in her eyes.

Cade tore his gaze from the green glow over the horizon and saw Lev close the door. He waited until Jamie was strapped back into her seat between Lev and Daymon. Then he flashed a thumbs up to Duncan and said one word into the comms: *Home.*

Epilogue

In a fraction of a nanosecond, the detonation had produced temperatures rivaling those on the sun's surface, instantly vaporizing Elvis, the device, the wrecker, and everything around him in a half a mile radius. Next a shockwave containing massive overpressures shot out to all points of the compass from ground zero, moving at a staggering speed. Then the roiling thermonuclear cloud sprouted and sucked a great deal of radioactive dust and debris skyward to forty thousand feet where it merged with the polar Jetstream and was carried far and wide east and north across broad swaths of Idaho and Montana.

On the ground from as far as the eye could see, if there had been a living soul to witness it, nothing moved atop the smooth glassed-over top soil.

On the periphery, dozens of miles northwest of ground zero, tens of thousands of dead migrating eastward from cities once high in populace were instantly blinded and irradiated and sent shambling away in clusters to all points of the compass.

West of Huntsville

In the dark of the Ogden Canyon Pass, the dead were arriving from the west in droves. And with each passing hour, hundreds of the walking corpses were being forced up and over the guard rail to the canyon floor below, where the ones that survived the fall started a slow crawling hunt for prey, oblivious of broken limbs or jutting bones or partial paralysis.

Meanwhile up at pass level, with each passing hour, their ranks no longer being thinned daily by the Huntsville bandits, the amassing dead were beginning to counter the weight of the stacked shipping containers, moving them a millimeter at a time behind each surge of newly arrived flesh and bone.

Oblivious to the ongoing battle between physics and insatiable hunger, the elderly full-sized male raccoon rattled out of the underbrush.

Quickly finding itself trapped among a forest of shuffling feet, a primeval spark flared deep in the coon's plum-sized brain and the twenty-pound creature took blind flight east. After being bashed countless times by bony knees and sharp-edged shinbones, the coon unwittingly climbed up a cold cadaver's back, where the contact of warm flesh and fur started a chain reaction of unimaginable proportions.

It was over in a matter of seconds, with the unlucky raccoon ending up in a dozen different pieces in a dozen distended stomachs.

But the ensuing melee the coon's mad dash had started widened the eight-inch gap between container and guardrail, and the long-delayed undead diaspora east was underway.

###

Thanks for reading *Warpath*. Look for a new novel in the *Surviving the Zombie Apocalypse* series in late 2014. Please feel free to Friend Shawn Chesser on Facebook.

ABOUT THE AUTHOR

Shawn Chesser, a practicing father, has been a zombie fanatic for decades. He likes his creatures shambling, trudging and moaning. As for fast, agile, screaming specimens ... not so much. He lives in Portland, Oregon, with his wife, two kids and three fish. This is his seventh novel.

CUSTOMERS ALSO PURCHASED:

JOHN O'BRIEN
NEW WORLD
SERIES

JAMES N. COOK
SURVIVING THE DEAD
SERIES

MARK TUFO
ZOMBIE FALLOUT
SERIES

ARMAND
ROSAMILLIA
DYING DAYS
SERIES

HEATH STALLCUP
THE MONSTER
SQUAD

Printed in Great Britain
by Amazon.co.uk, Ltd.,
Marston Gate.